RVEL

ISOM, Editor
LL, Associate Editor
Publication Design
LENA MAHINA, Production
te Manager, Digital Assests
nior Editor, Special Projects
Licensed Publishing
oduction & Special Projects
Print, Sales & Marketing
I, Editor in Chief

Manager AFK & Graphix Media, Scholastic
nior Designer, Scholastic

STAN LEE & STEVE DITKO

OHN NEE, JOE QUESADA,
d RICKEY PURDIN

MARVEL

imprint of Scholastic Inc., *Publishers since 1920.*
marks and/or registered trademarks of Scholastic Inc.

338-64804-1

21 22 23 24 25

113

, June 2021

blo Leon
riana Maher

LAUREN B
CAITLIN O'CONNE
ADAM DEL RE,
JOE FRONTIRRE with **SA**
JOE HOCHSTEIN, Associc
JENNIFER GRÜNWALD, Se
SVEN LARSEN, VP
JEFF YOUNGQUIST, VP Pr
DAVID GABRIEL, SVP
C.B. CEBULSK

MICHAEL PETRANEK, Executive Editor,
JESSICA MELTZER, Se

Spider-Man created by

With special thanks to **J**
NICK LOWE, an

ISBN 978-1-

10 9 8 7 6 5 4 3 2

Printed in the U.S.A.

First editio

Art by Pc
Letters by A

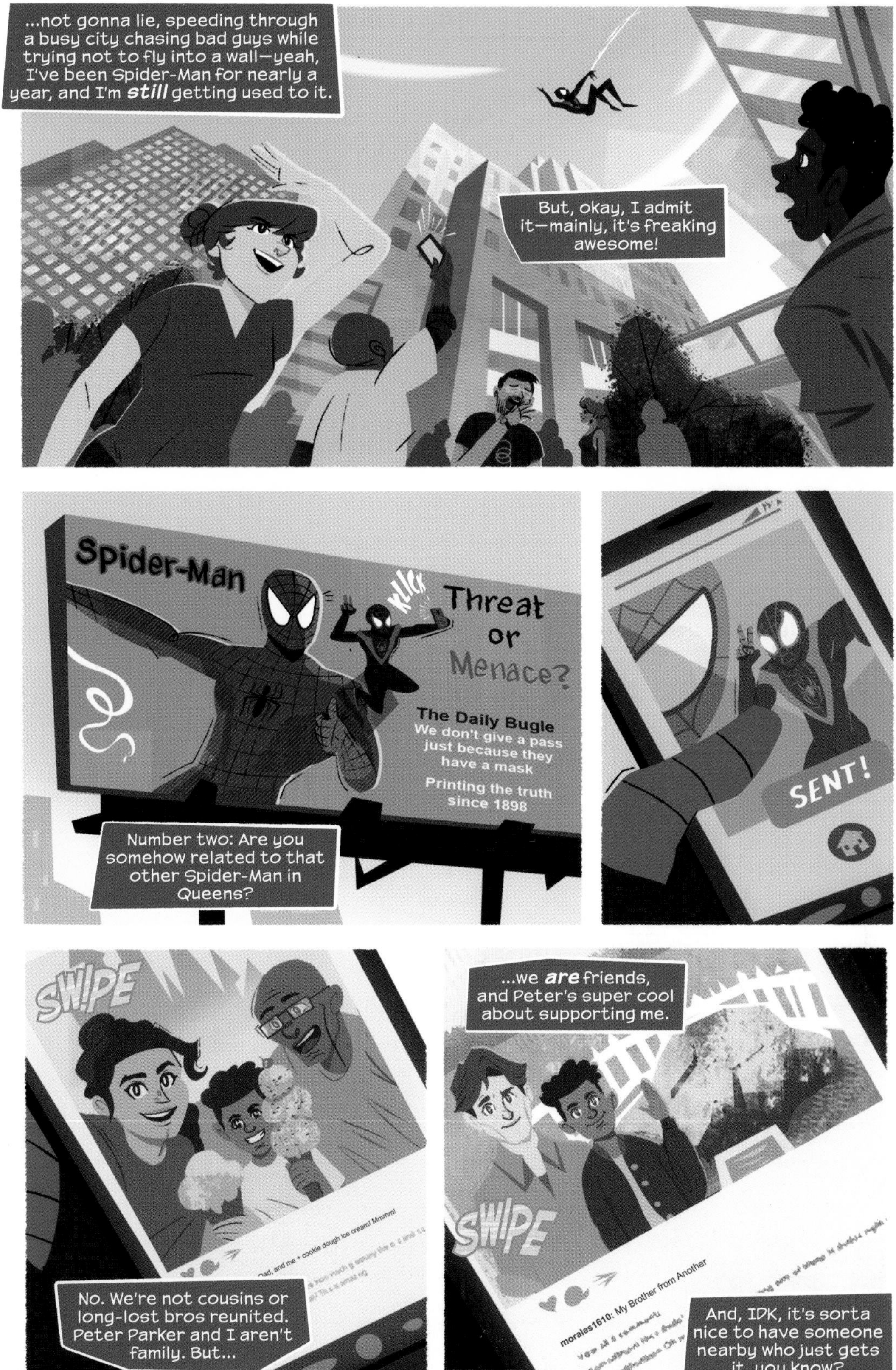
...not gonna lie, speeding through a busy city chasing bad guys while trying not to fly into a wall—yeah, I've been Spider-Man for nearly a year, and I'm still getting used to it.
But, okay, I admit it—mainly, it's freaking awesome!
Spider-Man
KLICK
Threat or Menace?
The Daily Bugle
We don't give a pass just because they have a mask
Printing the truth since 1898
Number two: Are you somehow related to that other Spider-Man in Queens?
SENT!
SWIPE
Dad, and me + cookie dough ice cream! Mmmm!
No. We're not cousins or long-lost bros reunited. Peter Parker and I aren't family. But...
...we are friends, and Peter's super cool about supporting me.
SWIPE
morales1610: My Brother from Another
And, IDK, it's sorta nice to have someone nearby who just gets it, you know?

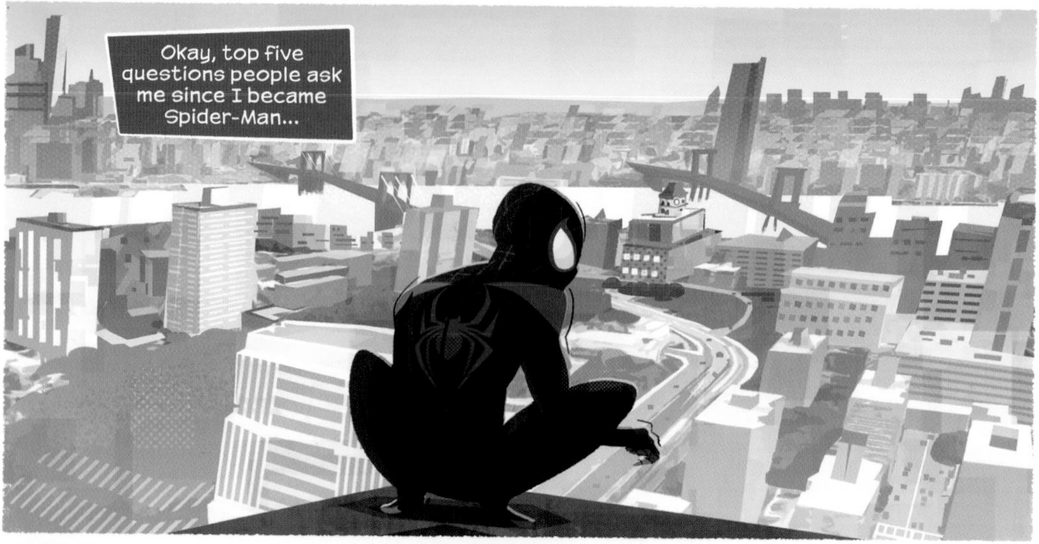
Okay, top five questions people ask me since I became Spider-Man...

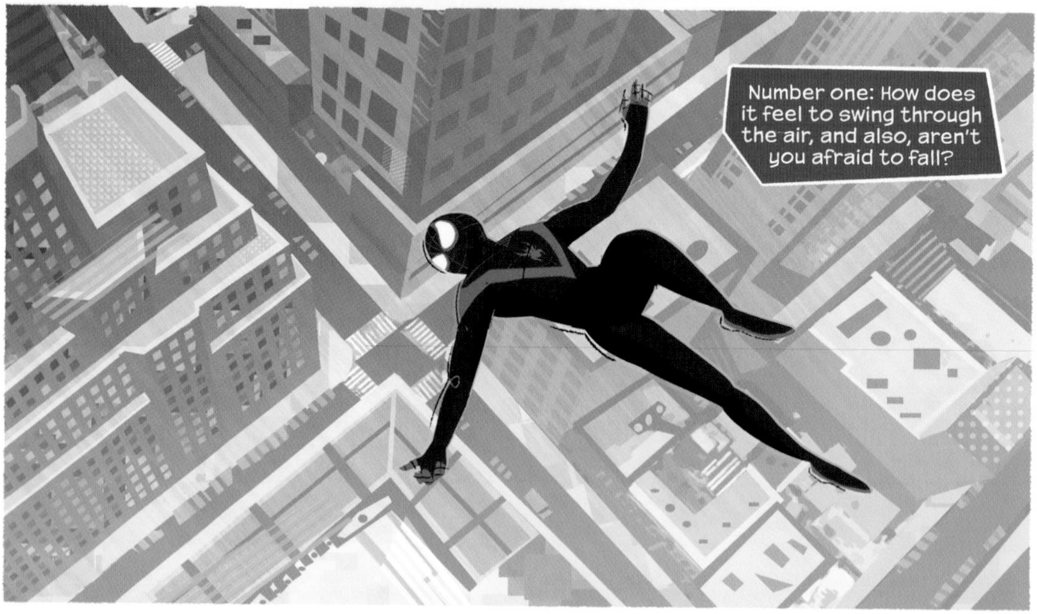
Number one: How does it feel to swing through the air, and also, aren't you afraid to fall?

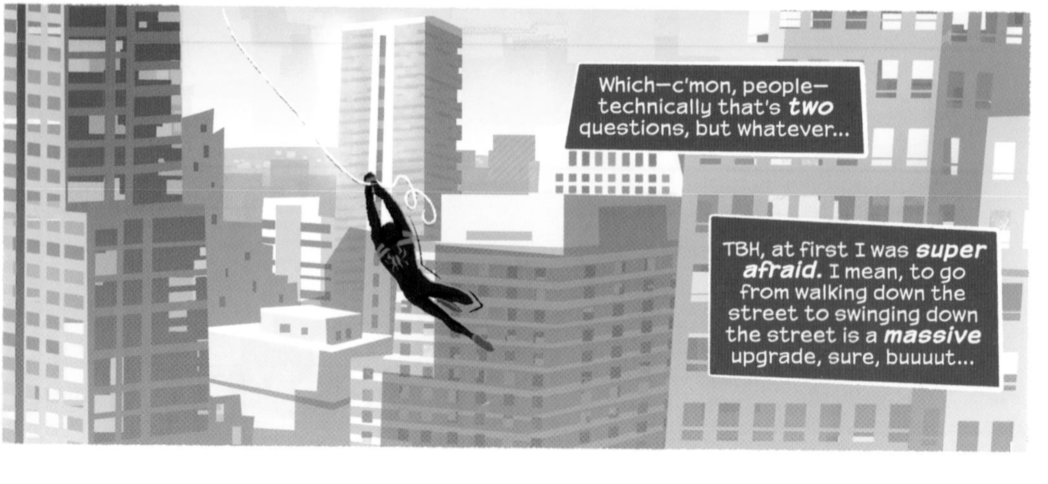
Which—c'mon, people—technically that's ***two*** questions, but whatever...
TBH, at first I was ***super afraid.*** I mean, to go from walking down the street to swinging down the street is a ***massive*** upgrade, sure, buuuut...

CHAPTER
ONE

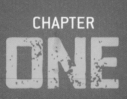

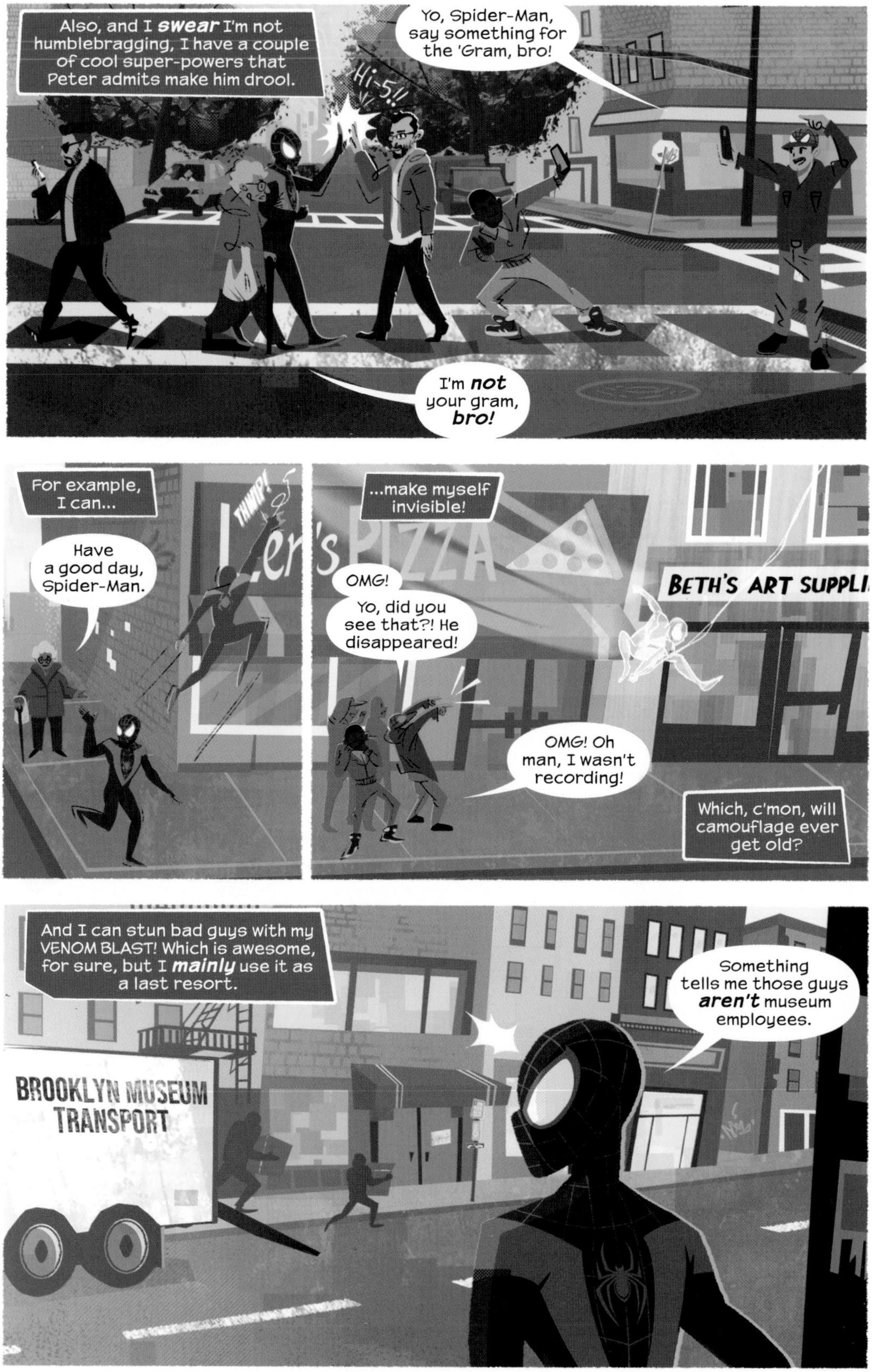
Also, and I **swear** I'm not humblebragging, I have a couple of cool super-powers that Peter admits make him drool.
Yo, Spider-Man, say something for the 'Gram, bro!
Hi-5!!
I'm **not** your gram, ***bro!***
For example, I can...
THWIP!
Have a good day, Spider-Man.
...make myself invisible!
OMG!
Yo, did you see that?! He disappeared!
BETH'S ART SUPPLI
OMG! Oh man, I wasn't recording!
Which, c'mon, will camouflage ever get old?
And I can stun bad guys with my VENOM BLAST! Which is awesome, for sure, but I ***mainly*** use it as a last resort.
BROOKLYN MUSEUM TRANSPORT
Something tells me those guys ***aren't*** museum employees.

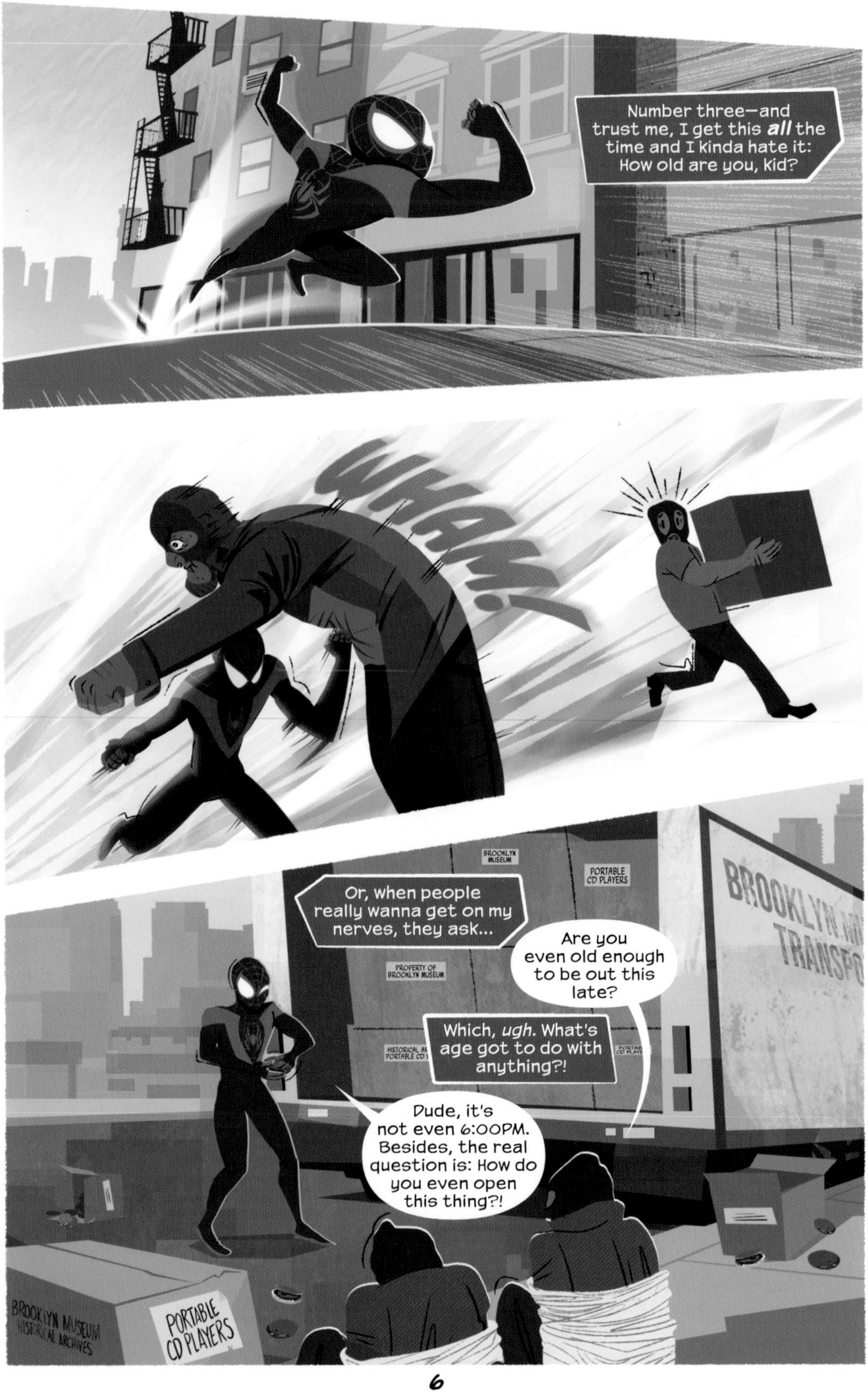
Number three—and trust me, I get this ***all*** the time and I kinda hate it: How old are you, kid?
WHAM!
BROOKLYN MUSEUM
PORTABLE CD PLAYERS
Or, when people really wanna get on my nerves, they ask...
Are you even old enough to be out this late?
PROPERTY OF BROOKLYN MUSEUM
Which, *ugh.* What's age got to do with anything?!
Dude, it's not even 6:00PM. Besides, the real question is: How do you even open this thing?!
BROOKLYN MUSEUM HISTORICAL ARCHIVES
PORTABLE CD PLAYERS

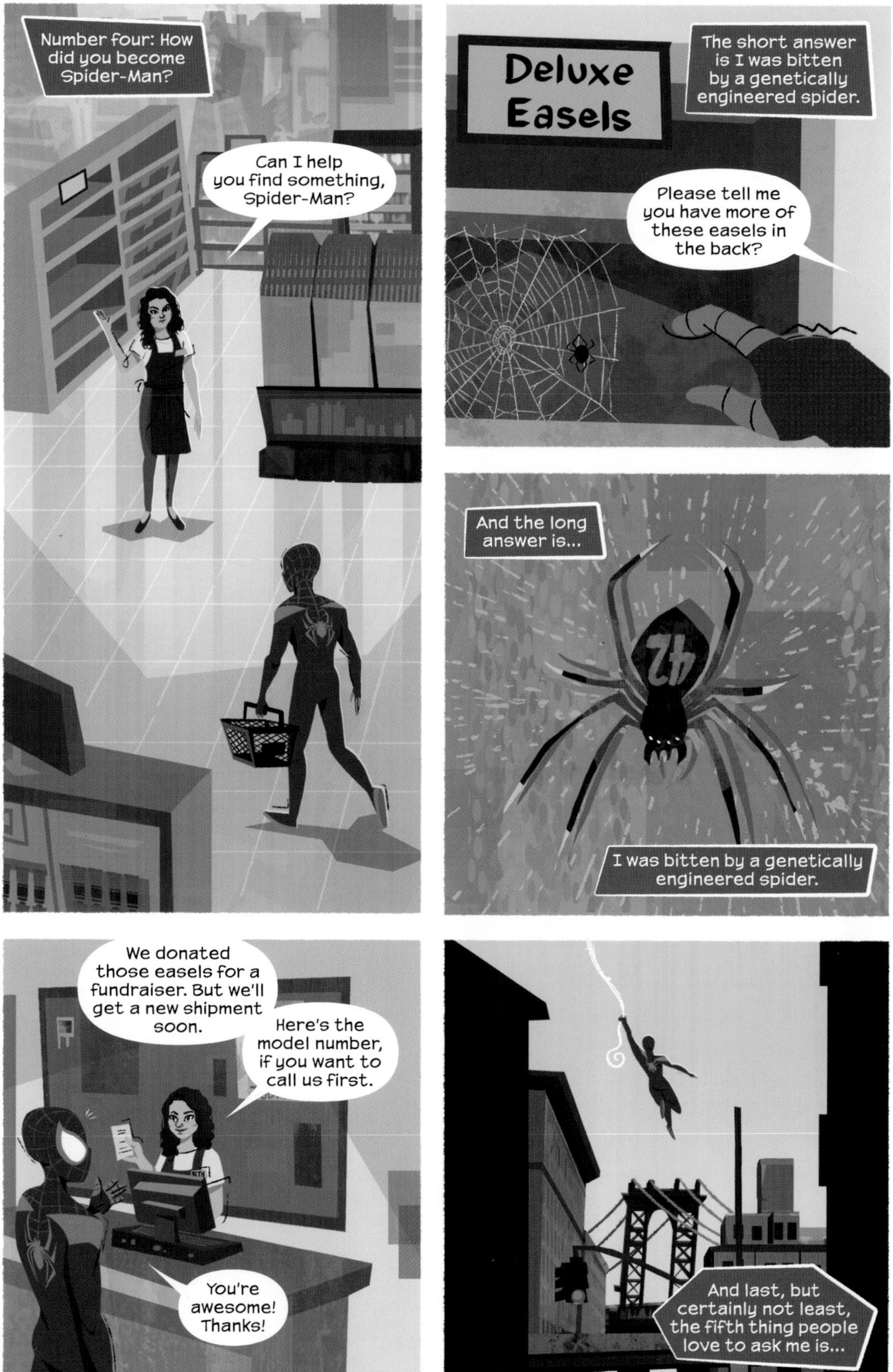
Number four: How did you become Spider-Man?
Can I help you find something, Spider-Man?
Deluxe Easels
The short answer is I was bitten by a genetically engineered spider.
Please tell me you have more of these easels in the back?
And the long answer is...
42
I was bitten by a genetically engineered spider.
We donated those easels for a fundraiser. But we'll get a new shipment soon.
Here's the model number, if you want to call us first.
You're awesome! Thanks!
And last, but certainly not least, the fifth thing people love to ask me is...

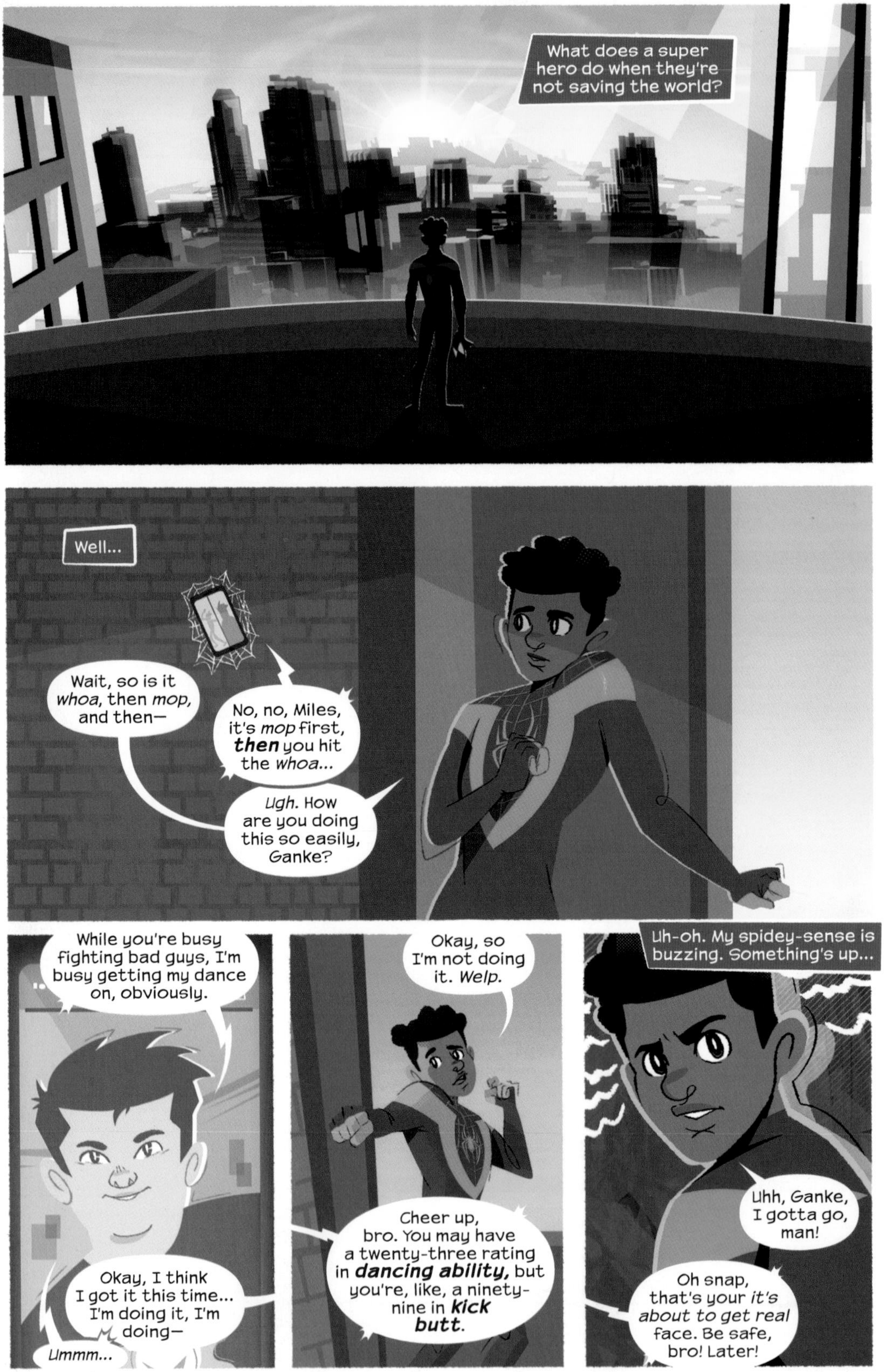

What does a super hero do when they're not saving the world?
Well...
Wait, so is it *whoa*, then *mop*, and then—
No, no, Miles, it's *mop* first, ***then*** you hit the *whoa*...
Ugh. How are you doing this so easily, Ganke?
While you're busy fighting bad guys, I'm busy getting my dance on, obviously.
Okay, I think I got it this time... I'm doing it, I'm doing—
Ummm...
Okay, so I'm not doing it. *Welp.*
Cheer up, bro. You may have a twenty-three rating in ***dancing ability,*** but you're, like, a ninety-nine in ***kick butt***.
Uh-oh. My spidey-sense is buzzing. Something's up...
Uhh, Ganke, I gotta go, man!
Oh snap, that's your *it's about to get real* face. Be safe, bro! Later!

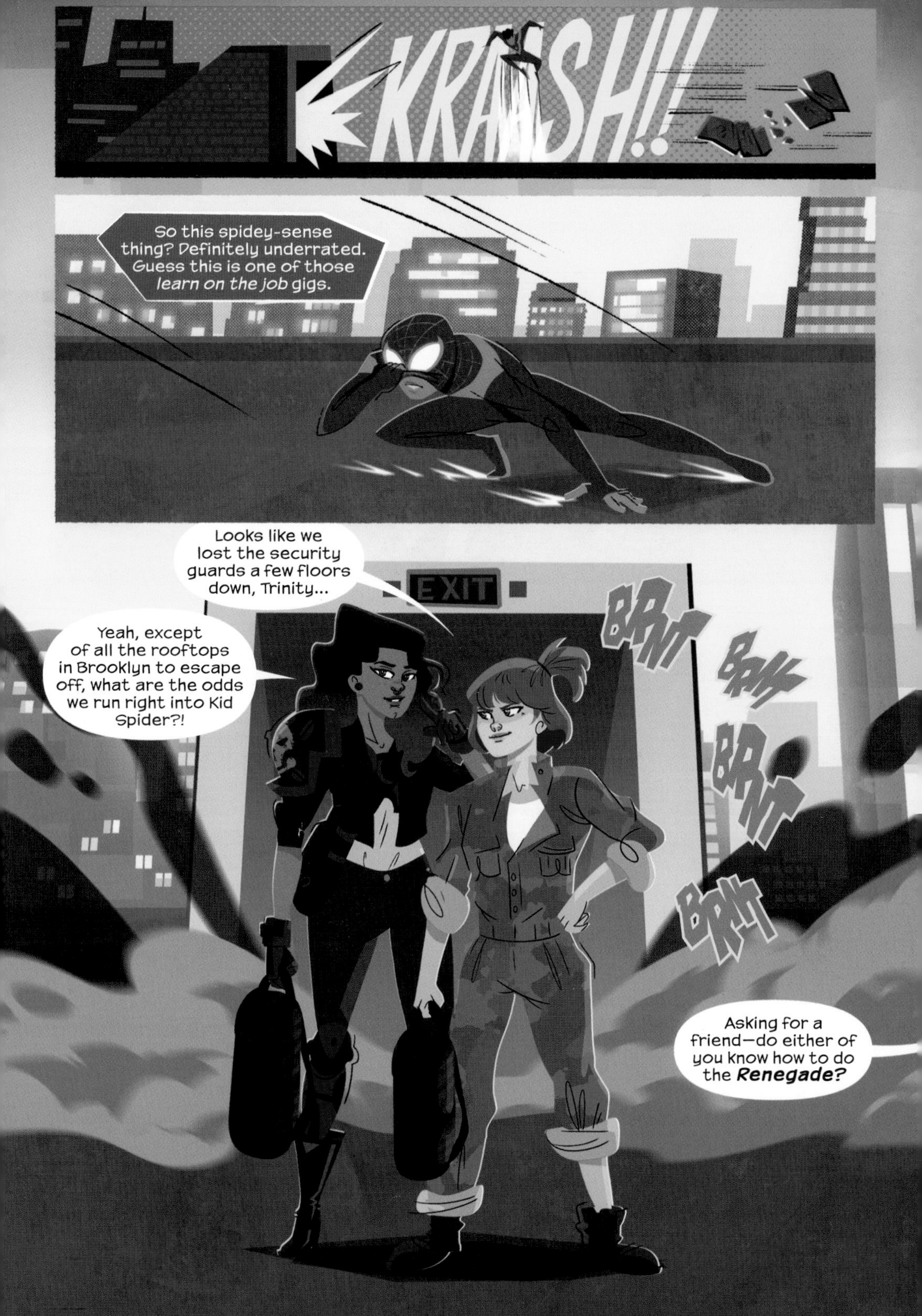
KRASH!!
So this spidey-sense thing? Definitely underrated. Guess this is one of those learn on the job gigs.
Looks like we lost the security guards a few floors down, Trinity...
Yeah, except of all the rooftops in Brooklyn to escape off, what are the odds we run right into Kid Spider?!
EXIT
BRNT
BRNT
BRNT
BRNT
Asking for a friend—do either of you know how to do the Renegade?

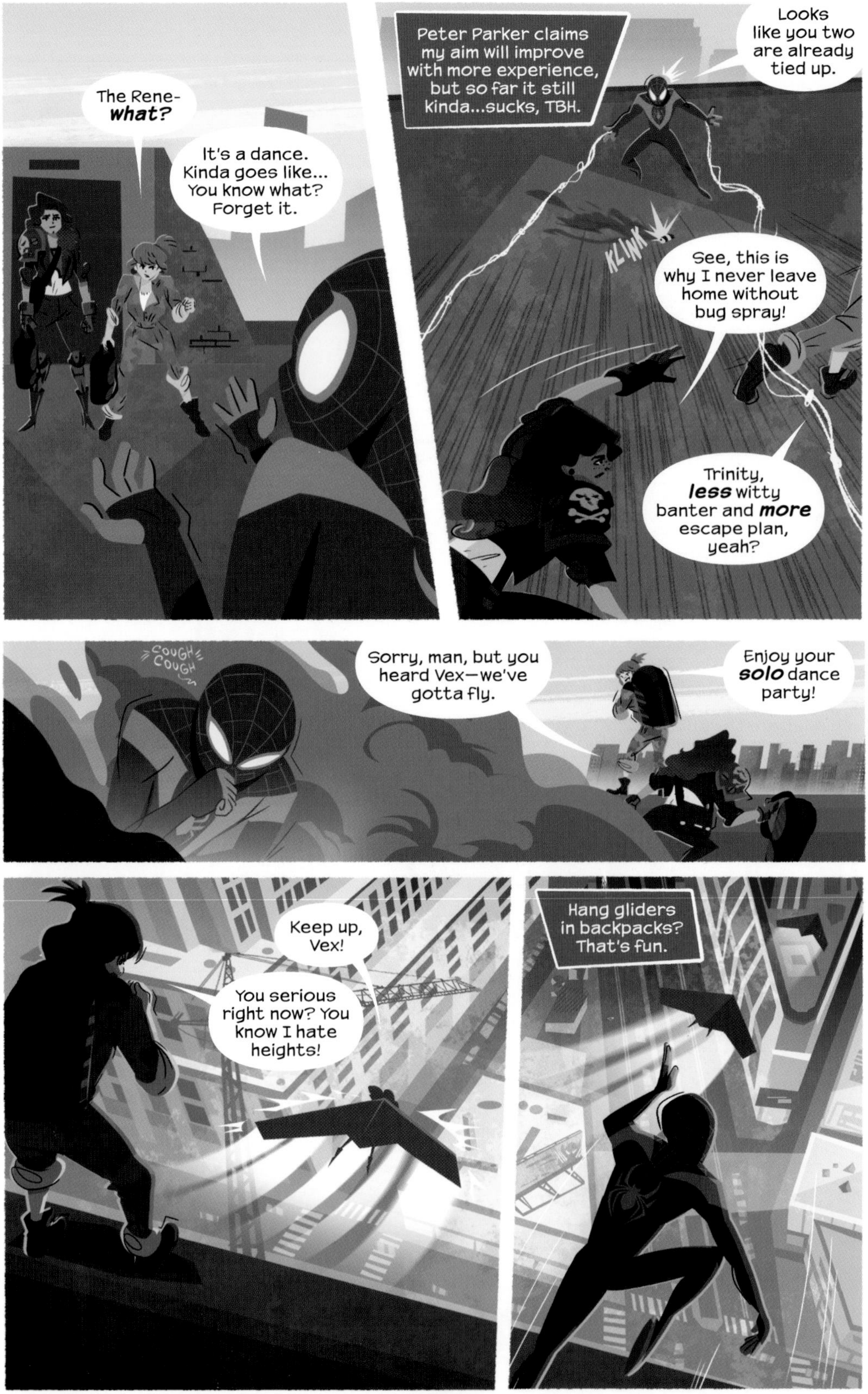
The Rene-*what?*
It's a dance. Kinda goes like... You know what? Forget it.
Peter Parker claims my aim will improve with more experience, but so far it still kinda...sucks, TBH.
Looks like you two are already tied up.
KLINK
See, this is why I never leave home without bug spray!
Trinity, *less* witty banter and *more* escape plan, yeah?
COUGH COUGH
Sorry, man, but you heard Vex—we've gotta fly.
Enjoy your *solo* dance party!
Keep up, Vex!
You serious right now? You know I hate heights!
Hang gliders in backpacks? That's fun.

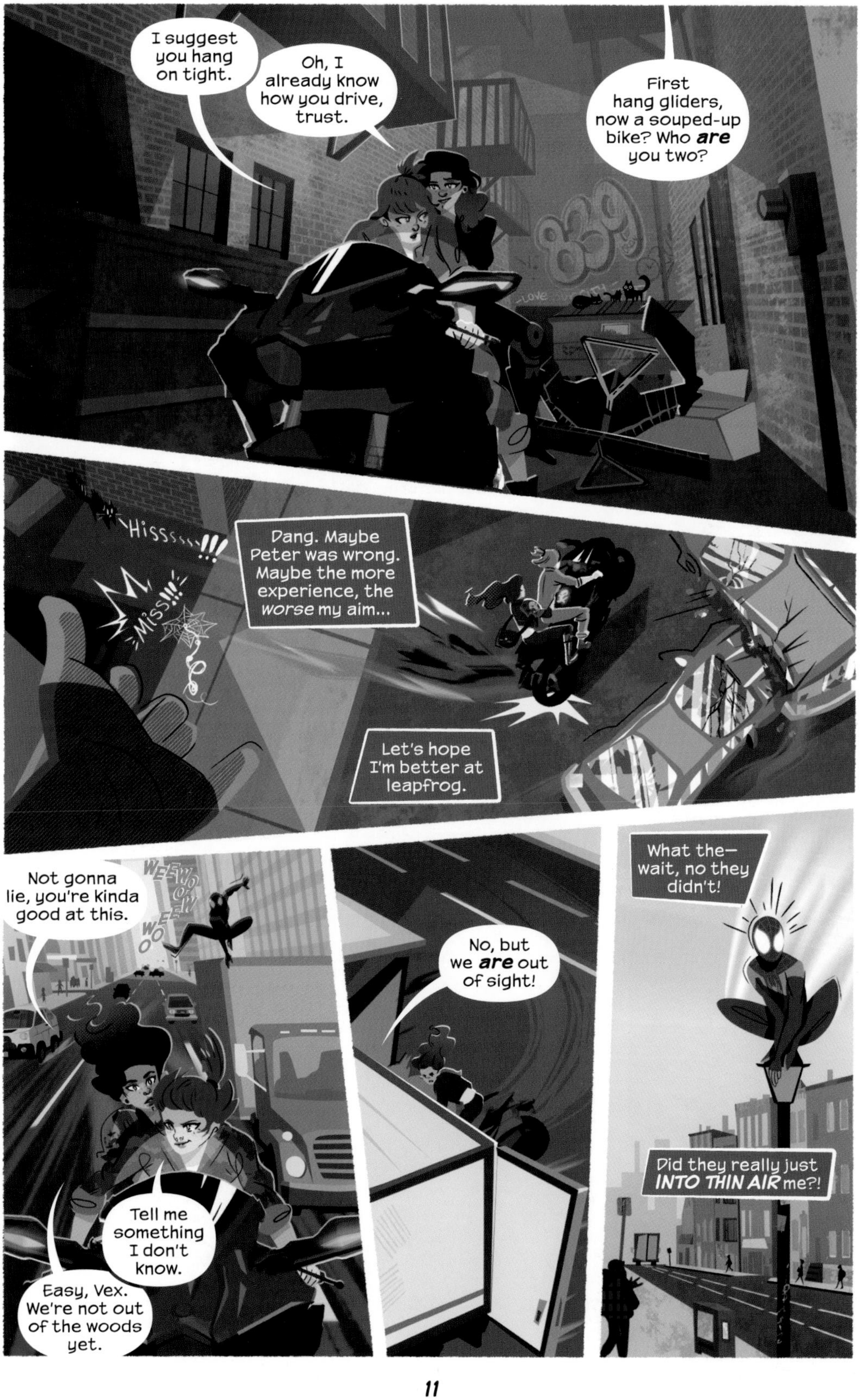

I suggest you hang on tight.
Oh, I already know how you drive, trust.
First hang gliders, now a souped-up bike? Who ***are*** you two?
Hissss!!!
Miss!!!
Dang. Maybe Peter was wrong. Maybe the more experience, the *worse* my aim...
Let's hope I'm better at leapfrog.
Not gonna lie, you're kinda good at this.
WEEWOO WEEWOO
Tell me something I don't know.
Easy, Vex. We're not out of the woods yet.
No, but we ***are*** out of sight!
What the—wait, no they didn't!
Did they really just **INTO THIN AIR** me?!

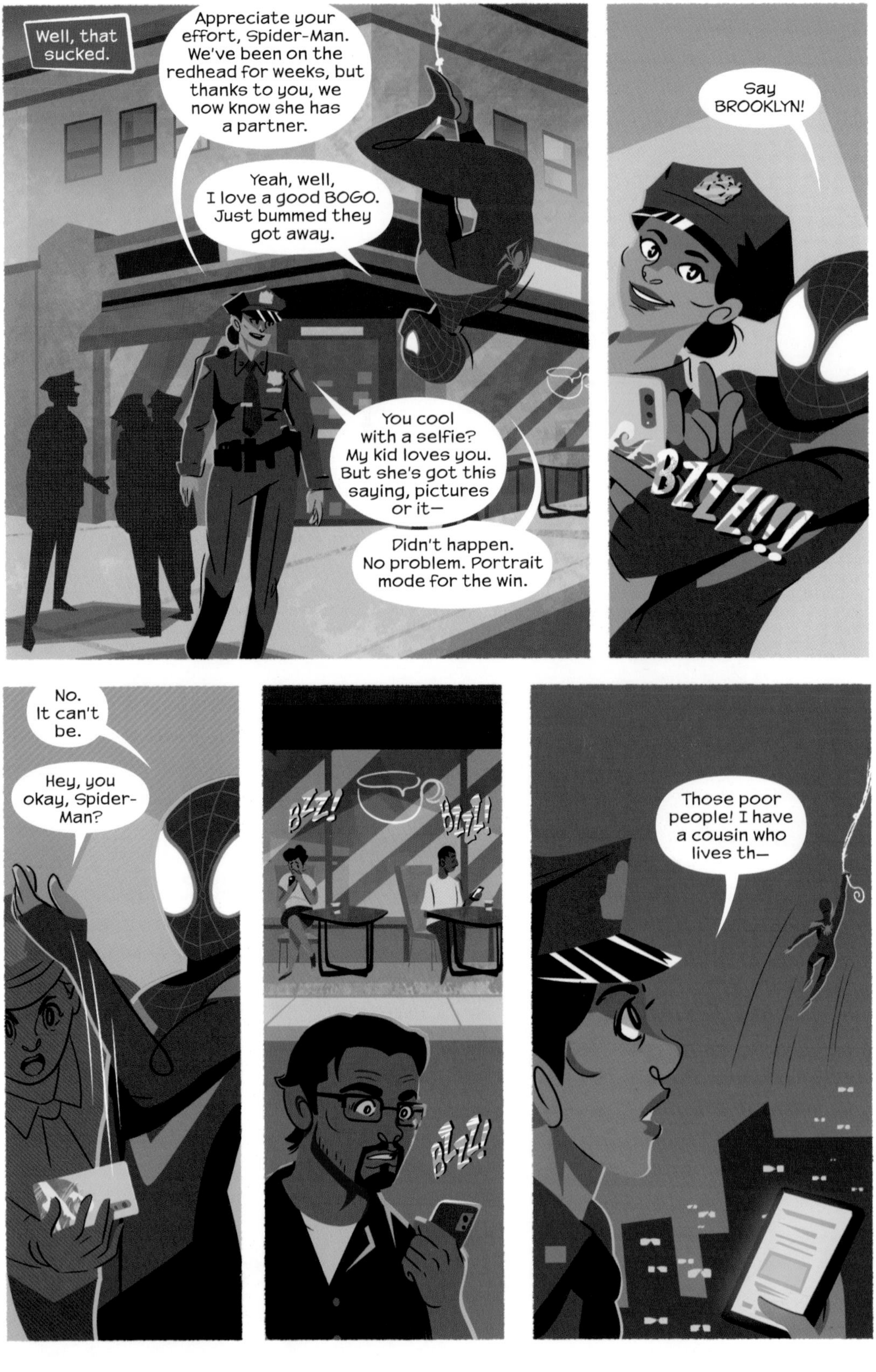
Well, that sucked.
Appreciate your effort, Spider-Man. We've been on the redhead for weeks, but thanks to you, we now know she has a partner.
Yeah, well, I love a good BOGO. Just bummed they got away.
You cool with a selfie? My kid loves you. But she's got this saying, pictures or it—
Didn't happen. No problem. Portrait mode for the win.
Say BROOKLYN!
BZZZ!!!
No. It can't be.
Hey, you okay, Spider-Man?
BZZ!
BZZZ!
BZZZ!
Those poor people! I have a cousin who lives th—

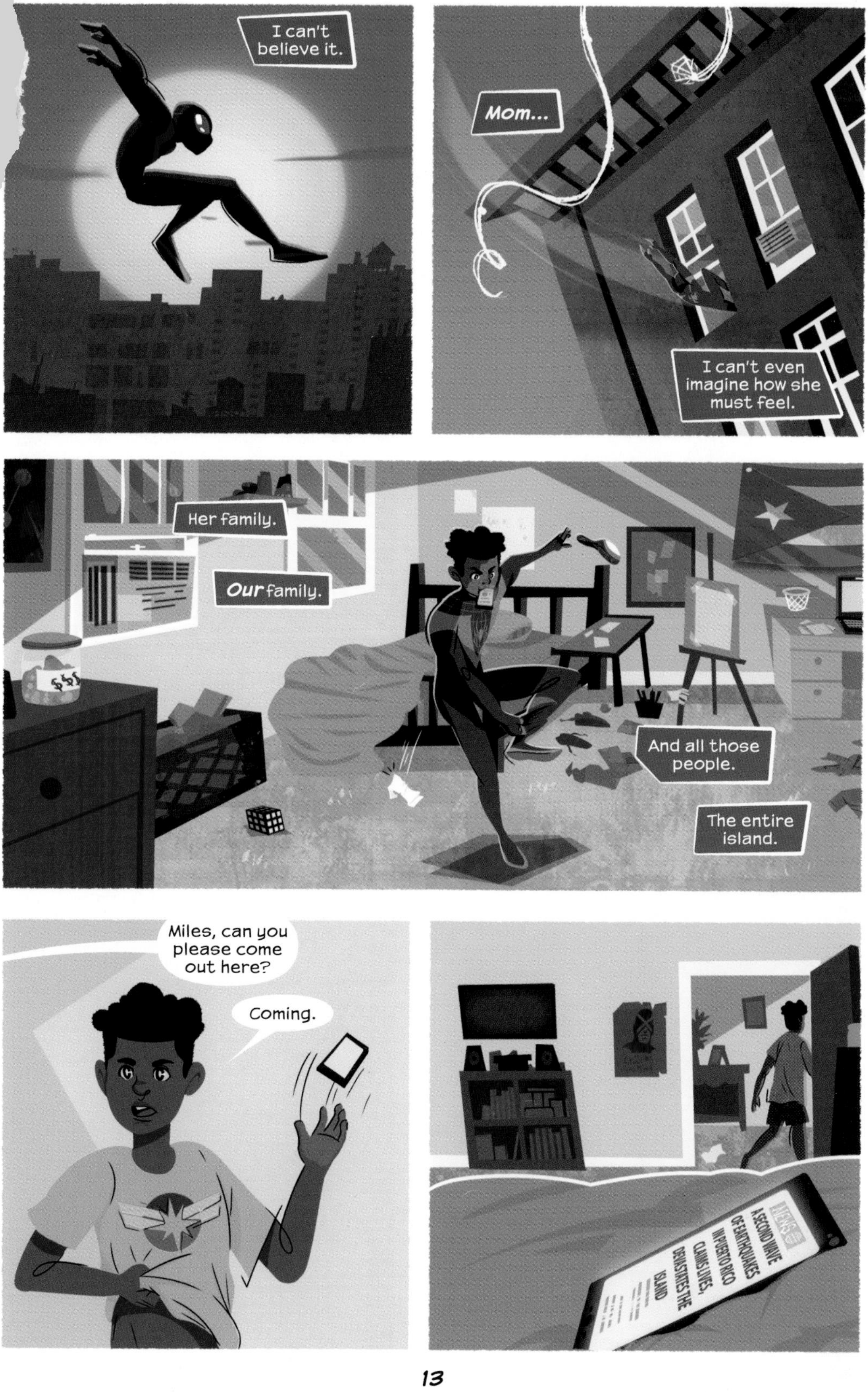

I can't believe it.
Mom...
I can't even imagine how she must feel.
Her family.
Our family.
And all those people.
The entire island.
Miles, can you please come out here?
Coming.
NEWS
A SECOND WAVE OF EARTHQUAKES IN PUERTO RICO CLAIMS LIVES, DEVASTATES THE ISLAND

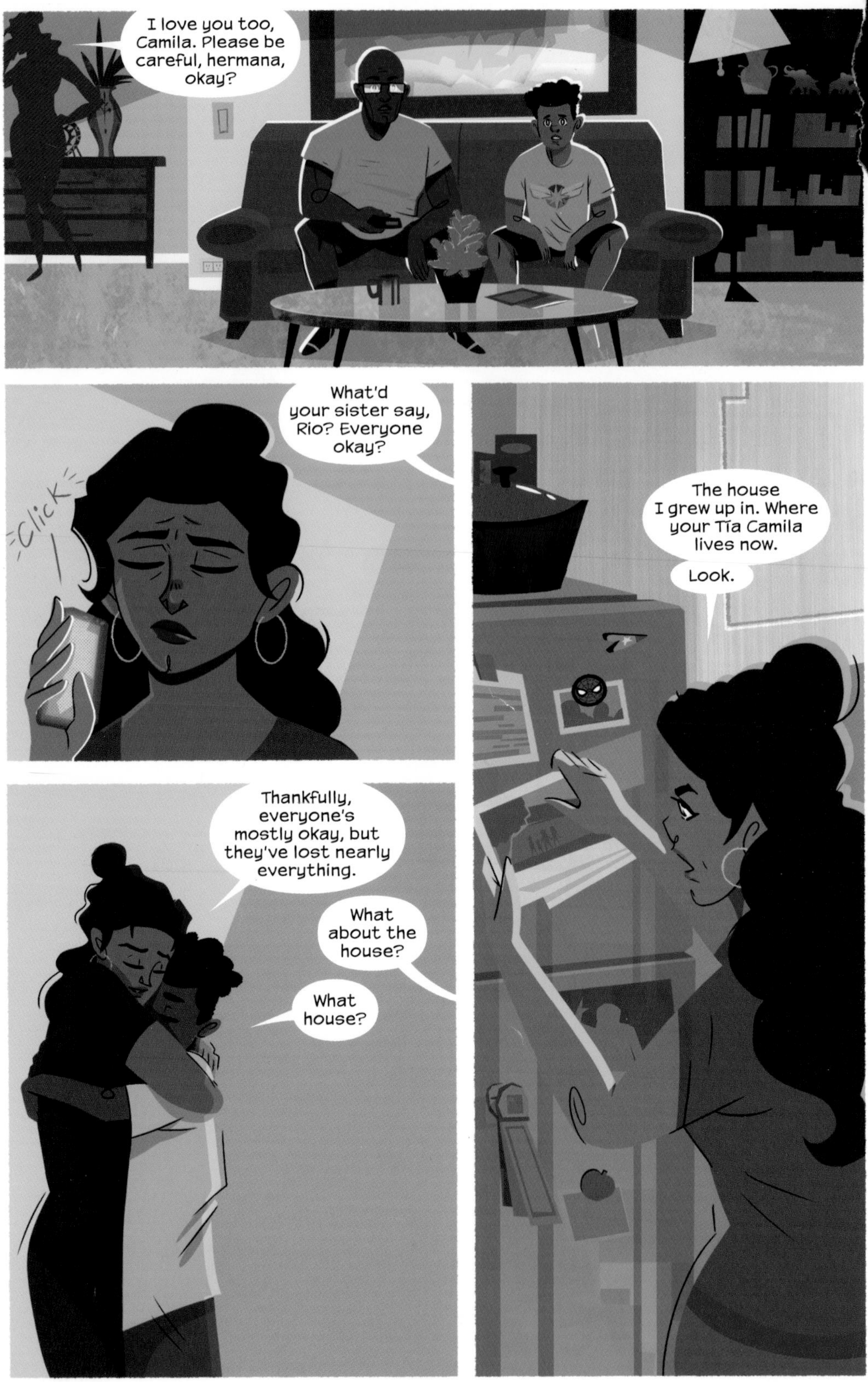

I love you too, Camila. Please be careful, hermana, okay?
What'd your sister say, Rio? Everyone okay?
Click
Thankfully, everyone's mostly okay, but they've lost nearly everything.
What about the house?
What house?
The house I grew up in. Where your Tía Camila lives now.
Look.

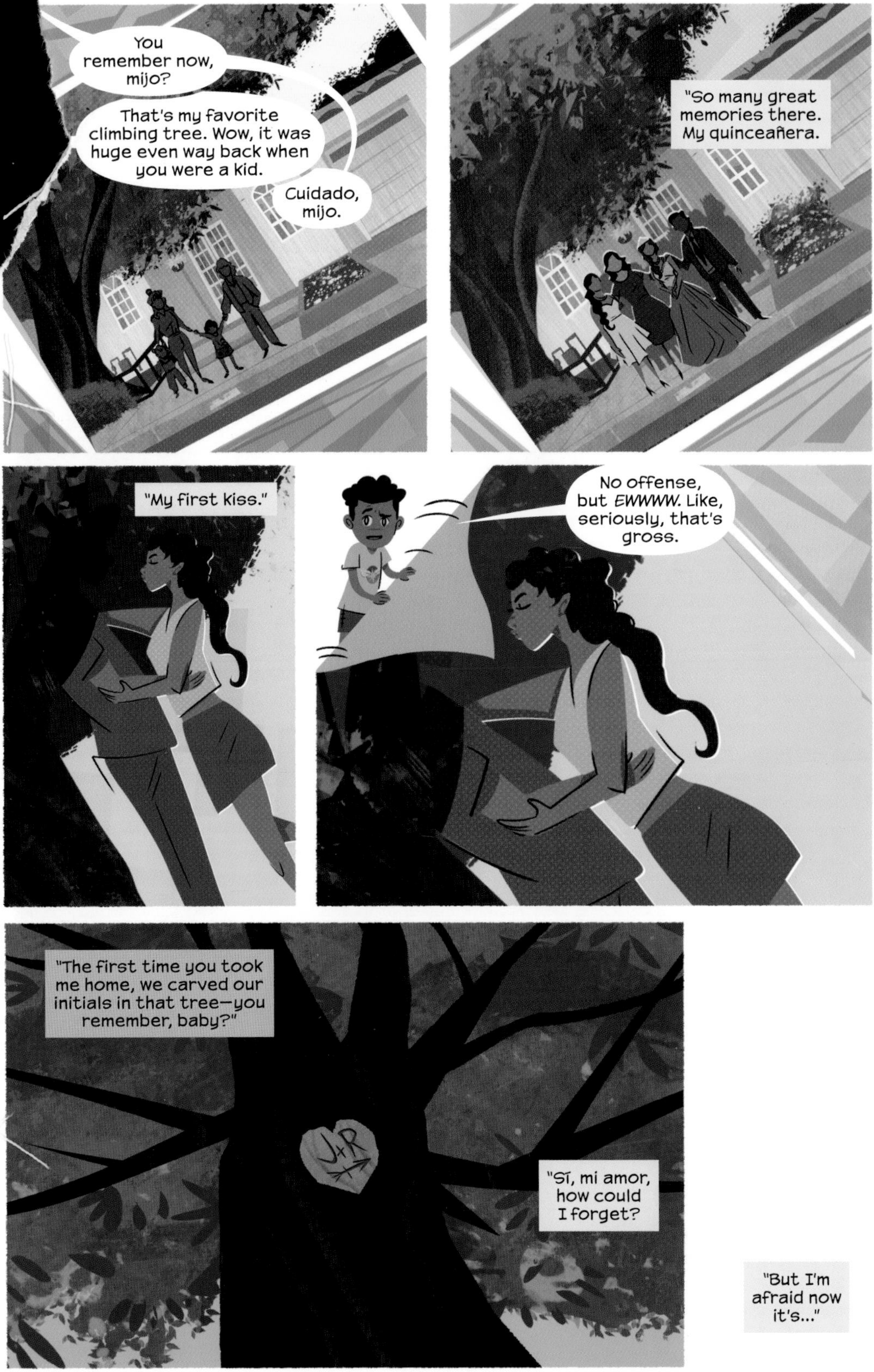
You remember now, mijo?
That's my favorite climbing tree. Wow, it was huge even way back when you were a kid.
Cuidado, mijo.
"So many great memories there. My quinceañera.
"My first kiss."
No offense, but EWWWW. Like, seriously, that's gross.
"The first time you took me home, we carved our initials in that tree—you remember, baby?"
J+R
"Sí, mi amor, how could I forget?
"But I'm afraid now it's..."

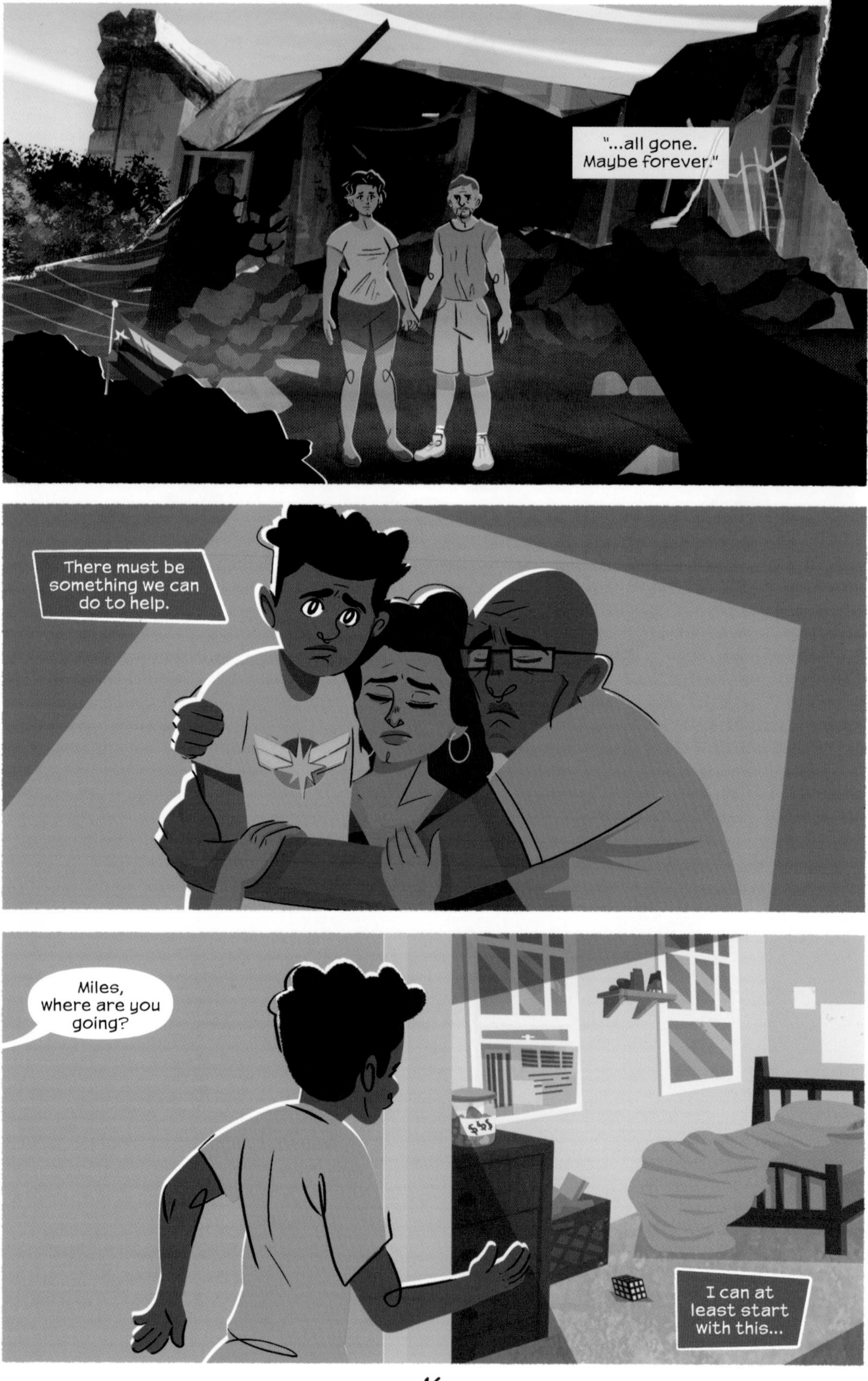
"...all gone. Maybe forever."
There must be something we can do to help.
Miles, where are you going?
I can at least start with this...

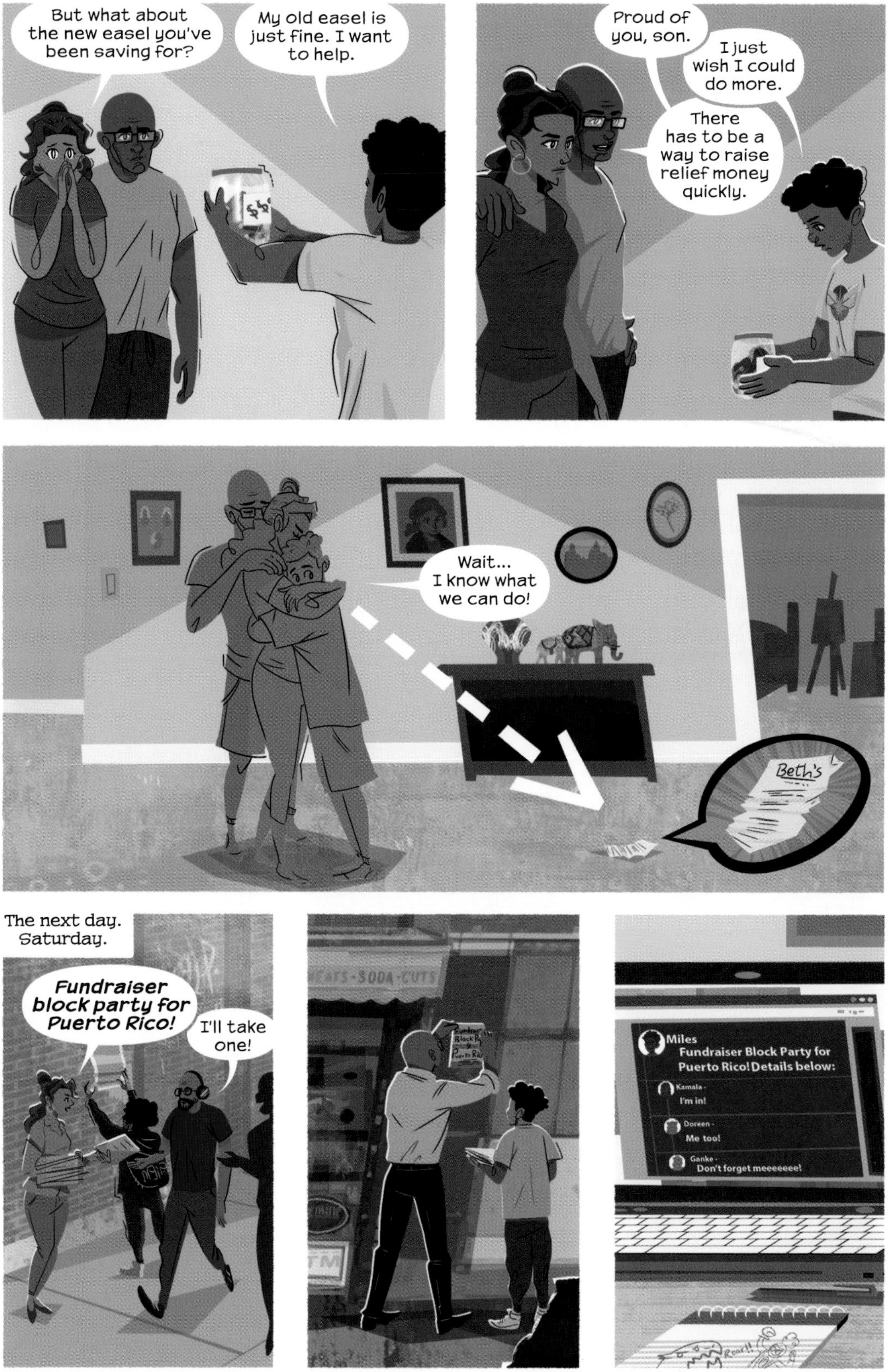
But what about the new easel you've been saving for?
My old easel is just fine. I want to help.
Proud of you, son.
I just wish I could do more.
There has to be a way to raise relief money quickly.
Wait... I know what we can do!
Beth's
The next day. Saturday.
Fundraiser block party for Puerto Rico!
I'll take one!
MEATS - SODA - CUTS
Fundraiser Block Party for Puerto Rico
Miles
Fundraiser Block Party for Puerto Rico! Details below:
Kamala -
I'm in!
Doreen -
Me too!
Ganke -
Don't forget meeeeeee!
Rear!!

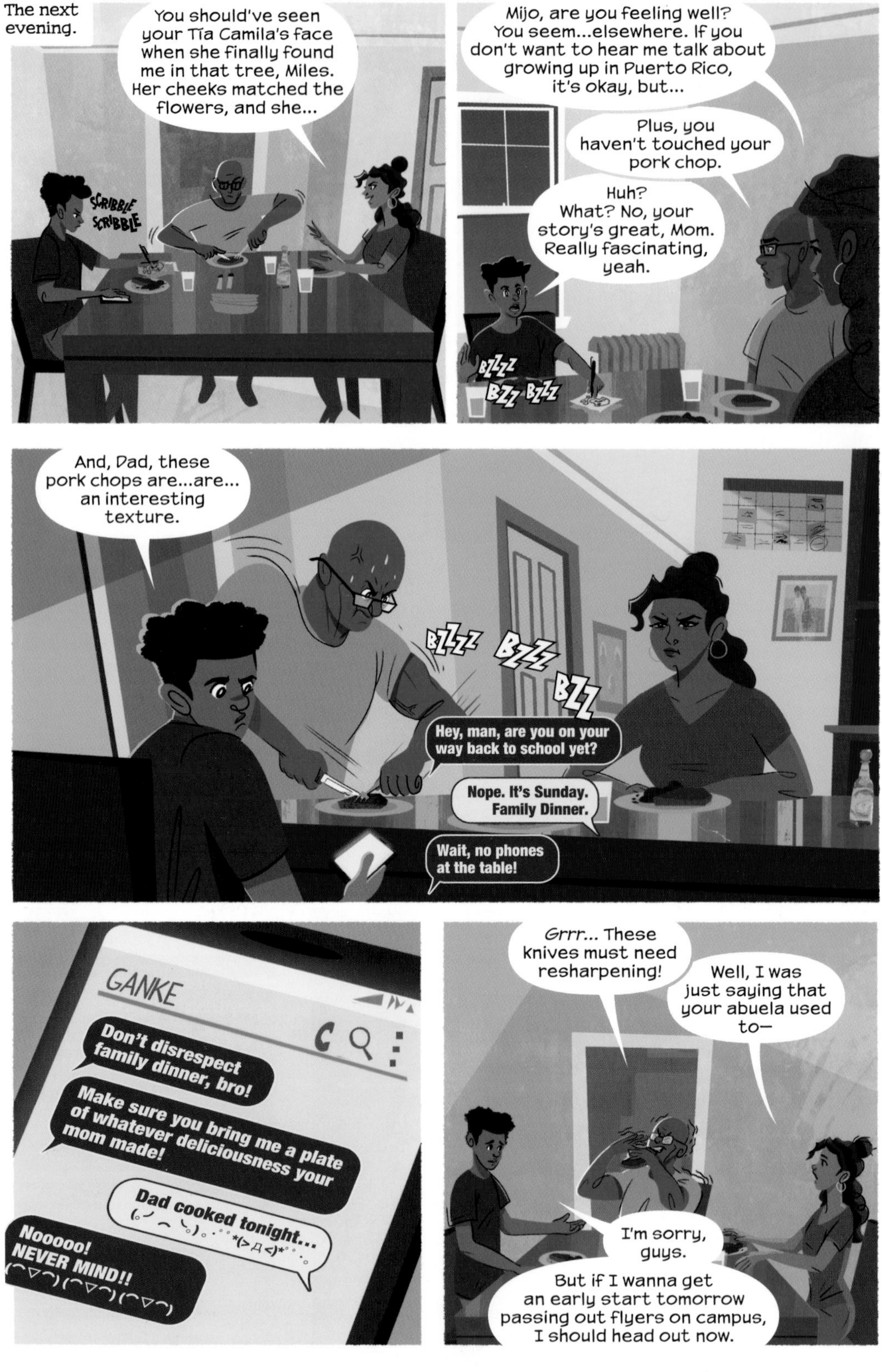
The next evening.
You should've seen your Tía Camila's face when she finally found me in that tree, Miles. Her cheeks matched the flowers, and she...
SCRIBBLE SCRIBBLE
Mijo, are you feeling well? You seem...elsewhere. If you don't want to hear me talk about growing up in Puerto Rico, it's okay, but...
Plus, you haven't touched your pork chop.
Huh? What? No, your story's great, Mom. Really fascinating, yeah.
BZZZZ BZZ BZZZ
And, Dad, these pork chops are...are... an interesting texture.
BZZZZ BZZZ BZZ
Hey, man, are you on your way back to school yet?
Nope. It's Sunday. Family Dinner.
Wait, no phones at the table!
GANKE
Don't disrespect family dinner, bro!
Make sure you bring me a plate of whatever deliciousness your mom made!
Dad cooked tonight... (｡╯︵╰｡)｡.°°*(>Д<)*°°.｡
Nooooo! NEVER MIND!! (⌒▽⌒)(⌒▽⌒)(⌒▽⌒)
Grrr... These knives must need resharpening!
Well, I was just saying that your abuela used to—
I'm sorry, guys.
But if I wanna get an early start tomorrow passing out flyers on campus, I should head out now.

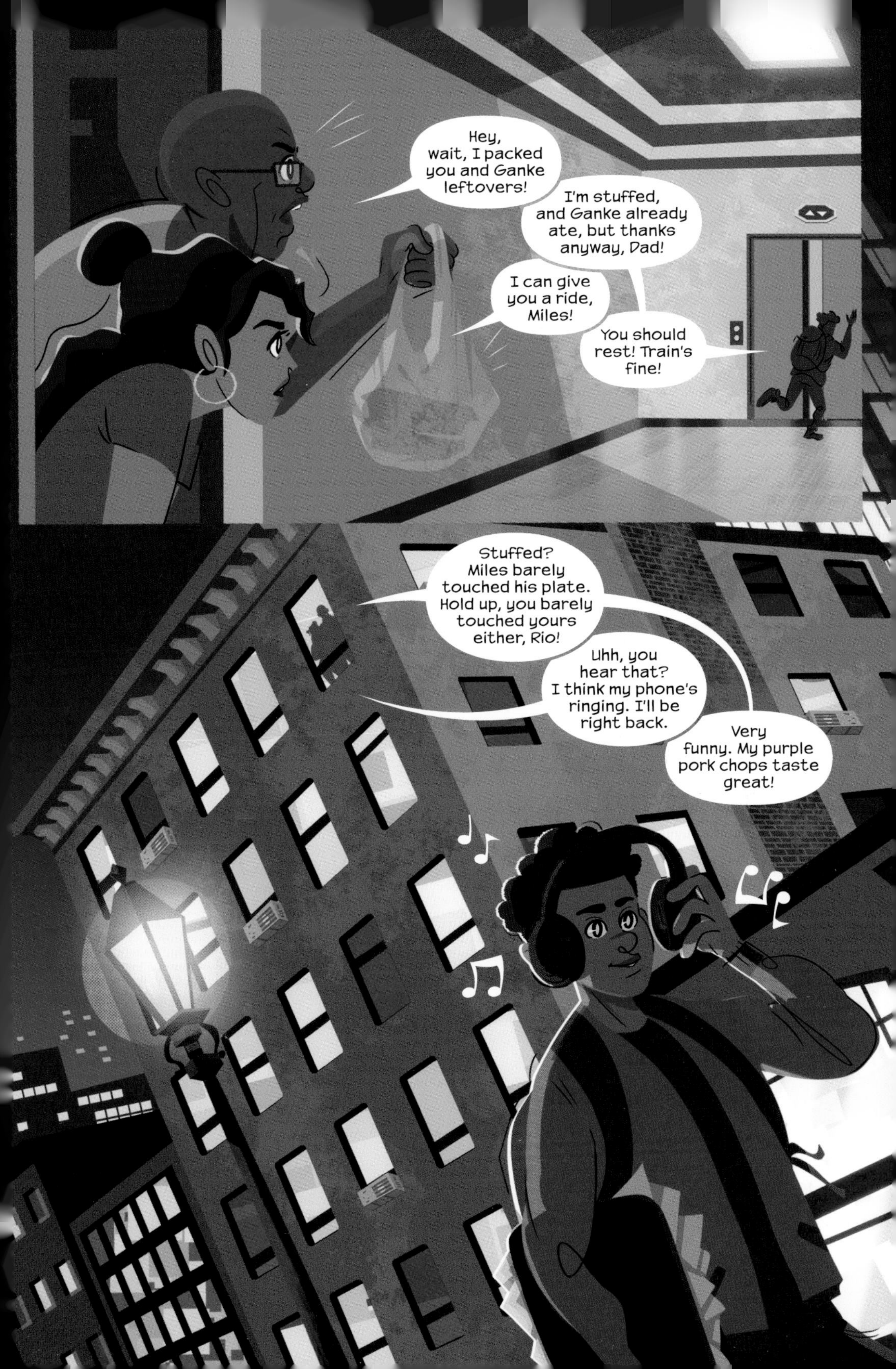
Hey, wait, I packed you and Ganke leftovers!
I'm stuffed, and Ganke already ate, but thanks anyway, Dad!
I can give you a ride, Miles!
You should rest! Train's fine!
Stuffed? Miles barely touched his plate. Hold up, you barely touched yours either, Rio!
Uhh, you hear that? I think my phone's ringing. I'll be right back.
Very funny. My purple pork chops taste great!

CHAPTER

TWO

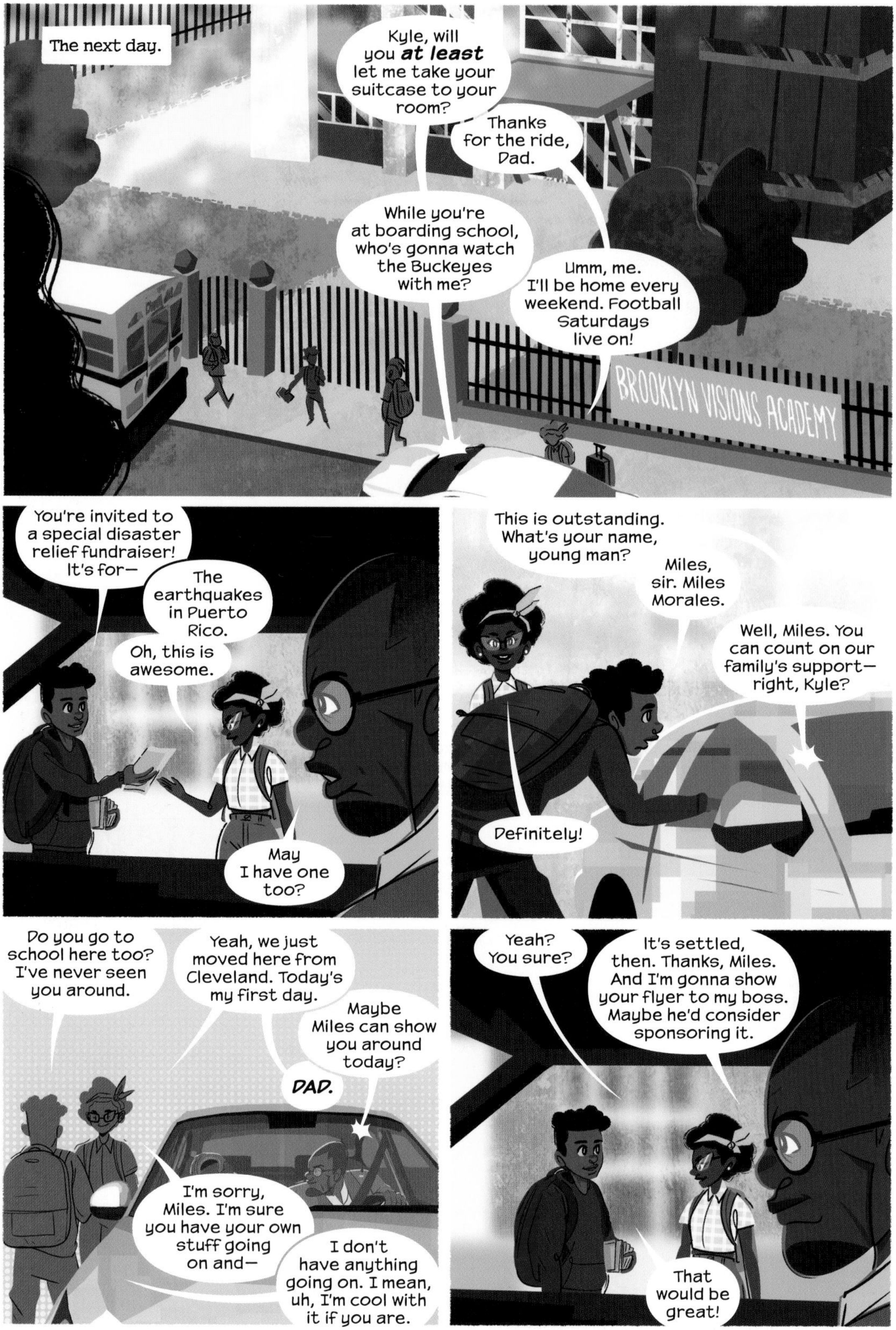
The next day.
Kyle, will you **at least** let me take your suitcase to your room?
Thanks for the ride, Dad.
While you're at boarding school, who's gonna watch the Buckeyes with me?
Umm, me. I'll be home every weekend. Football Saturdays live on!
BROOKLYN VISIONS ACADEMY
You're invited to a special disaster relief fundraiser! It's for—
The earthquakes in Puerto Rico.
Oh, this is awesome.
May I have one too?
This is outstanding. What's your name, young man?
Miles, sir. Miles Morales.
Well, Miles. You can count on our family's support—right, Kyle?
Definitely!
Do you go to school here too? I've never seen you around.
Yeah, we just moved here from Cleveland. Today's my first day.
Maybe Miles can show you around today?
DAD.
I'm sorry, Miles. I'm sure you have your own stuff going on and—
I don't have anything going on. I mean, uh, I'm cool with it if you are.
Yeah? You sure?
It's settled, then. Thanks, Miles. And I'm gonna show your flyer to my boss. Maybe he'd consider sponsoring it.
That would be great!

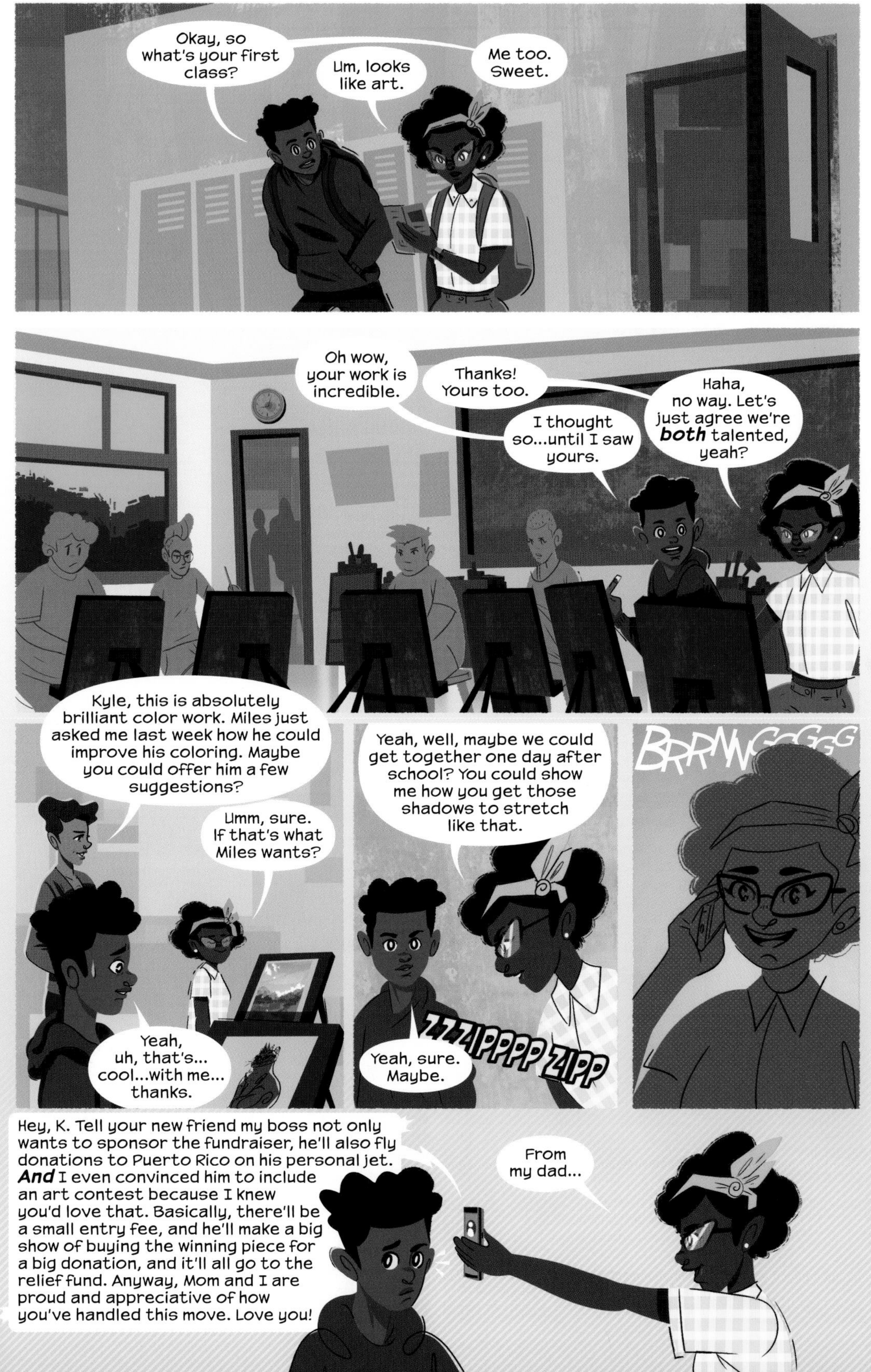

Okay, so what's your first class?
Um, looks like art.
Me too. Sweet.
Oh wow, your work is incredible.
Thanks! Yours too.
I thought so...until I saw yours.
Haha, no way. Let's just agree we're ***both*** talented, yeah?
Kyle, this is absolutely brilliant color work. Miles just asked me last week how he could improve his coloring. Maybe you could offer him a few suggestions?
Umm, sure. If that's what Miles wants?
Yeah, uh, that's... cool...with me... thanks.
Yeah, well, maybe we could get together one day after school? You could show me how you get those shadows to stretch like that.
ZZZIPPPP ZIPP
Yeah, sure. Maybe.
BRRRWGGGG
Hey, K. Tell your new friend my boss not only wants to sponsor the fundraiser, he'll also fly donations to Puerto Rico on his personal jet. ***And*** I even convinced him to include an art contest because I knew you'd love that. Basically, there'll be a small entry fee, and he'll make a big show of buying the winning piece for a big donation, and it'll all go to the relief fund. Anyway, Mom and I are proud and appreciative of how you've handled this move. Love you!
From my dad...

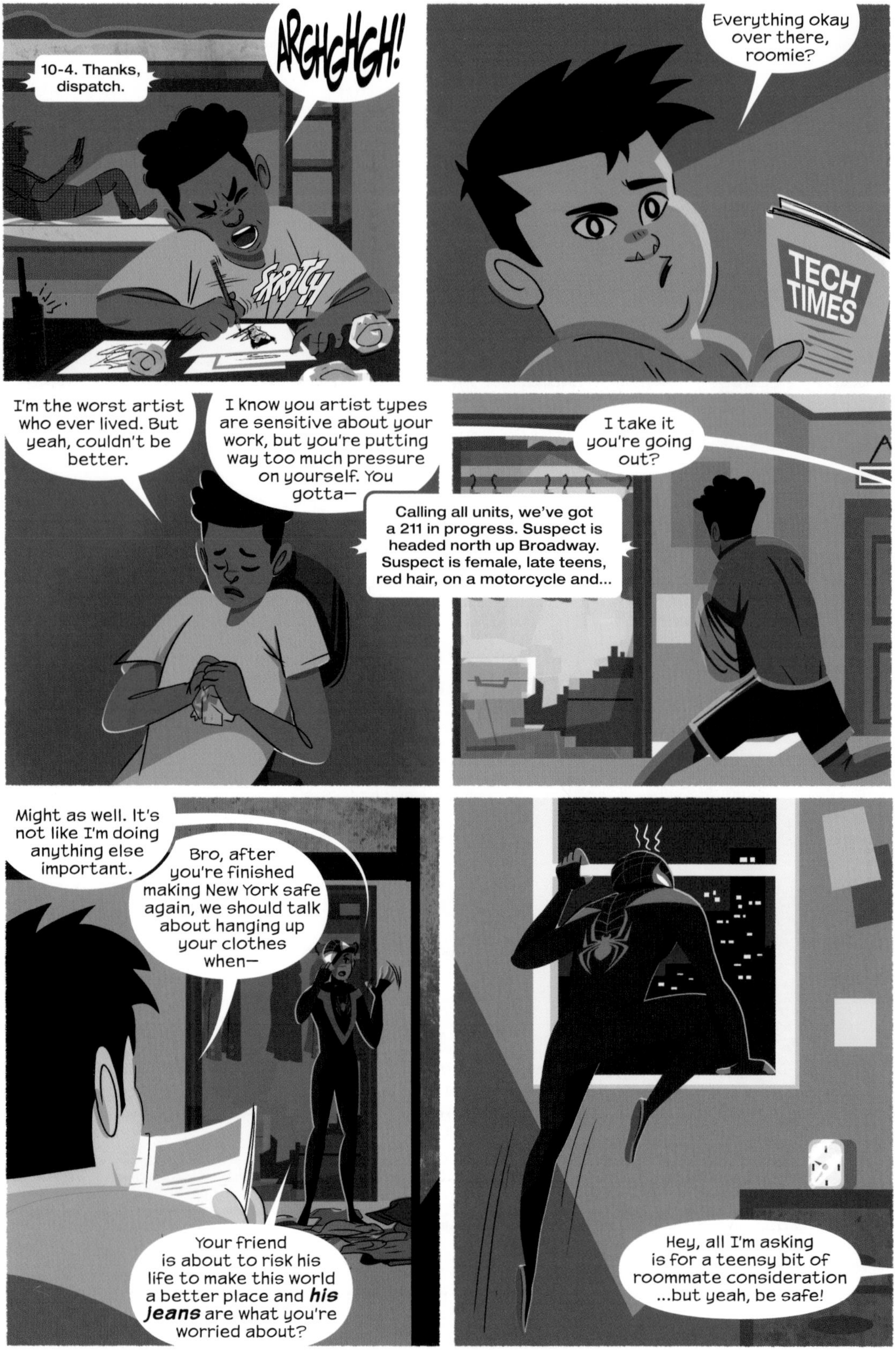
10-4. Thanks, dispatch.
ARGHGHGH!
SKRITCH
Everything okay over there, roomie?
TECH TIMES
I'm the worst artist who ever lived. But yeah, couldn't be better.
I know you artist types are sensitive about your work, but you're putting way too much pressure on yourself. You gotta—
I take it you're going out?
Calling all units, we've got a 211 in progress. Suspect is headed north up Broadway. Suspect is female, late teens, red hair, on a motorcycle and...
Might as well. It's not like I'm doing anything else important.
Bro, after you're finished making New York safe again, we should talk about hanging up your clothes when—
Your friend is about to risk his life to make this world a better place and ***his jeans*** are what you're worried about?
Hey, all I'm asking is for a teensy bit of roommate consideration ...but yeah, be safe!

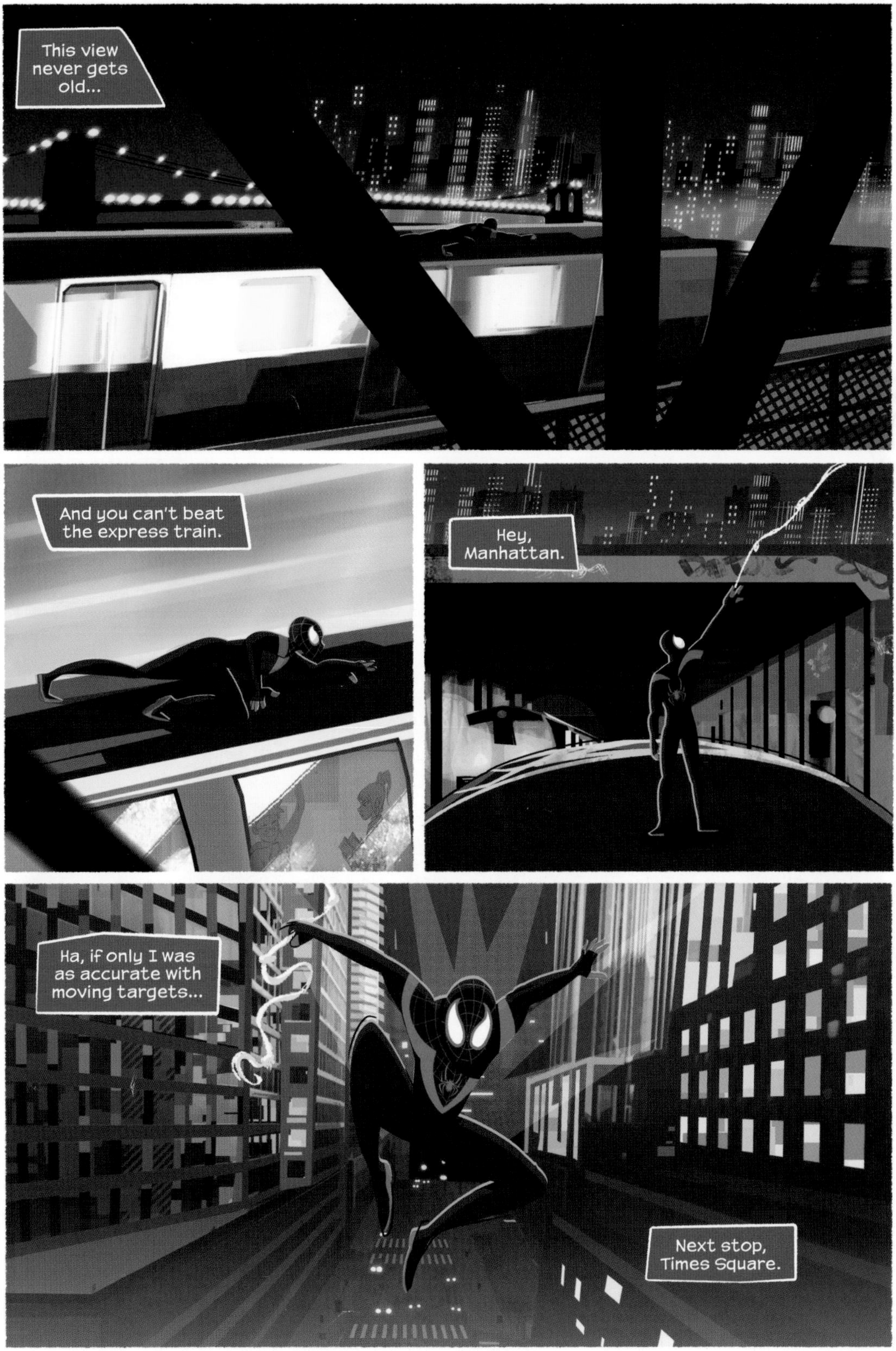
This view never gets old...
And you can't beat the express train.
Hey, Manhattan.
Ha, if only I was as accurate with moving targets...
Next stop, Times Square.

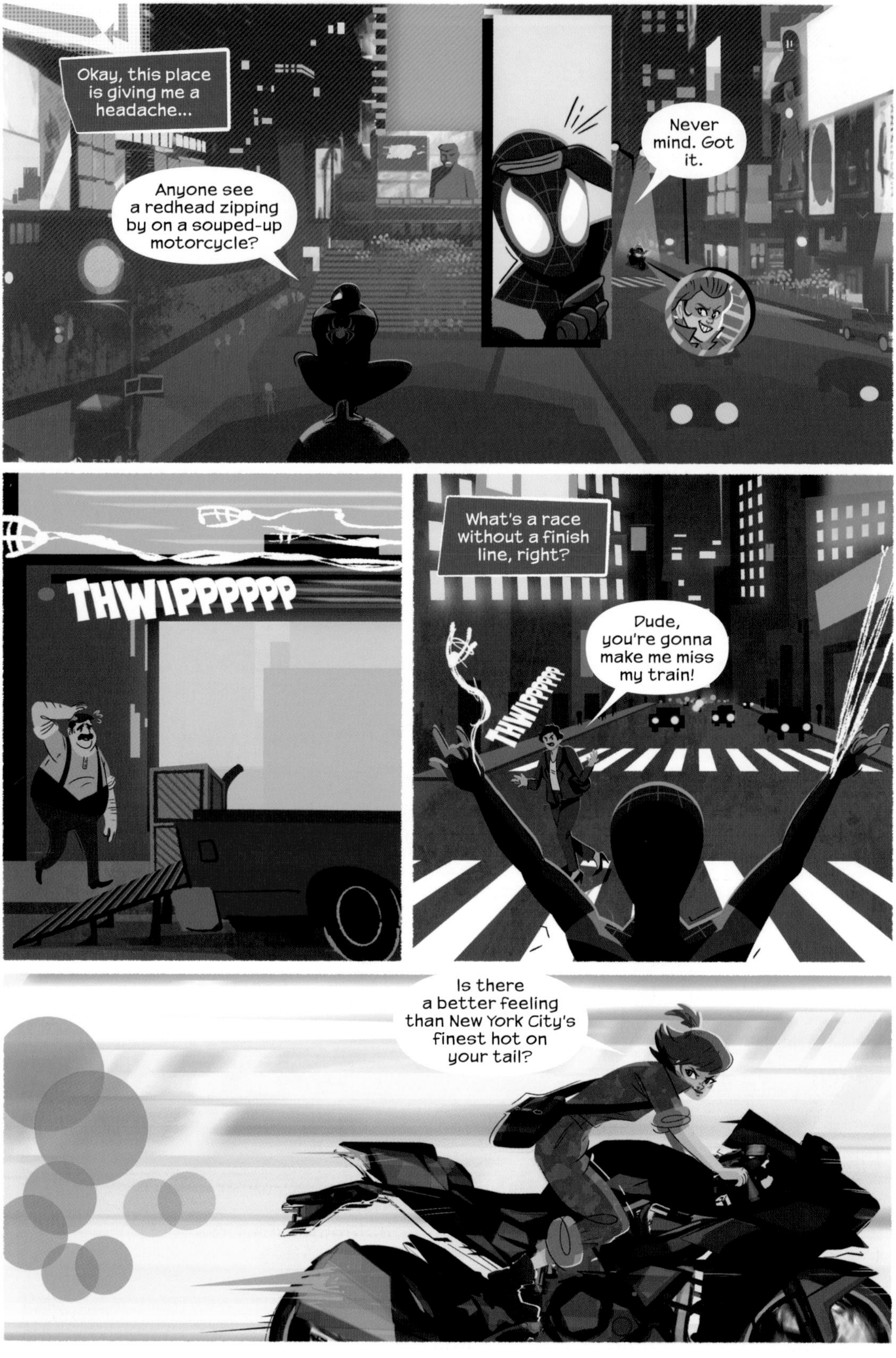
Okay, this place is giving me a headache...
Anyone see a redhead zipping by on a souped-up motorcycle?
Never mind. Got it.
THWIPPPPPP
What's a race without a finish line, right?
Dude, you're gonna make me miss my train!
THWIPPPPP
Is there a better feeling than New York City's finest hot on your tail?

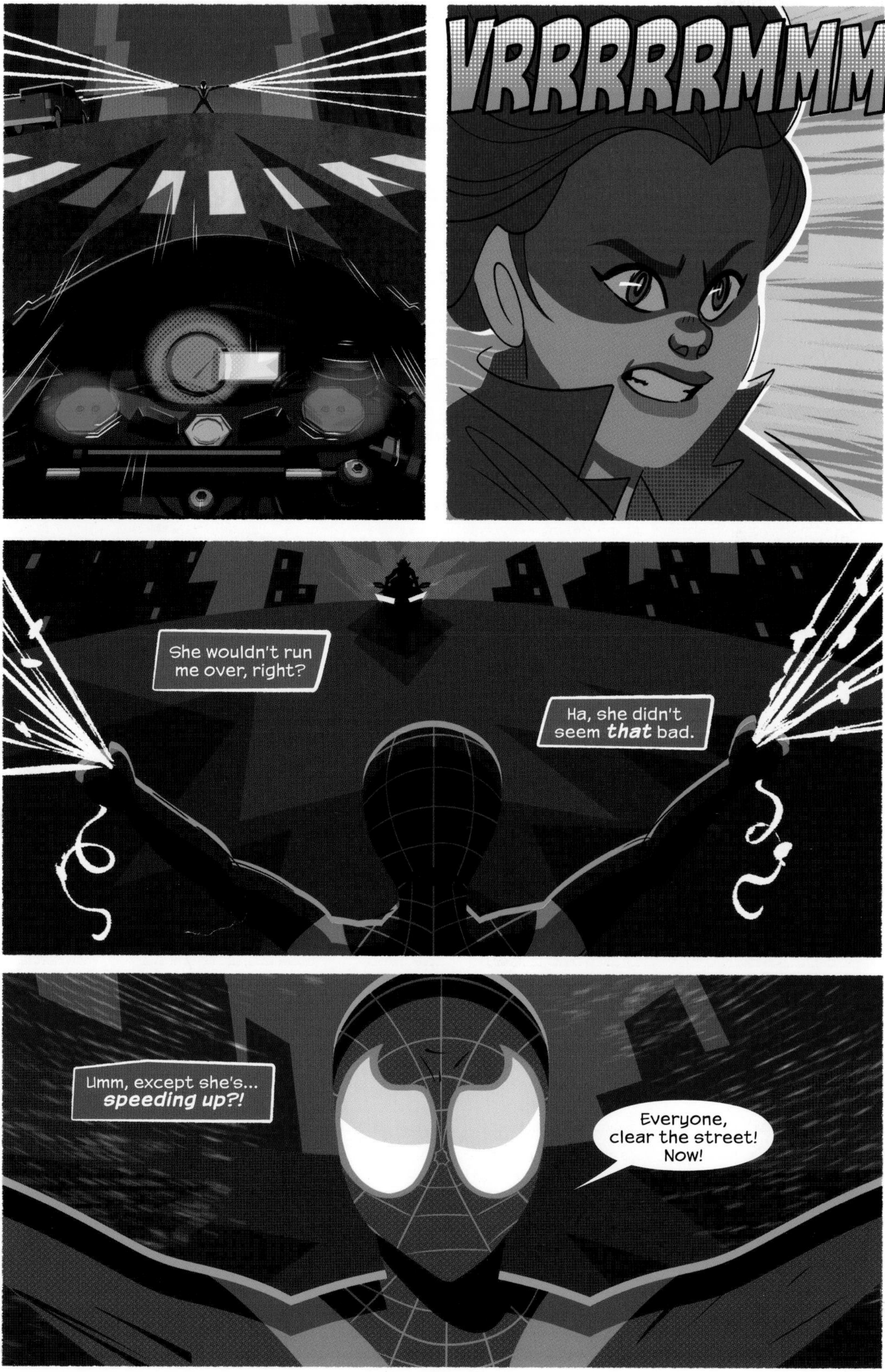
VRRRRRMMM
She wouldn't run me over, right?
Ha, she didn't seem ***that*** bad.
Umm, except she's... ***speeding up?!***
Everyone, clear the street! Now!

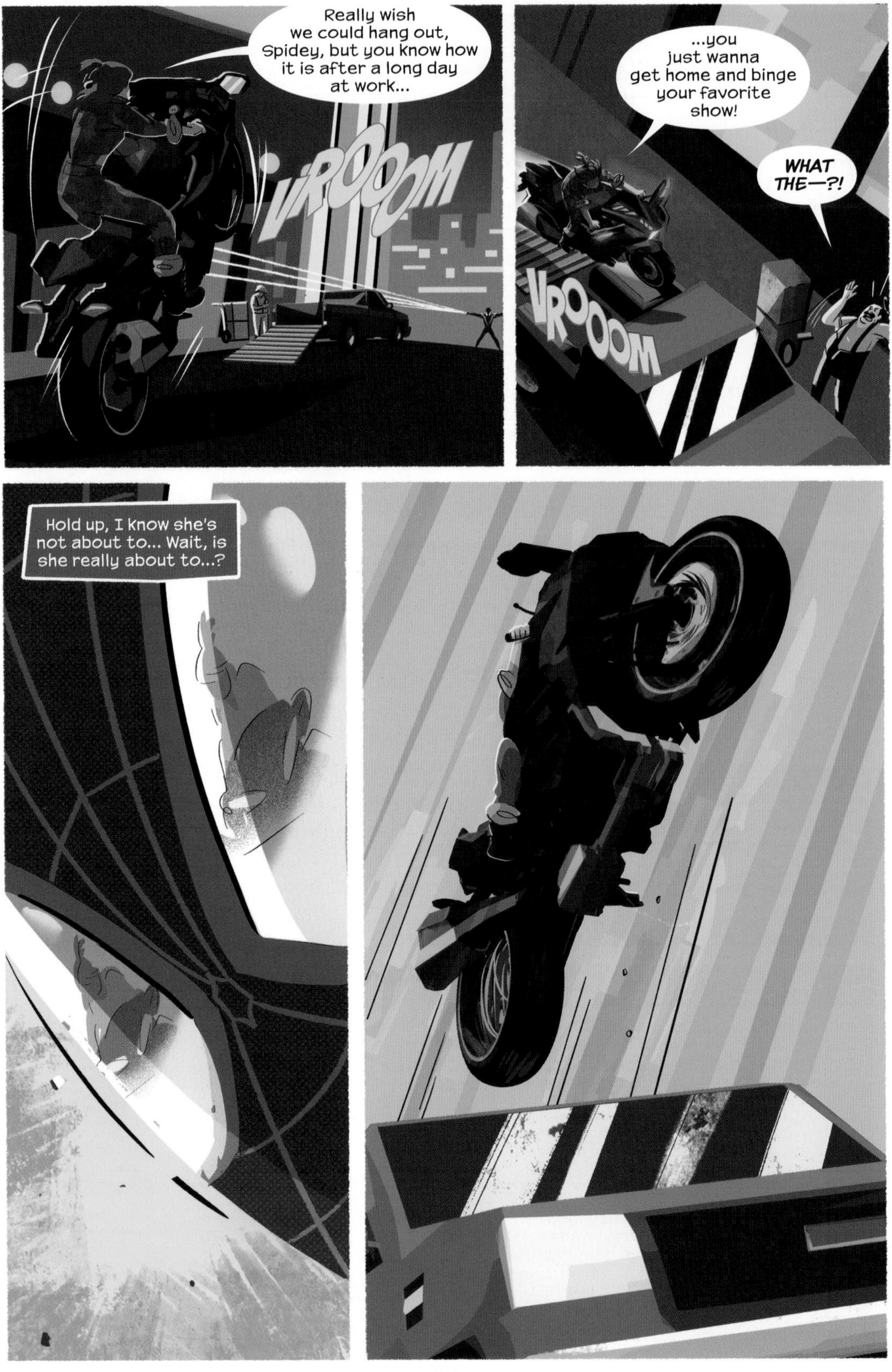
Really wish we could hang out, Spidey, but you know how it is after a long day at work...
VROOOM
...you just wanna get home and binge your favorite show!
WHAT THE—?!
VROOOM
Hold up, I know she's not about to... Wait, is she really about to...?

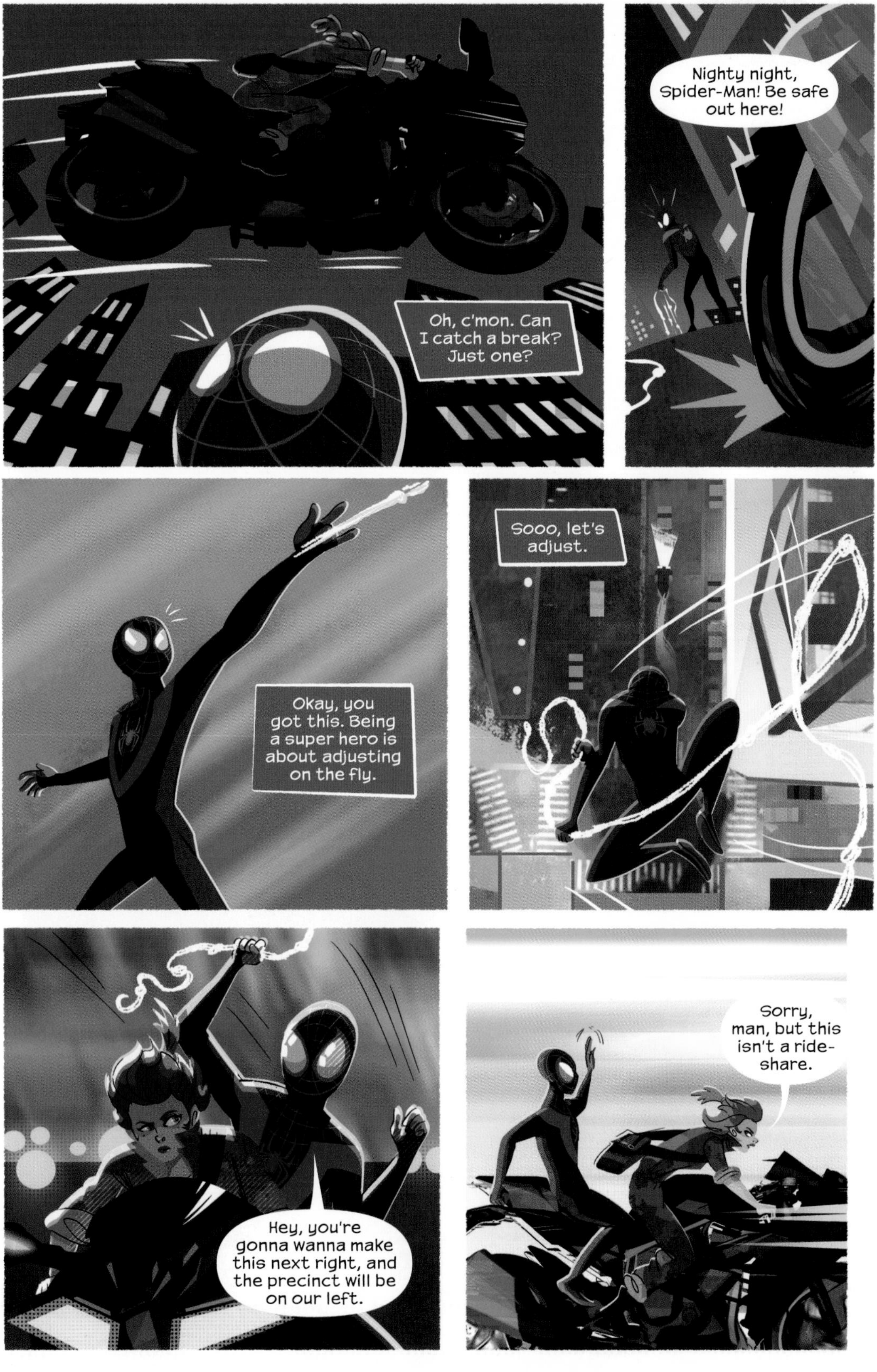
Oh, c'mon. Can I catch a break? Just one?
Nighty night, Spider-Man! Be safe out here!
Okay, you got this. Being a super hero is about adjusting on the fly.
Sooo, let's adjust.
Hey, you're gonna wanna make this next right, and the precinct will be on our left.
Sorry, man, but this isn't a ride-share.

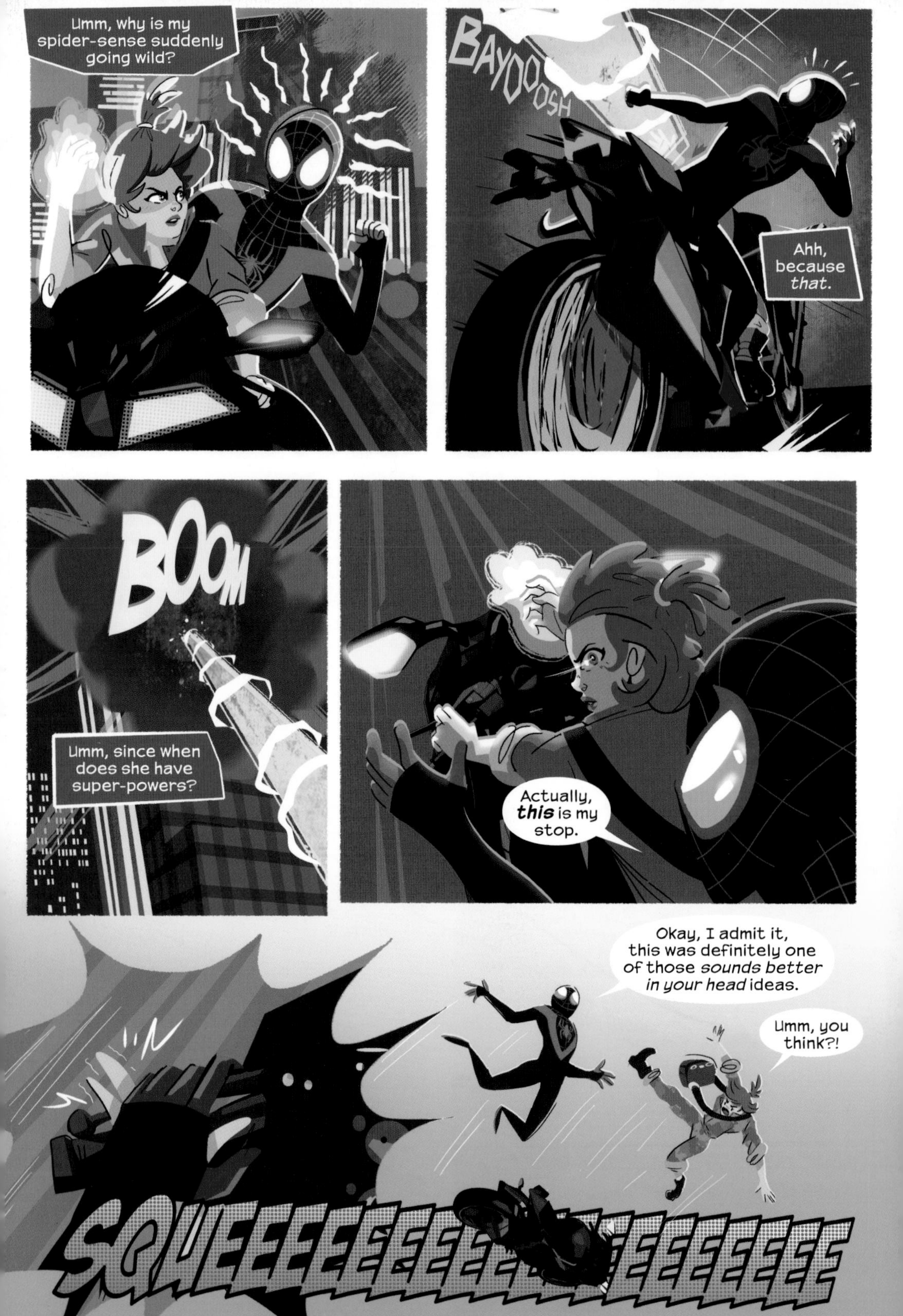
Umm, why is my spider-sense suddenly going wild?
BAYOOOOSH
Ahh, because *that*.
BOOM
Umm, since when does she have super-powers?
Actually, ***this*** is my stop.
Okay, I admit it, this was definitely one of those *sounds better in your head* ideas.
Umm, you think?!
SQUEEEEEEEEEEEEEEEEEEE

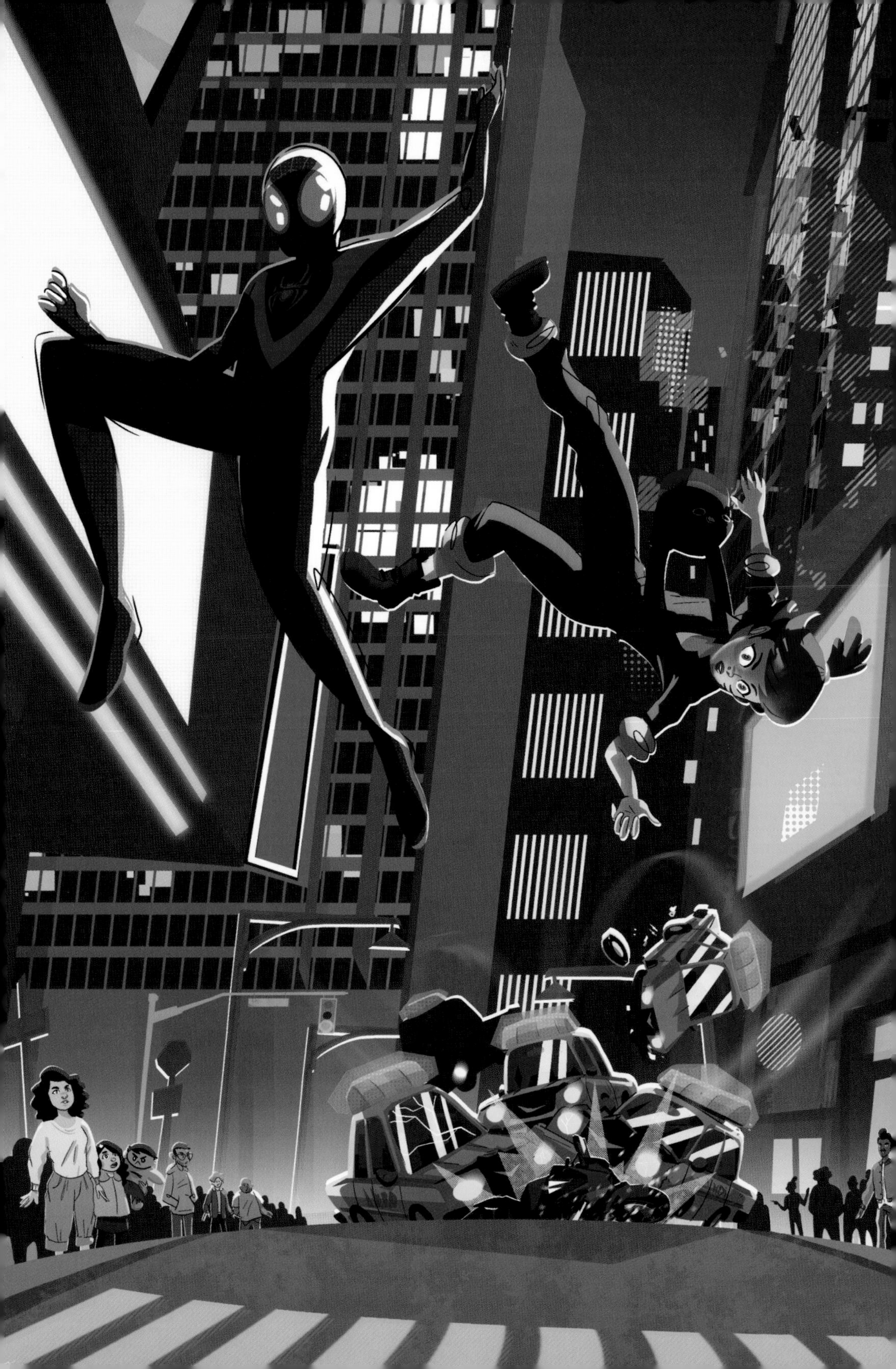

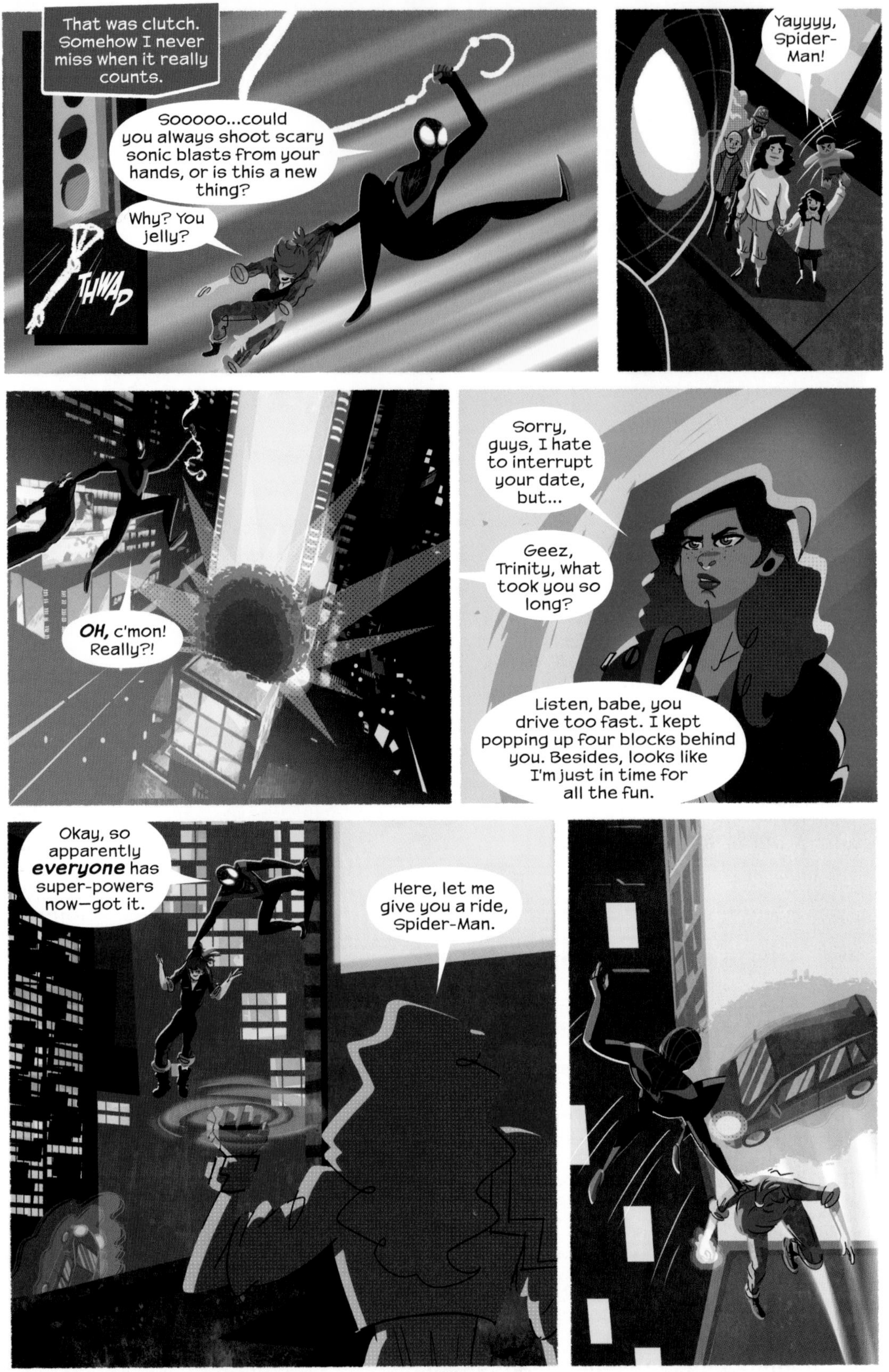
That was clutch. Somehow I never miss when it really counts.
Sooooo...could you always shoot scary sonic blasts from your hands, or is this a new thing?
Why? You jelly?
THWAP
Yayyyy, Spider-Man!
OH, c'mon! Really?!
Sorry, guys, I hate to interrupt your date, but...
Geez, Trinity, what took you so long?
Listen, babe, you drive too fast. I kept popping up four blocks behind you. Besides, looks like I'm just in time for all the fun.
Okay, so apparently everyone has super-powers now—got it.
Here, let me give you a ride, Spider-Man.

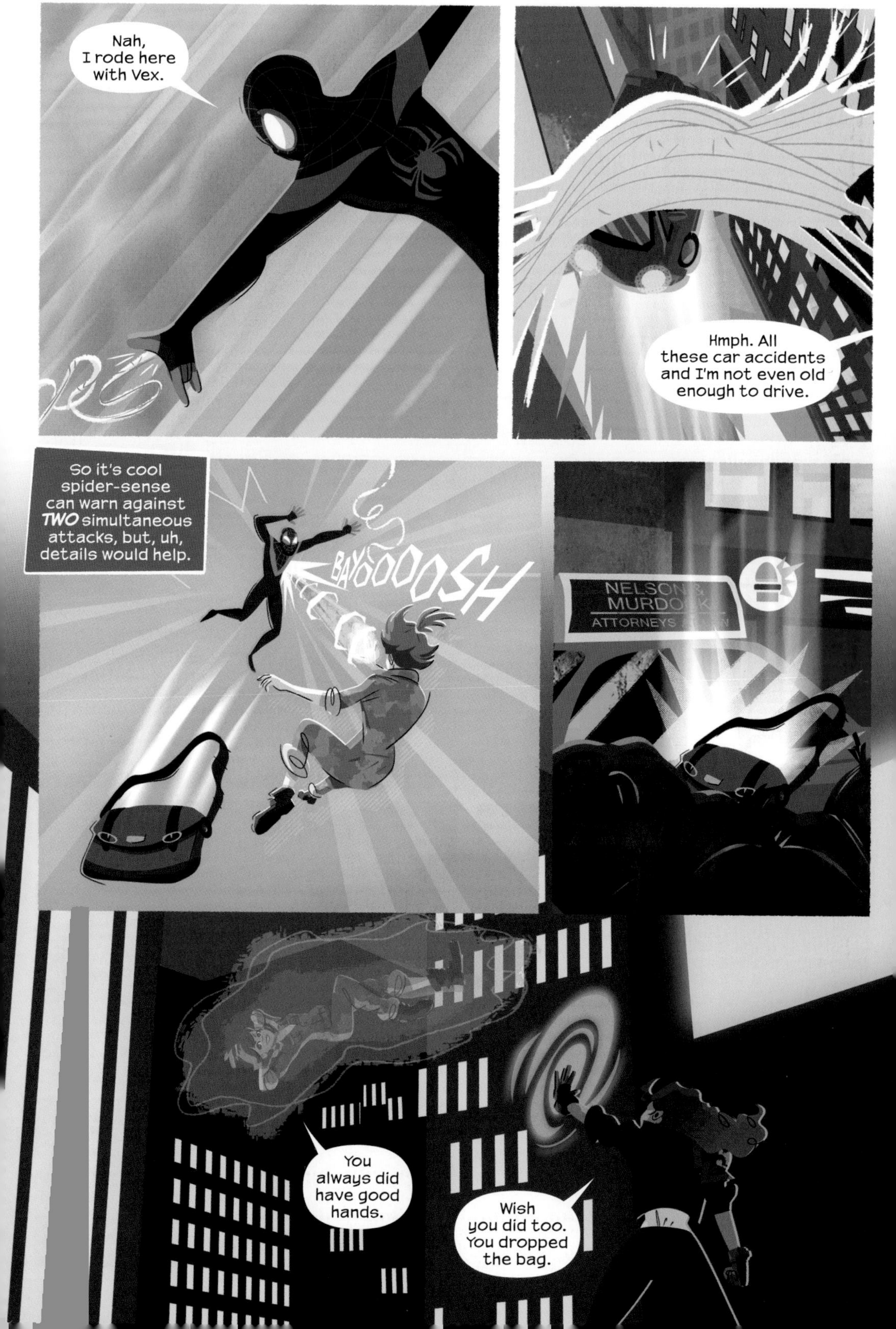
Nah, I rode here with Vex.
Hmph. All these car accidents and I'm not even old enough to drive.
So it's cool spider-sense can warn against **TWO** simultaneous attacks, but, uh, details would help.
BAYOOOOOSH
NELSON & MURDOCK
ATTORNEYS
You always did have good hands.
Wish you did too. You dropped the bag.

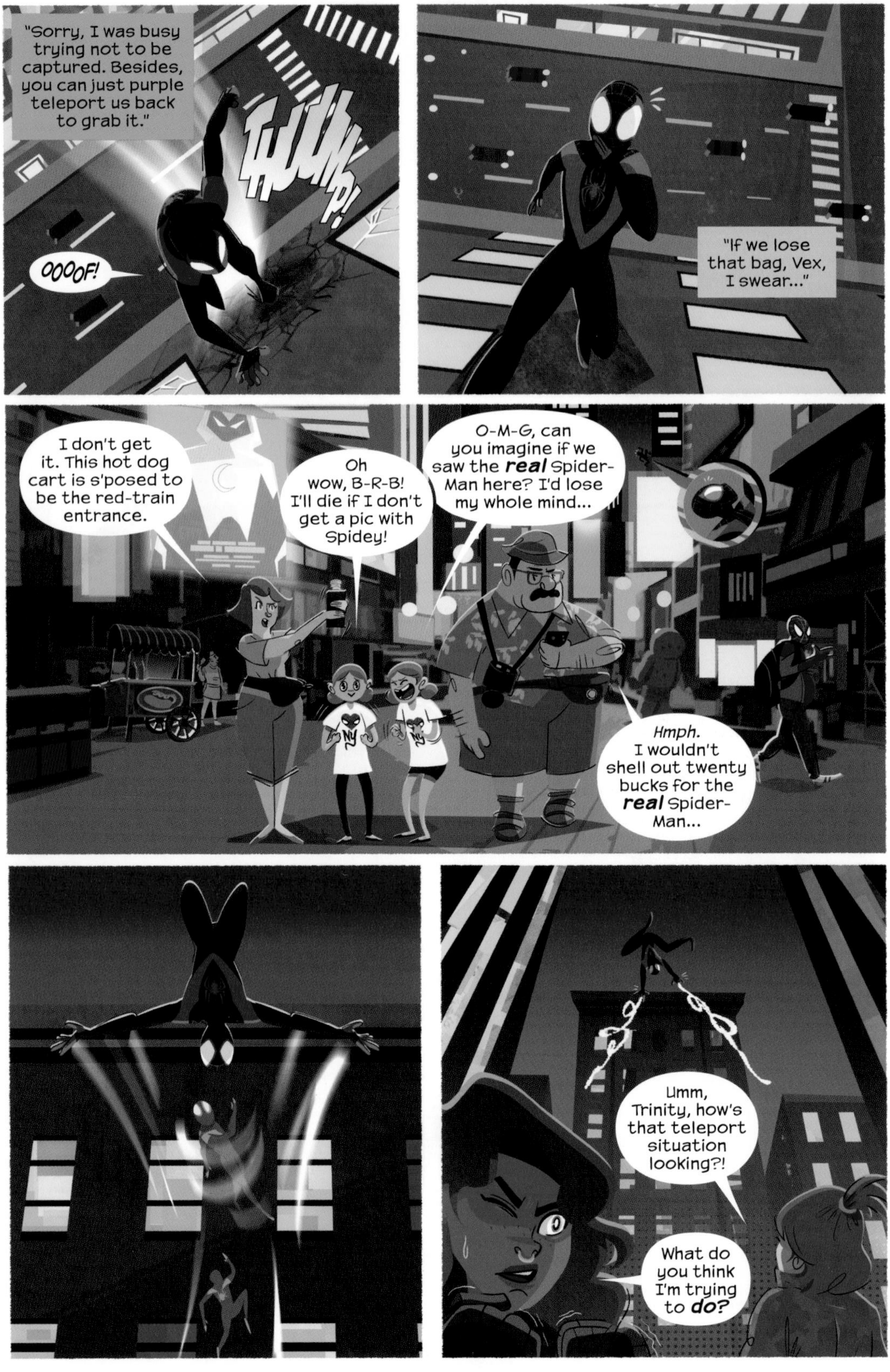
"Sorry, I was busy trying not to be captured. Besides, you can just purple teleport us back to grab it."
THUMP!
OOOOF!
"If we lose that bag, Vex, I swear..."
I don't get it. This hot dog cart is s'posed to be the red-train entrance.
Oh wow, B-R-B! I'll die if I don't get a pic with Spidey!
O-M-G, can you imagine if we saw the ***real*** Spider-Man here? I'd lose my whole mind...
Hmph. I wouldn't shell out twenty bucks for the ***real*** Spider-Man...
Umm, Trinity, how's that teleport situation looking?!
What do you think I'm trying to ***do?***

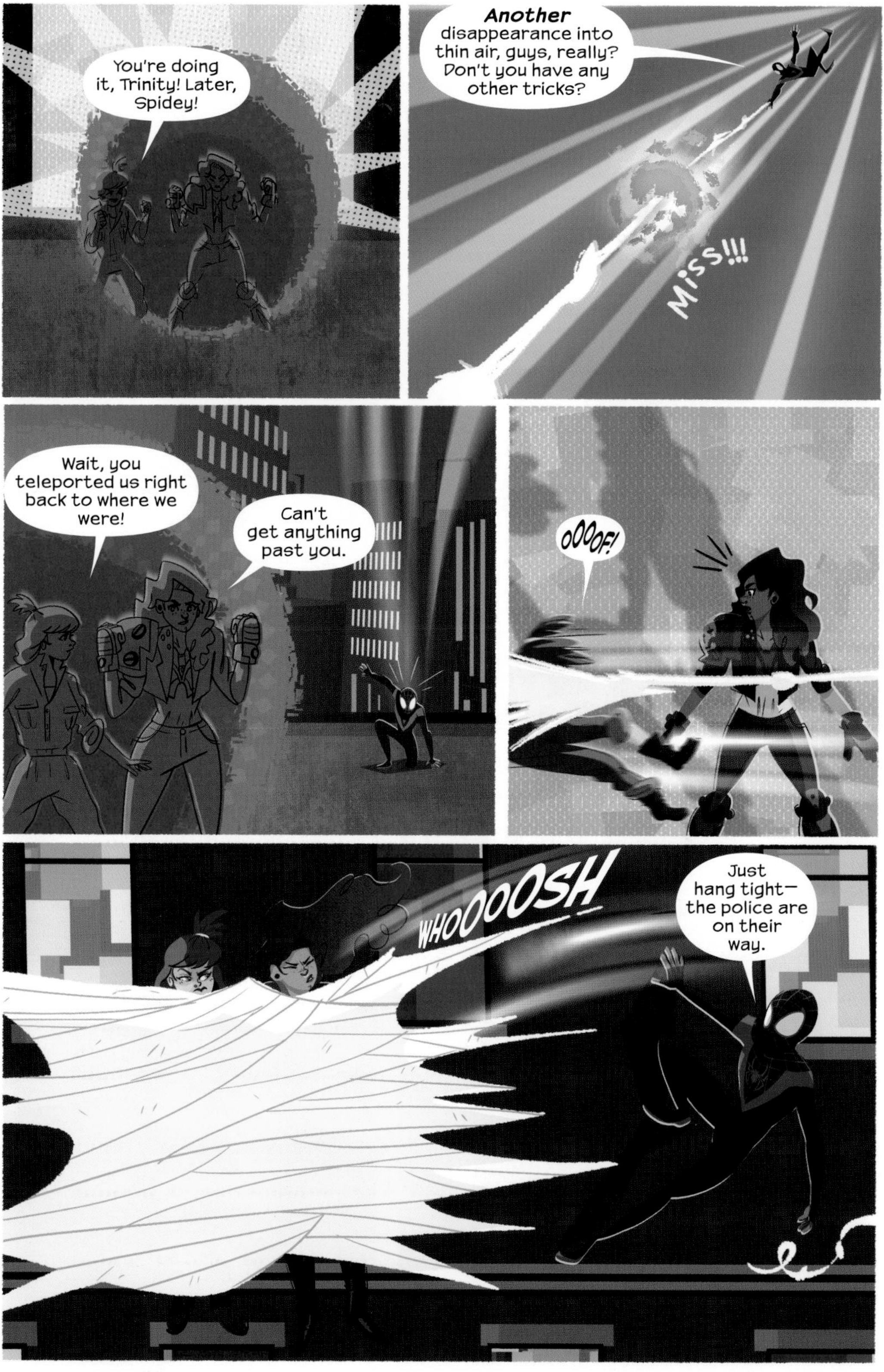
You're doing it, Trinity! Later, Spidey!
Another disappearance into thin air, guys, really? Don't you have any other tricks?
MISS!!!
Wait, you teleported us right back to where we were!
Can't get anything past you.
OOOOF!
WHOOOOSH
Just hang tight— the police are on their way.

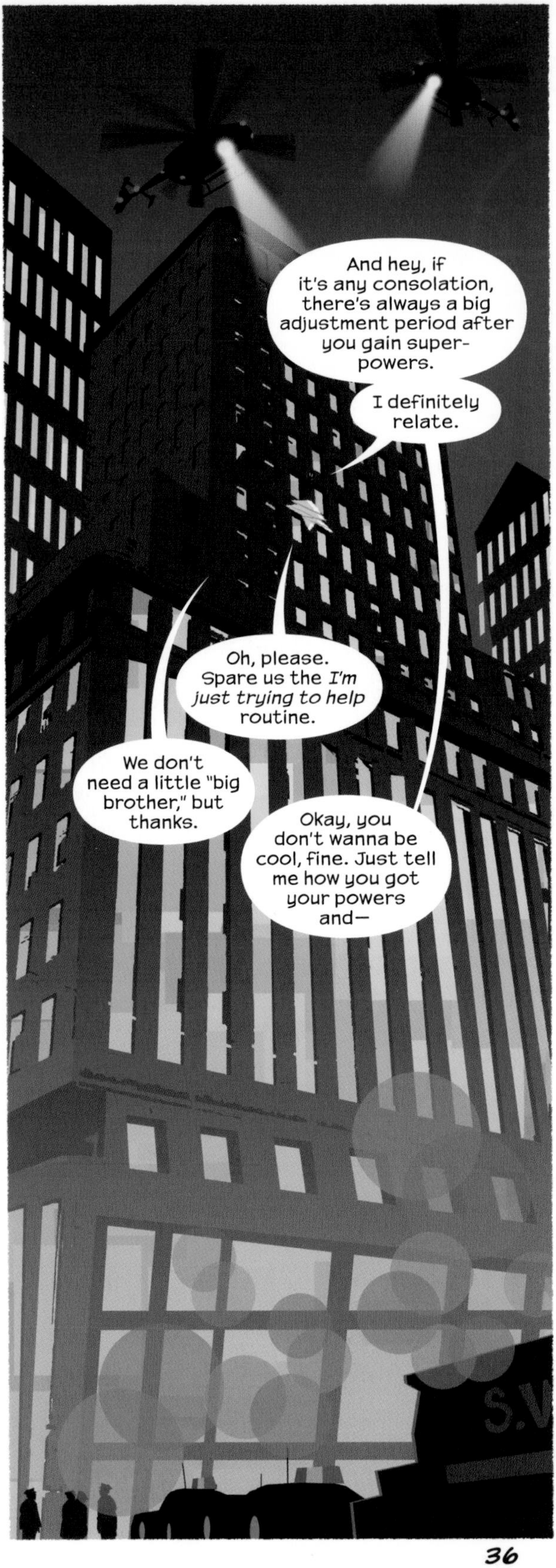
And hey, if it's any consolation, there's always a big adjustment period after you gain super-powers.
I definitely relate.
Oh, please. Spare us the *I'm just trying to help* routine.
We don't need a little "big brother," but thanks.
Okay, you don't wanna be cool, fine. Just tell me how you got your powers and—
S.V
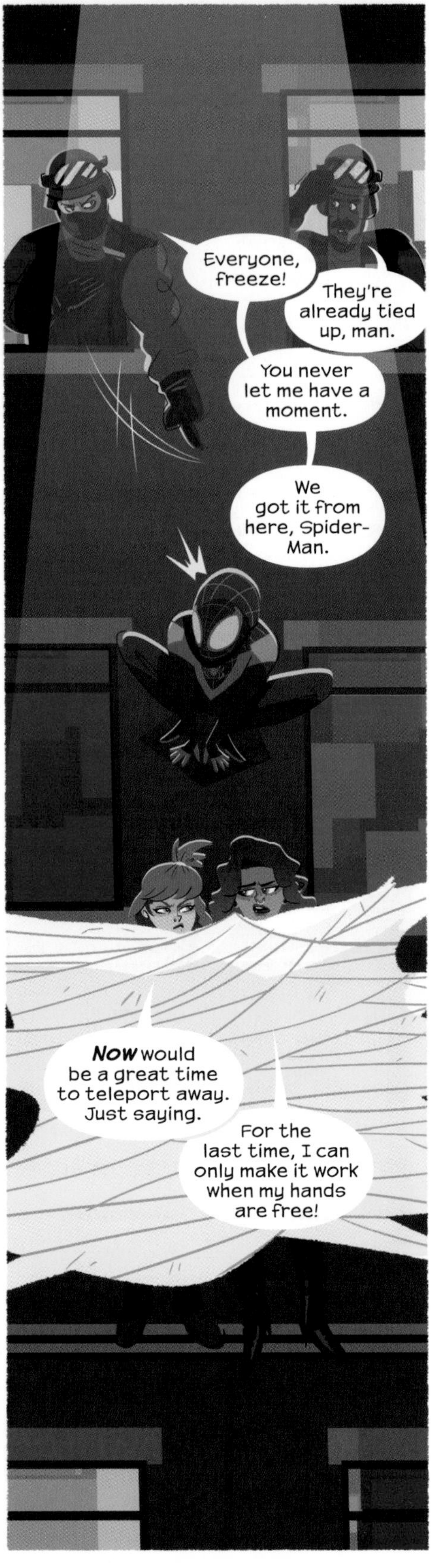
Everyone, freeze!
They're already tied up, man.
You never let me have a moment.
We got it from here, Spider-Man.
NOW would be a great time to teleport away. Just saying.
For the last time, I can only make it work when my hands are free!

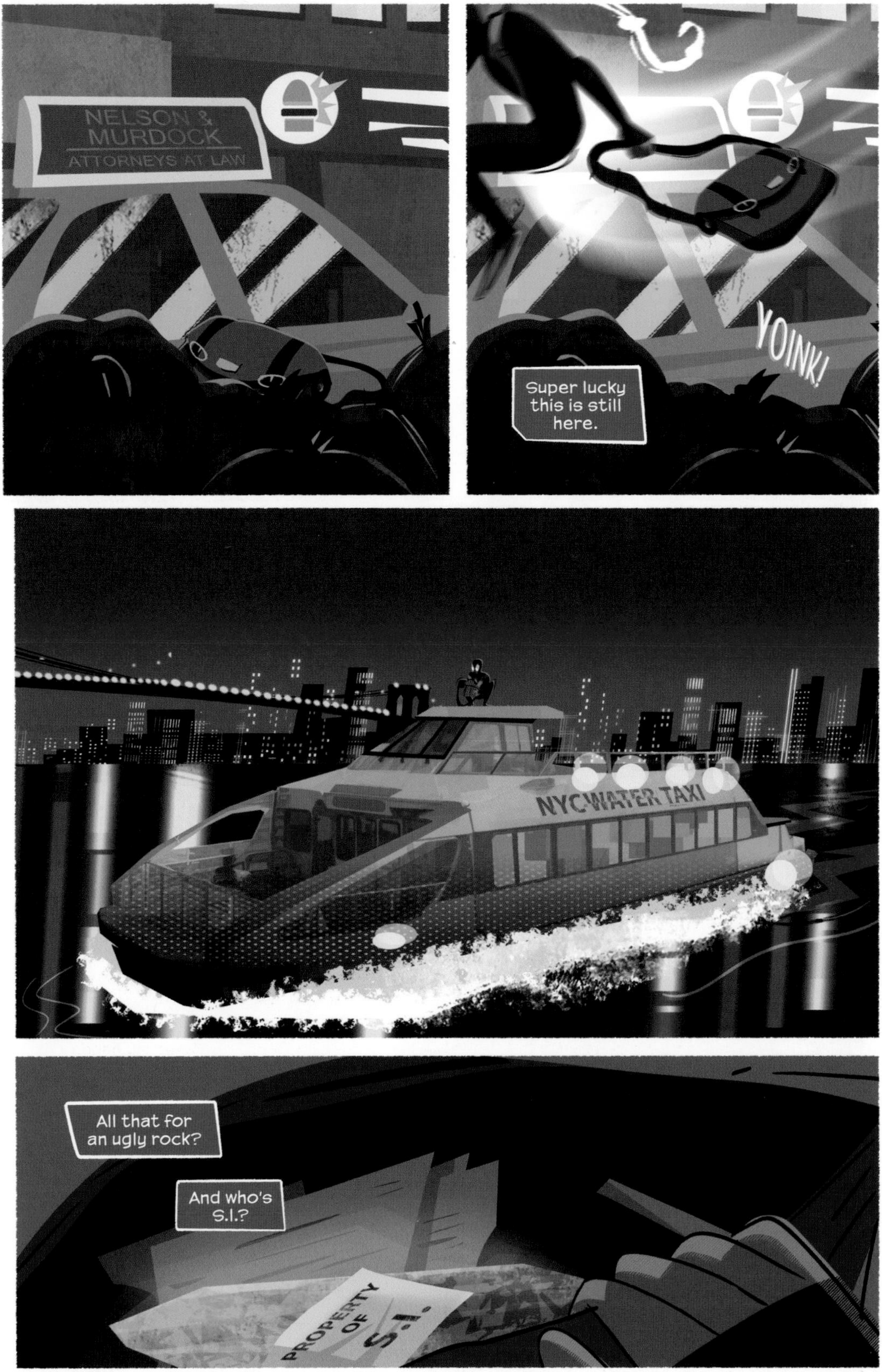
NELSON & MURDOCK
ATTORNEYS AT LAW
Super lucky this is still here.
YOINK!
NYC WATER TAXI
All that for an ugly rock?
And who's S.I.?
PROPERTY OF S.I.

CHAPTER

THREE

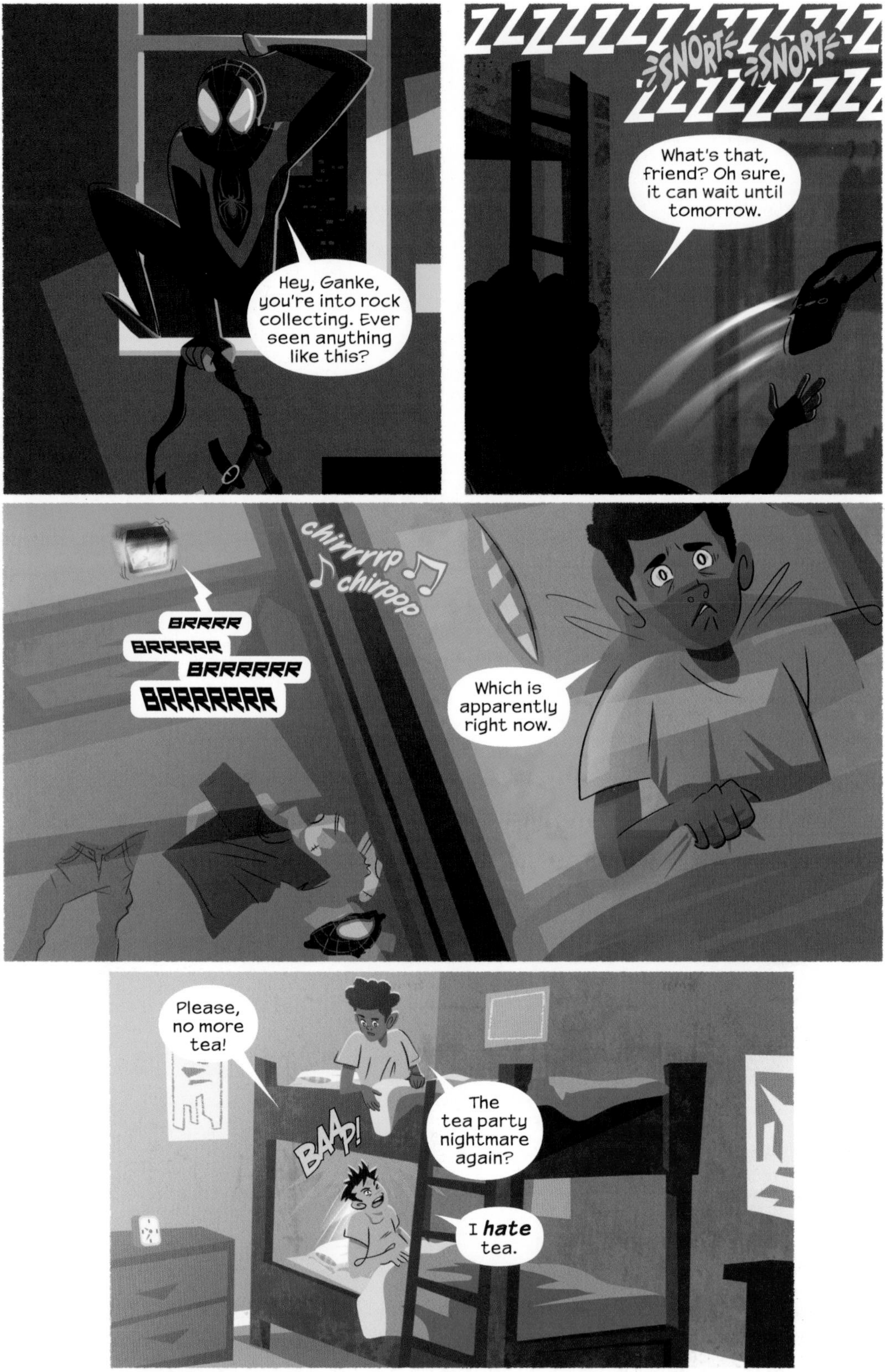
Hey, Ganke, you're into rock collecting. Ever seen anything like this?
ZZZZZZZ SNORT ZZZ SNORT Z
ZZZZZZZZZ
What's that, friend? Oh sure, it can wait until tomorrow.
BRRRR
BRRRRR
BRRRRRR
BRRRRRRR
chirrrrrp chirppp
Which is apparently right now.
Please, no more tea!
BAAP!
The tea party nightmare again?
I *hate* tea.

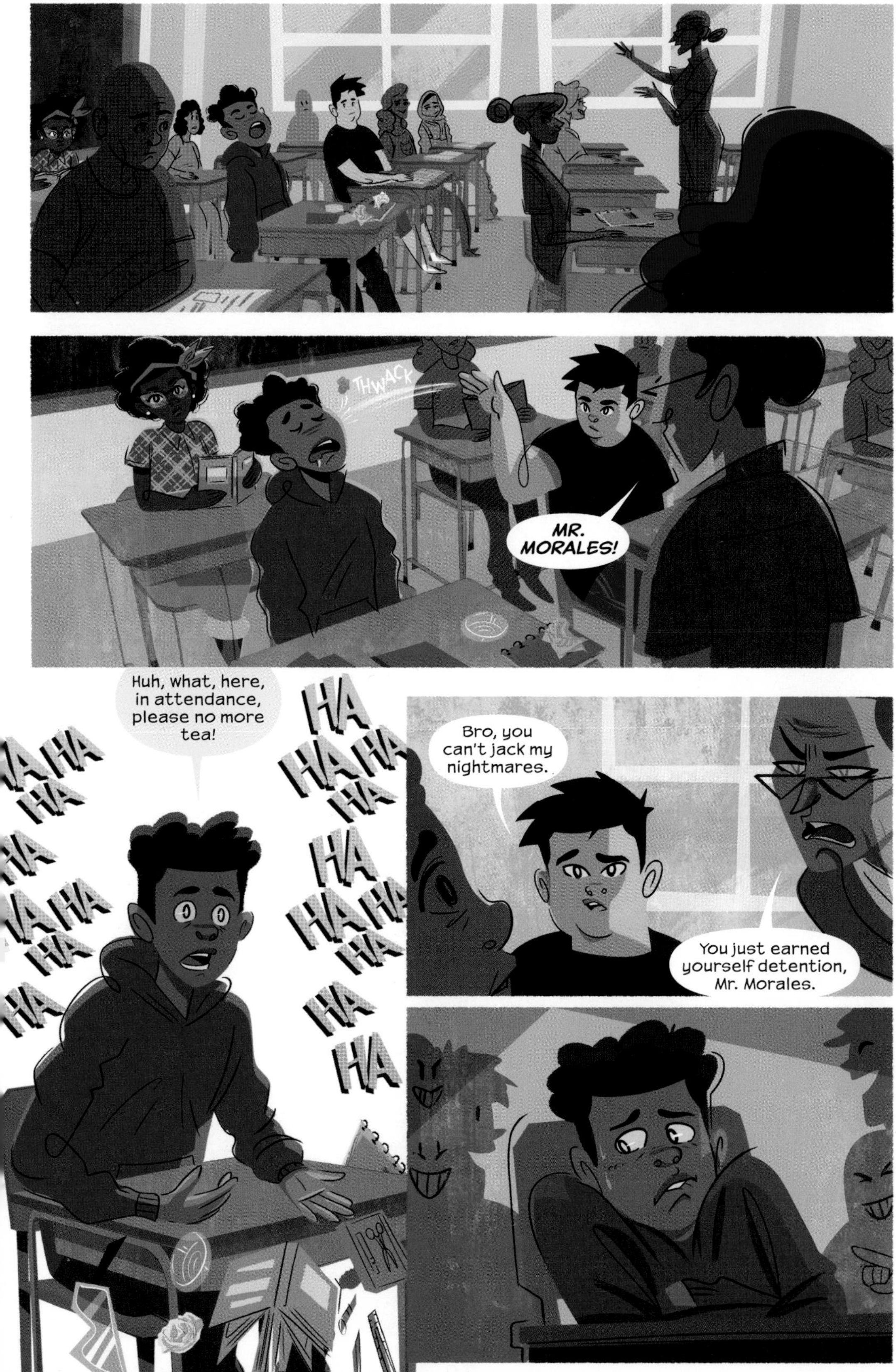
THWACK
MR. MORALES!
Huh, what, here, in attendance, please no more tea!
HA HA HA
HA HA HA
HA HA HA
HA HA HA
Bro, you can't jack my nightmares.
You just earned yourself detention, Mr. Morales.

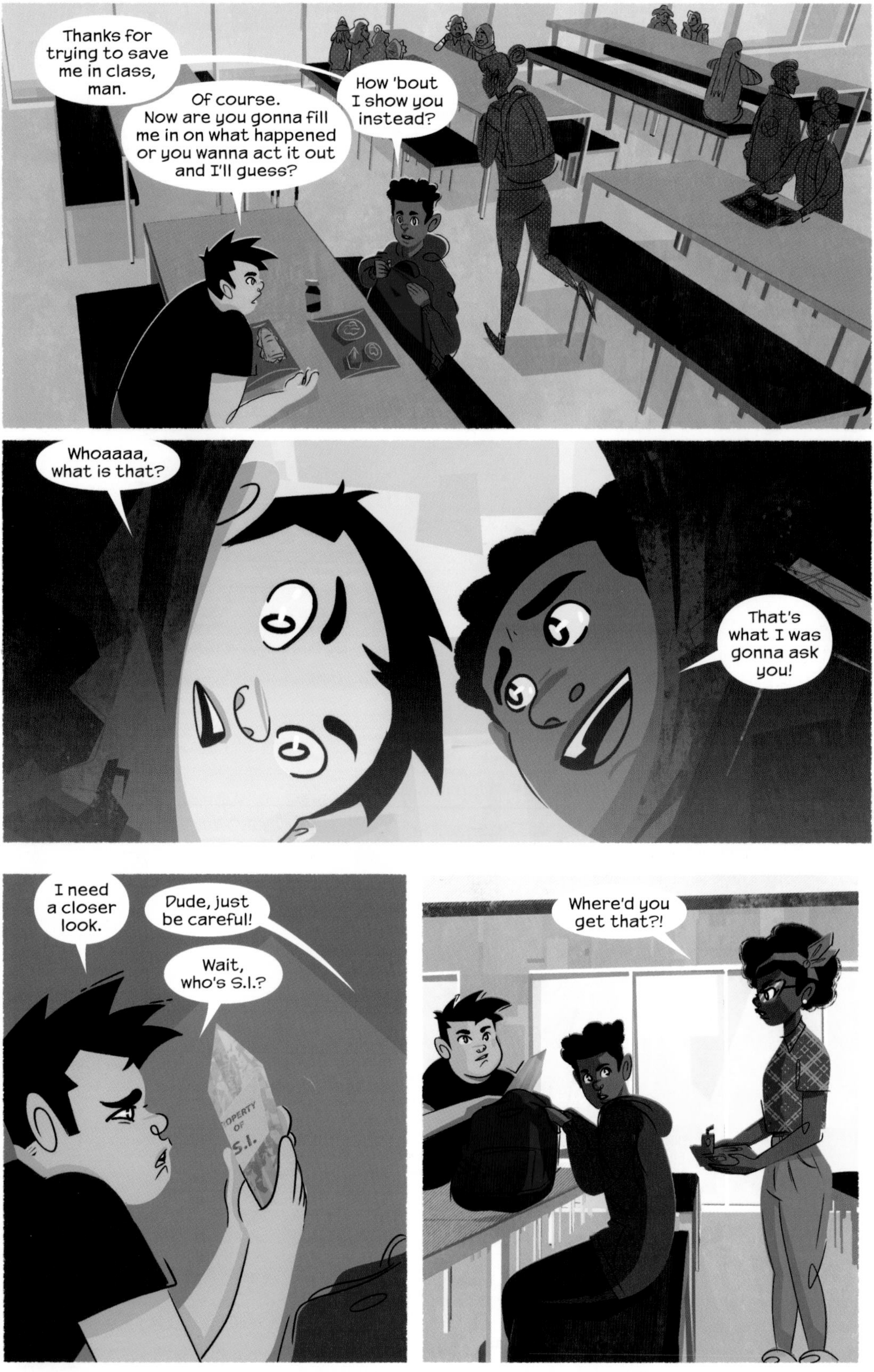
Thanks for trying to save me in class, man.
Of course. Now are you gonna fill me in on what happened or you wanna act it out and I'll guess?
How 'bout I show you instead?
Whoaaaa, what is that?
That's what I was gonna ask you!
I need a closer look.
Dude, just be careful!
Wait, who's S.I.?
PROPERTY OF S.I.
Where'd you get that?!

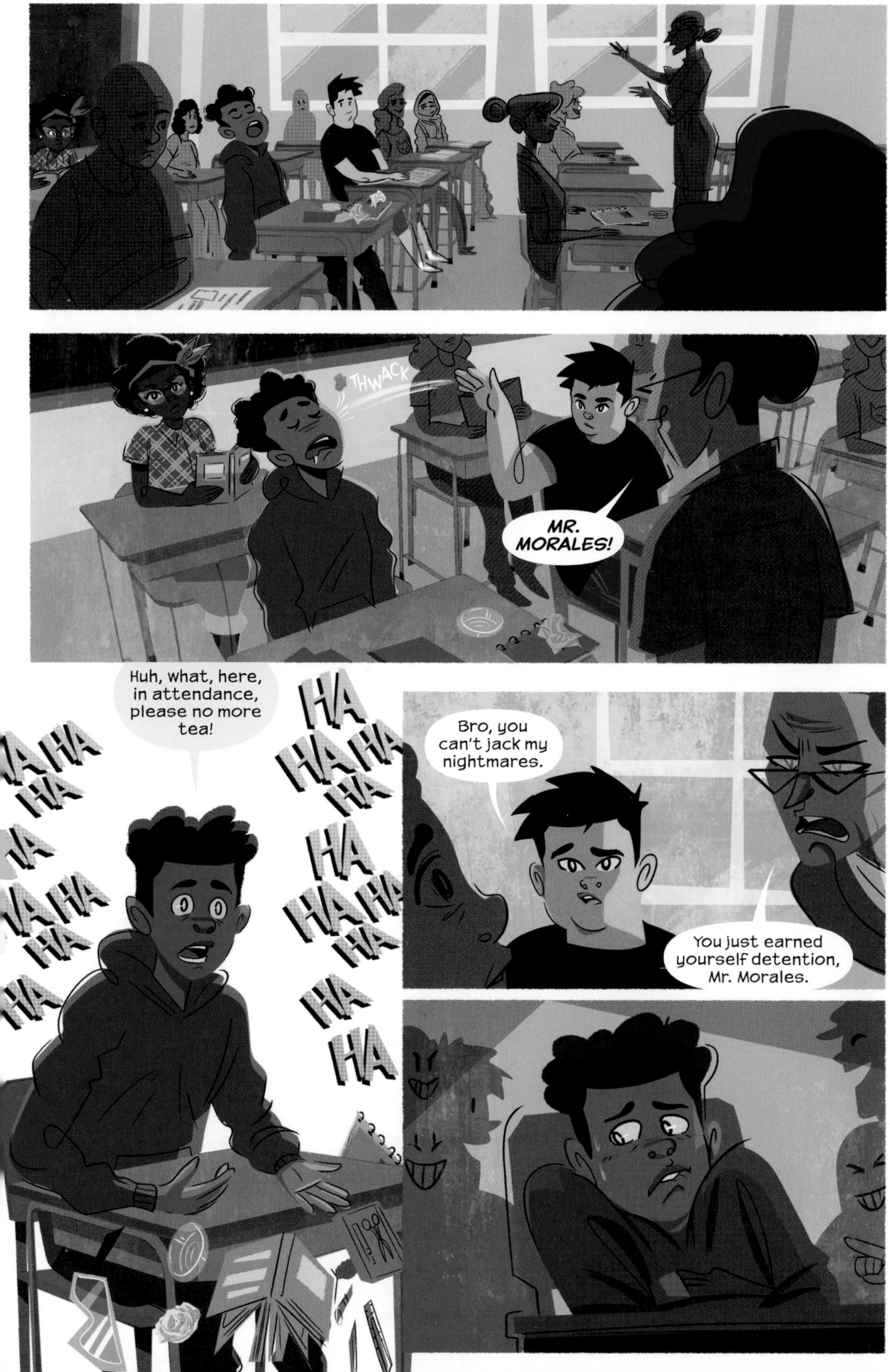
THWACK
MR. MORALES!
Huh, what, here, in attendance, please no more tea!
HA HA HA HA HA HA HA HA HA HA HA HA HA HA HA HA HA HA HA
Bro, you can't jack my nightmares.
You just earned yourself detention, Mr. Morales.

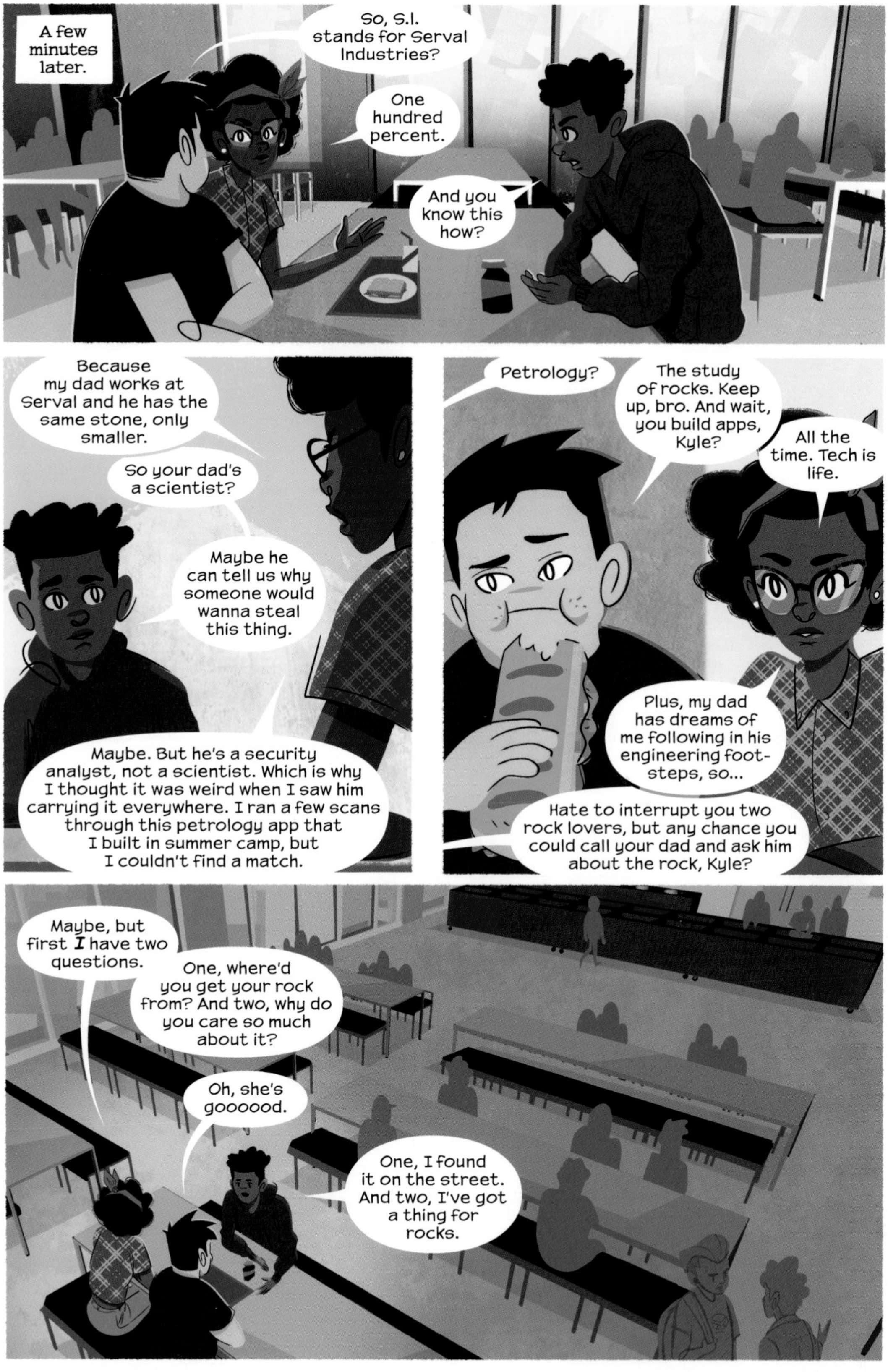
A few minutes later.
So, S.I. stands for Serval Industries?
One hundred percent.
And you know this how?
Because my dad works at Serval and he has the same stone, only smaller.
So your dad's a scientist?
Maybe he can tell us why someone would wanna steal this thing.
Maybe. But he's a security analyst, not a scientist. Which is why I thought it was weird when I saw him carrying it everywhere. I ran a few scans through this petrology app that I built in summer camp, but I couldn't find a match.
Petrology?
The study of rocks. Keep up, bro. And wait, you build apps, Kyle?
All the time. Tech is life.
Plus, my dad has dreams of me following in his engineering foot-steps, so...
Hate to interrupt you two rock lovers, but any chance you could call your dad and ask him about the rock, Kyle?
Maybe, but first **I** have two questions.
One, where'd you get your rock from? And two, why do you care so much about it?
Oh, she's goooood.
One, I found it on the street. And two, I've got a thing for rocks.

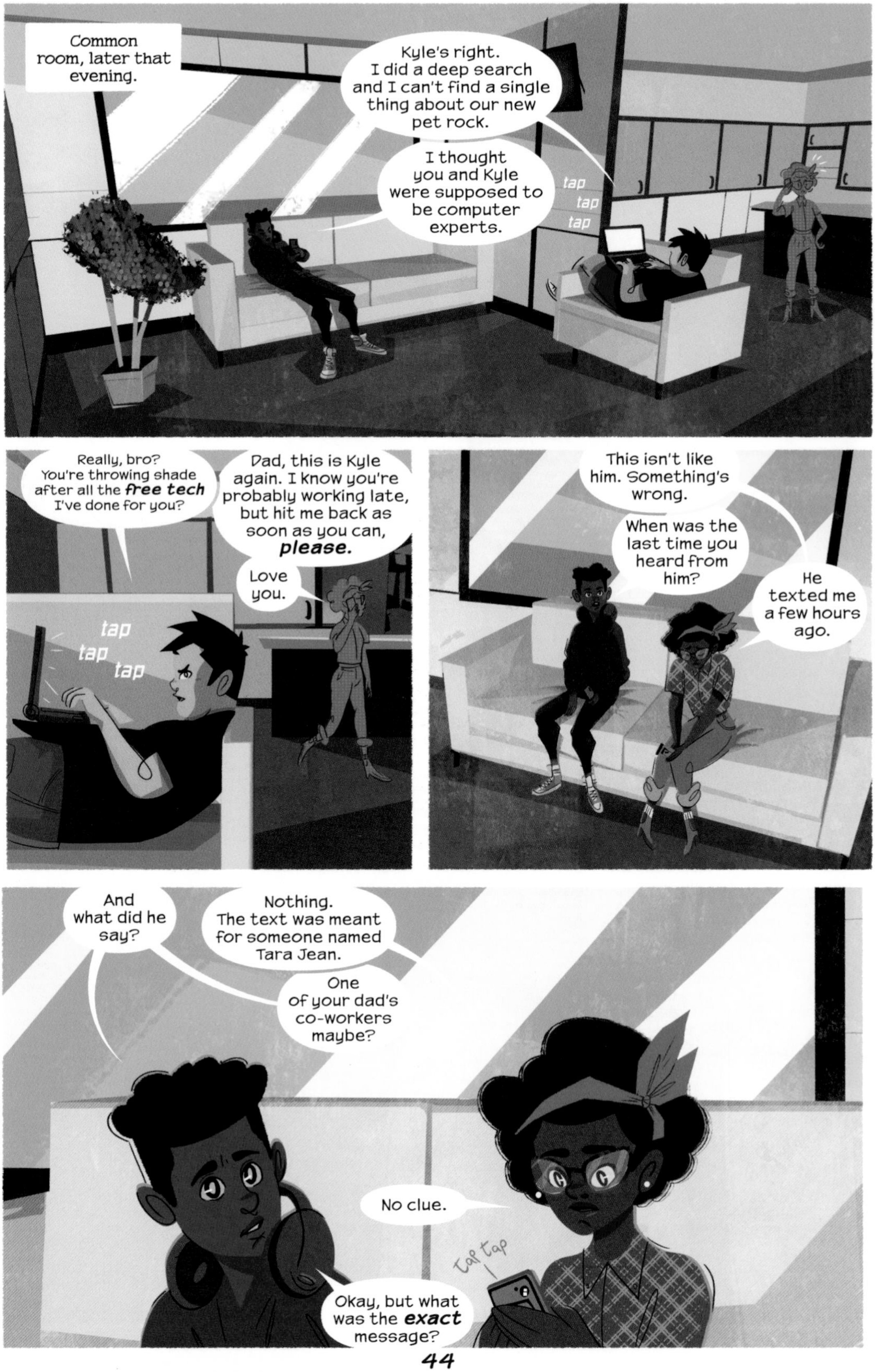
Common room, later that evening.
Kyle's right. I did a deep search and I can't find a single thing about our new pet rock.
I thought you and Kyle were supposed to be computer experts.
tap tap tap
Really, bro? You're throwing shade after all the **free tech** I've done for you?
Dad, this is Kyle again. I know you're probably working late, but hit me back as soon as you can, **please.**
Love you.
tap tap tap
This isn't like him. Something's wrong.
When was the last time you heard from him?
He texted me a few hours ago.
And what did he say?
Nothing. The text was meant for someone named Tara Jean.
One of your dad's co-workers maybe?
No clue.
Okay, but what was the **exact** message?
Tap tap

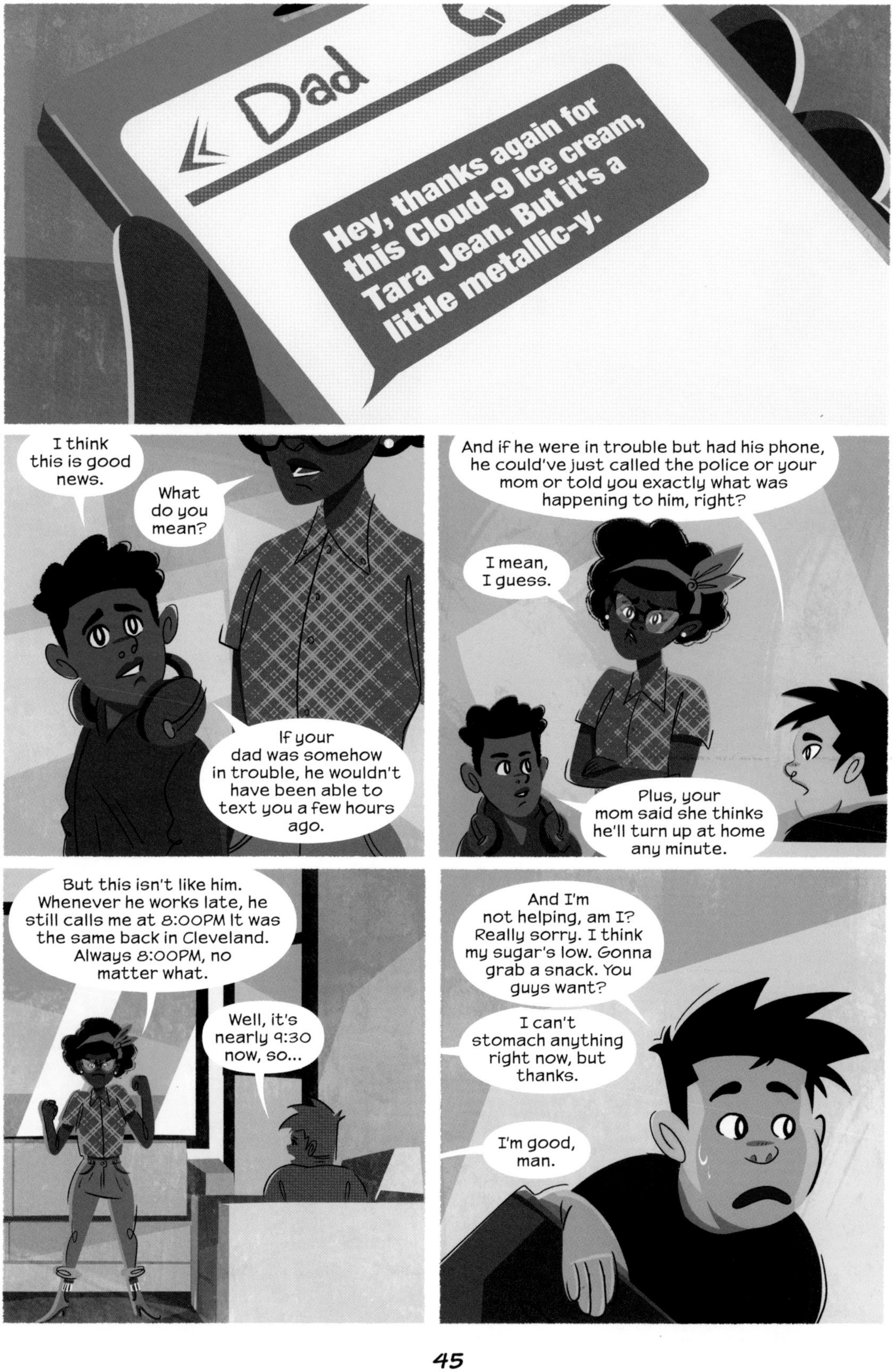
Dad
Hey, thanks again for this Cloud-9 ice cream, Tara Jean. But it's a little metallic-y.
I think this is good news.
What do you mean?
If your dad was somehow in trouble, he wouldn't have been able to text you a few hours ago.
And if he were in trouble but had his phone, he could've just called the police or your mom or told you exactly what was happening to him, right?
I mean, I guess.
Plus, your mom said she thinks he'll turn up at home any minute.
But this isn't like him. Whenever he works late, he still calls me at 8:00PM It was the same back in Cleveland. Always 8:00PM, no matter what.
Well, it's nearly 9:30 now, so...
And I'm not helping, am I? Really sorry. I think my sugar's low. Gonna grab a snack. You guys want?
I can't stomach anything right now, but thanks.
I'm good, man.

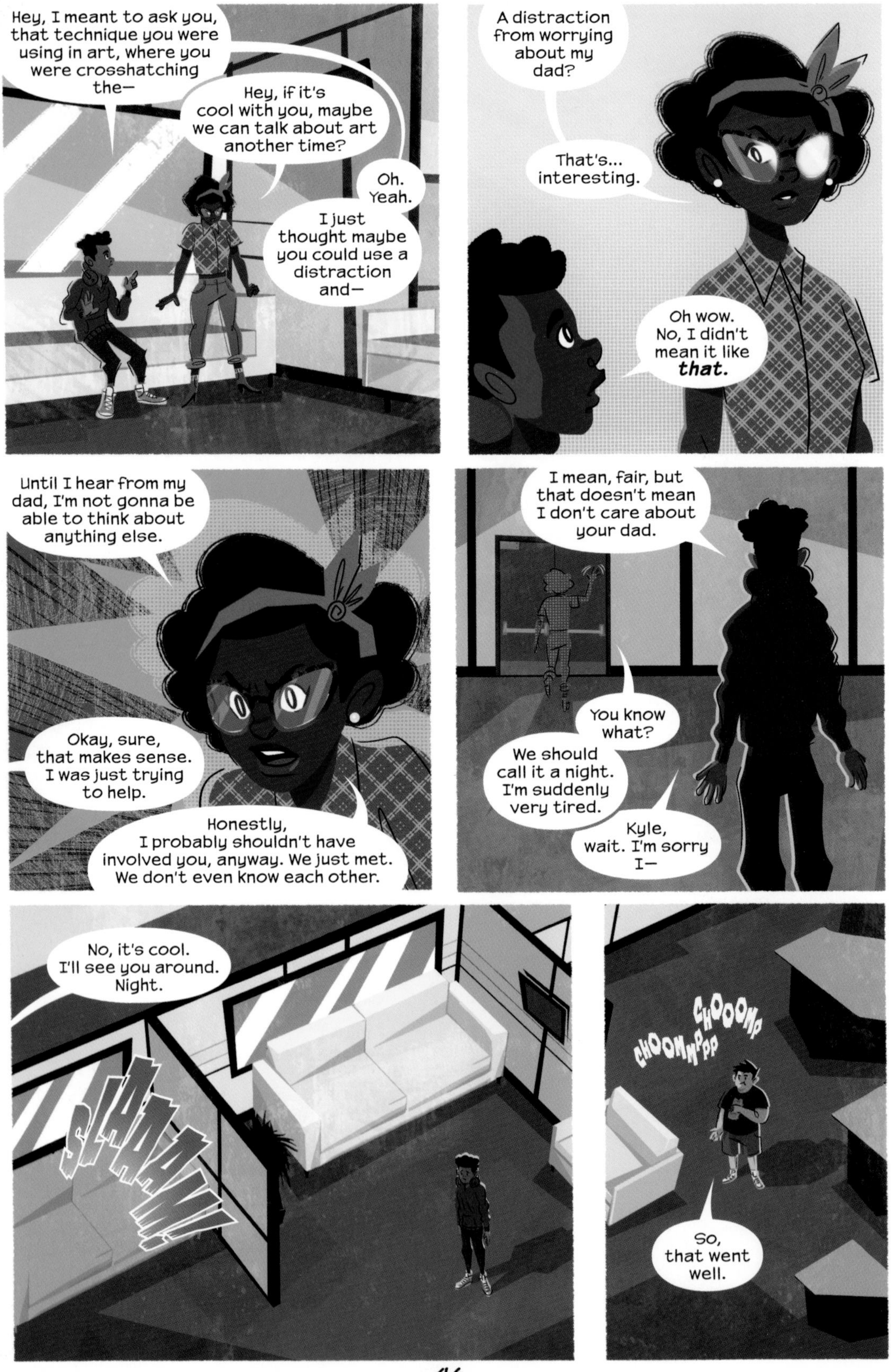

Hey, I meant to ask you, that technique you were using in art, where you were crosshatching the—
Hey, if it's cool with you, maybe we can talk about art another time?
Oh. Yeah.
I just thought maybe you could use a distraction and—
A distraction from worrying about my dad?
That's... interesting.
Oh wow. No, I didn't mean it like *that.*
Until I hear from my dad, I'm not gonna be able to think about anything else.
Okay, sure, that makes sense. I was just trying to help.
Honestly, I probably shouldn't have involved you, anyway. We just met. We don't even know each other.
I mean, fair, but that doesn't mean I don't care about your dad.
You know what?
We should call it a night. I'm suddenly very tired.
Kyle, wait. I'm sorry I—
No, it's cool. I'll see you around. Night.
SLAAAM!!
CHOOOMP
CHOOMMPPP
So, that went well.

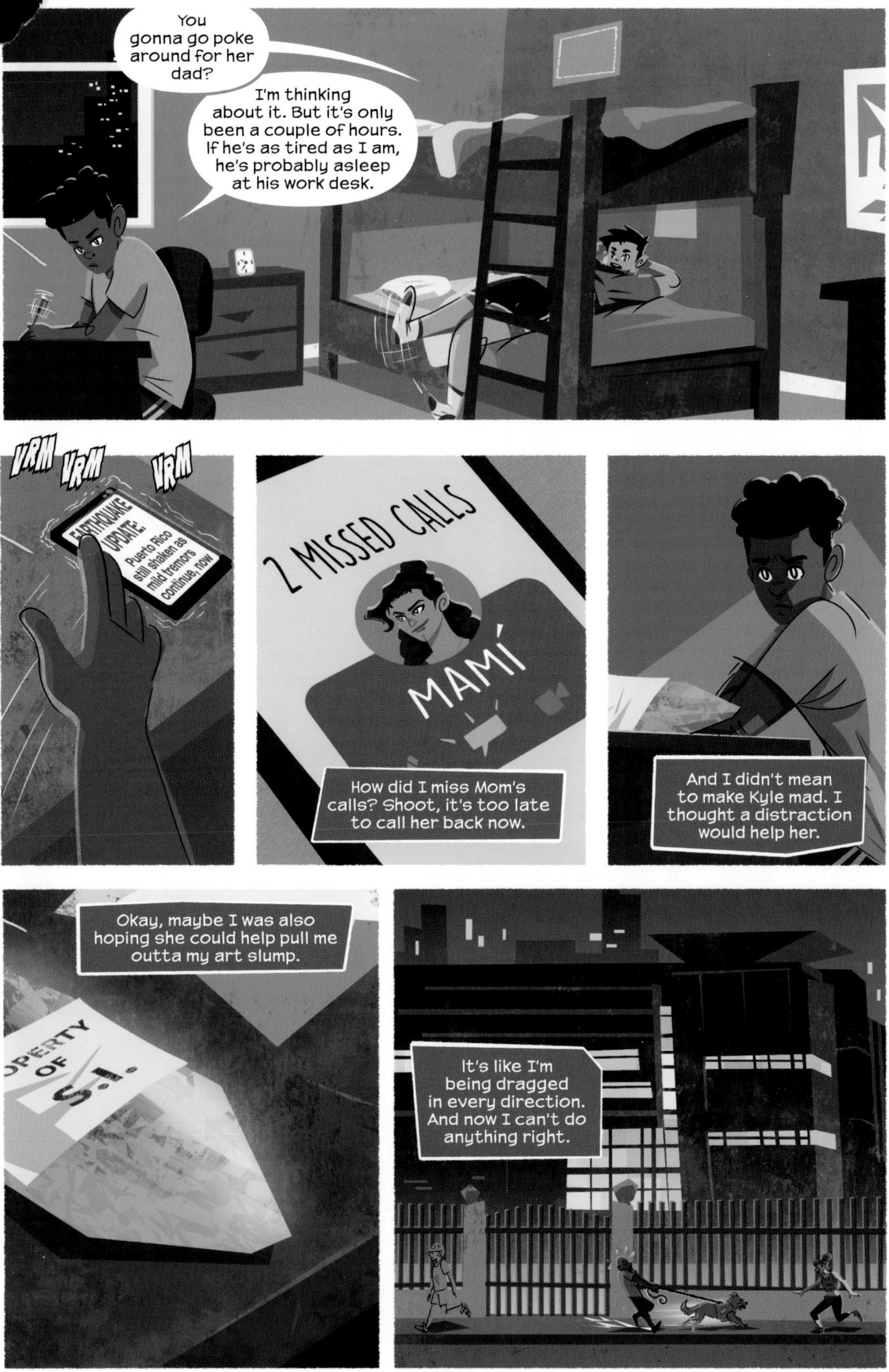
You gonna go poke around for her dad?
I'm thinking about it. But it's only been a couple of hours. If he's as tired as I am, he's probably asleep at his work desk.
VRM
VRM
VRM
EARTHQUAKE UPDATE:
Puerto Rico still shaken as mild tremors continue, now
2 MISSED CALLS
MAMÍ
How did I miss Mom's calls? Shoot, it's too late to call her back now.
And I didn't mean to make Kyle mad. I thought a distraction would help her.
Okay, maybe I was also hoping she could help pull me outta my art slump.
OPERTY OF S.I.
It's like I'm being dragged in every direction. And now I can't do anything right.

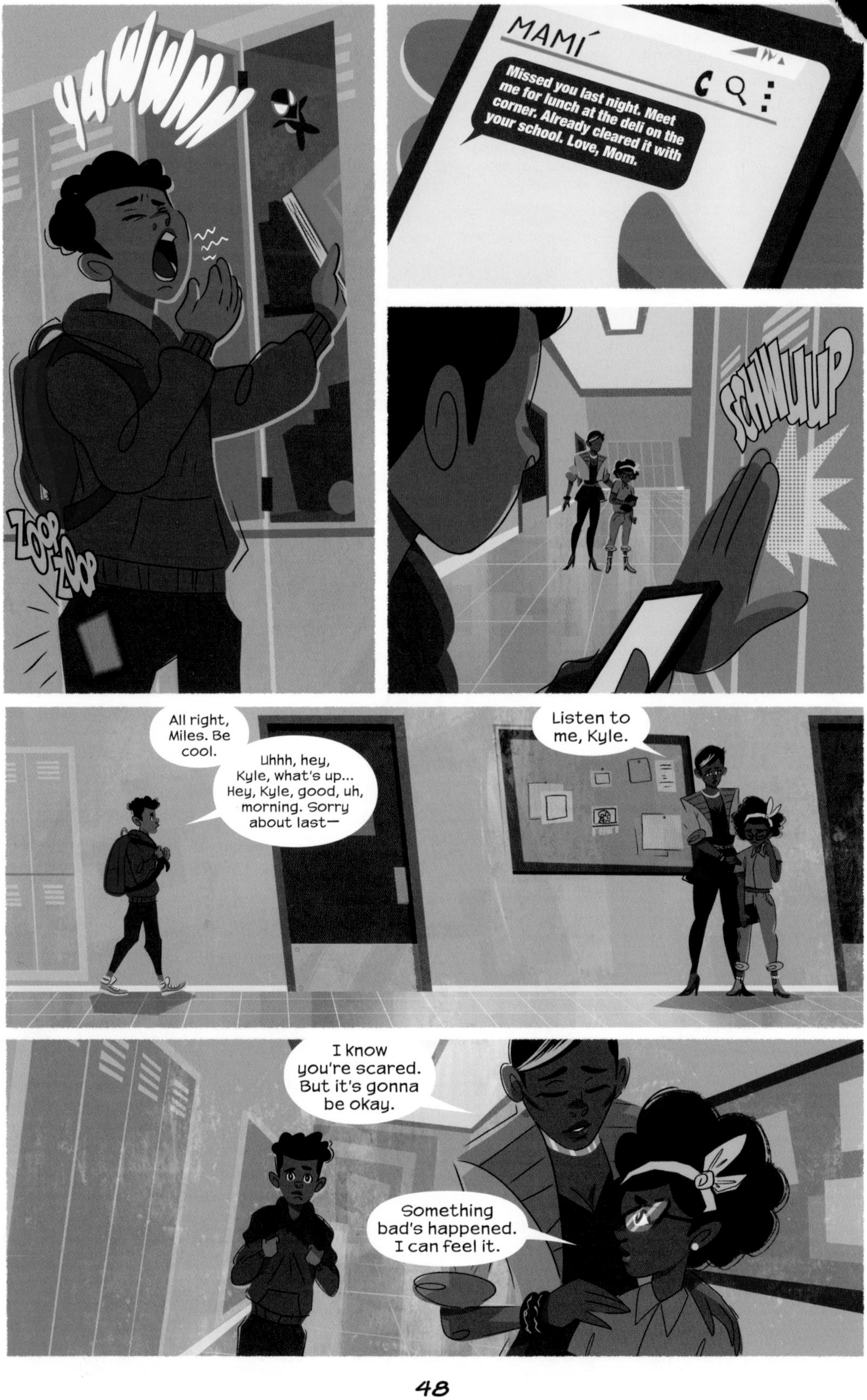
YAWWNN
ZOOP ZOOP
MAMÍ
Missed you last night. Meet me for lunch at the deli on the corner. Already cleared it with your school. Love, Mom.
SCHWUUP
All right, Miles. Be cool.
Uhhh, hey, Kyle, what's up... Hey, Kyle, good, uh, morning. Sorry about last—
Listen to me, Kyle.
I know you're scared. But it's gonna be okay.
Something bad's happened. I can feel it.

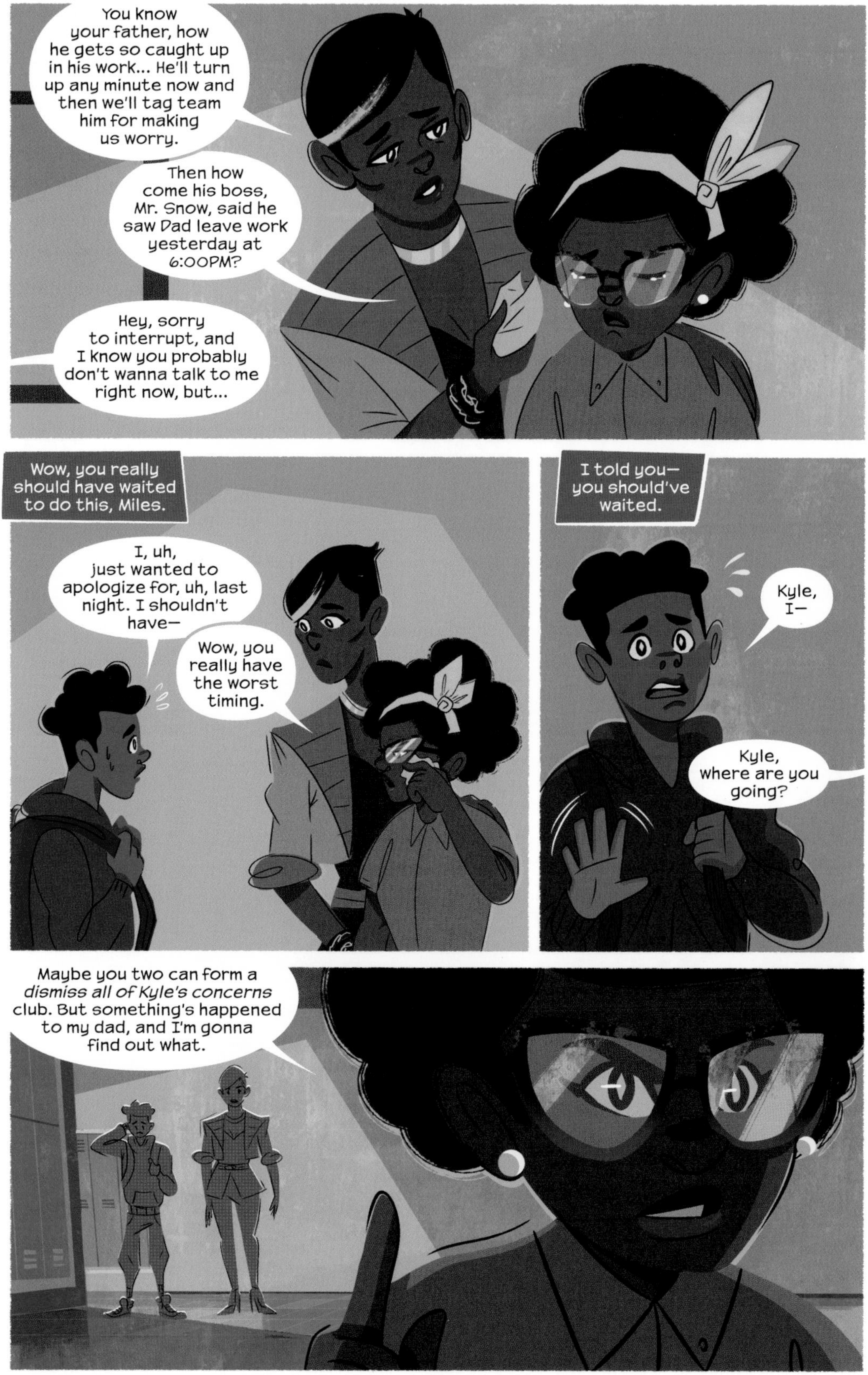
You know your father, how he gets so caught up in his work... He'll turn up any minute now and then we'll tag team him for making us worry.
Then how come his boss, Mr. Snow, said he saw Dad leave work yesterday at 6:00PM?
Hey, sorry to interrupt, and I know you probably don't wanna talk to me right now, but...
Wow, you really should have waited to do this, Miles.
I, uh, just wanted to apologize for, uh, last night. I shouldn't have—
Wow, you really have the worst timing.
I told you— you should've waited.
Kyle, I—
Kyle, where are you going?
Maybe you two can form a *dismiss all of Kyle's concerns* club. But something's happened to my dad, and I'm gonna find out what.

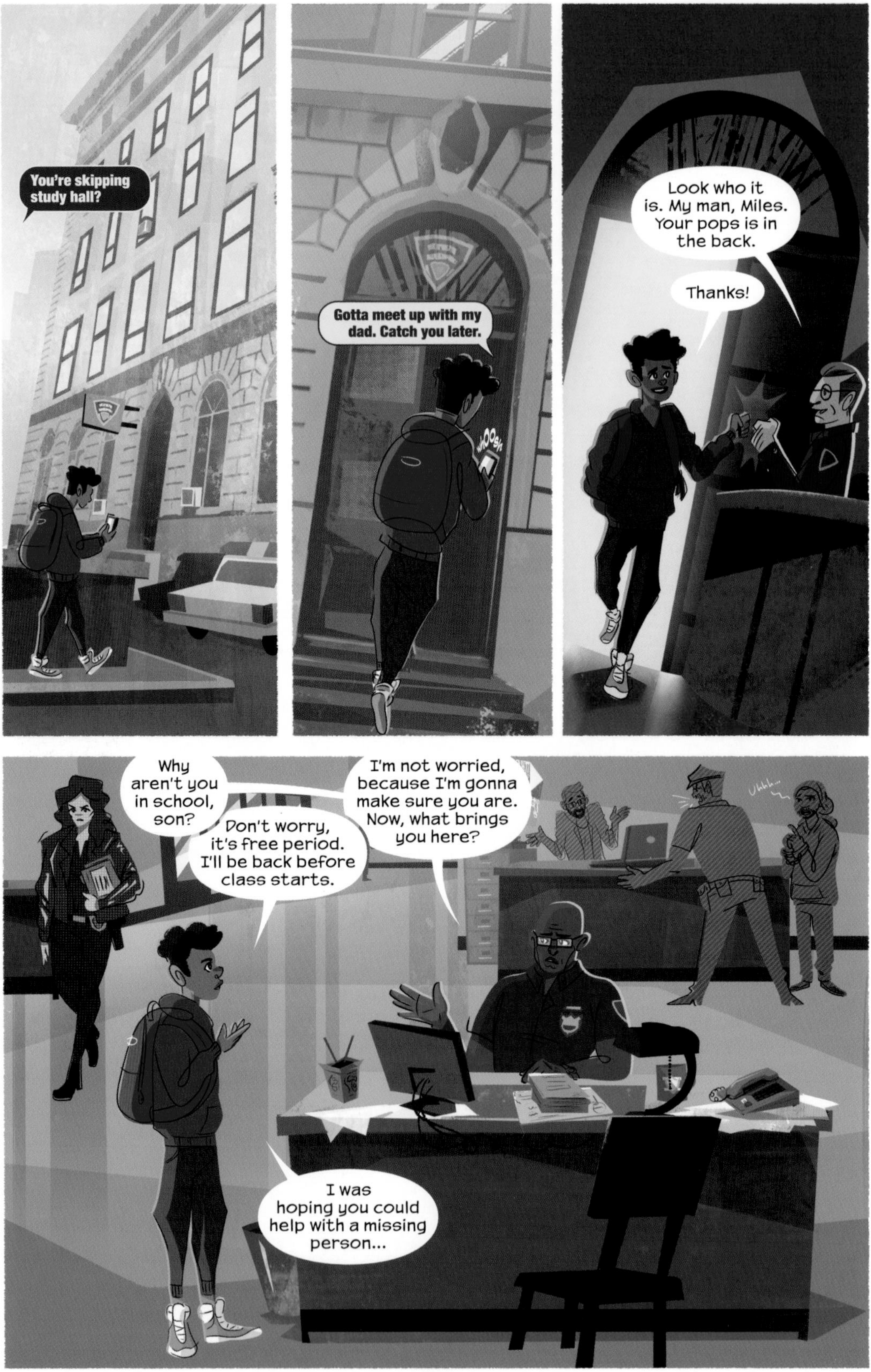
You're skipping study hall?
Gotta meet up with my dad. Catch you later.
WHOOSH
Look who it is. My man, Miles. Your pops is in the back.
Thanks!
Why aren't you in school, son?
Don't worry, it's free period. I'll be back before class starts.
I'm not worried, because I'm gonna make sure you are. Now, what brings you here?
I was hoping you could help with a missing person...

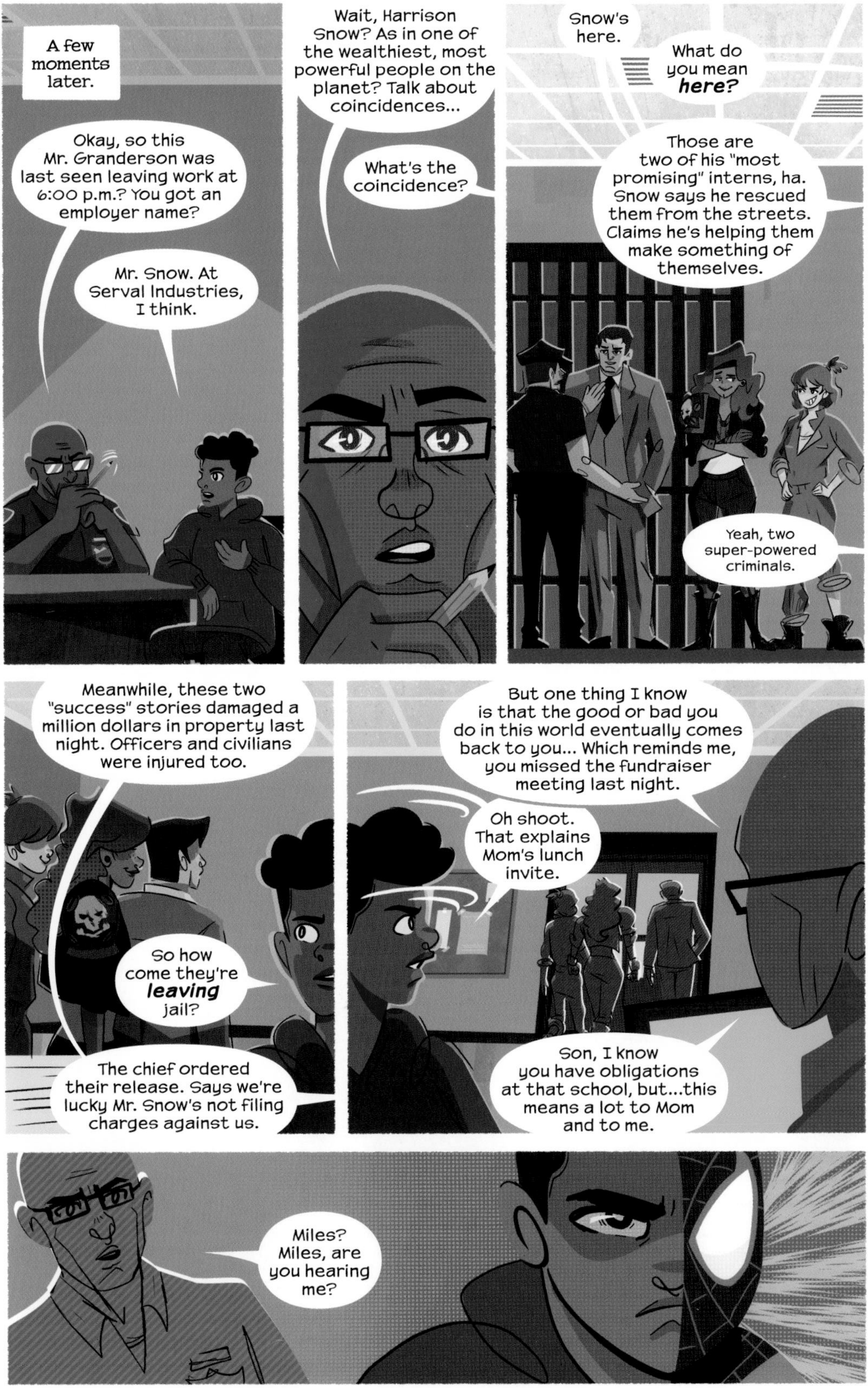
A few moments later.
Okay, so this Mr. Granderson was last seen leaving work at 6:00 p.m.? You got an employer name?
Mr. Snow. At Serval Industries, I think.
Wait, Harrison Snow? As in one of the wealthiest, most powerful people on the planet? Talk about coincidences...
What's the coincidence?
Snow's here.
What do you mean *here?*
Those are two of his "most promising" interns, ha. Snow says he rescued them from the streets. Claims he's helping them make something of themselves.
Yeah, two super-powered criminals.
Meanwhile, these two "success" stories damaged a million dollars in property last night. Officers and civilians were injured too.
So how come they're *leaving* jail?
The chief ordered their release. Says we're lucky Mr. Snow's not filing charges against us.
But one thing I know is that the good or bad you do in this world eventually comes back to you... Which reminds me, you missed the fundraiser meeting last night.
Oh shoot. That explains Mom's lunch invite.
Son, I know you have obligations at that school, but...this means a lot to Mom and to me.
Miles? Miles, are you hearing me?

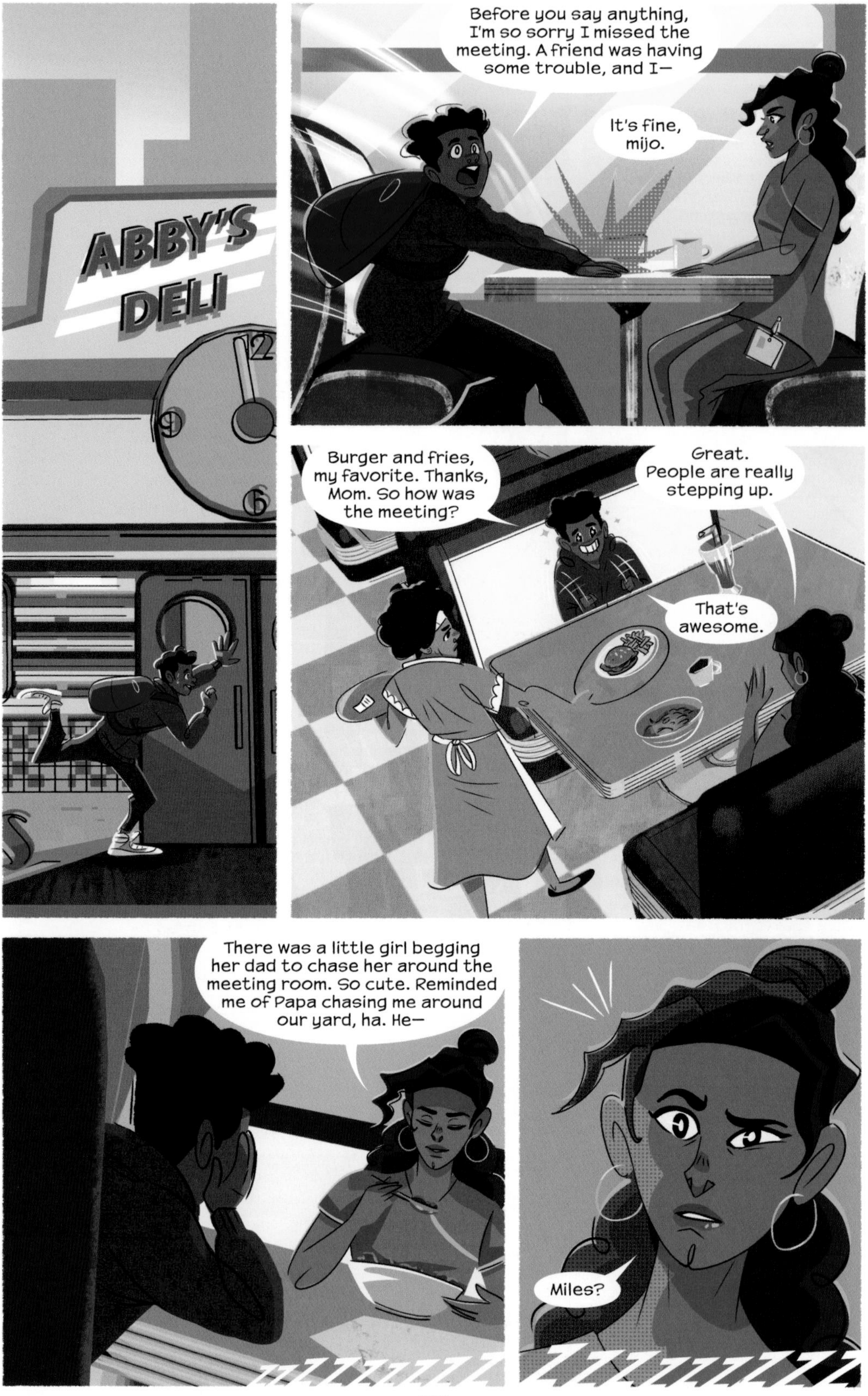
ABBY'S DELI
Before you say anything, I'm so sorry I missed the meeting. A friend was having some trouble, and I—
It's fine, mijo.
Burger and fries, my favorite. Thanks, Mom. So how was the meeting?
Great. People are really stepping up.
That's awesome.
There was a little girl begging her dad to chase her around the meeting room. So cute. Reminded me of Papa chasing me around our yard, ha. He—
Miles?
ZZZZZZZZZZ
ZZZZZZZZZZZZZ

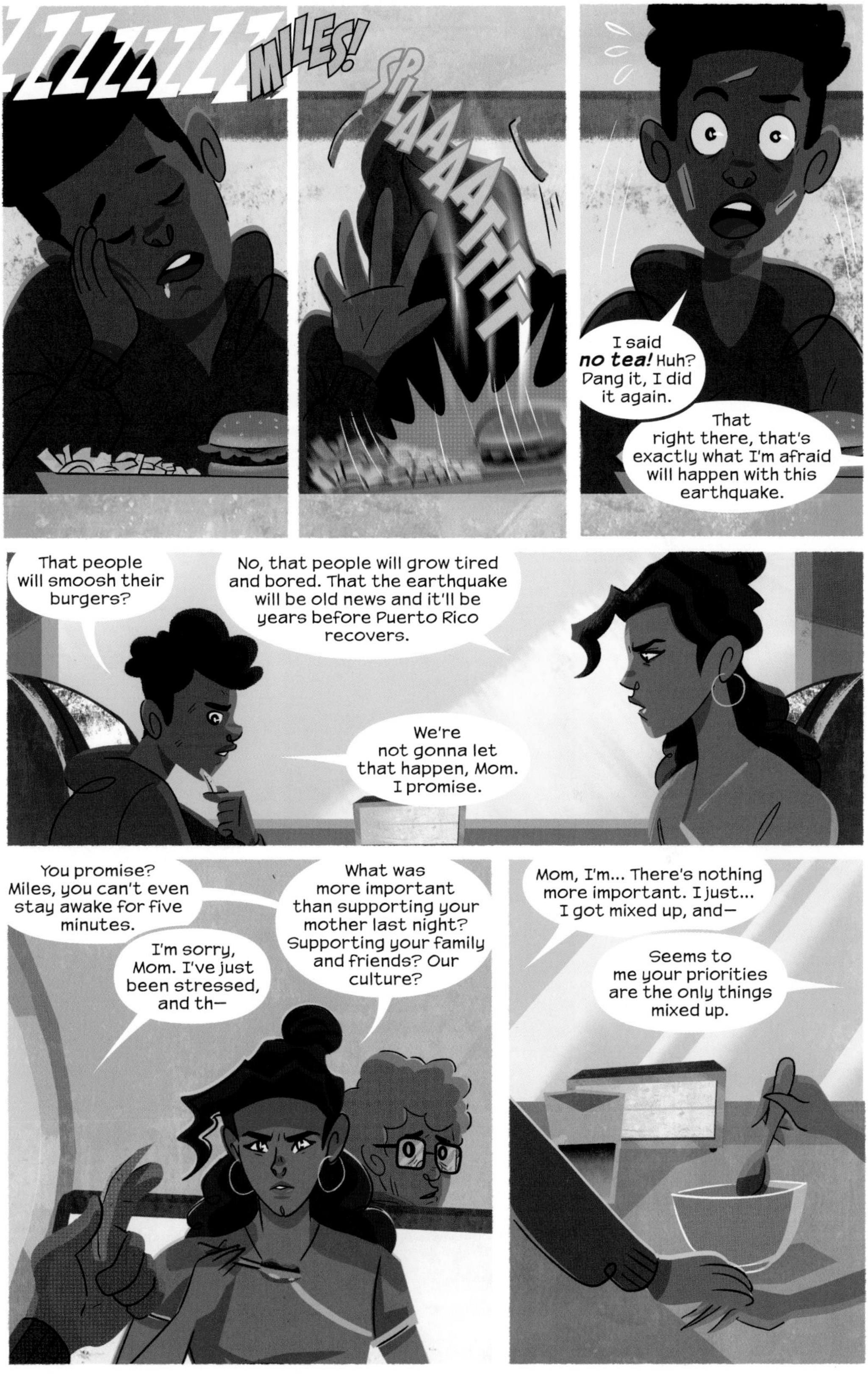
ZZZZZZZZ
MILES!
SPLAAAATTT
I said no tea! Huh? Dang it, I did it again.
That right there, that's exactly what I'm afraid will happen with this earthquake.
That people will smoosh their burgers?
No, that people will grow tired and bored. That the earthquake will be old news and it'll be years before Puerto Rico recovers.
We're not gonna let that happen, Mom. I promise.
You promise? Miles, you can't even stay awake for five minutes.
I'm sorry, Mom. I've just been stressed, and th—
What was more important than supporting your mother last night? Supporting your family and friends? Our culture?
Mom, I'm... There's nothing more important. I just... I got mixed up, and—
Seems to me your priorities are the only things mixed up.

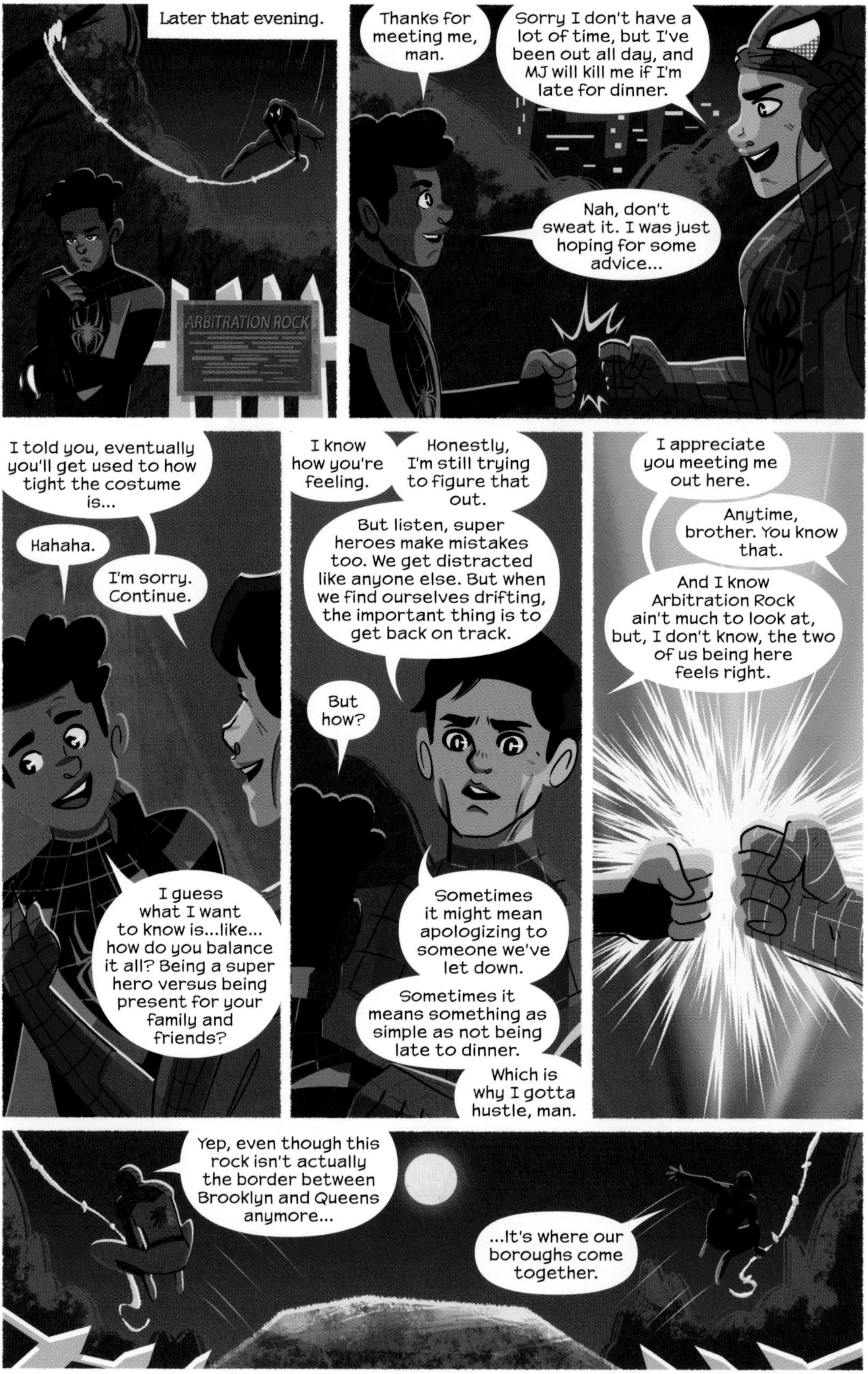
Later that evening.
ARBITRATION ROCK
Thanks for meeting me, man.
Sorry I don't have a lot of time, but I've been out all day, and MJ will kill me if I'm late for dinner.
Nah, don't sweat it. I was just hoping for some advice...
I told you, eventually you'll get used to how tight the costume is...
Hahaha.
I'm sorry. Continue.
I guess what I want to know is...like... how do you balance it all? Being a super hero versus being present for your family and friends?
I know how you're feeling.
Honestly, I'm still trying to figure that out.
But listen, super heroes make mistakes too. We get distracted like anyone else. But when we find ourselves drifting, the important thing is to get back on track.
But how?
Sometimes it might mean apologizing to someone we've let down.
Sometimes it means something as simple as not being late to dinner.
Which is why I gotta hustle, man.
I appreciate you meeting me out here.
Anytime, brother. You know that.
And I know Arbitration Rock ain't much to look at, but, I don't know, the two of us being here feels right.
Yep, even though this rock isn't actually the border between Brooklyn and Queens anymore...
...It's where our boroughs come together.

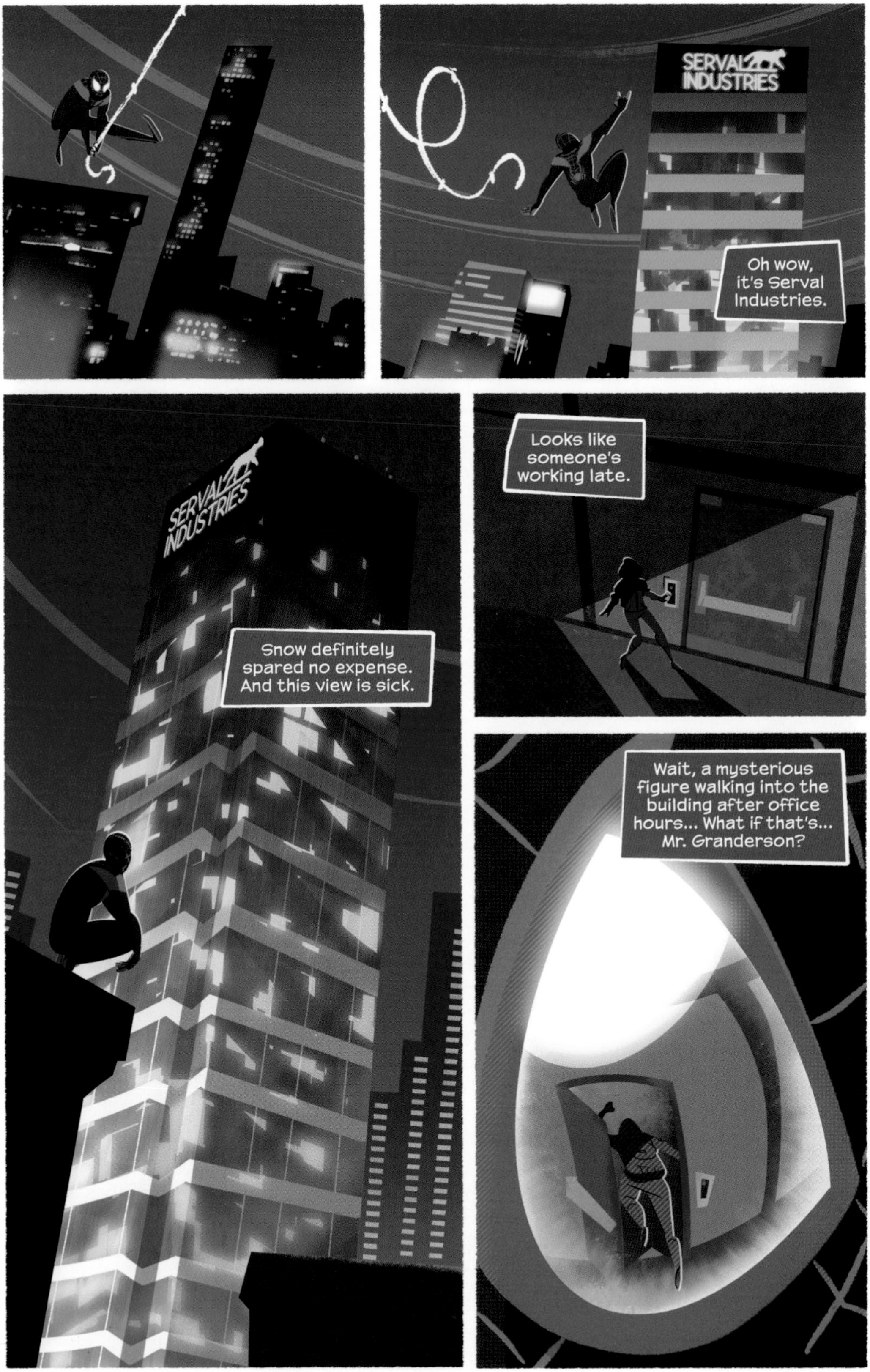
SERVAL INDUSTRIES
Oh wow, it's Serval Industries.
SERVAL INDUSTRIES
Snow definitely spared no expense. And this view is sick.
Looks like someone's working late.
Wait, a mysterious figure walking into the building after office hours... What if that's... Mr. Granderson?

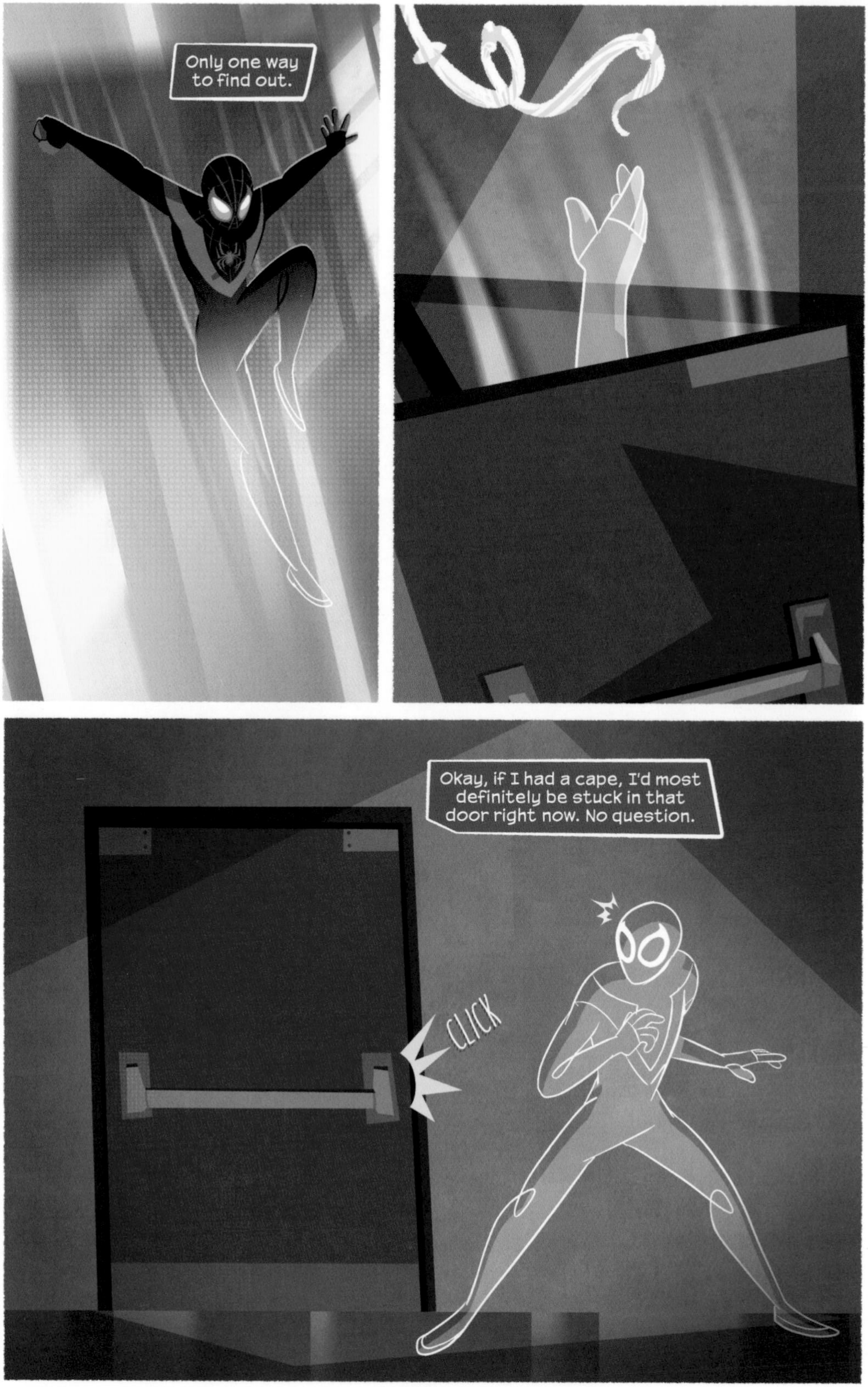
Only one way to find out.
Okay, if I had a cape, I'd most definitely be stuck in that door right now. No question.
CLICK

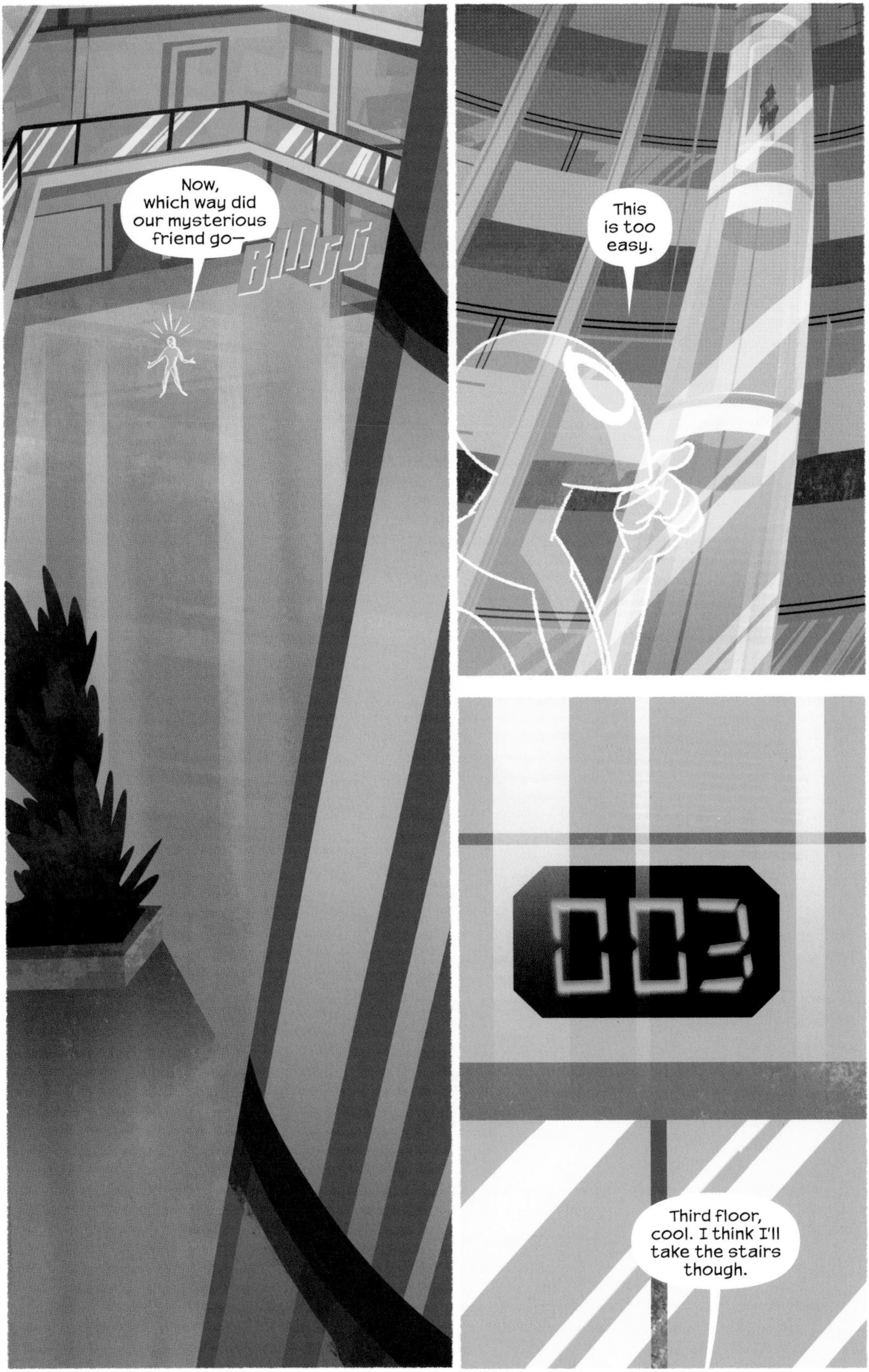
Now, which way did our mysterious friend go—
BINGO
This is too easy.
Third floor, cool. I think I'll take the stairs though.

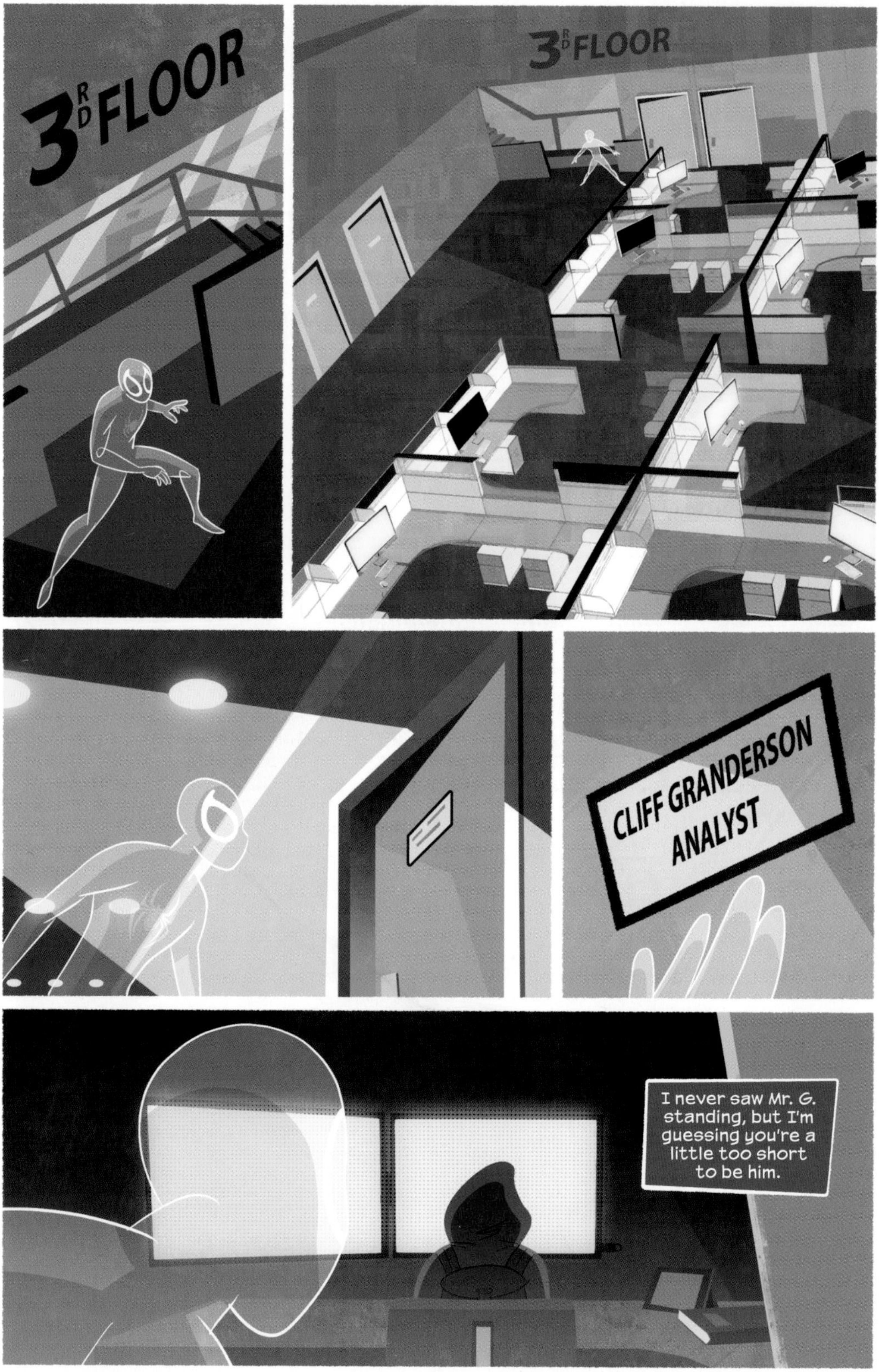
3RD FLOOR
3RD FLOOR
CLIFF GRANDERSON
ANALYST
I never saw Mr. G. standing, but I'm guessing you're a little too short to be him.

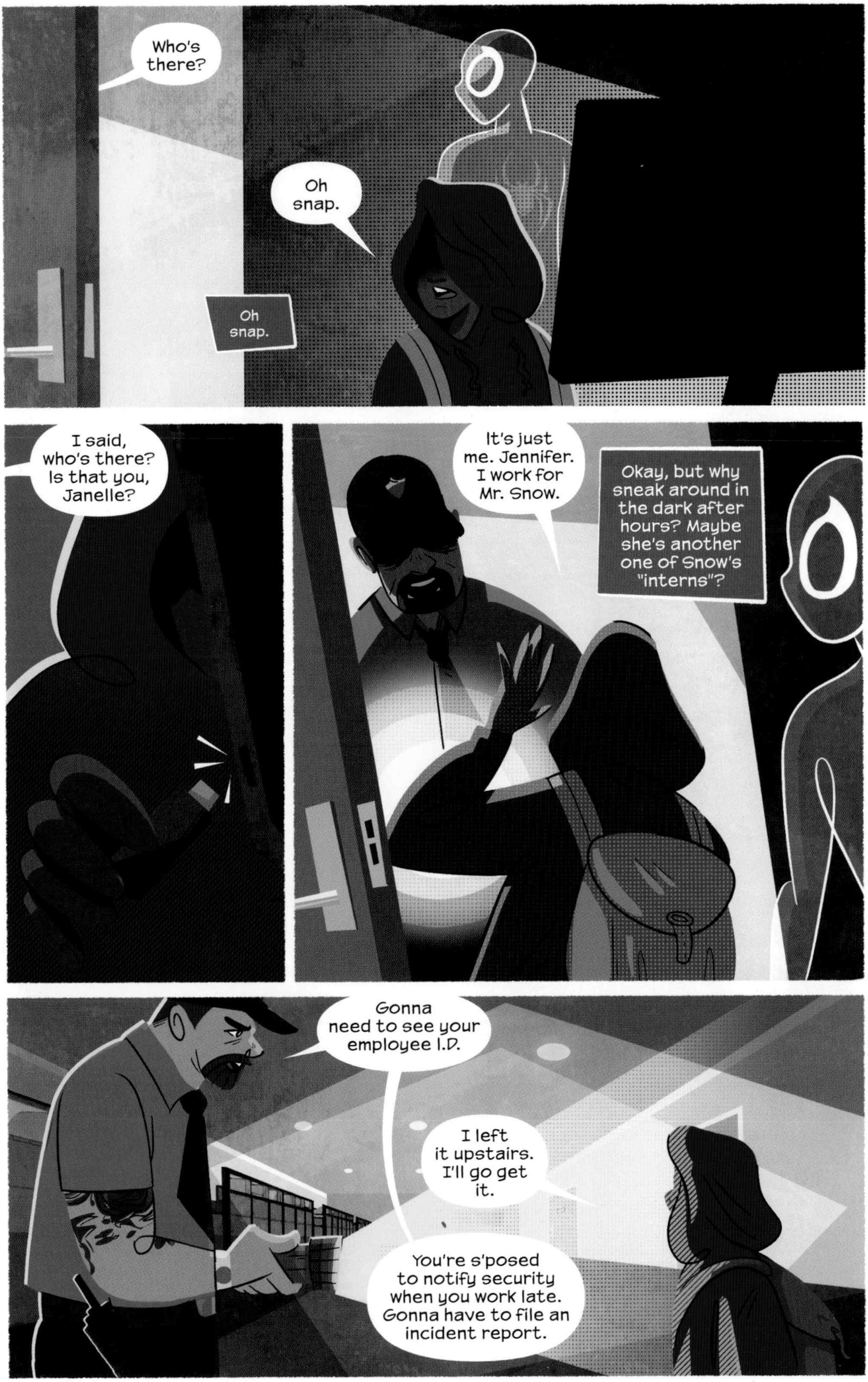
Who's there?
Oh snap.
Oh snap.
I said, who's there? Is that you, Janelle?
It's just me. Jennifer. I work for Mr. Snow.
Okay, but why sneak around in the dark after hours? Maybe she's another one of Snow's "interns"?
Gonna need to see your employee I.D.
I left it upstairs. I'll go get it.
You're s'posed to notify security when you work late. Gonna have to file an incident report.

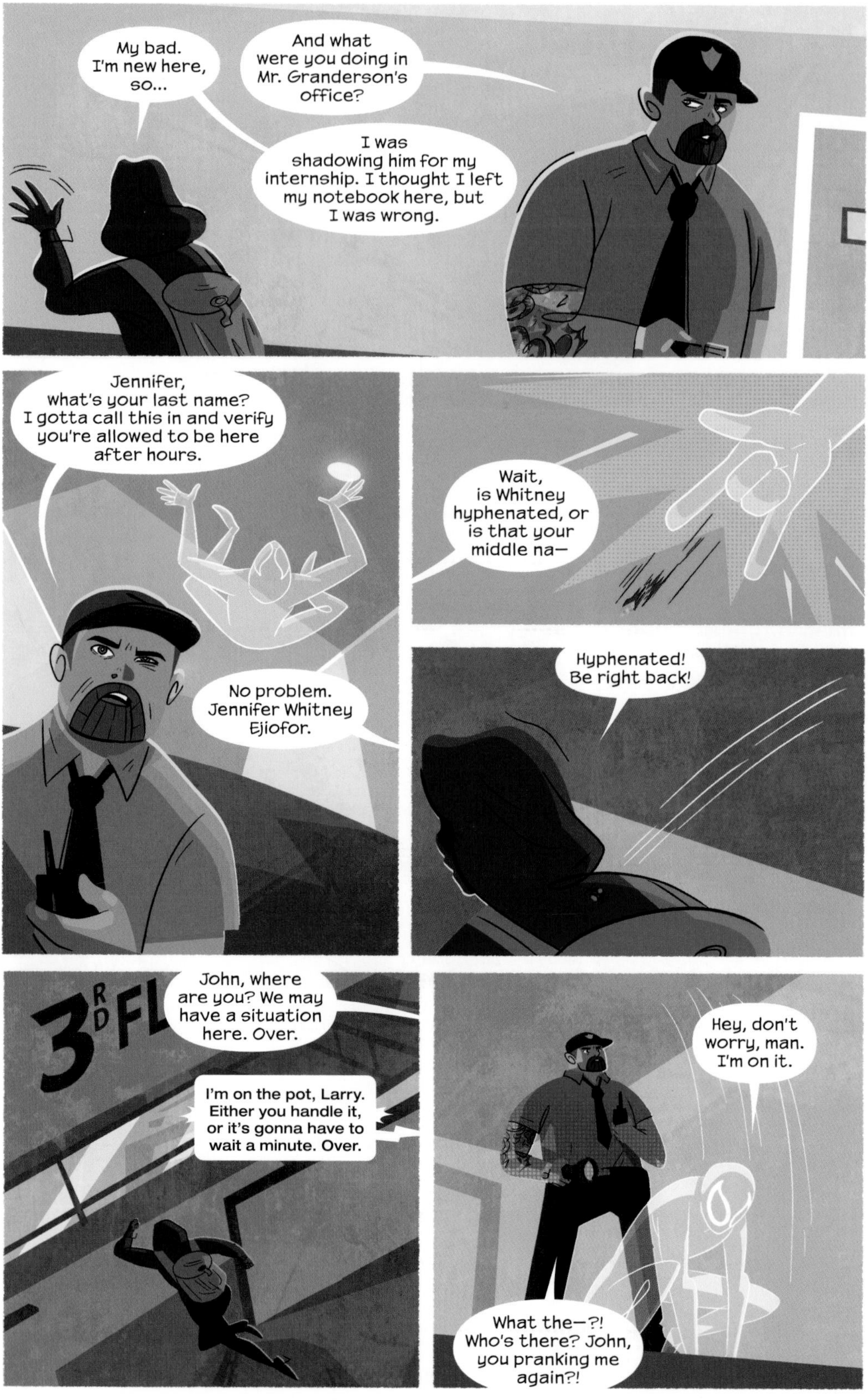
My bad. I'm new here, so...
And what were you doing in Mr. Granderson's office?
I was shadowing him for my internship. I thought I left my notebook here, but I was wrong.
Jennifer, what's your last name? I gotta call this in and verify you're allowed to be here after hours.
No problem. Jennifer Whitney Ejiofor.
Wait, is Whitney hyphenated, or is that your middle na—
Hyphenated! Be right back!
3RD FL
John, where are you? We may have a situation here. Over.
I'm on the pot, Larry. Either you handle it, or it's gonna have to wait a minute. Over.
Hey, don't worry, man. I'm on it.
What the—?! Who's there? John, you pranking me again?!

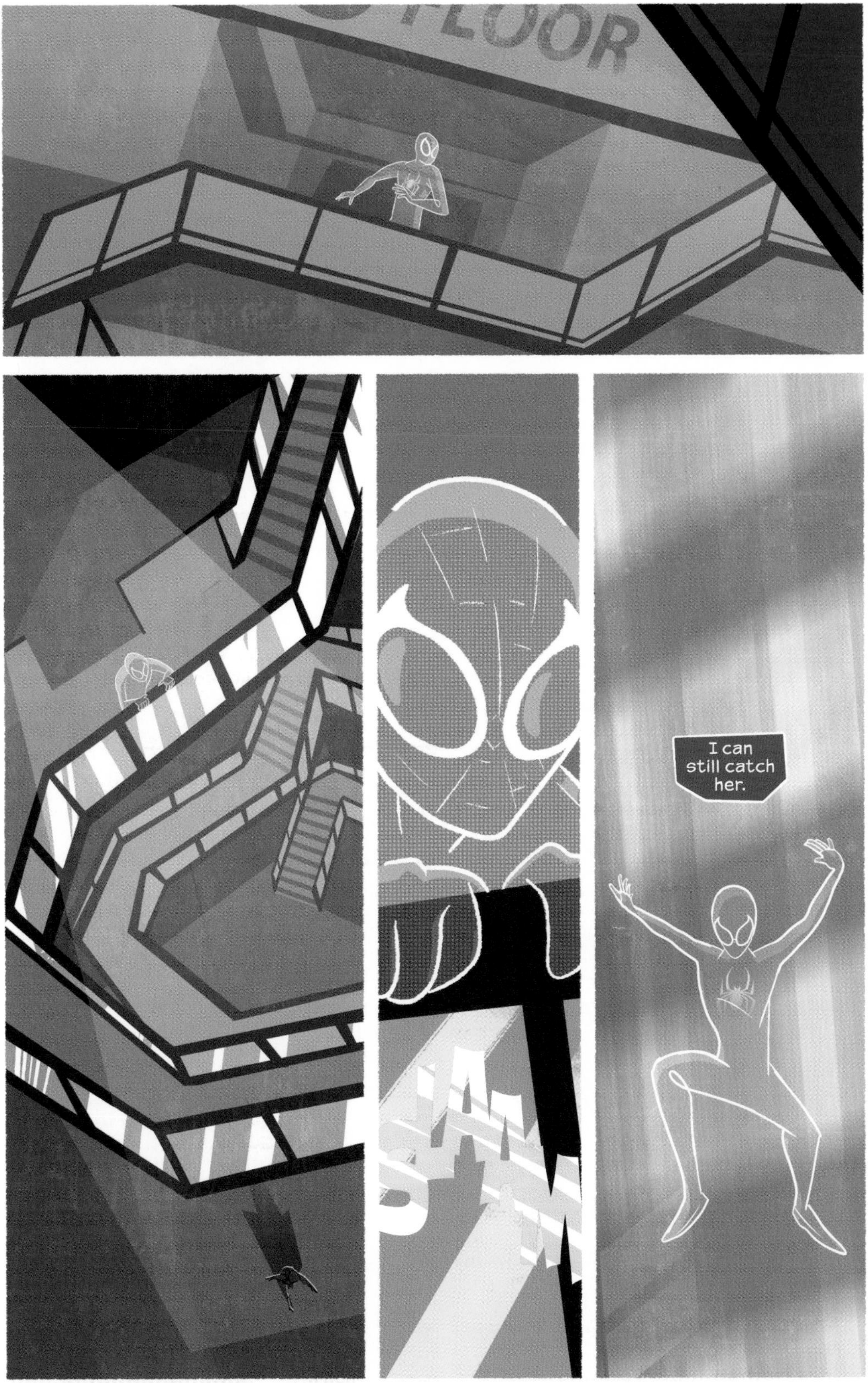
FLOOR
I can still catch her.

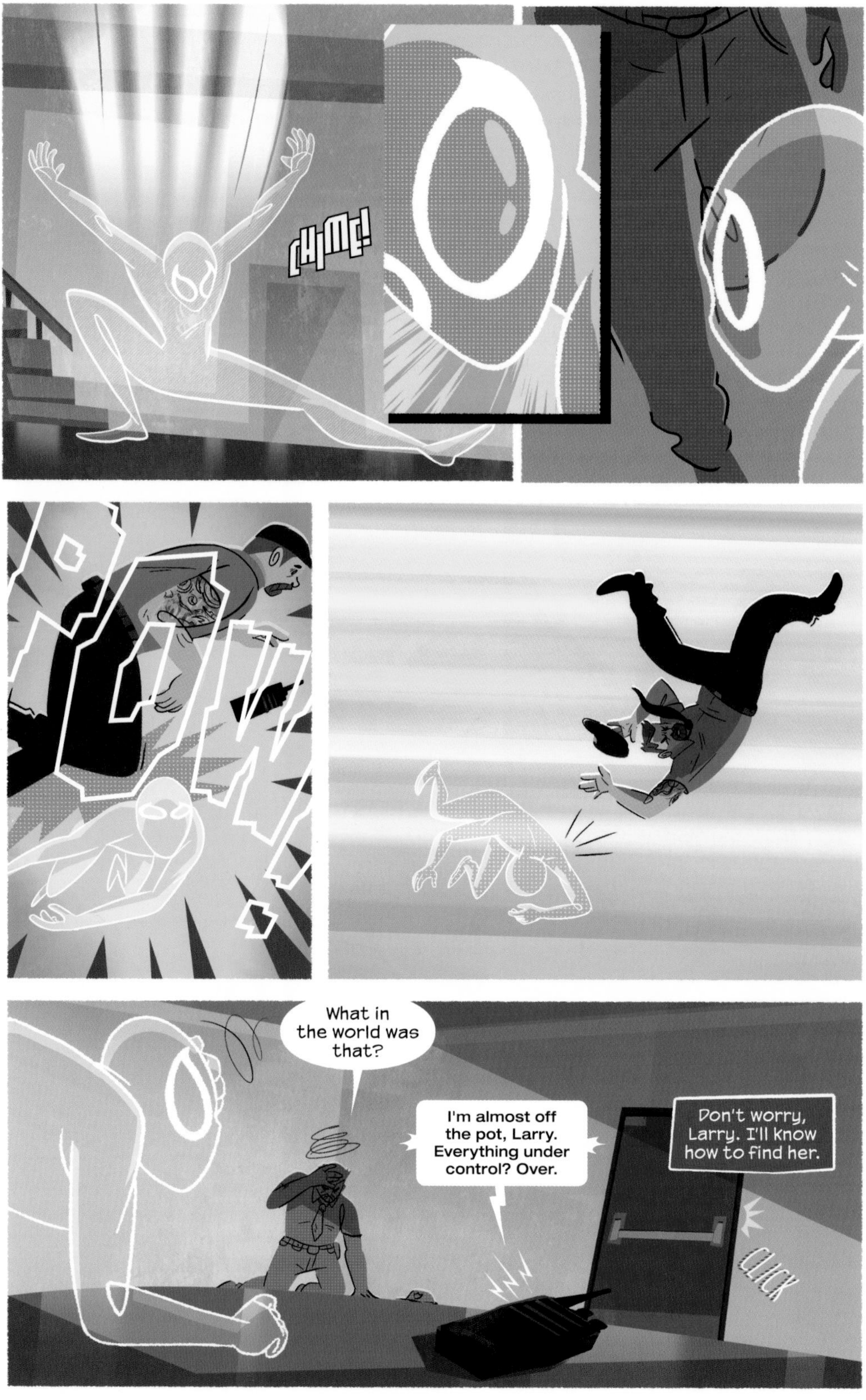
CHIME!
What in the world was that?
I'm almost off the pot, Larry. Everything under control? Over.
Don't worry, Larry. I'll know how to find her.
CLICK

CHAPTER
FOUR

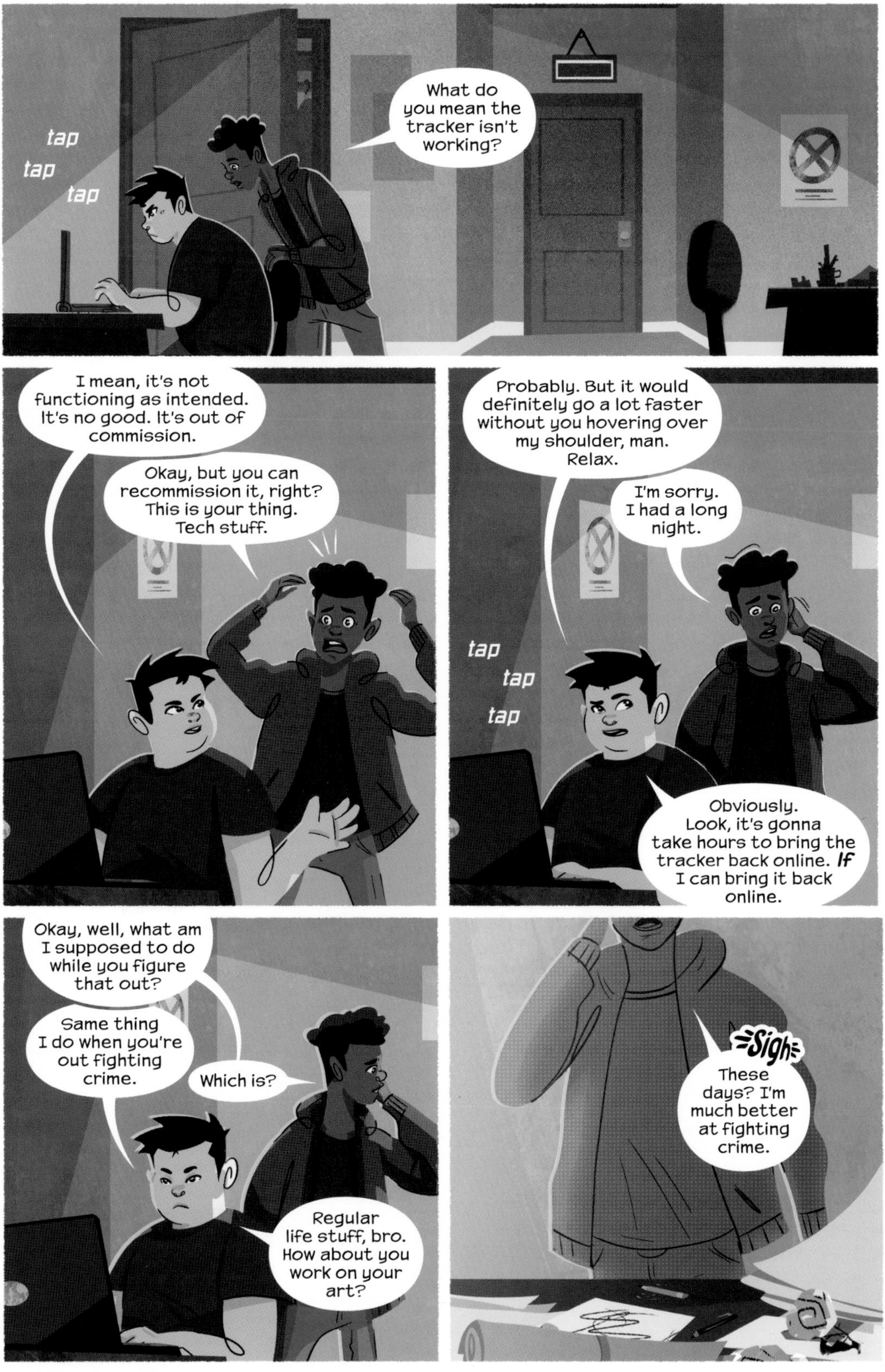
tap
tap
tap
What do you mean the tracker isn't working?
I mean, it's not functioning as intended. It's no good. It's out of commission.
Okay, but you can recommission it, right? This is your thing. Tech stuff.
Probably. But it would definitely go a lot faster without you hovering over my shoulder, man. Relax.
I'm sorry. I had a long night.
tap
tap
tap
Obviously. Look, it's gonna take hours to bring the tracker back online. *If* I can bring it back online.
Okay, well, what am I supposed to do while you figure that out?
Same thing I do when you're out fighting crime.
Which is?
Regular life stuff, bro. How about you work on your art?
Sigh
These days? I'm much better at fighting crime.

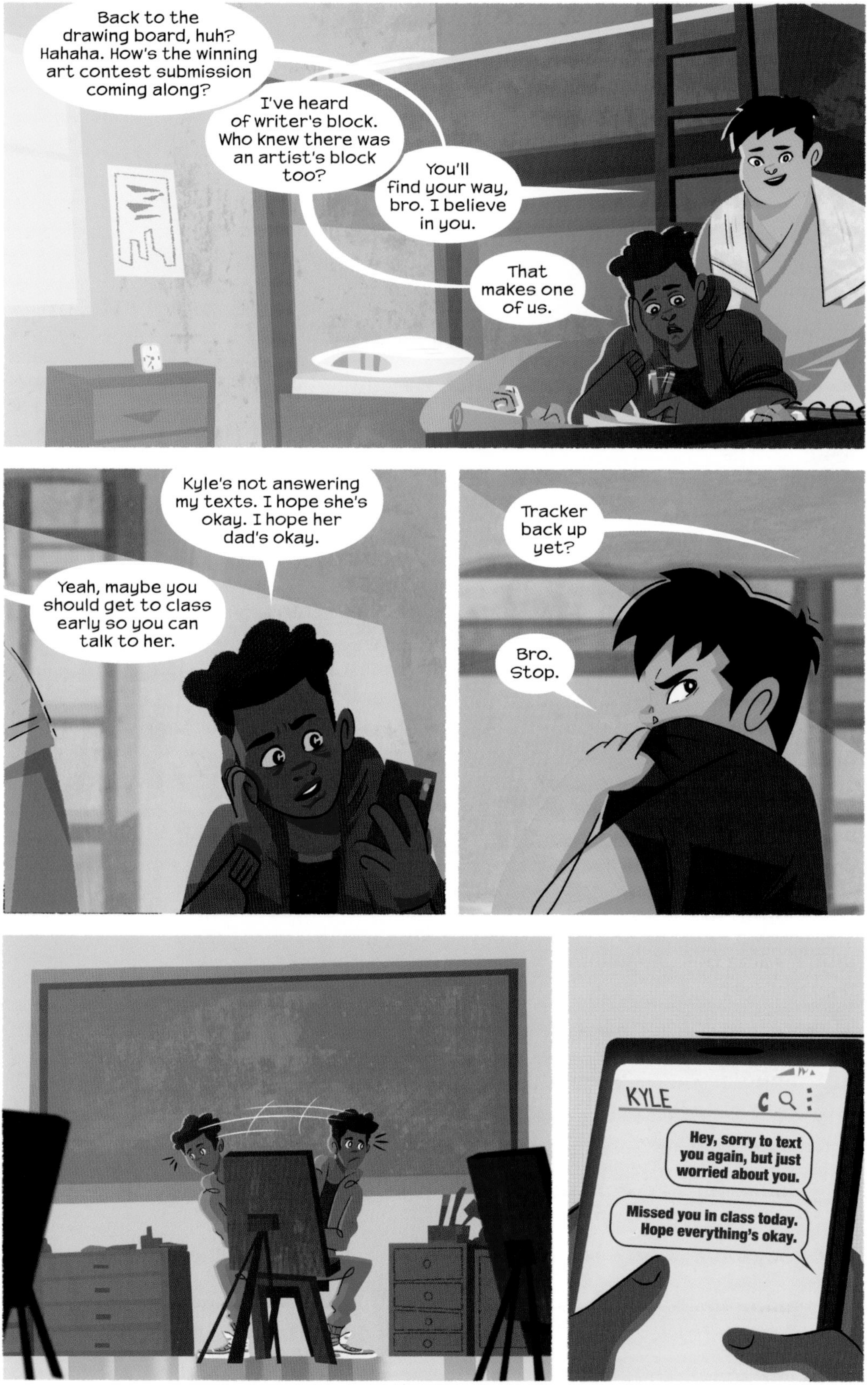
Back to the drawing board, huh? Hahaha. How's the winning art contest submission coming along?
I've heard of writer's block. Who knew there was an artist's block too?
You'll find your way, bro. I believe in you.
That makes one of us.
Kyle's not answering my texts. I hope she's okay. I hope her dad's okay.
Yeah, maybe you should get to class early so you can talk to her.
Tracker back up yet?
Bro. Stop.
KYLE
Hey, sorry to text you again, but just worried about you.
Missed you in class today. Hope everything's okay.

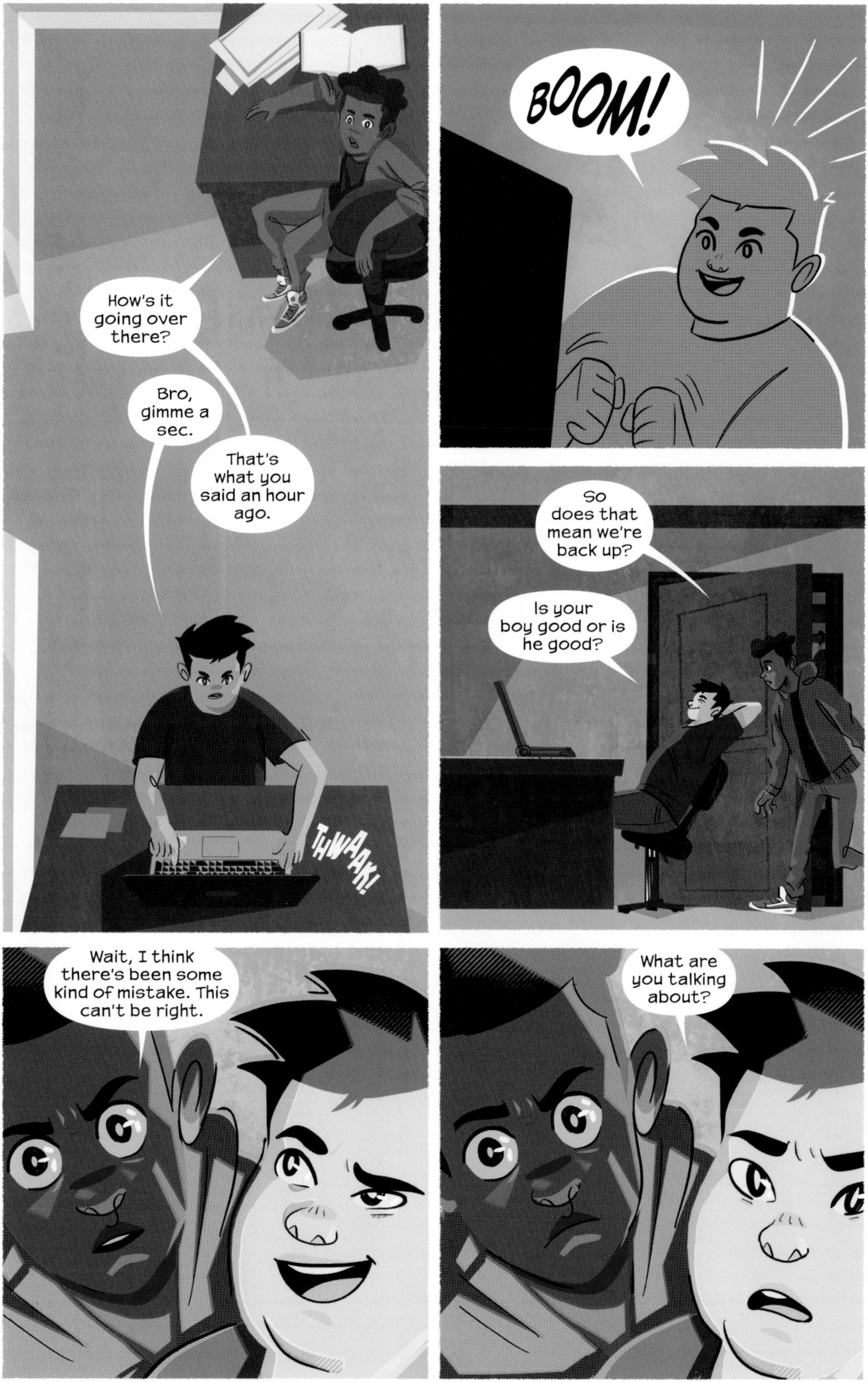
How's it going over there?
Bro, gimme a sec.
That's what you said an hour ago.
THWAAK!
BOOM!
So does that mean we're back up?
Is your boy good or is he good?
Wait, I think there's been some kind of mistake. This can't be right.
What are you talking about?

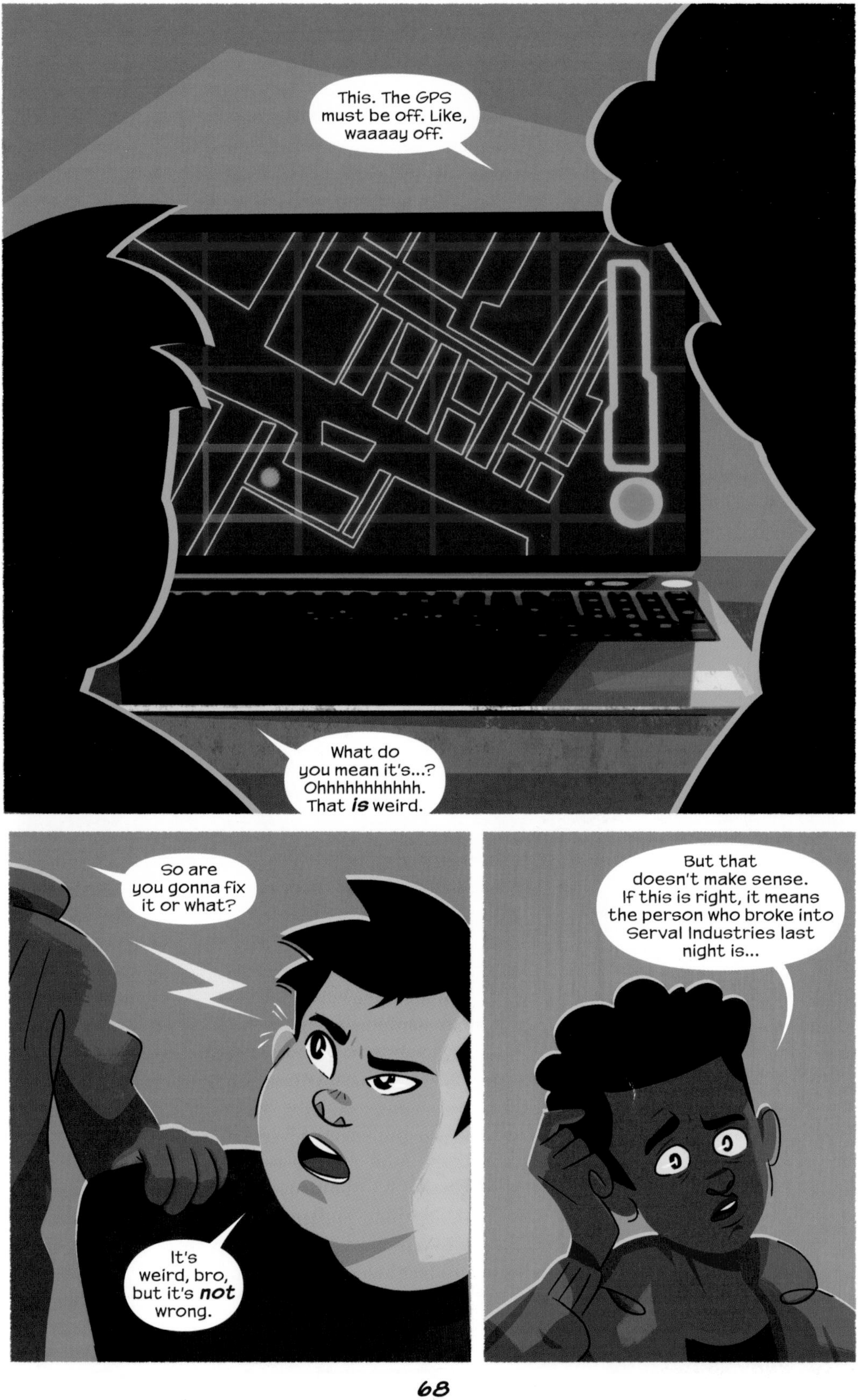
This. The GPS must be off. Like, waaaay off.
What do you mean it's...? Ohhhhhhhhhhh. That ***is*** weird.
So are you gonna fix it or what?
It's weird, bro, but it's ***not*** wrong.
But that doesn't make sense. If this is right, it means the person who broke into Serval Industries last night is...

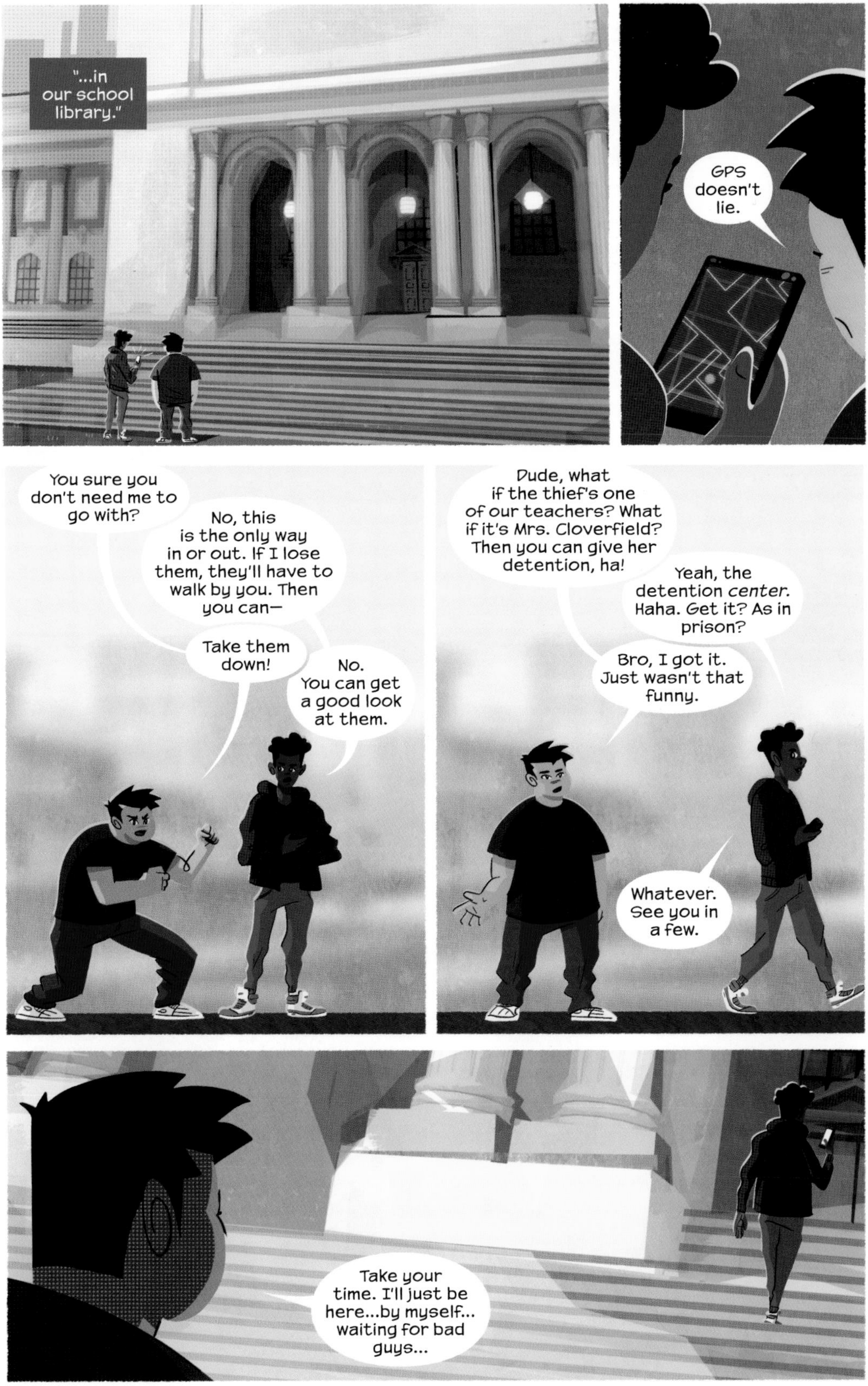
"...in our school library."
GPS doesn't lie.
You sure you don't need me to go with?
No, this is the only way in or out. If I lose them, they'll have to walk by you. Then you can—
Take them down!
No. You can get a good look at them.
Dude, what if the thief's one of our teachers? What if it's Mrs. Cloverfield? Then you can give her detention, ha!
Yeah, the detention *center.* Haha. Get it? As in prison?
Bro, I got it. Just wasn't that funny.
Whatever. See you in a few.
Take your time. I'll just be here...by myself... waiting for bad guys...

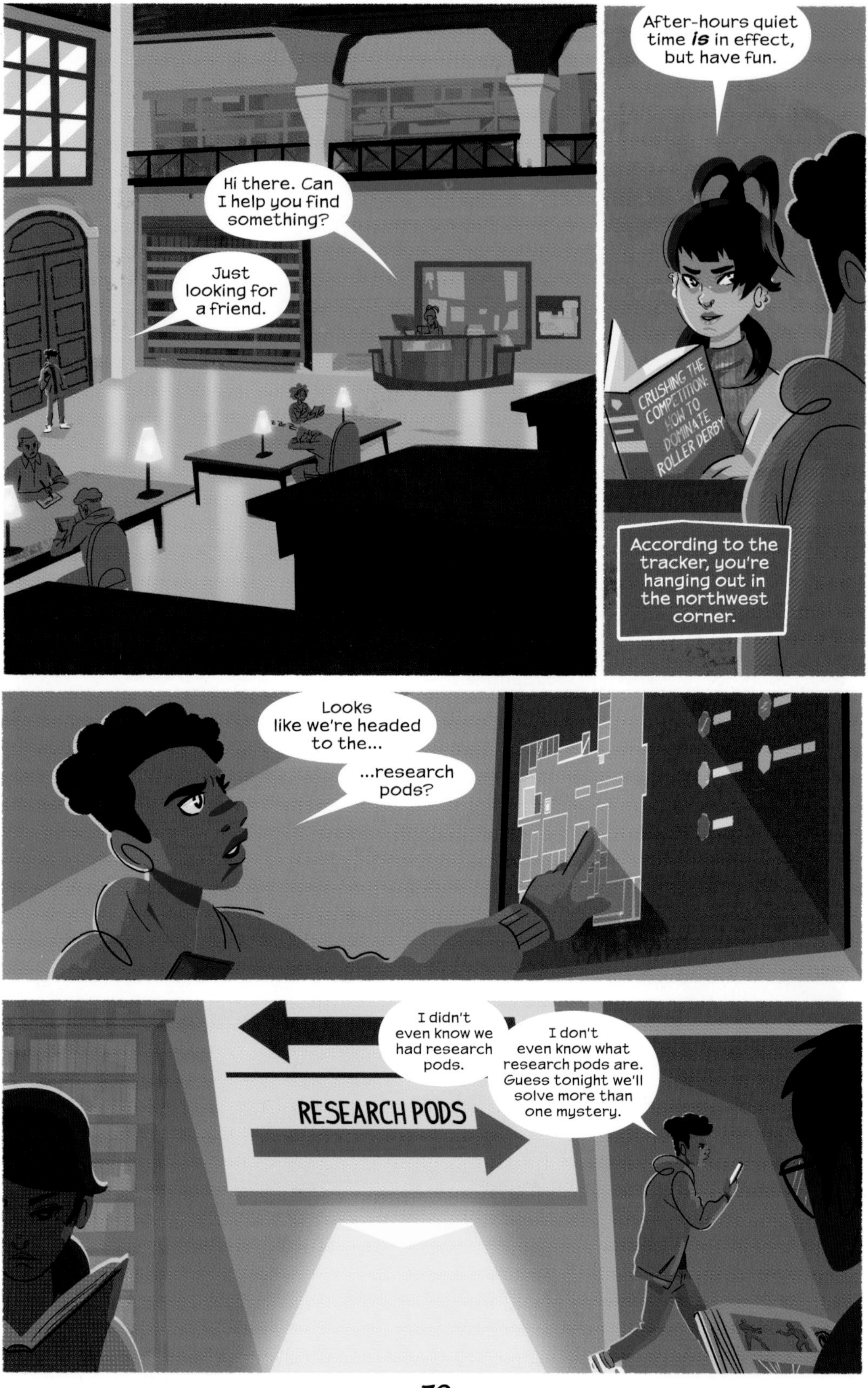
Hi there. Can I help you find something?
Just looking for a friend.
After-hours quiet time *is* in effect, but have fun.
CRUSHING THE COMPETITION: HOW TO DOMINATE ROLLER DERBY
According to the tracker, you're hanging out in the northwest corner.
Looks like we're headed to the...
...research pods?
RESEARCH PODS
I didn't even know we had research pods.
I don't even know what research pods are. Guess tonight we'll solve more than one mystery.

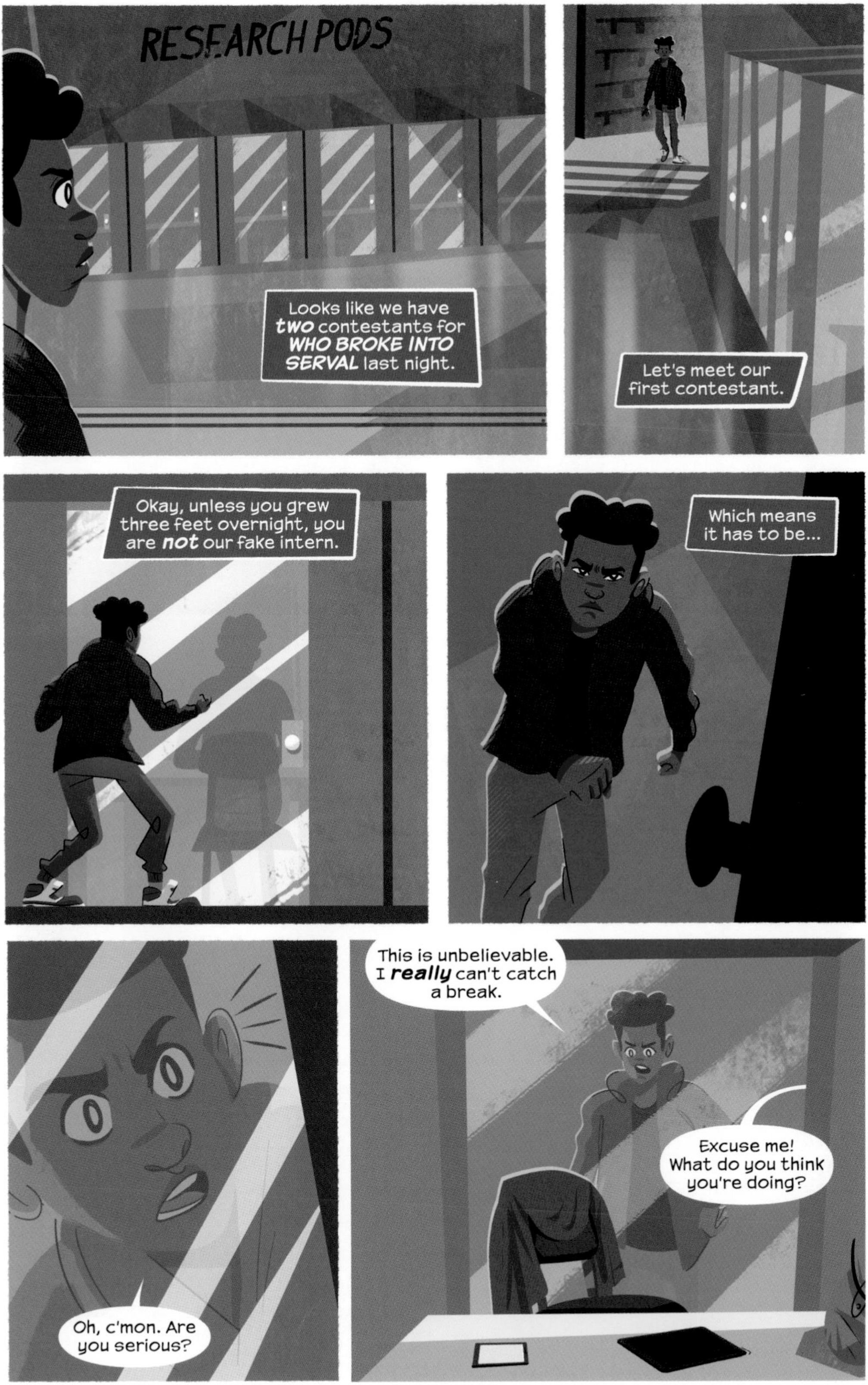
RESEARCH PODS
Looks like we have two contestants for WHO BROKE INTO SERVAL last night.
Let's meet our first contestant.
Okay, unless you grew three feet overnight, you are not our fake intern.
Which means it has to be...
Oh, c'mon. Are you serious?
This is unbelievable. I really can't catch a break.
Excuse me! What do you think you're doing?

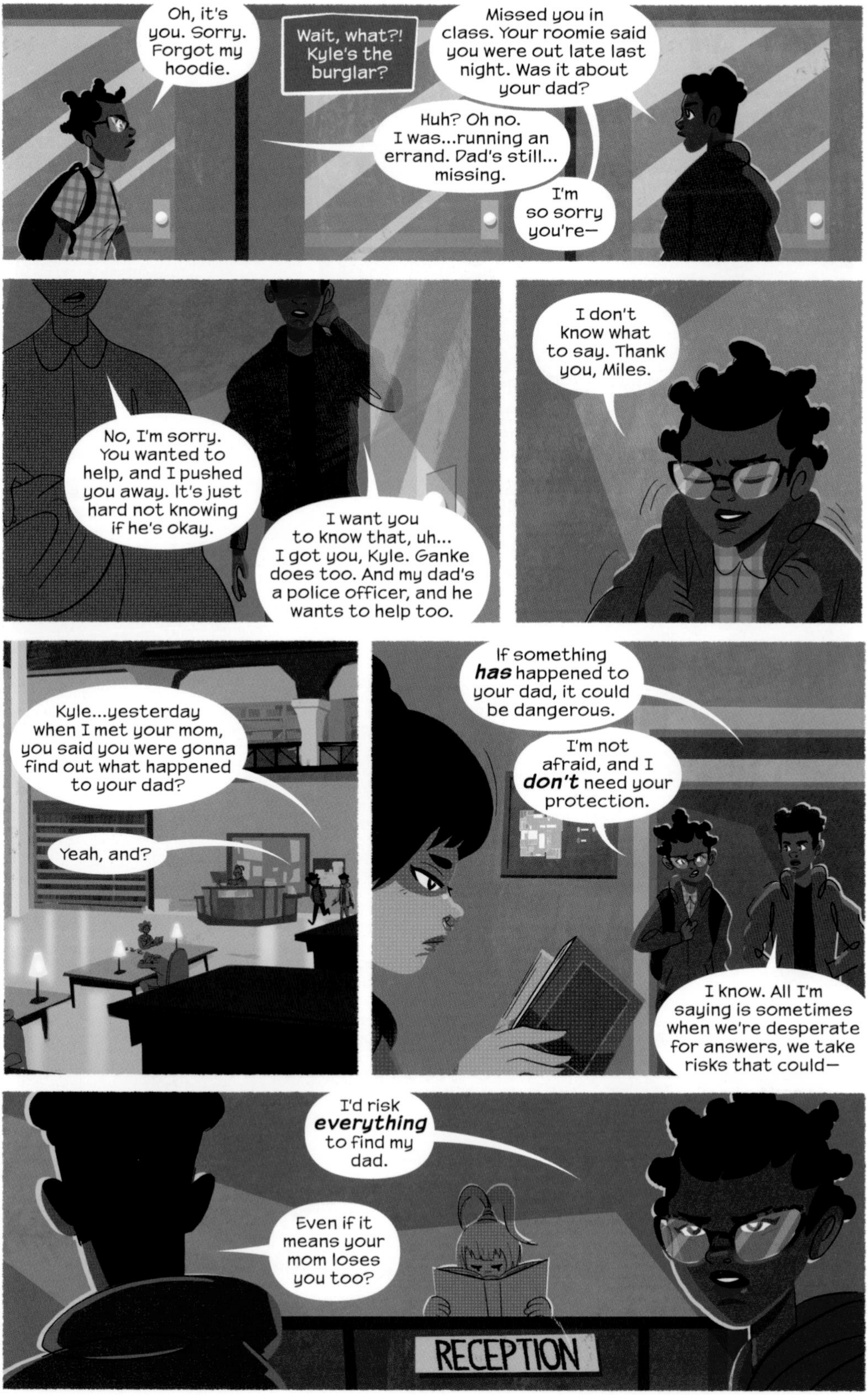

Oh, it's you. Sorry. Forgot my hoodie.
Wait, what?! Kyle's the burglar?
Missed you in class. Your roomie said you were out late last night. Was it about your dad?
Huh? Oh no. I was...running an errand. Dad's still... missing.
I'm so sorry you're—
No, I'm sorry. You wanted to help, and I pushed you away. It's just hard not knowing if he's okay.
I want you to know that, uh... I got you, Kyle. Ganke does too. And my dad's a police officer, and he wants to help too.
I don't know what to say. Thank you, Miles.
Kyle...yesterday when I met your mom, you said you were gonna find out what happened to your dad?
Yeah, and?
If something **has** happened to your dad, it could be dangerous.
I'm not afraid, and I **don't** need your protection.
I know. All I'm saying is sometimes when we're desperate for answers, we take risks that could—
I'd risk **everything** to find my dad.
Even if it means your mom loses you too?
RECEPTION

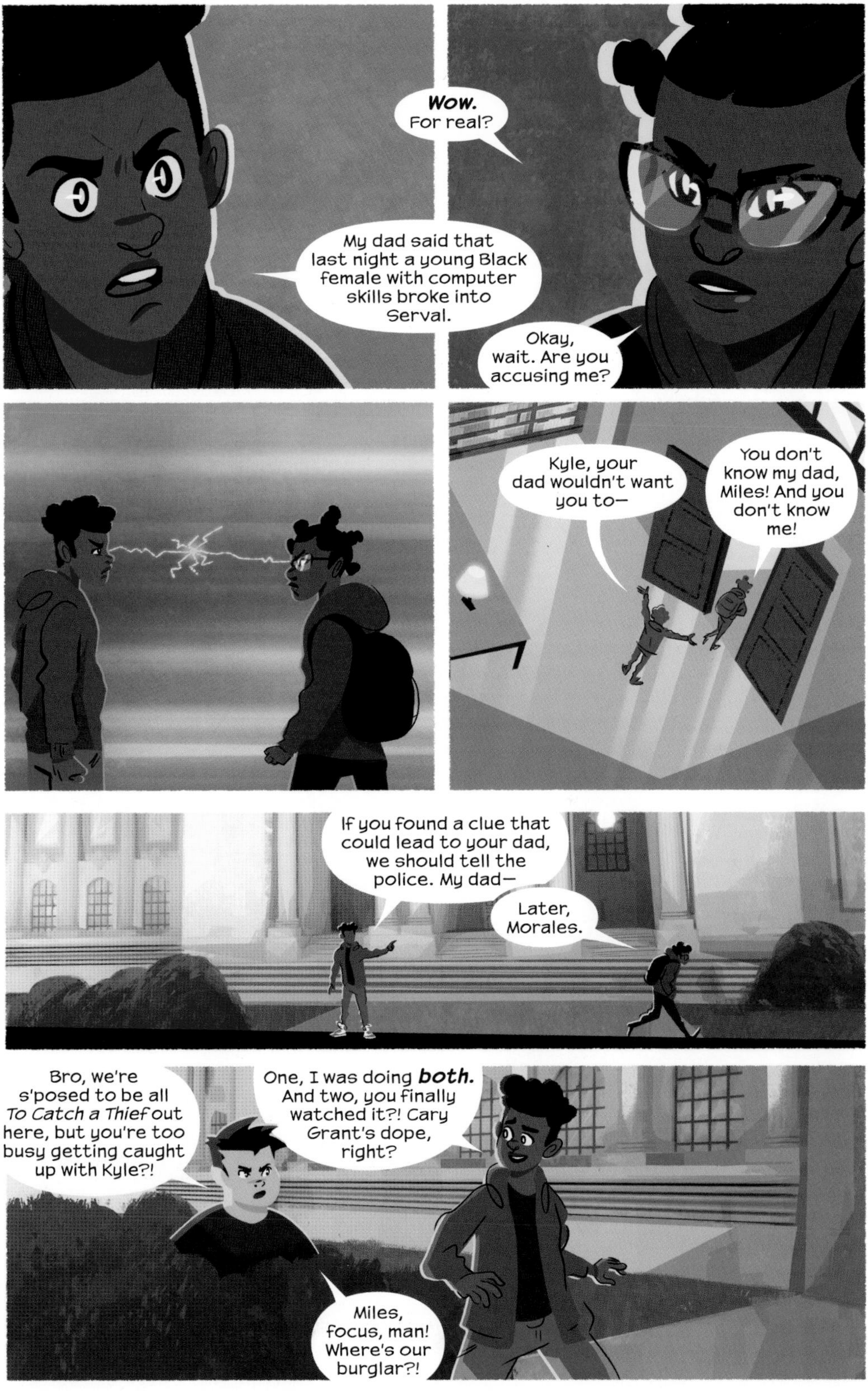
Wow. For real?
My dad said that last night a young Black female with computer skills broke into Serval.
Okay, wait. Are you accusing me?
Kyle, your dad wouldn't want you to—
You don't know my dad, Miles! And you don't know me!
If you found a clue that could lead to your dad, we should tell the police. My dad—
Later, Morales.
Bro, we're s'posed to be all *To Catch a Thief* out here, but you're too busy getting caught up with Kyle?!
One, I was doing **both.** And two, you finally watched it?! Cary Grant's dope, right?
Miles, focus, man! Where's our burglar?!

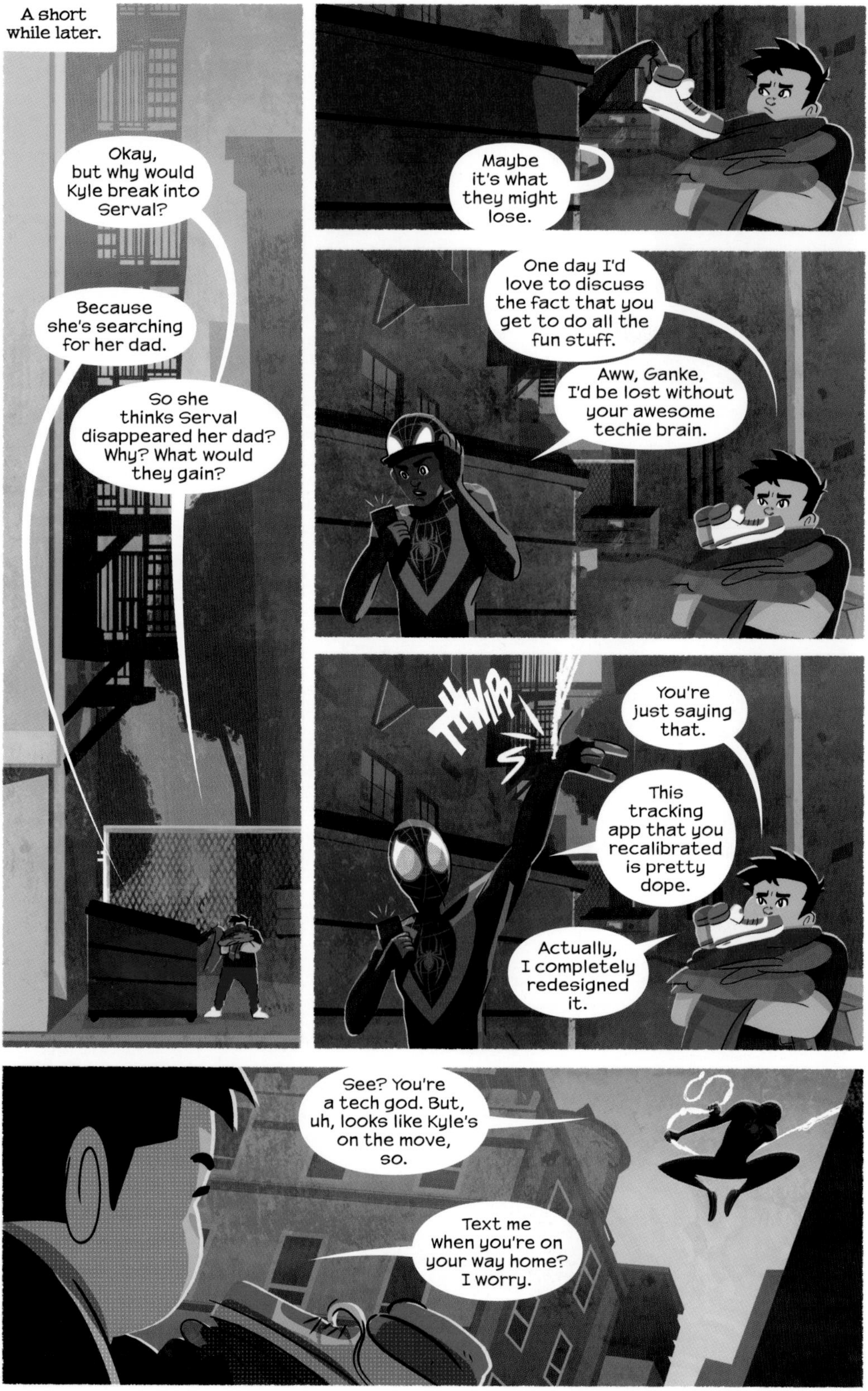
A short while later.
Okay, but why would Kyle break into Serval?
Because she's searching for her dad.
So she thinks Serval disappeared her dad? Why? What would they gain?
Maybe it's what they might lose.
One day I'd love to discuss the fact that you get to do all the fun stuff.
Aww, Ganke, I'd be lost without your awesome techie brain.
THWIPP
You're just saying that.
This tracking app that you recalibrated is pretty dope.
Actually, I completely redesigned it.
See? You're a tech god. But, uh, looks like Kyle's on the move, so.
Text me when you're on your way home? I worry.

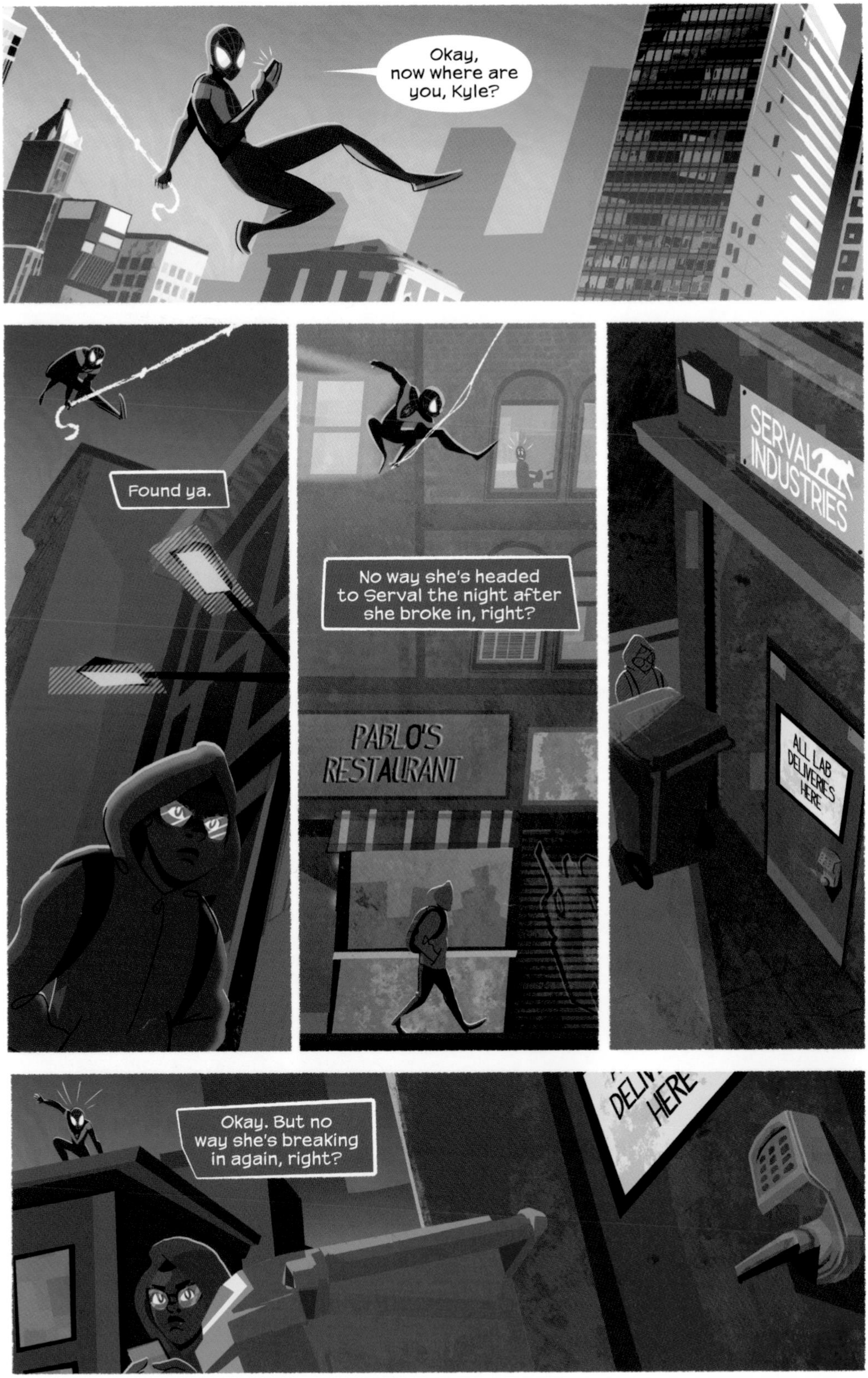
Okay, now where are you, Kyle?
Found ya.
No way she's headed to Serval the night after she broke in, right?
PABLO'S RESTAURANT
SERVAL INDUSTRIES
ALL LAB DELIVERIES HERE
Okay. But no way she's breaking in again, right?

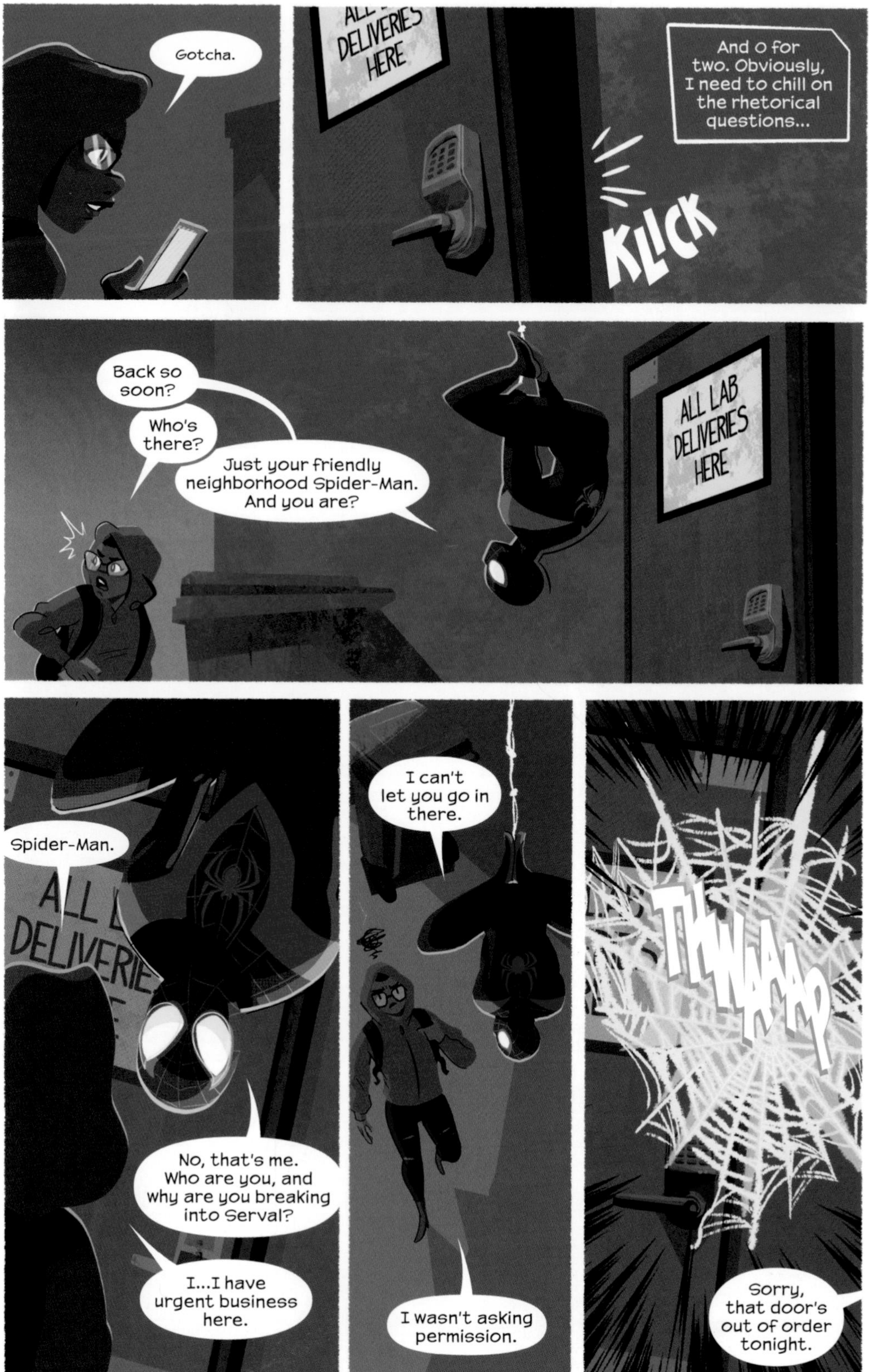

Gotcha.
DELIVERIES HERE
And 0 for two. Obviously, I need to chill on the rhetorical questions...
KLICK
Back so soon?
Who's there?
Just your friendly neighborhood Spider-Man. And you are?
ALL LAB DELIVERIES HERE
Spider-Man.
No, that's me. Who are you, and why are you breaking into Serval?
I...I have urgent business here.
I can't let you go in there.
I wasn't asking permission.
THWAAAP
Sorry, that door's out of order tonight.

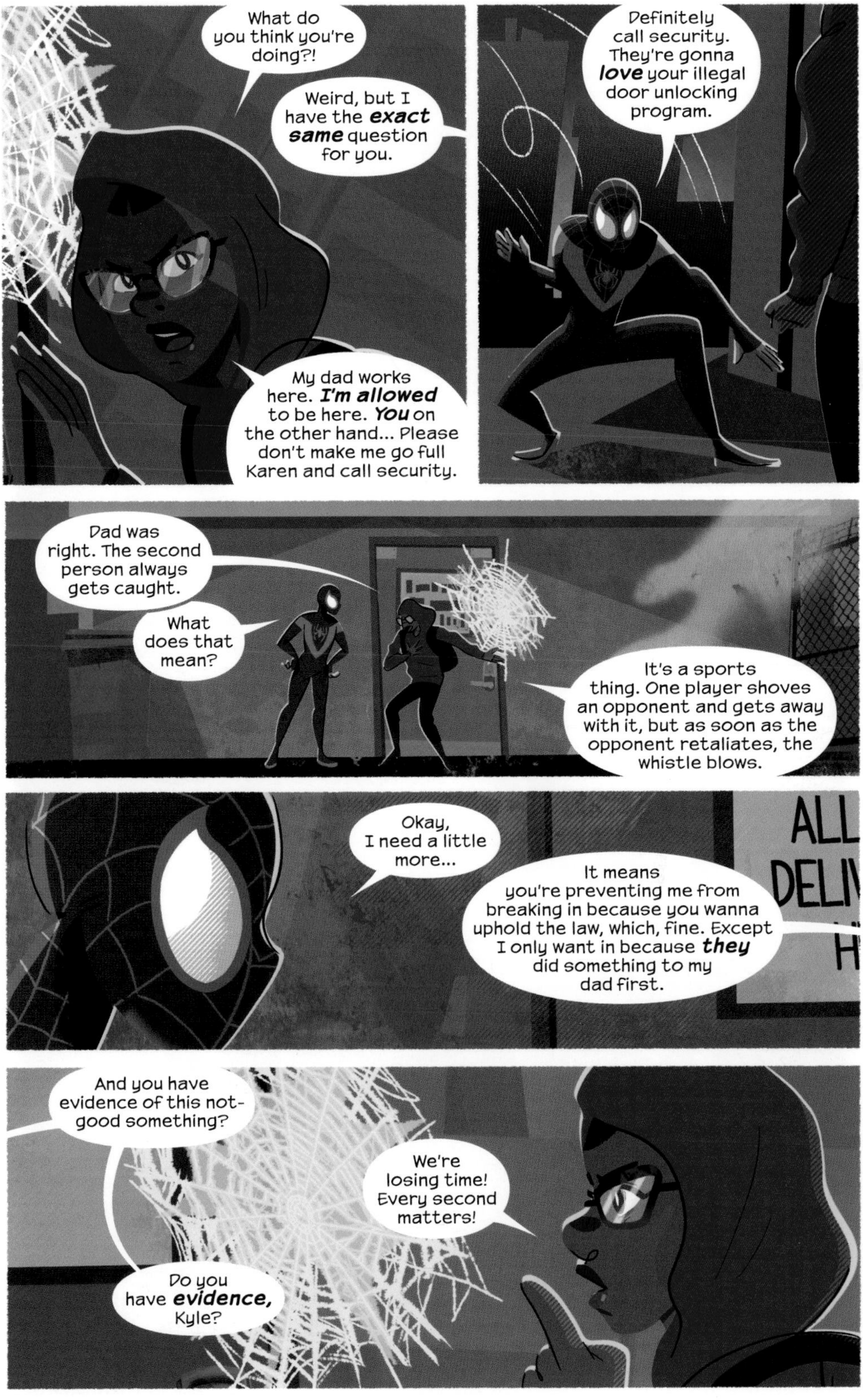

What do you think you're doing?!
Weird, but I have the *exact same* question for you.
Definitely call security. They're gonna *love* your illegal door unlocking program.
My dad works here. *I'm allowed* to be here. *You* on the other hand... Please don't make me go full Karen and call security.
Dad was right. The second person always gets caught.
What does that mean?
It's a sports thing. One player shoves an opponent and gets away with it, but as soon as the opponent retaliates, the whistle blows.
Okay, I need a little more...
It means you're preventing me from breaking in because you wanna uphold the law, which, fine. Except I only want in because *they* did something to my dad first.
And you have evidence of this not-good something?
We're losing time! Every second matters!
Do you have *evidence,* Kyle?

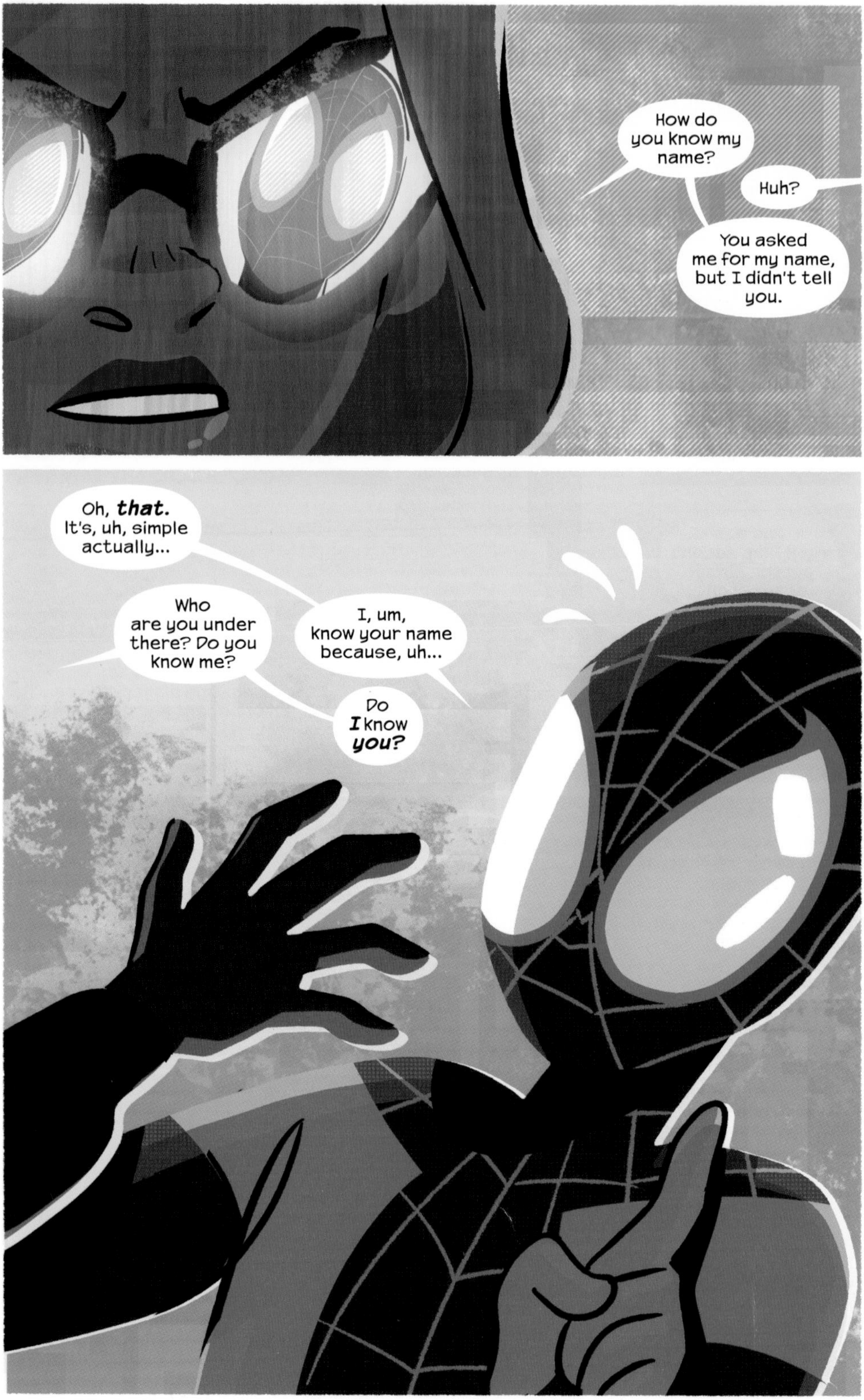
How do you know my name?
Huh?
You asked me for my name, but I didn't tell you.
Oh, **that.** It's, uh, simple actually...
I, um, know your name because, uh...
Who are you under there? Do you know me?
Do ***I*** know ***you?***

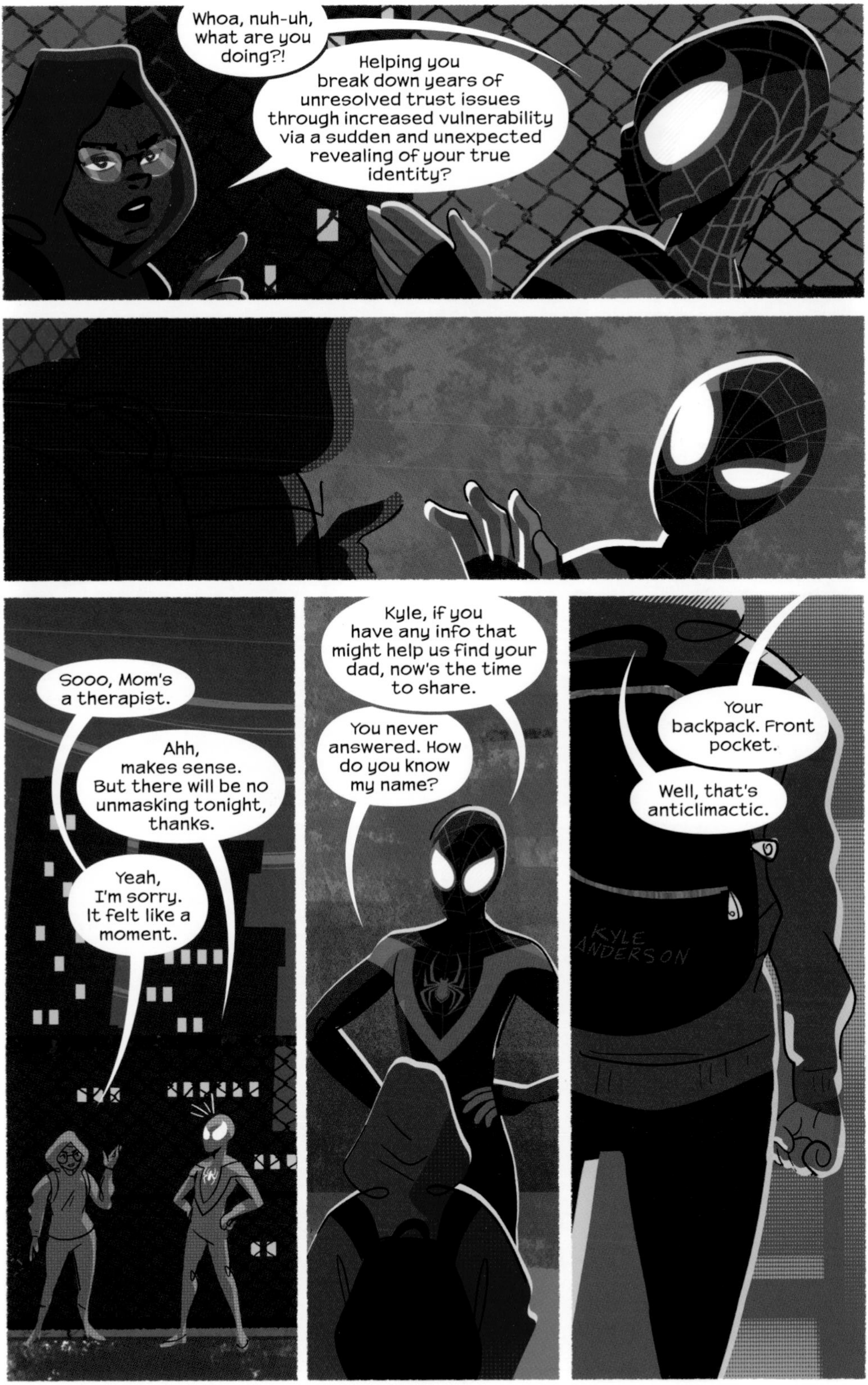
Whoa, nuh-uh, what are you doing?!
Helping you break down years of unresolved trust issues through increased vulnerability via a sudden and unexpected revealing of your true identity?
Sooo, Mom's a therapist.
Ahh, makes sense. But there will be no unmasking tonight, thanks.
Yeah, I'm sorry. It felt like a moment.
Kyle, if you have any info that might help us find your dad, now's the time to share.
You never answered. How do you know my name?
Your backpack. Front pocket.
Well, that's anticlimactic.
KYLE ANDERSON

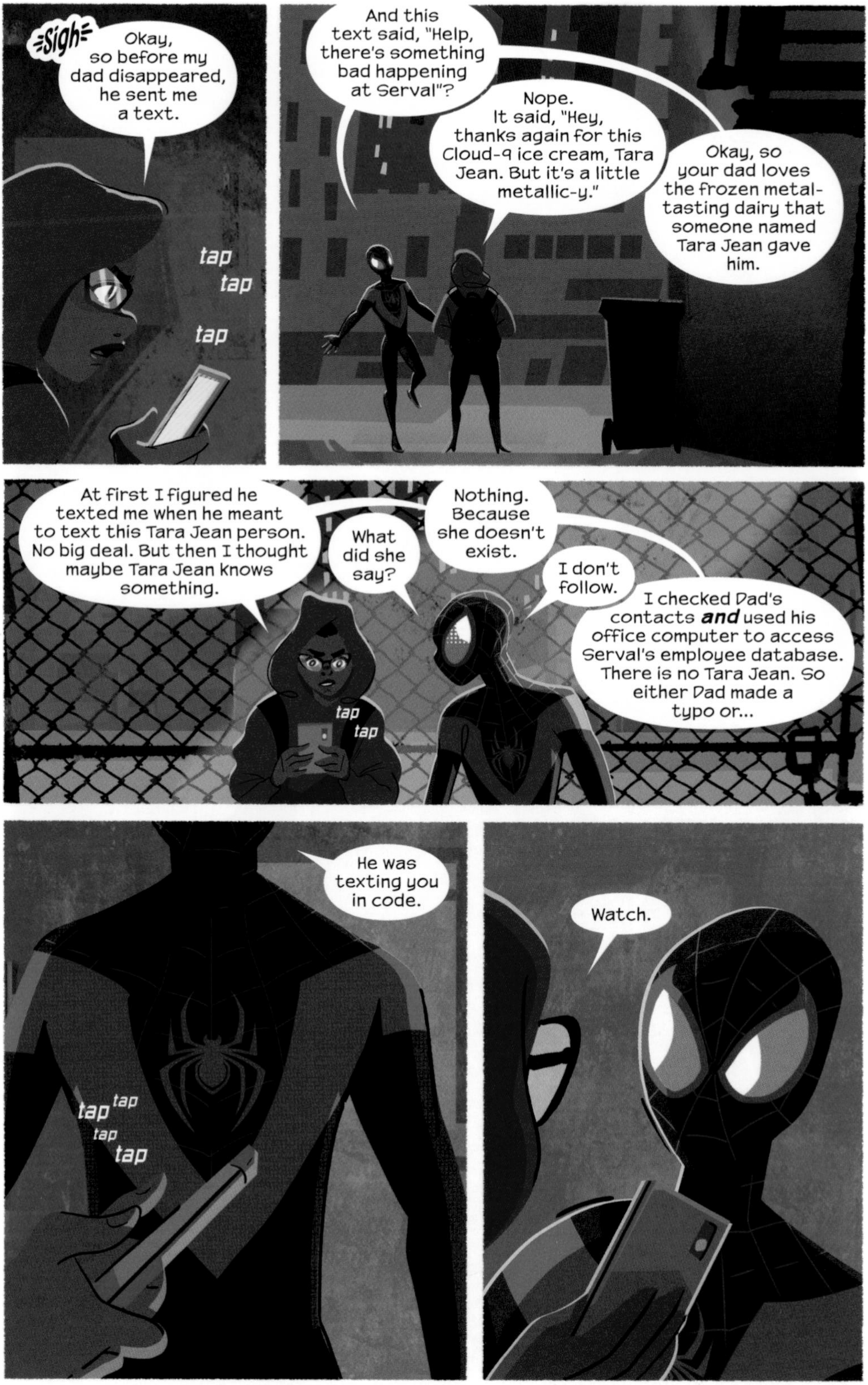
Sigh
Okay, so before my dad disappeared, he sent me a text.
tap tap tap
And this text said, "Help, there's something bad happening at Serval"?
Nope. It said, "Hey, thanks again for this Cloud-9 ice cream, Tara Jean. But it's a little metallic-y."
Okay, so your dad loves the frozen metal-tasting dairy that someone named Tara Jean gave him.
At first I figured he texted me when he meant to text this Tara Jean person. No big deal. But then I thought maybe Tara Jean knows something.
What did she say?
Nothing. Because she doesn't exist.
I don't follow.
I checked Dad's contacts **and** used his office computer to access Serval's employee database. There is no Tara Jean. So either Dad made a typo or...
tap tap
He was texting you in code.
tap tap tap tap
Watch.

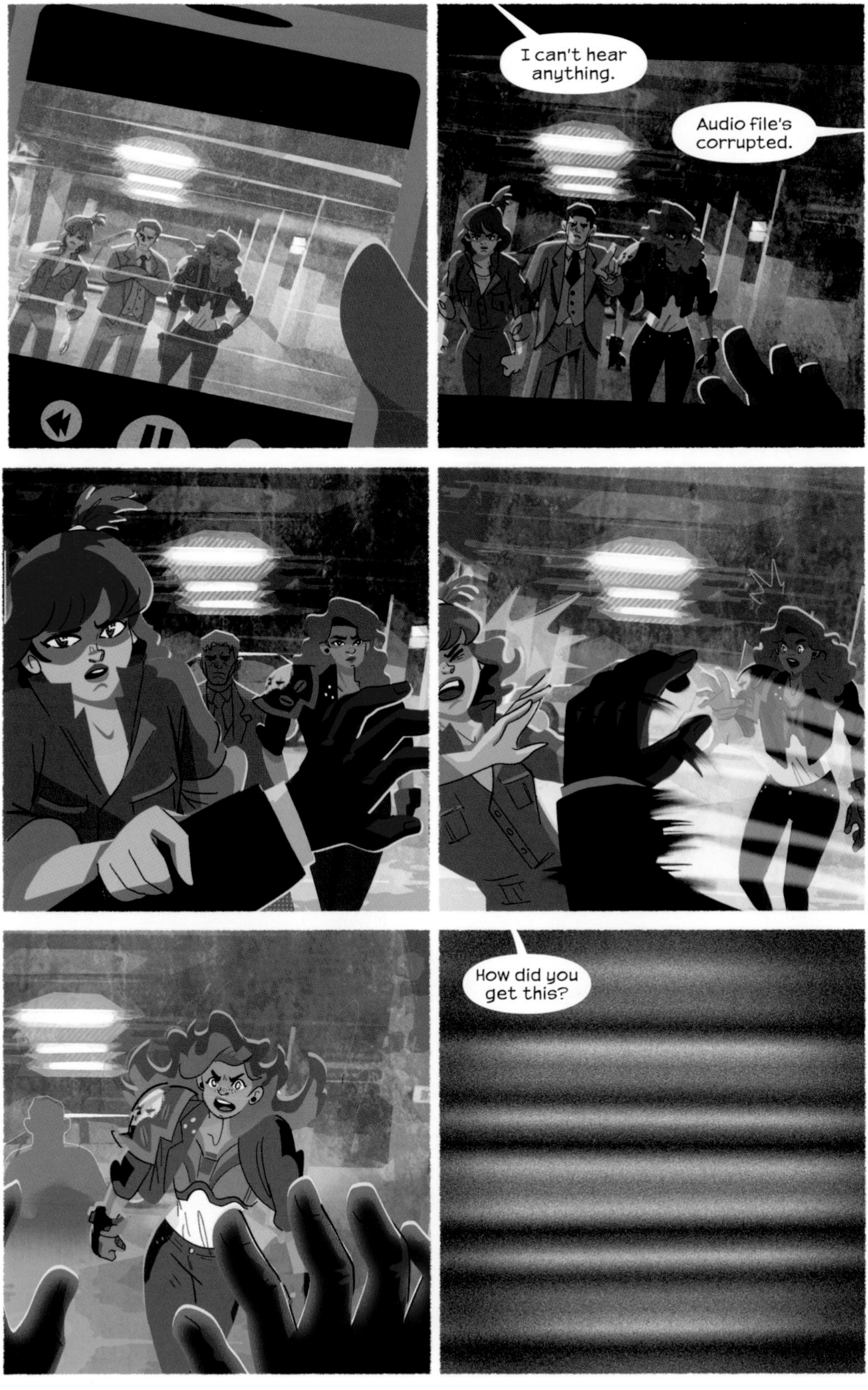
I can't hear anything.
Audio file's corrupted.
How did you get this?

CHAPTER

FIVE

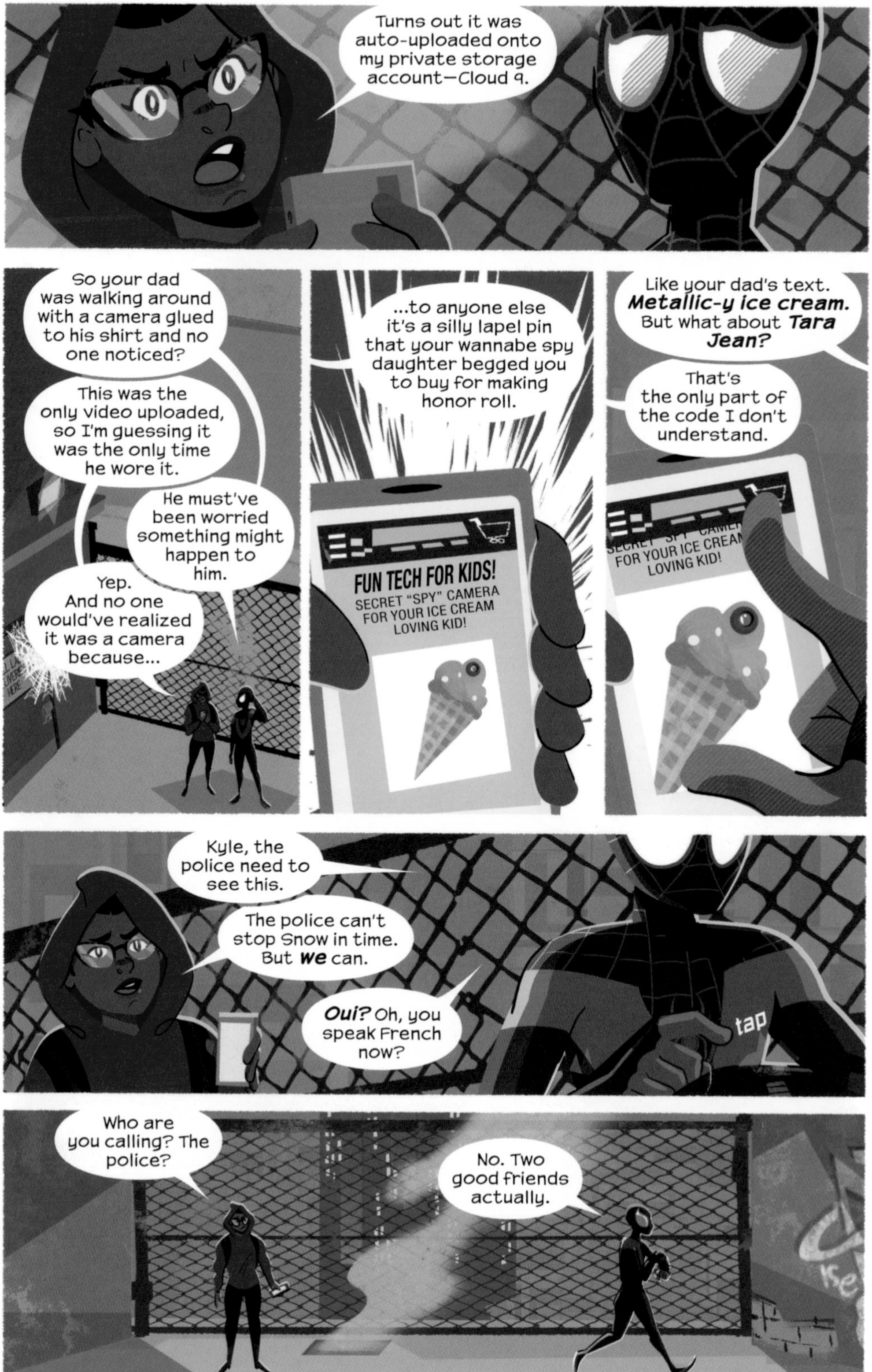
Turns out it was auto-uploaded onto my private storage account—Cloud 9.
So your dad was walking around with a camera glued to his shirt and no one noticed?
This was the only video uploaded, so I'm guessing it was the only time he wore it.
He must've been worried something might happen to him.
Yep. And no one would've realized it was a camera because...
...to anyone else it's a silly lapel pin that your wannabe spy daughter begged you to buy for making honor roll.
FUN TECH FOR KIDS!
SECRET "SPY" CAMERA FOR YOUR ICE CREAM LOVING KID!
Like your dad's text. ***Metallic-y ice cream.*** But what about ***Tara Jean?***
That's the only part of the code I don't understand.
FOR YOUR ICE CREAM LOVING KID!
Kyle, the police need to see this.
The police can't stop Snow in time. But ***we*** can.
Oui? Oh, you speak French now?
tap
Who are you calling? The police?
No. Two good friends actually.

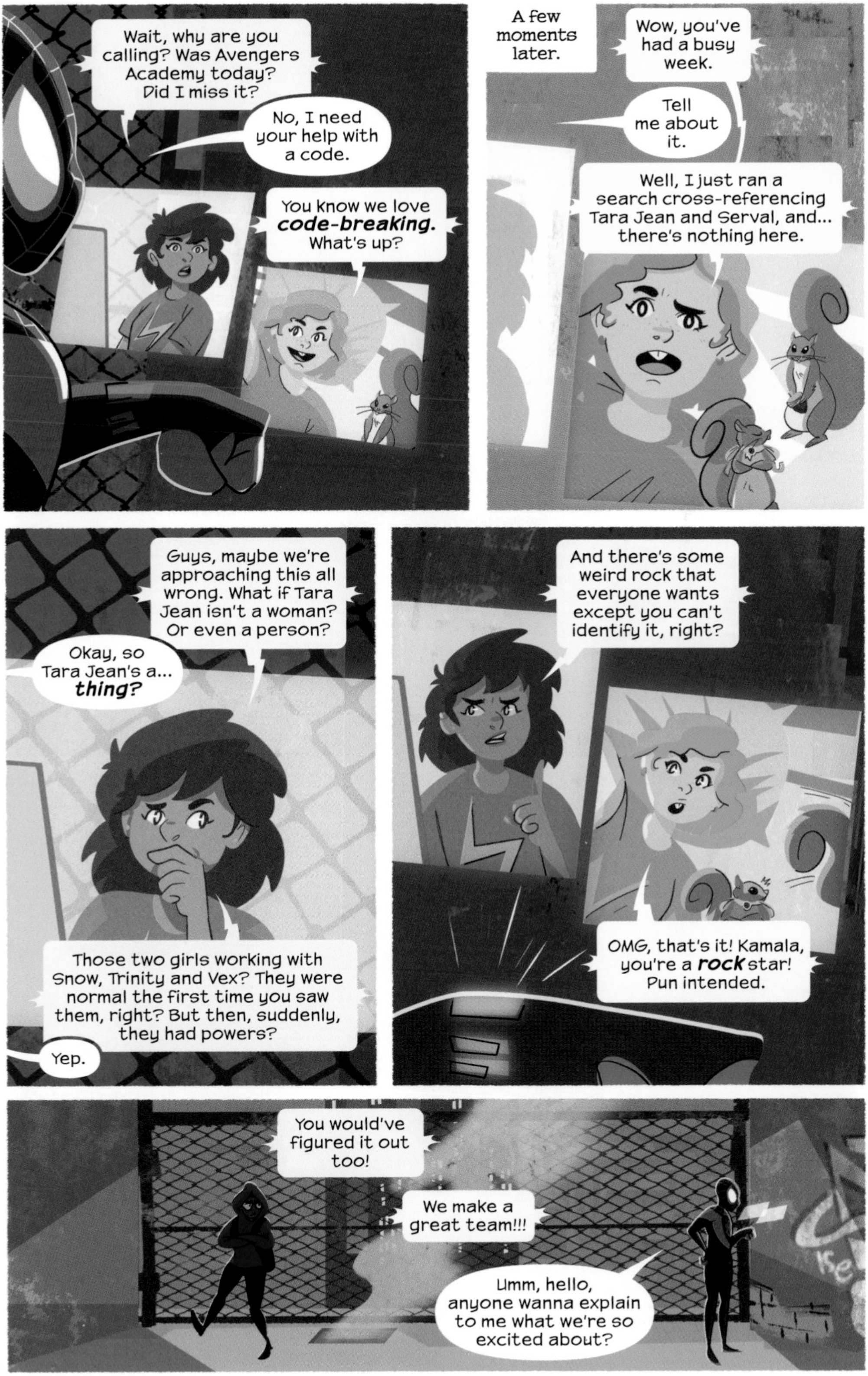
Wait, why are you calling? Was Avengers Academy today? Did I miss it?
No, I need your help with a code.
You know we love **code-breaking.** What's up?
A few moments later.
Wow, you've had a busy week.
Tell me about it.
Well, I just ran a search cross-referencing Tara Jean and Serval, and... there's nothing here.
Guys, maybe we're approaching this all wrong. What if Tara Jean isn't a woman? Or even a person?
Okay, so Tara Jean's a... ***thing?***
Those two girls working with Snow, Trinity and Vex? They were normal the first time you saw them, right? But then, suddenly, they had powers?
Yep.
And there's some weird rock that everyone wants except you can't identify it, right?
OMG, that's it! Kamala, you're a ***rock*** star! Pun intended.
You would've figured it out too!
We make a great team!!!
Umm, hello, anyone wanna explain to me what we're so excited about?

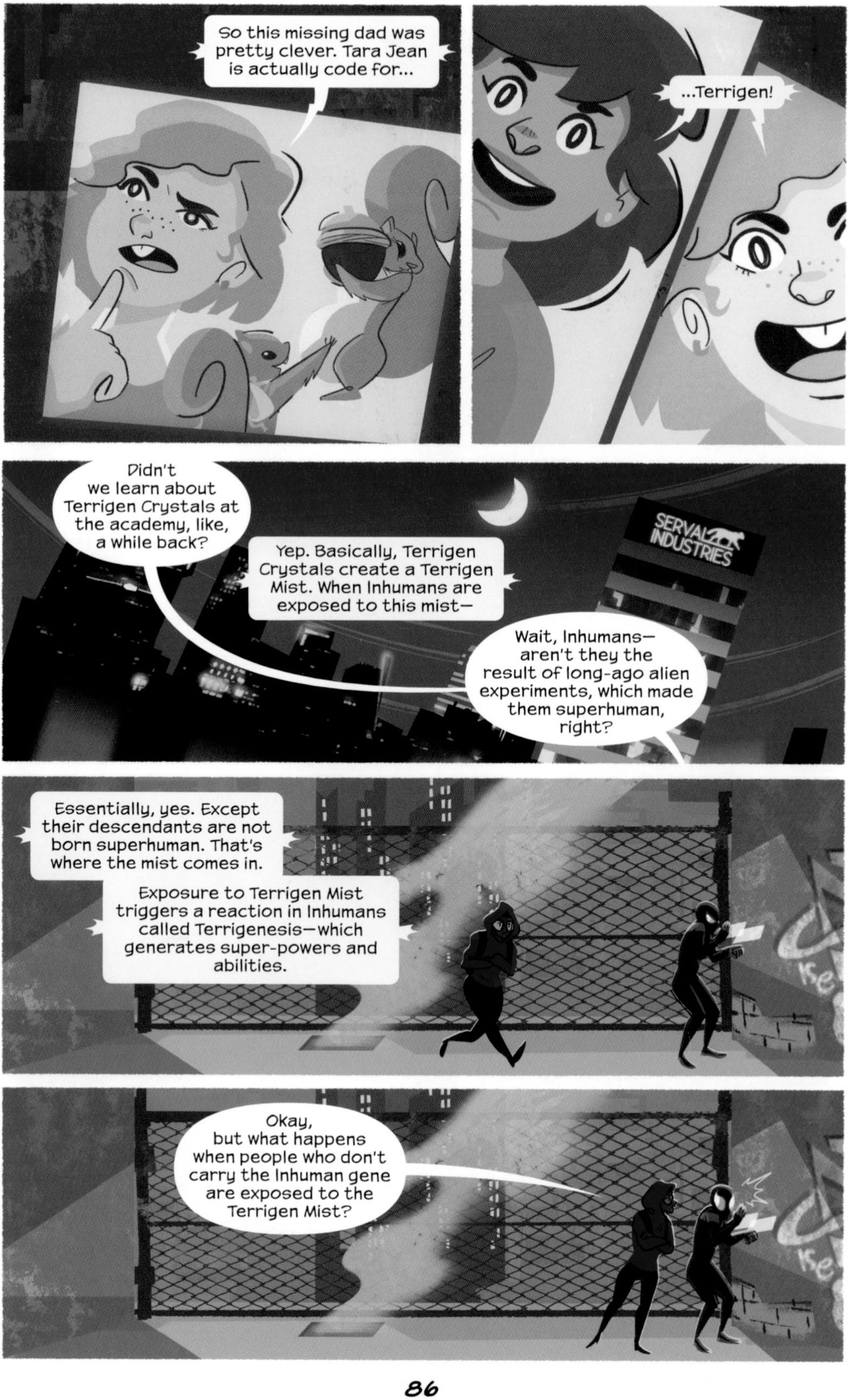
So this missing dad was pretty clever. Tara Jean is actually code for...
...Terrigen!
Didn't we learn about Terrigen Crystals at the academy, like, a while back?
Yep. Basically, Terrigen Crystals create a Terrigen Mist. When Inhumans are exposed to this mist—
SERVAL INDUSTRIES
Wait, Inhumans—aren't they the result of long-ago alien experiments, which made them superhuman, right?
Essentially, yes. Except their descendants are not born superhuman. That's where the mist comes in.
Exposure to Terrigen Mist triggers a reaction in Inhumans called Terrigenesis—which generates super-powers and abilities.
Okay, but what happens when people who don't carry the Inhuman gene are exposed to the Terrigen Mist?

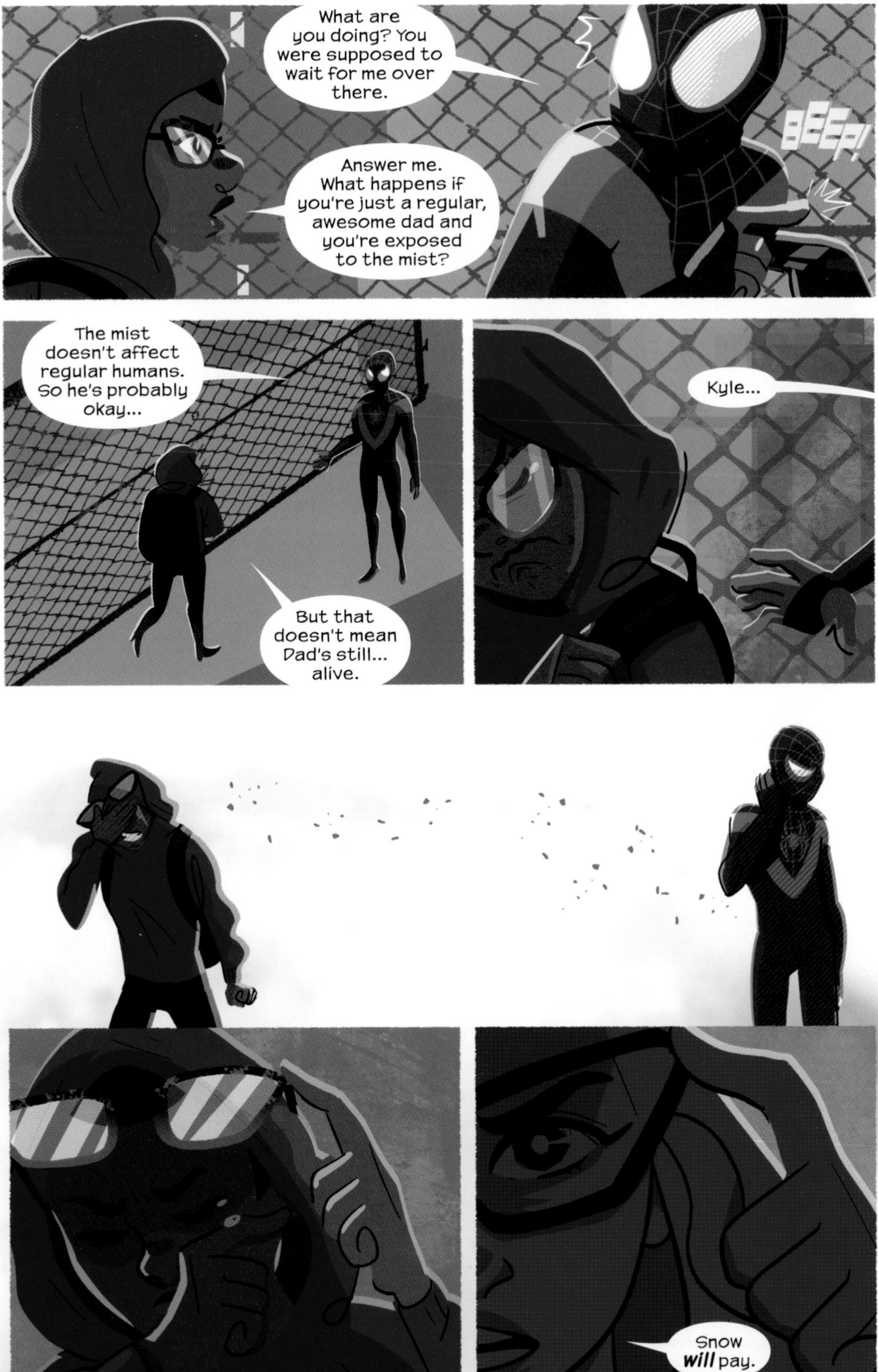

What are you doing? You were supposed to wait for me over there.
BEEP!
Answer me. What happens if you're just a regular, awesome dad and you're exposed to the mist?
The mist doesn't affect regular humans. So he's probably okay...
But that doesn't mean Dad's still... alive.
Kyle...
Snow **will** pay.

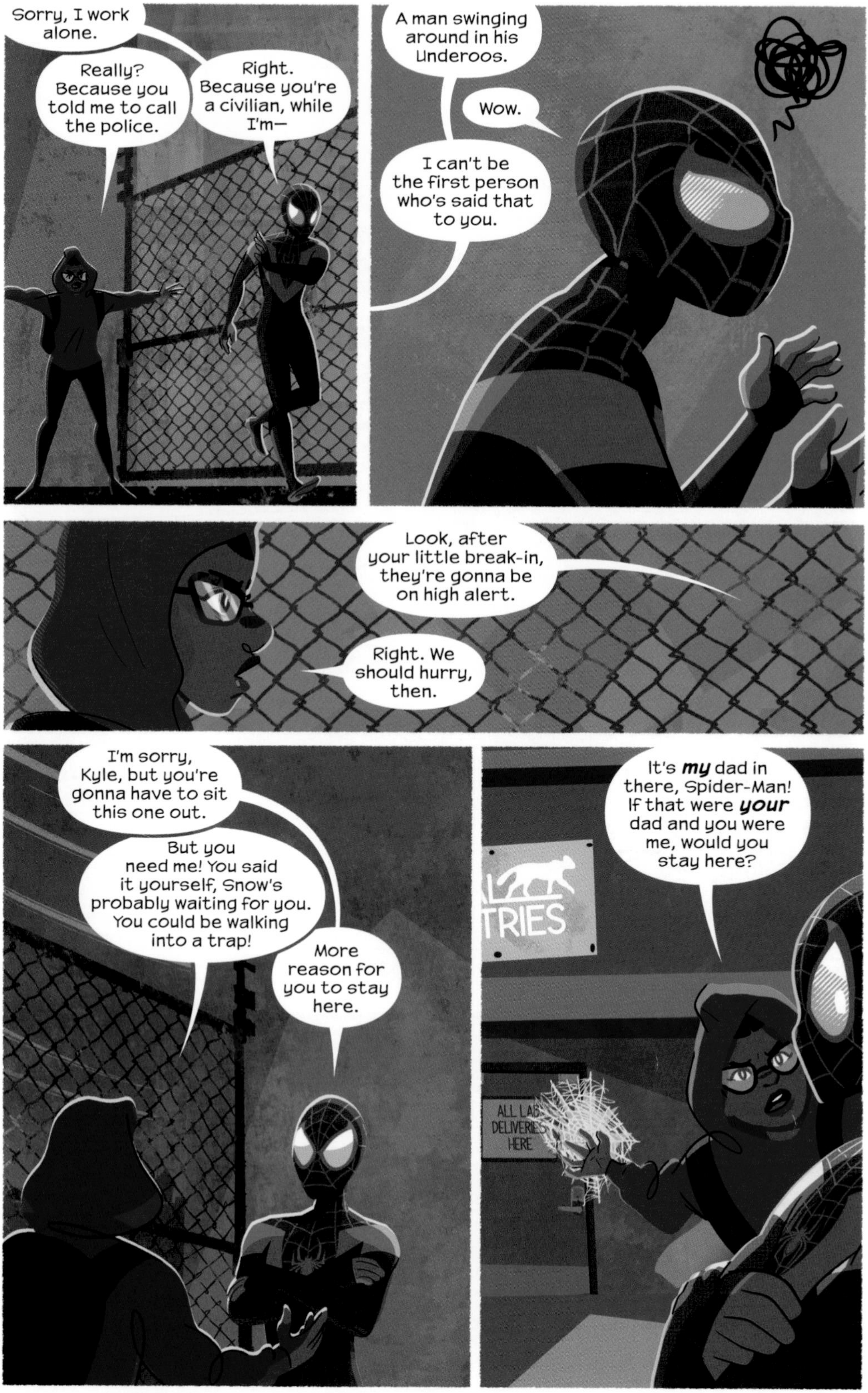
Sorry, I work alone.
Really? Because you told me to call the police.
Right. Because you're a civilian, while I'm—
A man swinging around in his Underoos.
Wow.
I can't be the first person who's said that to you.
Look, after your little break-in, they're gonna be on high alert.
Right. We should hurry, then.
I'm sorry, Kyle, but you're gonna have to sit this one out.
But you need me! You said it yourself, Snow's probably waiting for you. You could be walking into a trap!
More reason for you to stay here.
It's ***my*** dad in there, Spider-Man! If that were ***your*** dad and you were me, would you stay here?
ALL LAB
DELIVERIES
HERE

I can't believe I'm doing this... What's your number?

Why?

I'll call you if...I don't know... I need backup or whatever.

You're not gonna call. You're just trying to get rid of me.

Look, it's this or I glue you to the wall with webbing.

Call me!

So the Terrigen Crystals explain Trinity's and Vex's new powers. But what if they're only the beginning?

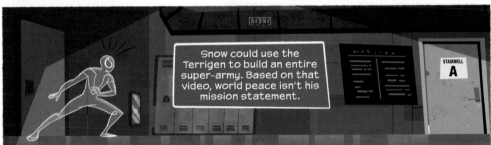

Snow could use the Terrigen to build an entire super-army. Based on that video, world peace isn't his mission statement.

STAIRWELL A

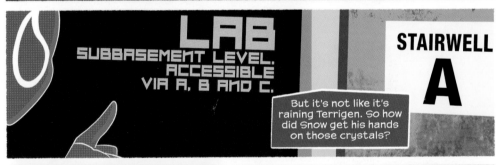

LAB
SUBBASEMENT LEVEL. ACCESSIBLE VIA A, B AND C.

STAIRWELL A

But it's not like it's raining Terrigen. So how did Snow get his hands on those crystals?

LAB →

I think it's time I ask Snow myself.

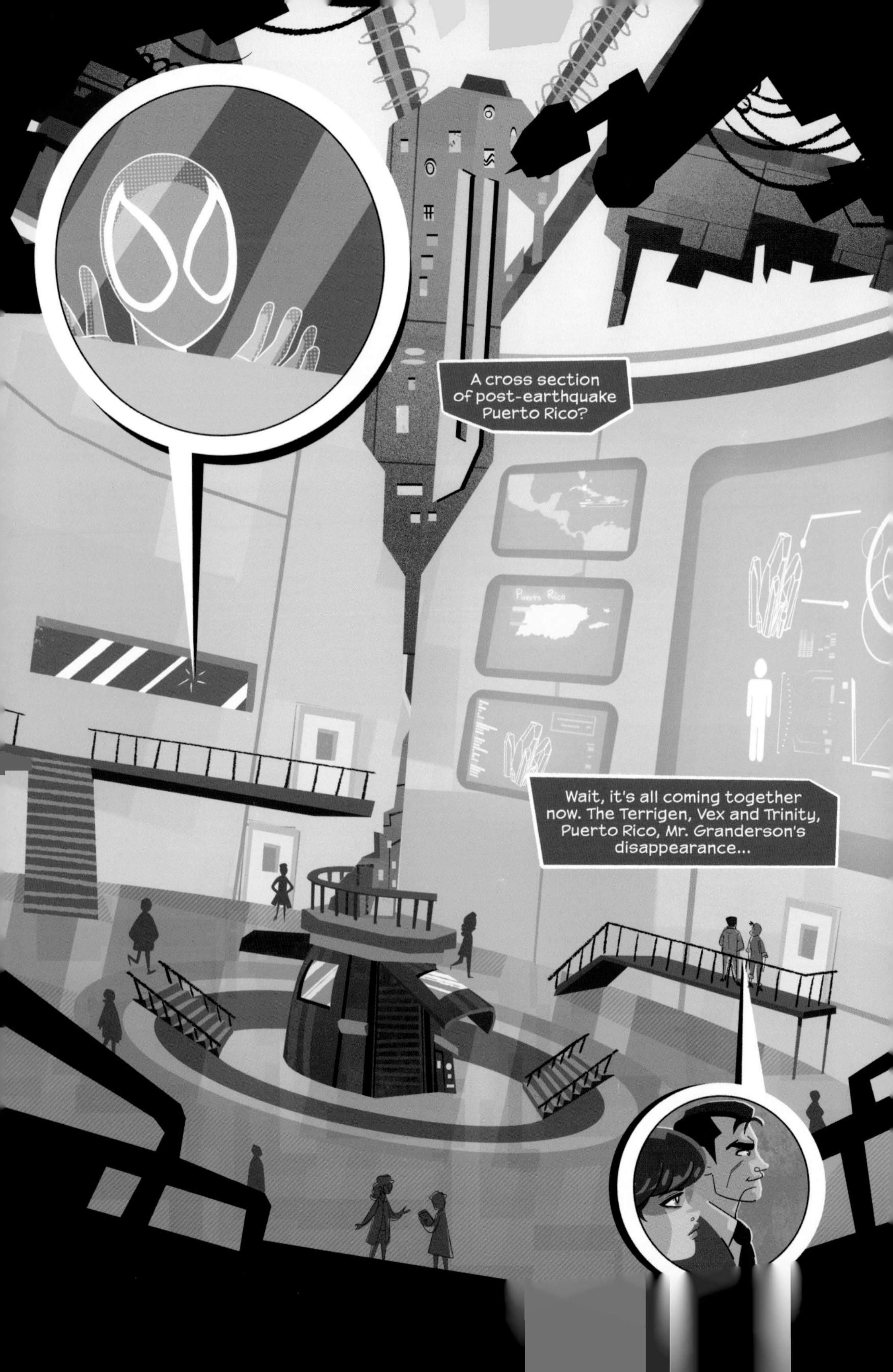
A cross section
of post-earthquake
Puerto Rico?
Puerto Rico
Wait, it's all coming together
now. The Terrigen, Vex and Trinity,
Puerto Rico, Mr. Granderson's
disappearance...

What if it's not a coincidence that Terrigen Crystals started showing up right after the earthquakes?

Wait, is that why Snow's flying the relief supplies to Puerto Rico on his private jet? To extract Terrigen?

Is he sponsoring our fundraiser so no one suspects his actual reason for visiting the island?

What if the Terrigen is *from* Puerto Rico?

And I'm the reason Mr. Granderson asked his boss to contribute.

What if it was buried so deep it took two massive earthquakes to unearth it?

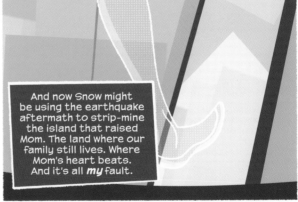

And now Snow might be using the earthquake aftermath to strip-mine the island that raised Mom. The land where our family still lives. Where Mom's heart beats. And it's all *my* fault.

What the—?!

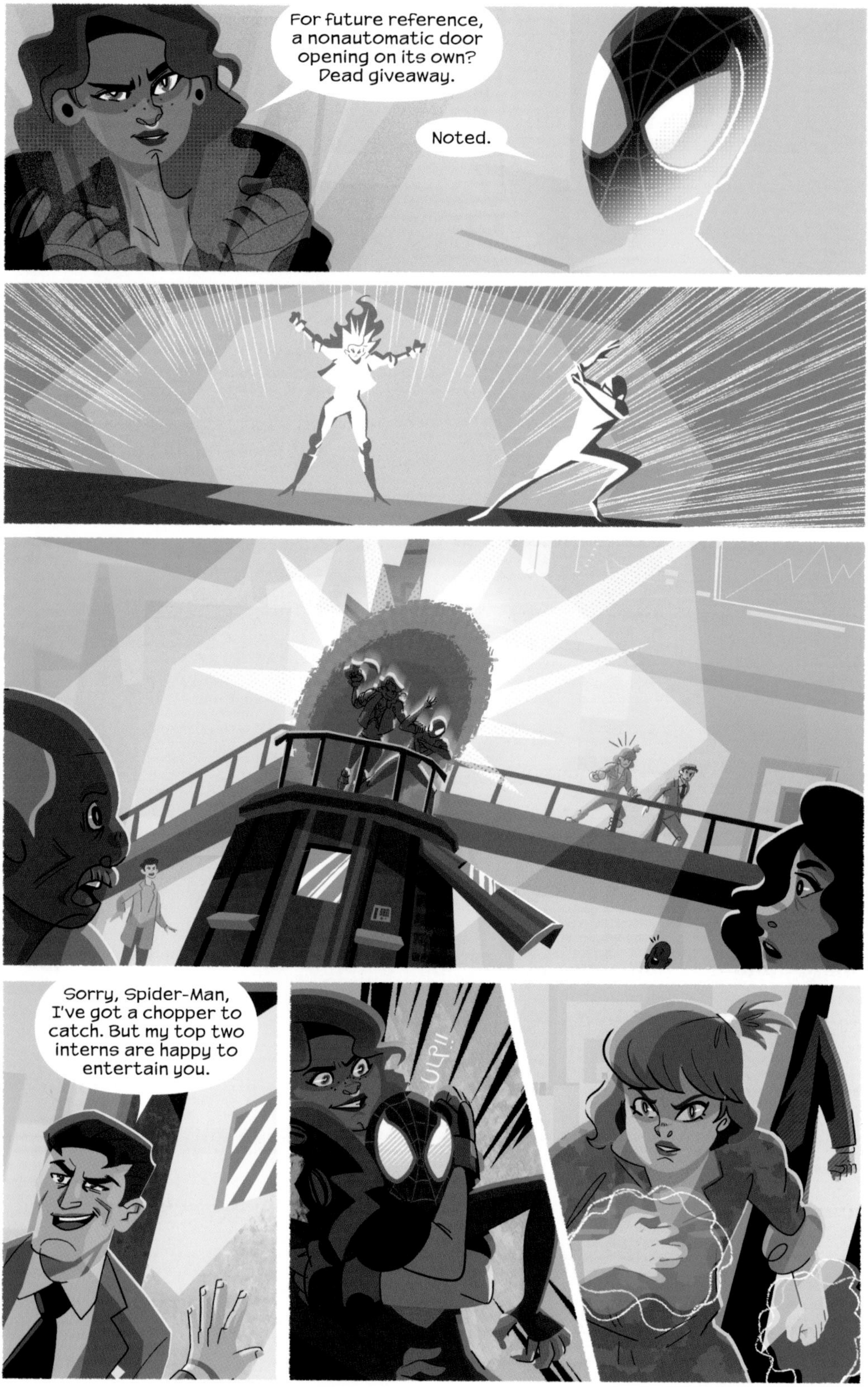
For future reference, a nonautomatic door opening on its own? Dead giveaway.
Noted.
Sorry, Spider-Man, I've got a chopper to catch. But my top two interns are happy to entertain you.
ULP!!

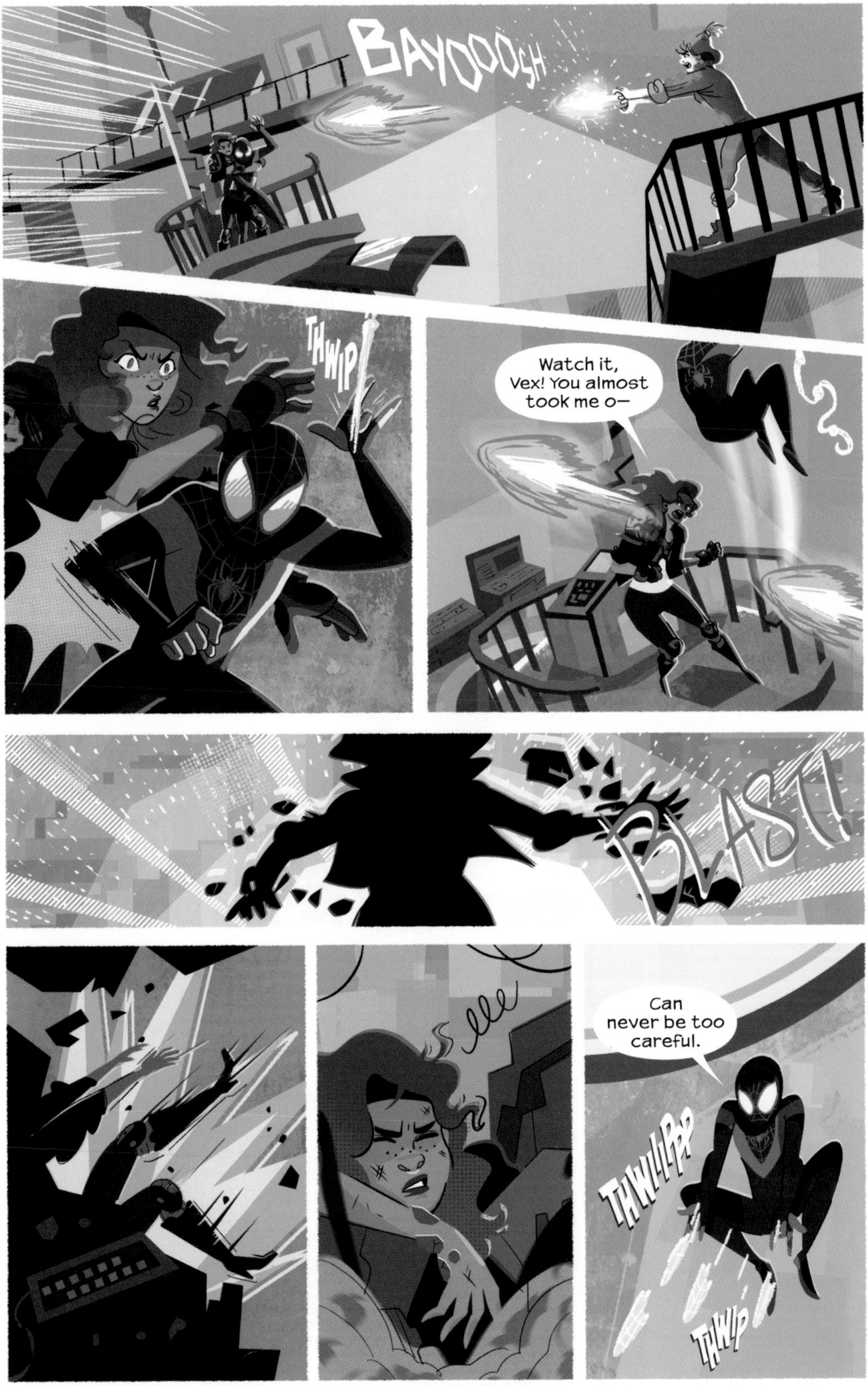
BAYOOOSH
THWIP
Watch it, Vex! You almost took me o—
BLAST!
Can never be too careful.
THWIIIPP
THWIP

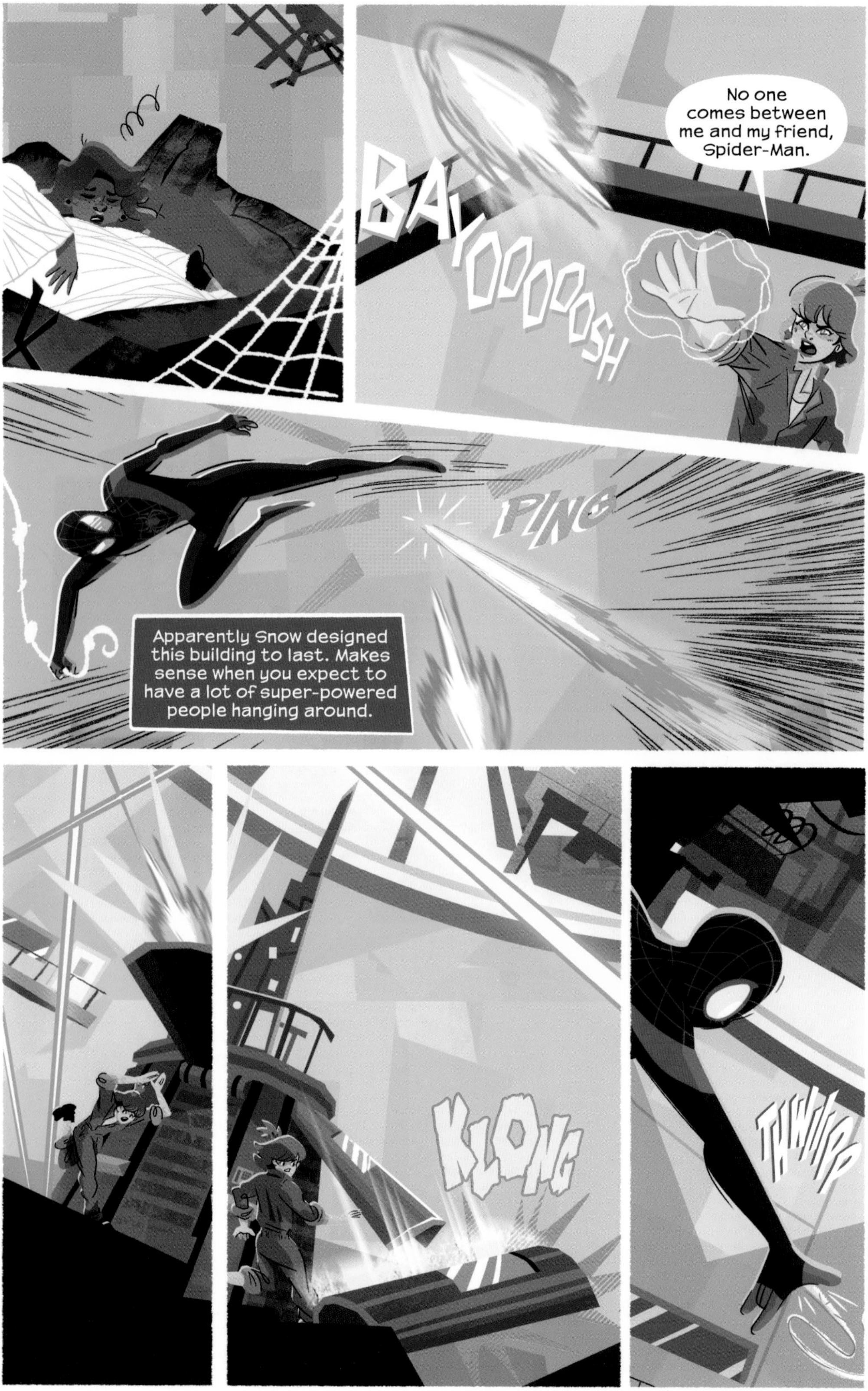
BAYOOOOOSH
No one comes between me and my friend, Spider-Man.
PING
Apparently Snow designed this building to last. Makes sense when you expect to have a lot of super-powered people hanging around.
KLONG
THWIP

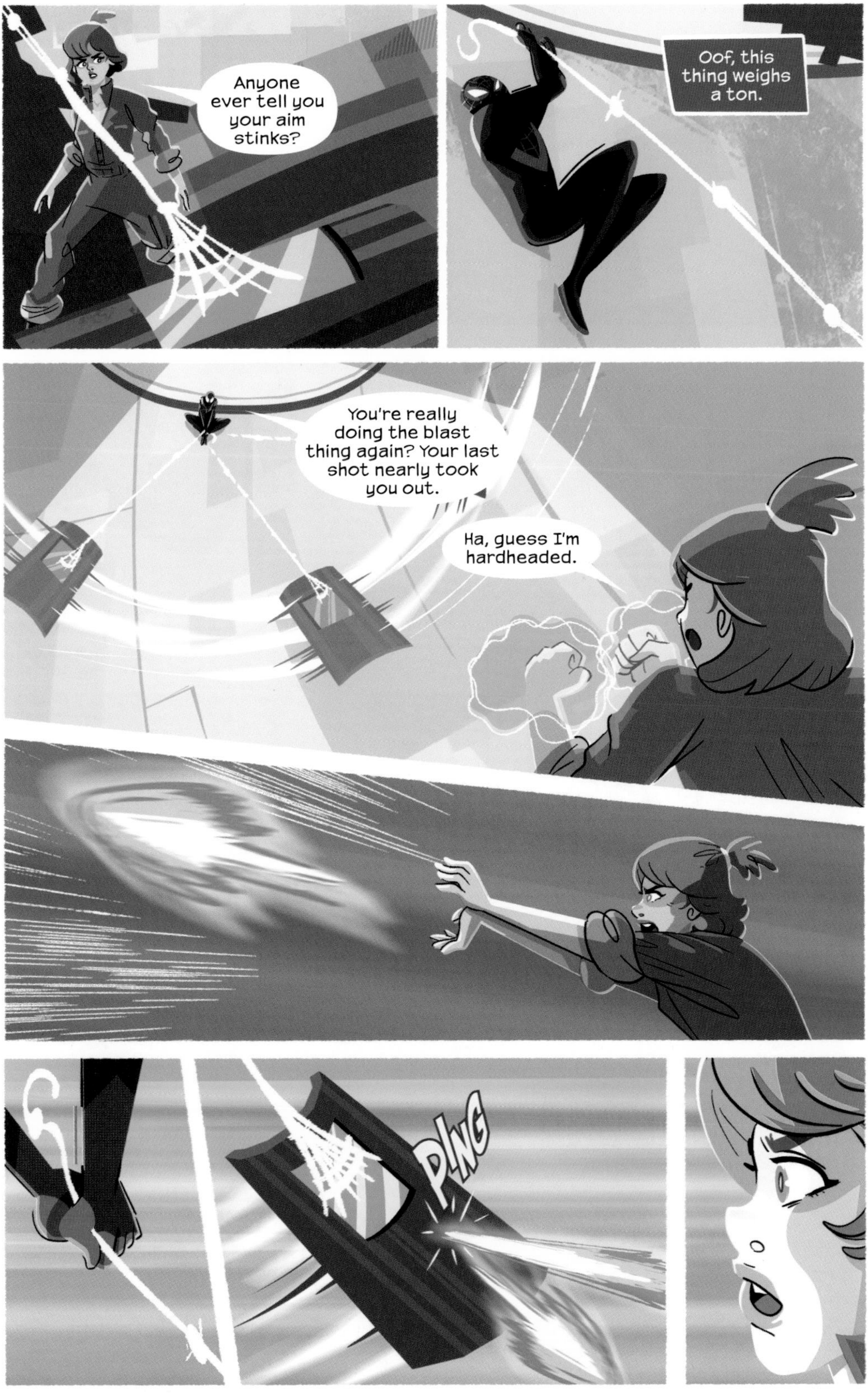
Anyone ever tell you your aim stinks?
Oof, this thing weighs a ton.
You're really doing the blast thing again? Your last shot nearly took you out.
Ha, guess I'm hardheaded.
PING

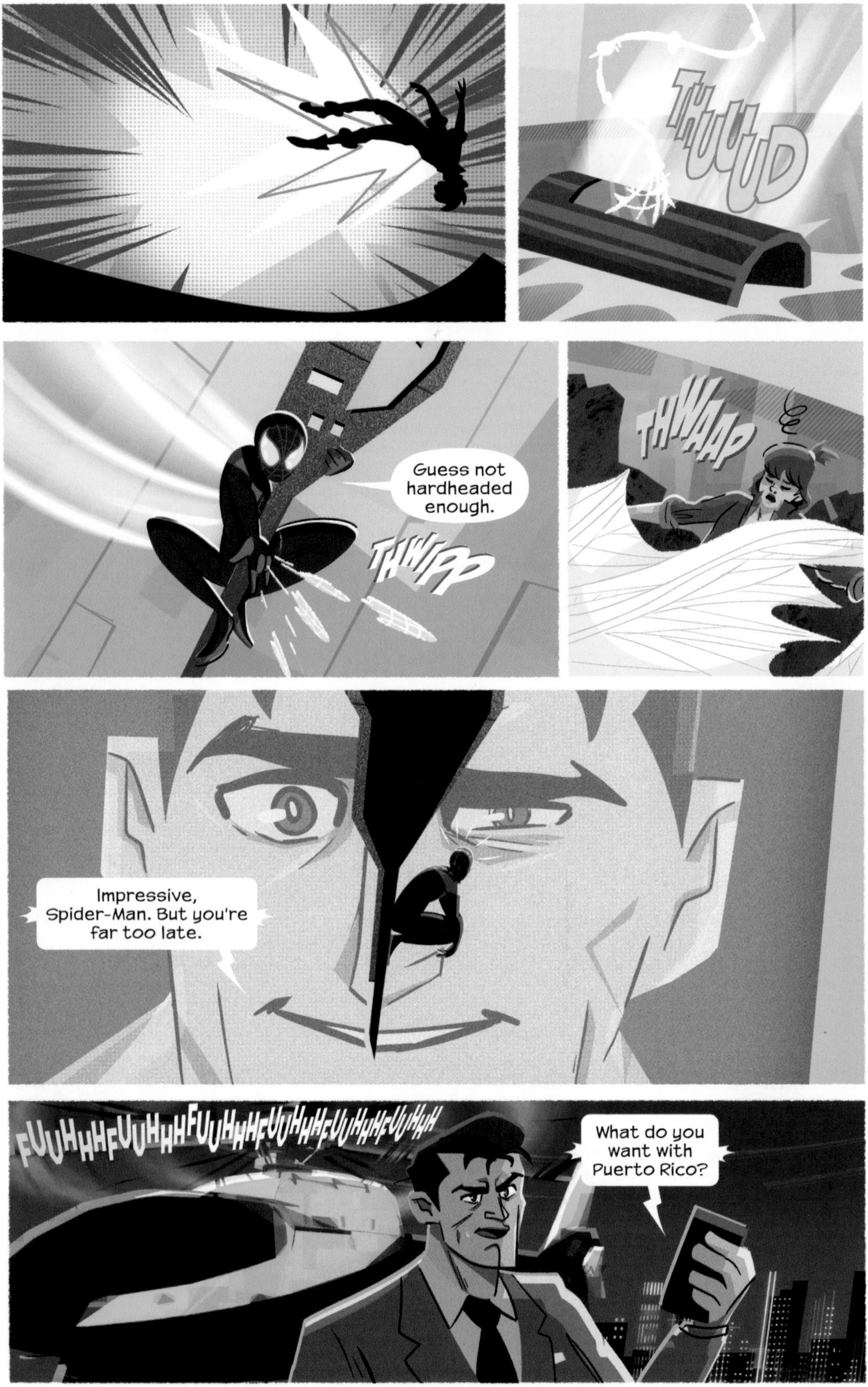
THUUUD
Guess not hardheaded enough.
THWIPP
THWAAP
Impressive, Spider-Man. But you're far too late.
FUUHHHFUUHHHFUUHHHFUUHHHFUUHHHFUUHHH
What do you want with Puerto Rico?

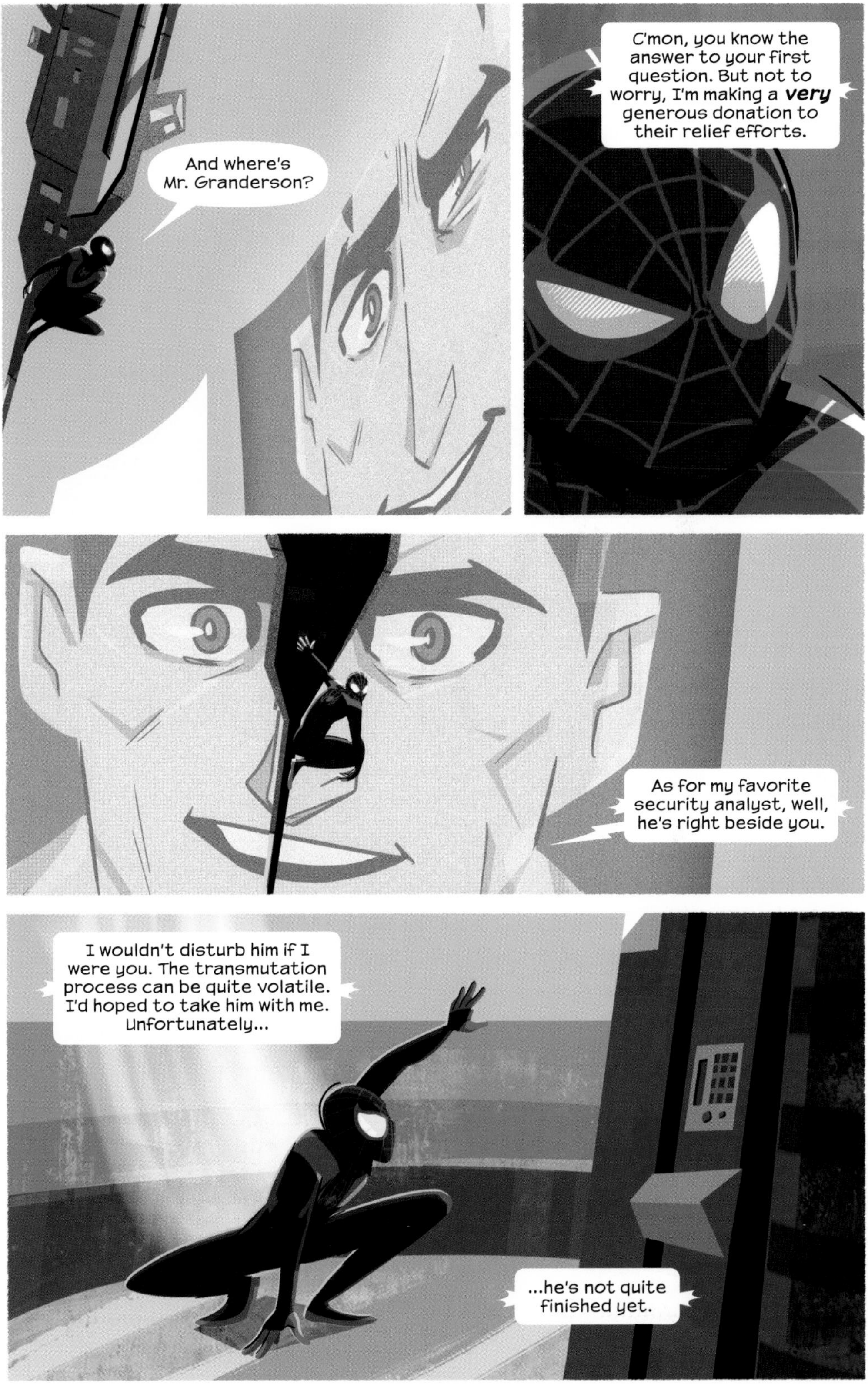
And where's Mr. Granderson?
C'mon, you know the answer to your first question. But not to worry, I'm making a **very** generous donation to their relief efforts.
As for my favorite security analyst, well, he's right beside you.
I wouldn't disturb him if I were you. The transmutation process can be quite volatile. I'd hoped to take him with me. Unfortunately...
...he's not quite finished yet.

CHAPTER

SIX

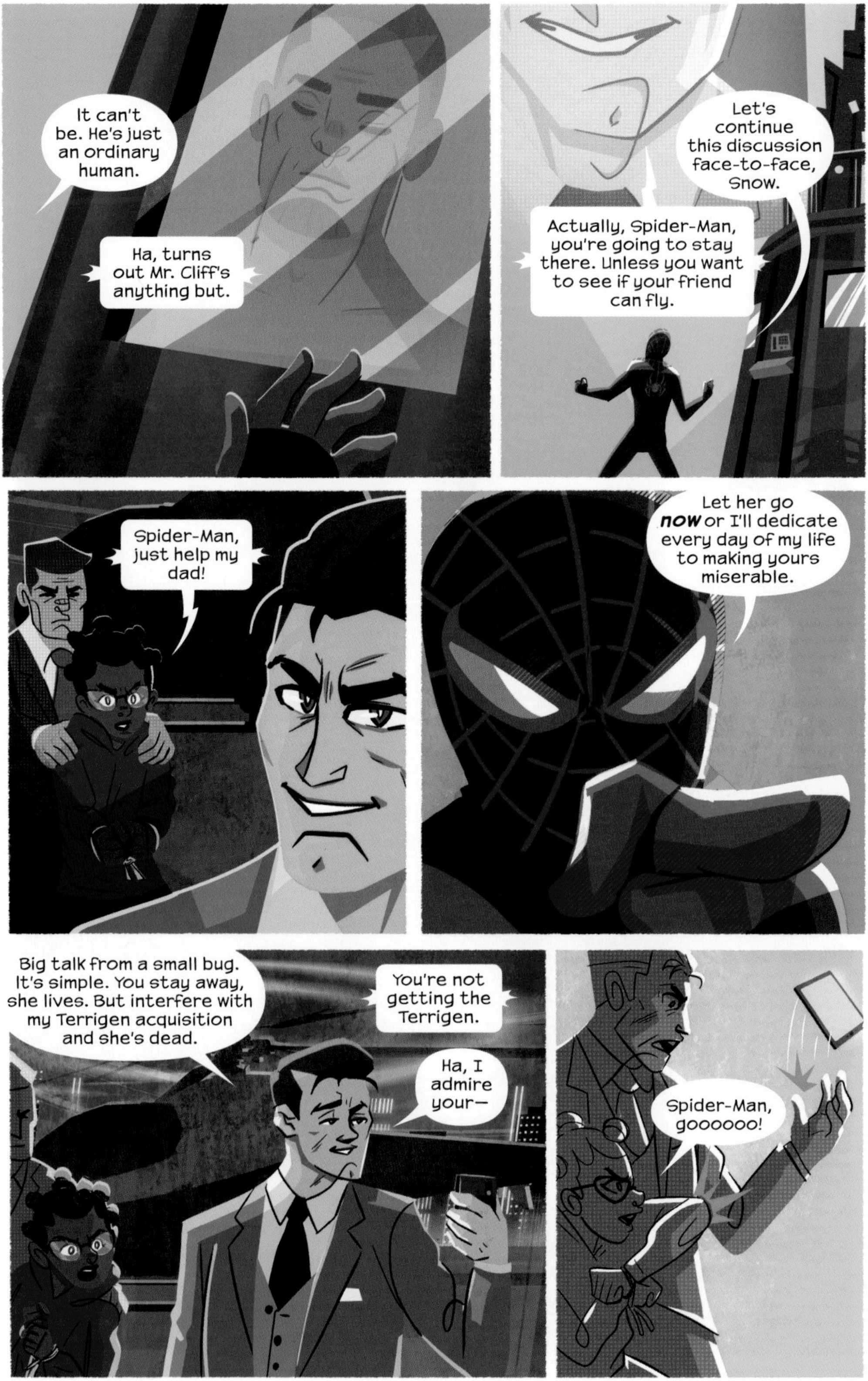
It can't be. He's just an ordinary human.
Ha, turns out Mr. Cliff's anything but.
Let's continue this discussion face-to-face, Snow.
Actually, Spider-Man, you're going to stay there. Unless you want to see if your friend can fly.
Spider-Man, just help my dad!
Let her go **NOW** or I'll dedicate every day of my life to making yours miserable.
Big talk from a small bug. It's simple. You stay away, she lives. But interfere with my Terrigen acquisition and she's dead.
You're not getting the Terrigen.
Ha, I admire your—
Spider-Man, goooooo!

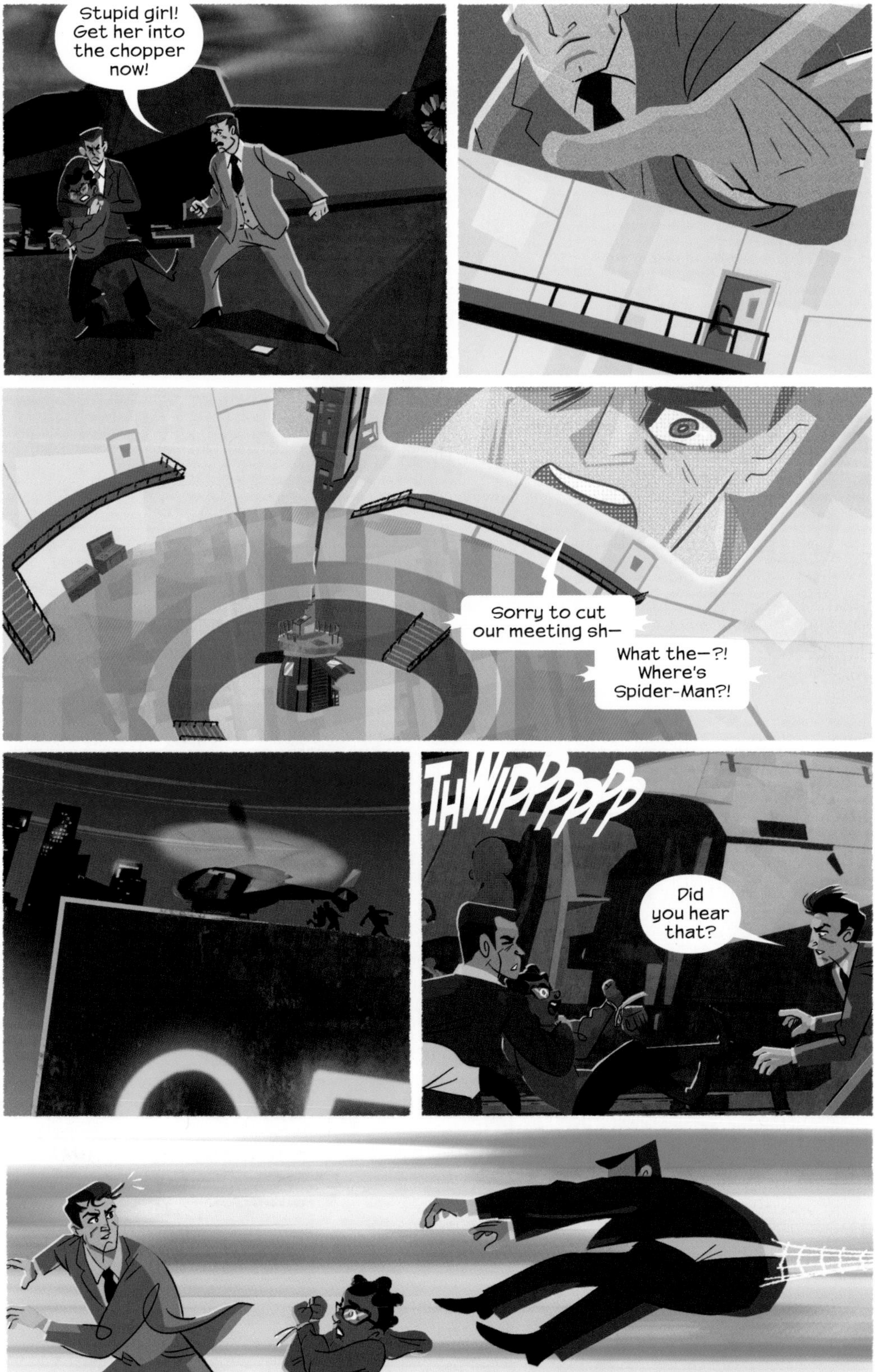
Stupid girl! Get her into the chopper now!
Sorry to cut our meeting sh—
What the—?! Where's Spider-Man?!
THWIPPPPPP
Did you hear that?

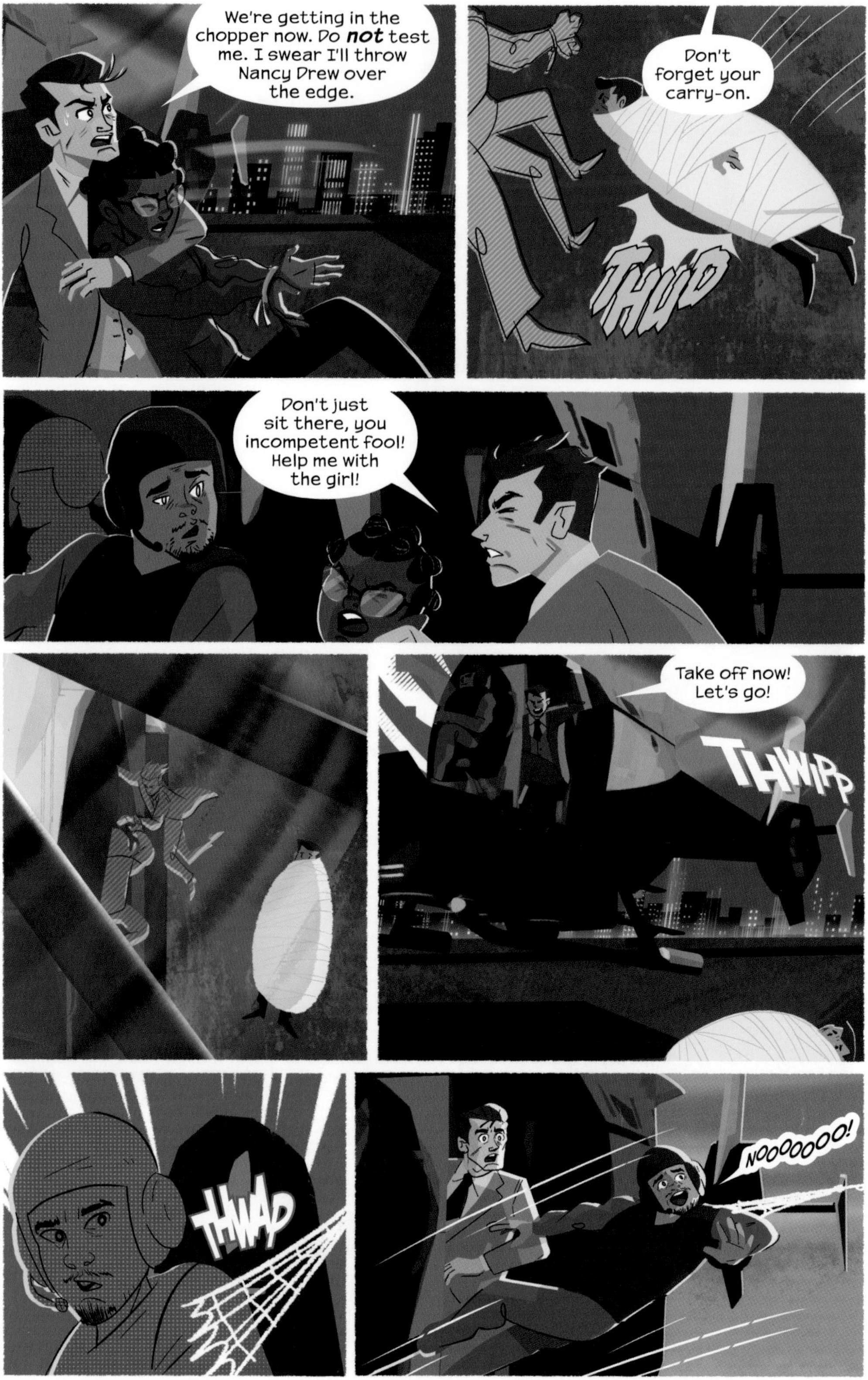
We're getting in the chopper now. Do **not** test me. I swear I'll throw Nancy Drew over the edge.
Don't forget your carry-on.
THUD
Don't just sit there, you incompetent fool! Help me with the girl!
Take off now! Let's go!
THWIPP
THWAP
NOOOOOOO!

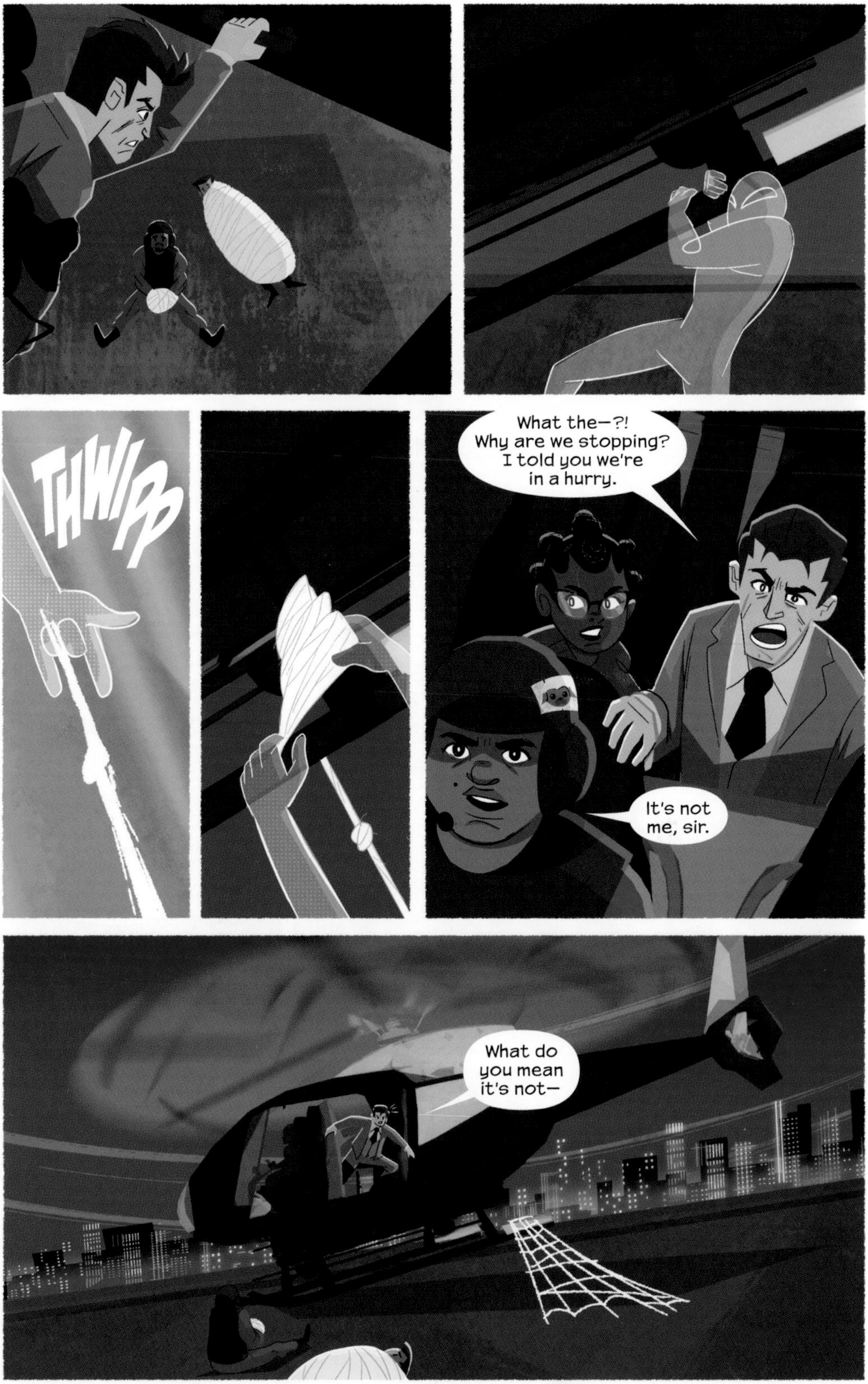
THWIPP
What the—?! Why are we stopping? I told you we're in a hurry.
It's not me, sir.
What do you mean it's not—

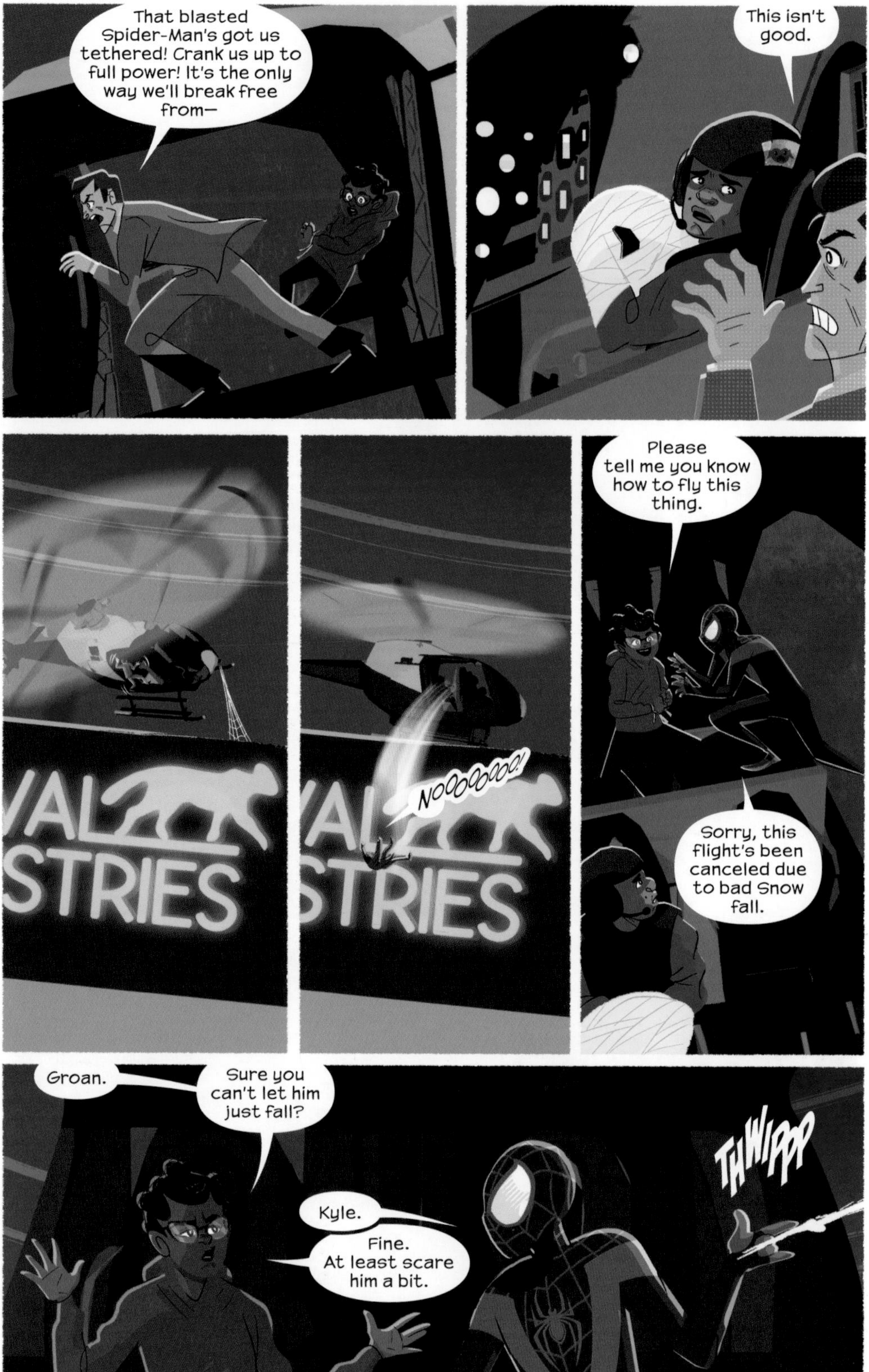
That blasted Spider-Man's got us tethered! Crank us up to full power! It's the only way we'll break free from—
This isn't good.
VAL
STRIES
VAL
STRIES
NOOOOOOOO!
Please tell me you know how to fly this thing.
Sorry, this flight's been canceled due to bad Snow fall.
Groan.
Sure you can't let him just fall?
Kyle.
Fine. At least scare him a bit.
THWIPPP

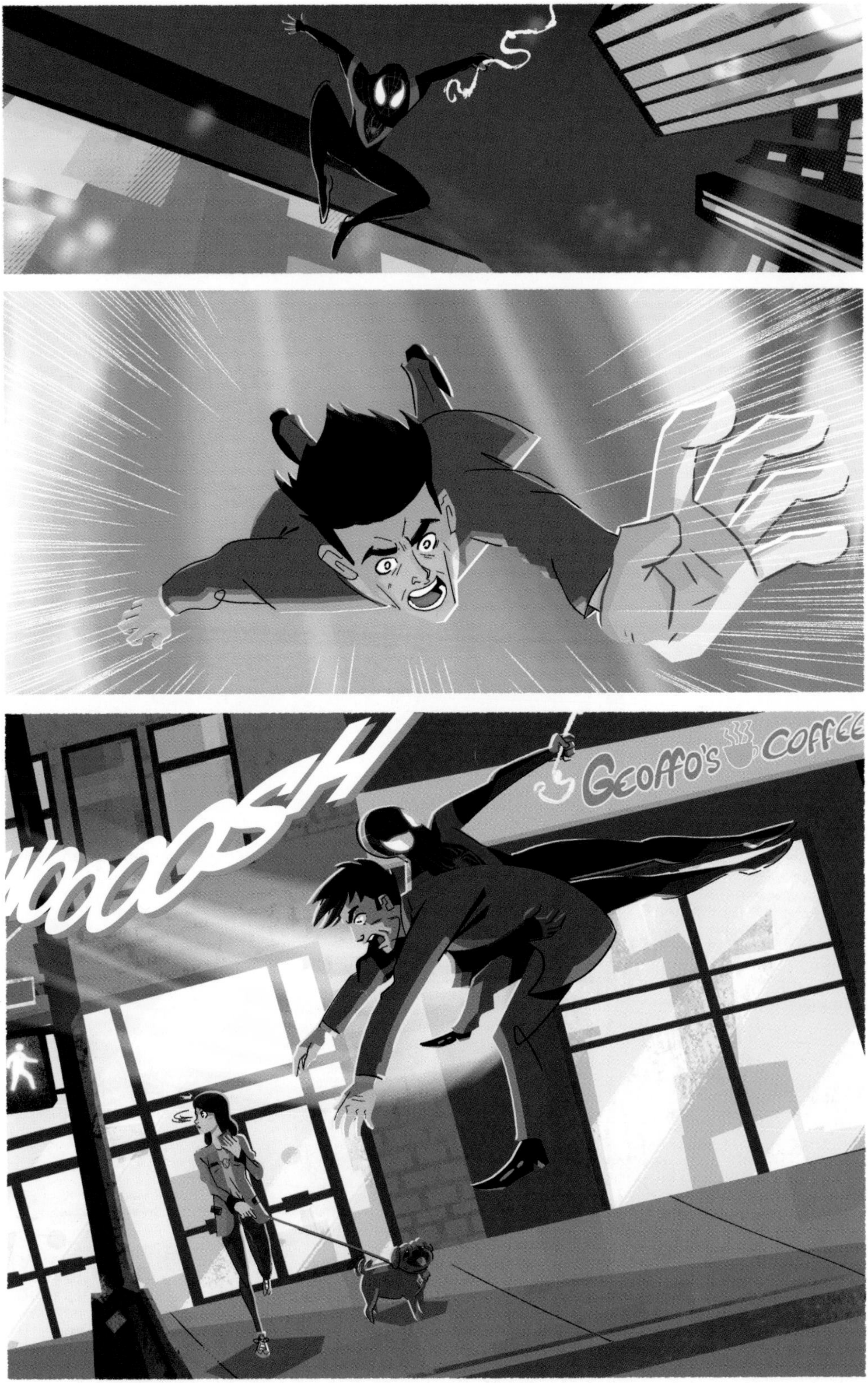
WOOOOOSH
GEOFFO'S COFFEE

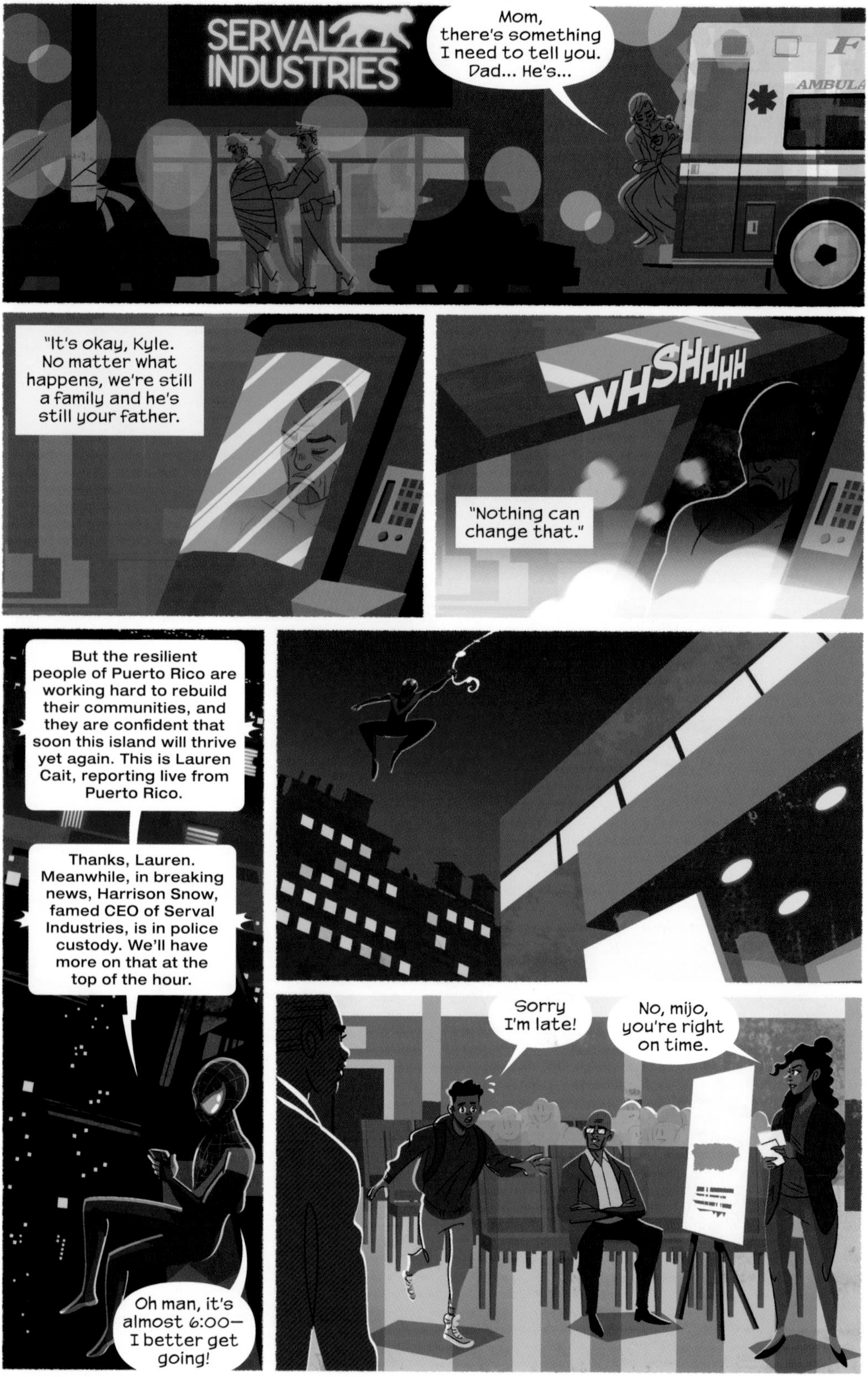
SERVAL INDUSTRIES
Mom, there's something I need to tell you. Dad... He's...
"It's okay, Kyle. No matter what happens, we're still a family and he's still your father.
WHSHHHH
"Nothing can change that."
But the resilient people of Puerto Rico are working hard to rebuild their communities, and they are confident that soon this island will thrive yet again. This is Lauren Cait, reporting live from Puerto Rico.
Thanks, Lauren. Meanwhile, in breaking news, Harrison Snow, famed CEO of Serval Industries, is in police custody. We'll have more on that at the top of the hour.
Oh man, it's almost 6:00—I better get going!
Sorry I'm late!
No, mijo, you're right on time.

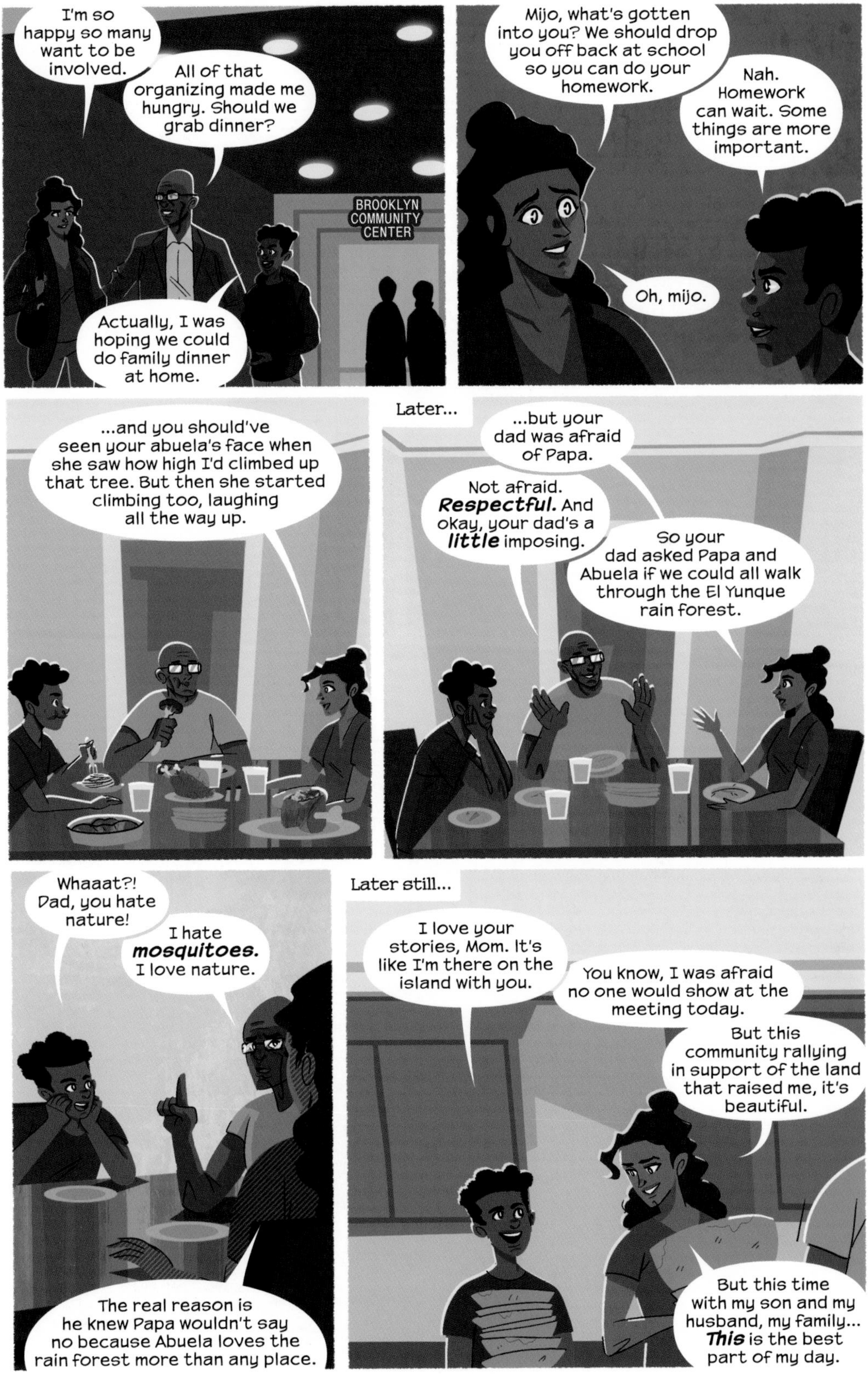

I'm so happy so many want to be involved.
All of that organizing made me hungry. Should we grab dinner?
BROOKLYN COMMUNITY CENTER
Actually, I was hoping we could do family dinner at home.
Mijo, what's gotten into you? We should drop you off back at school so you can do your homework.
Nah. Homework can wait. Some things are more important.
Oh, mijo.
...and you should've seen your abuela's face when she saw how high I'd climbed up that tree. But then she started climbing too, laughing all the way up.
Later...
...but your dad was afraid of Papa.
Not afraid. ***Respectful.*** And okay, your dad's a ***little*** imposing.
So your dad asked Papa and Abuela if we could all walk through the El Yunque rain forest.
Whaaat?! Dad, you hate nature!
I hate ***mosquitoes.*** I love nature.
The real reason is he knew Papa wouldn't say no because Abuela loves the rain forest more than any place.
Later still...
I love your stories, Mom. It's like I'm there on the island with you.
You know, I was afraid no one would show at the meeting today.
But this community rallying in support of the land that raised me, it's beautiful.
But this time with my son and my husband, my family... ***This*** is the best part of my day.

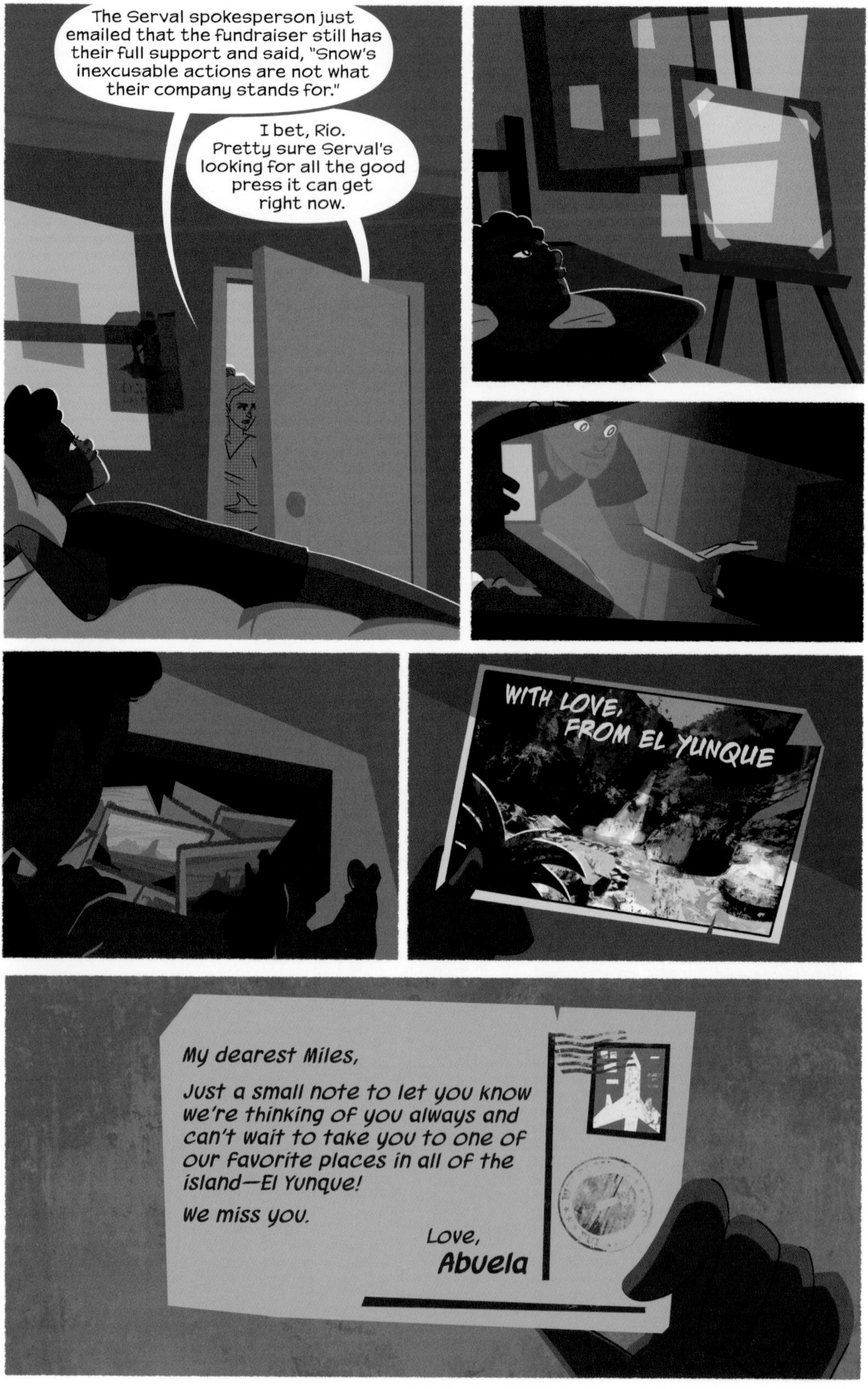
The Serval spokesperson just emailed that the fundraiser still has their full support and said, "Snow's inexcusable actions are not what their company stands for."
I bet, Rio. Pretty sure Serval's looking for all the good press it can get right now.
WITH LOVE, FROM EL YUNQUE
My dearest Miles,
Just a small note to let you know we're thinking of you always and can't wait to take you to one of our favorite places in all of the island—El Yunque!
We miss you.
Love,
Abuela

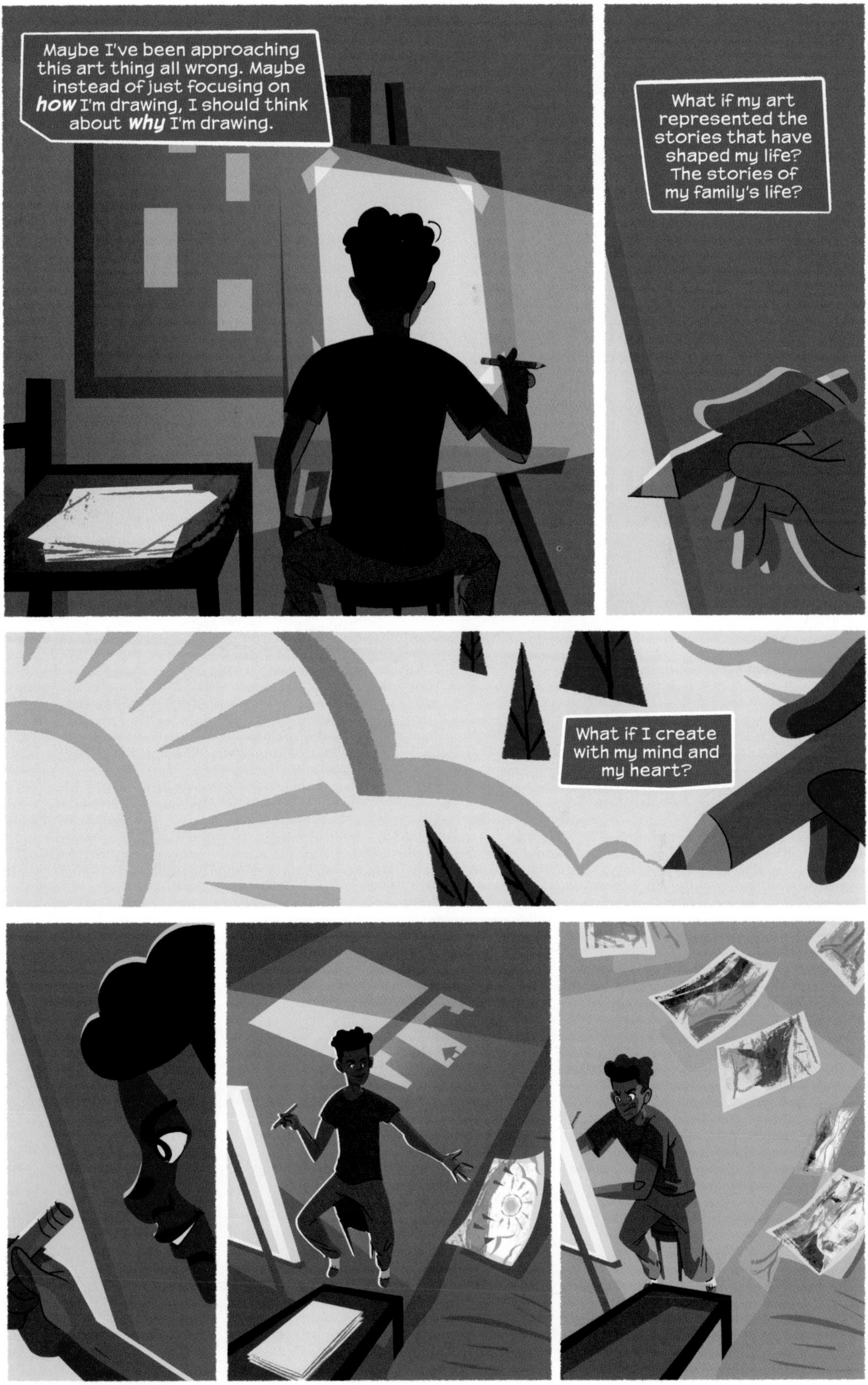
Maybe I've been approaching this art thing all wrong. Maybe instead of just focusing on **how** I'm drawing, I should think about **why** I'm drawing.
What if my art represented the stories that have shaped my life? The stories of my family's life?
What if I create with my mind and my heart?

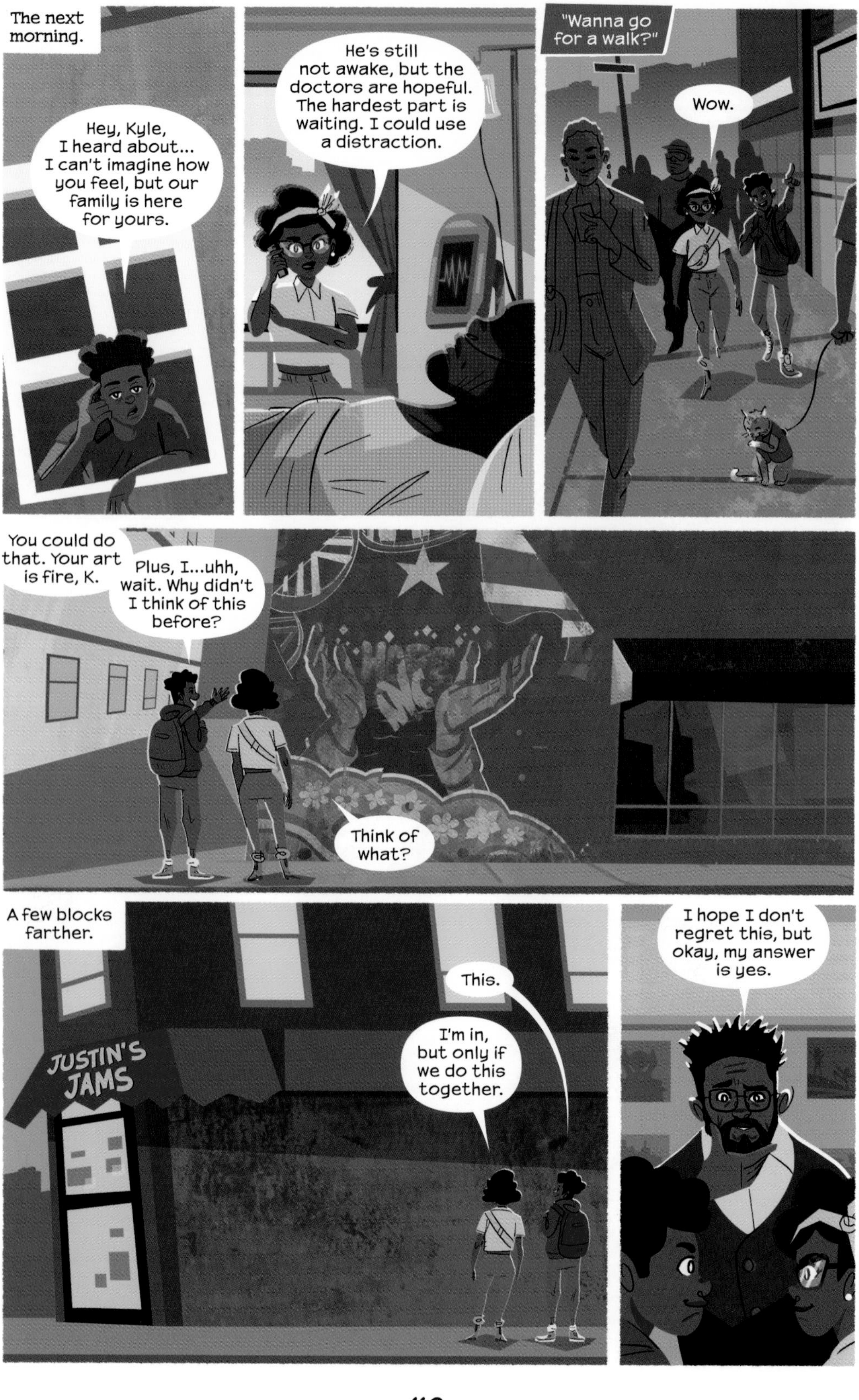
The next morning.
Hey, Kyle, I heard about... I can't imagine how you feel, but our family is here for yours.
He's still not awake, but the doctors are hopeful. The hardest part is waiting. I could use a distraction.
"Wanna go for a walk?"
Wow.
You could do that. Your art is fire, K.
Plus, I...uhh, wait. Why didn't I think of this before?
Think of what?
A few blocks farther.
JUSTIN'S JAMS
This.
I'm in, but only if we do this together.
I hope I don't regret this, but okay, my answer is yes.

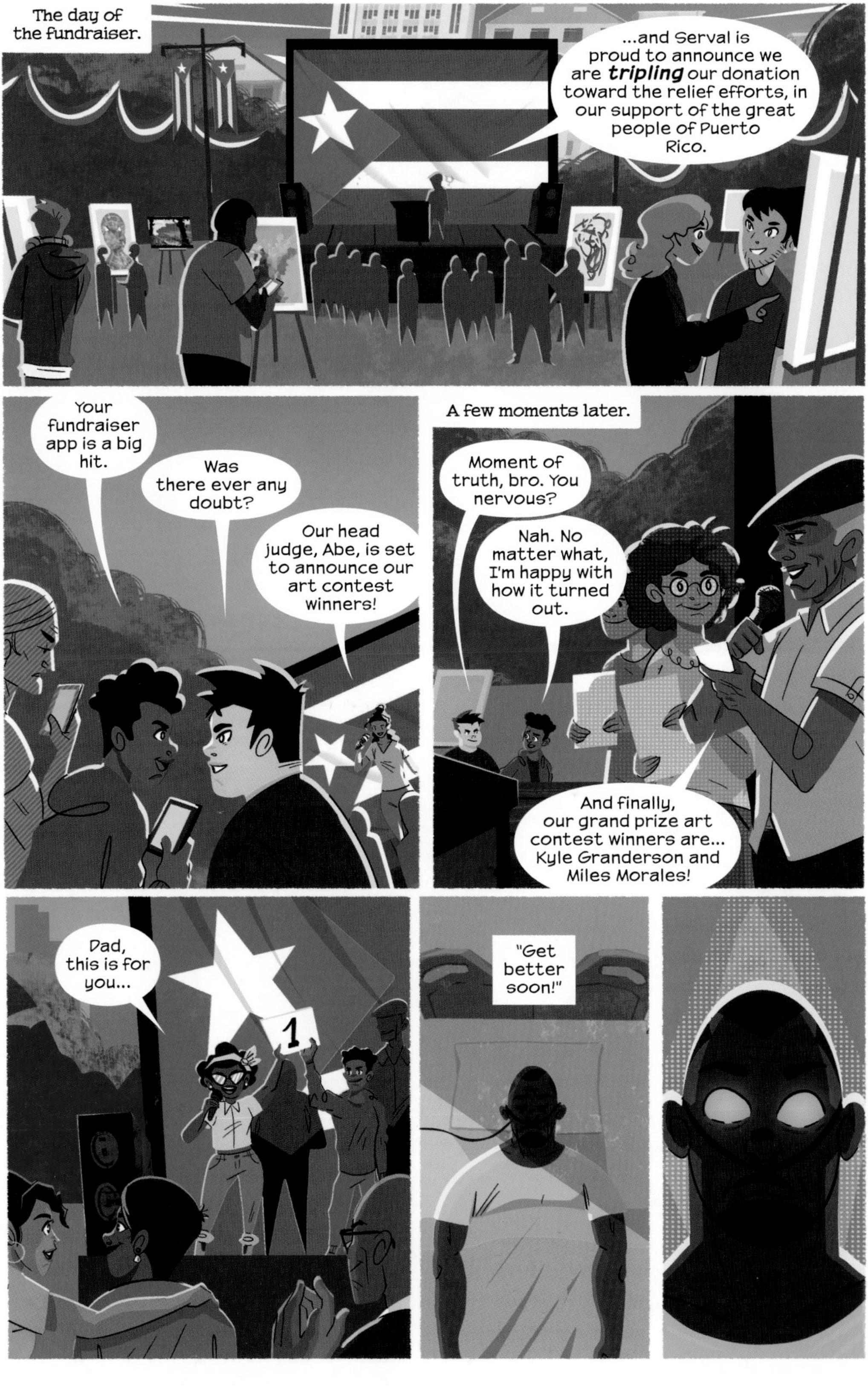
The day of the fundraiser.
...and Serval is proud to announce we are ***tripling*** our donation toward the relief efforts, in our support of the great people of Puerto Rico.
Your fundraiser app is a big hit.
Was there ever any doubt?
Our head judge, Abe, is set to announce our art contest winners!
A few moments later.
Moment of truth, bro. You nervous?
Nah. No matter what, I'm happy with how it turned out.
And finally, our grand prize art contest winners are... Kyle Granderson and Miles Morales!
Dad, this is for you...
1
"Get better soon!"

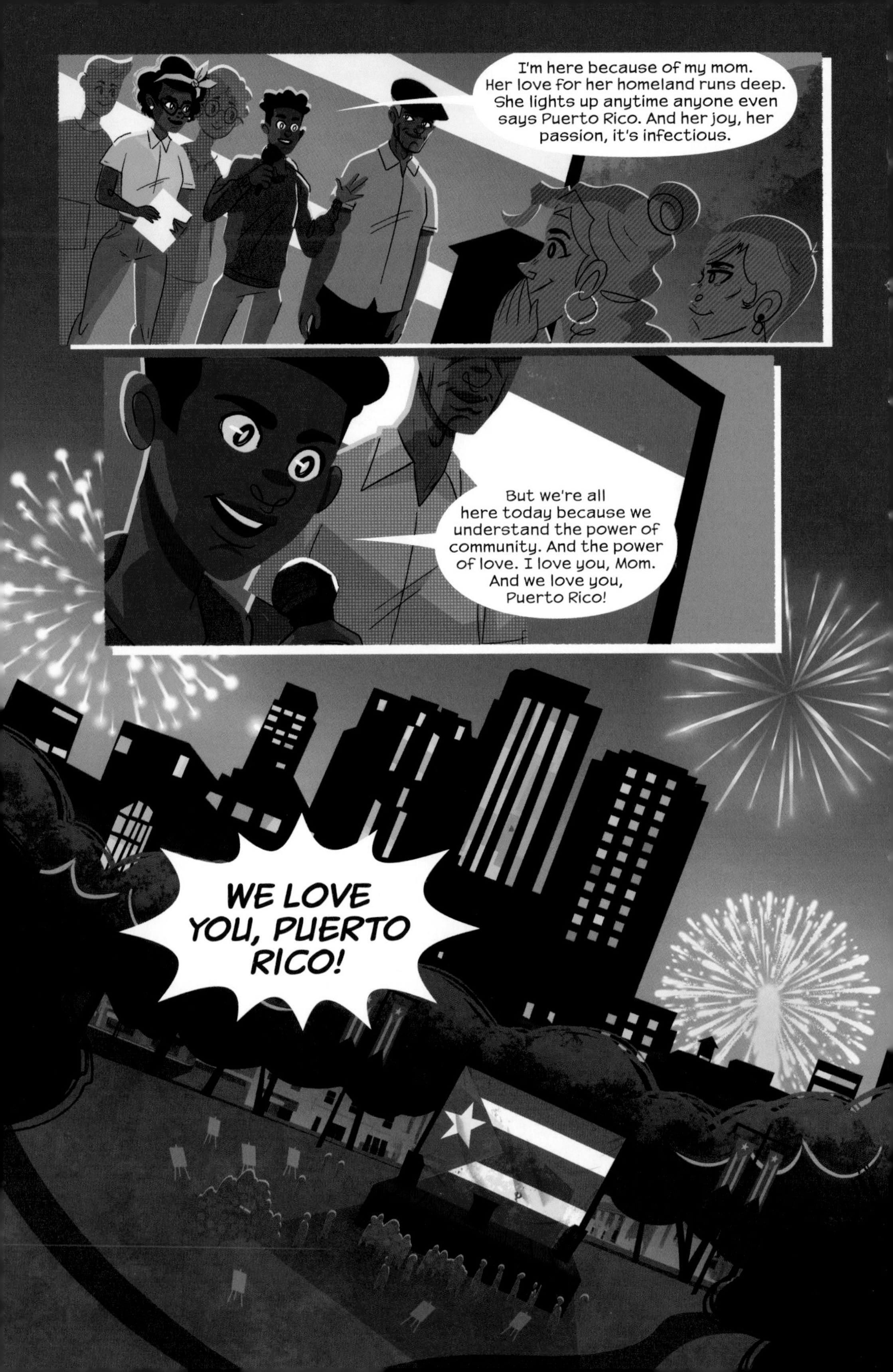
I'm here because of my mom. Her love for her homeland runs deep. She lights up anytime anyone even says Puerto Rico. And her joy, her passion, it's infectious.
But we're all here today because we understand the power of community. And the power of love. I love you, Mom. And we love you, Puerto Rico!
WE LOVE YOU, PUERTO RICO!

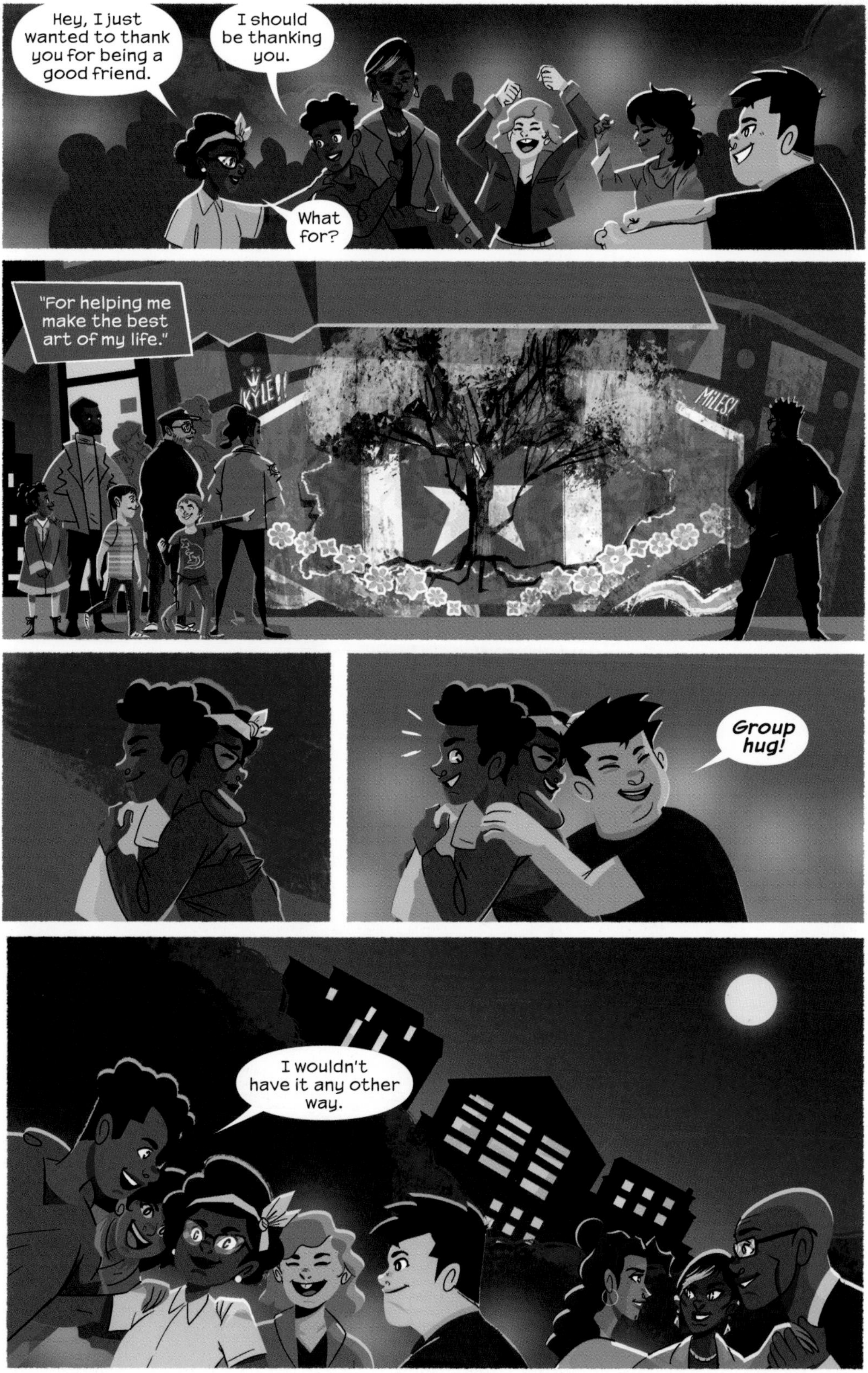
Hey, I just wanted to thank you for being a good friend.
I should be thanking you.
What for?
"For helping me make the best art of my life."
KYLE!!
MILES!
Group hug!
I wouldn't have it any other way.

To every young super hero in the making,
the power is already within you.
—JR

To the future super heroes out there,
we need your uplifting stories more than ever.
—PL

JUSTIN A. REYNOLDS has always wanted to be a writer. *Opposite of Always*, his debut novel, was an Indies Introduce selection and a School Library Journal Best Book, has been translated into seventeen languages and is being developed for film with Paramount Players. His second novel, *Early Departures*, arrived September 2020. Justin hangs out in northeast Ohio with his family and likes it and is probably somewhere, right now, dancing terribly. You can find him at justinareynolds.com.

PABLO LEON is an artist and designer whose clients include Warner Brothers Animation, OddBot Inc., Puny Entertainment, Bento Box Entertainment, and more. His original comic story *The Journey*, about the true accounts of people migrating from Latin America to the United States, was a 2019 Eisner Award nominee. He lives in Los Angeles, California.

CHECK OUT A SNEAK PEEK OF

MS. MARVEL
STRETCHED THIN

COMING **FALL 2021!**

WRITTEN BY
NADIA SHAMMAS

ILLUSTRATED BY
NABI H. ALI

LAYOUTS BY
GEOFFO

LETTERS BY
VC's JOE CARAMAGNA

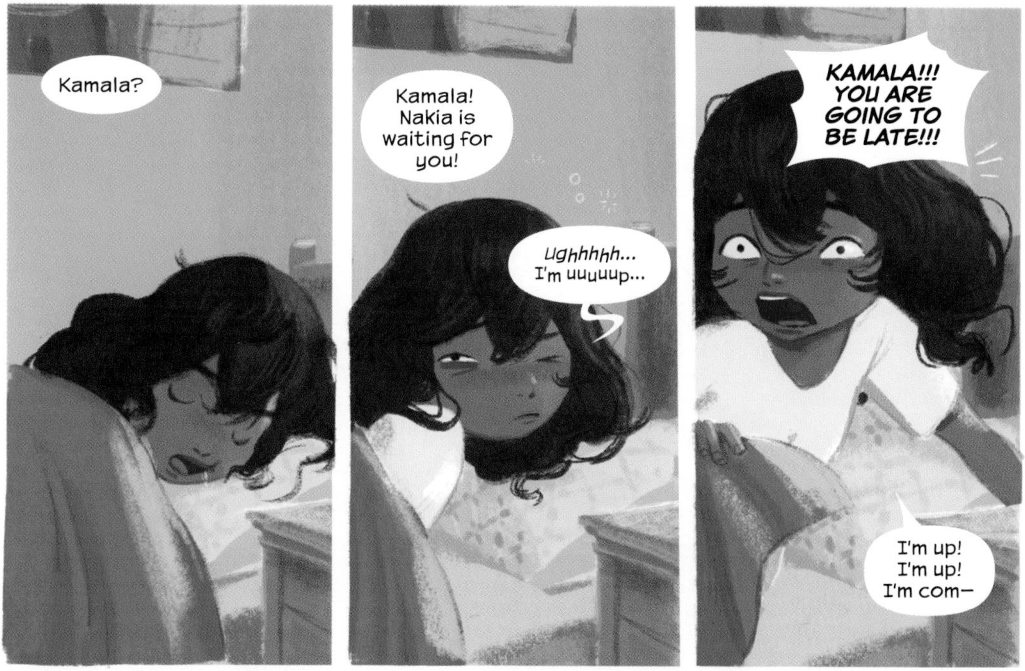
Kamala?
Kamala! Nakia is waiting for you!
Ughhhhh... I'm uuuuup...
KAMALA!!! YOU ARE GOING TO BE LATE!!!
I'm up! I'm up! I'm com—

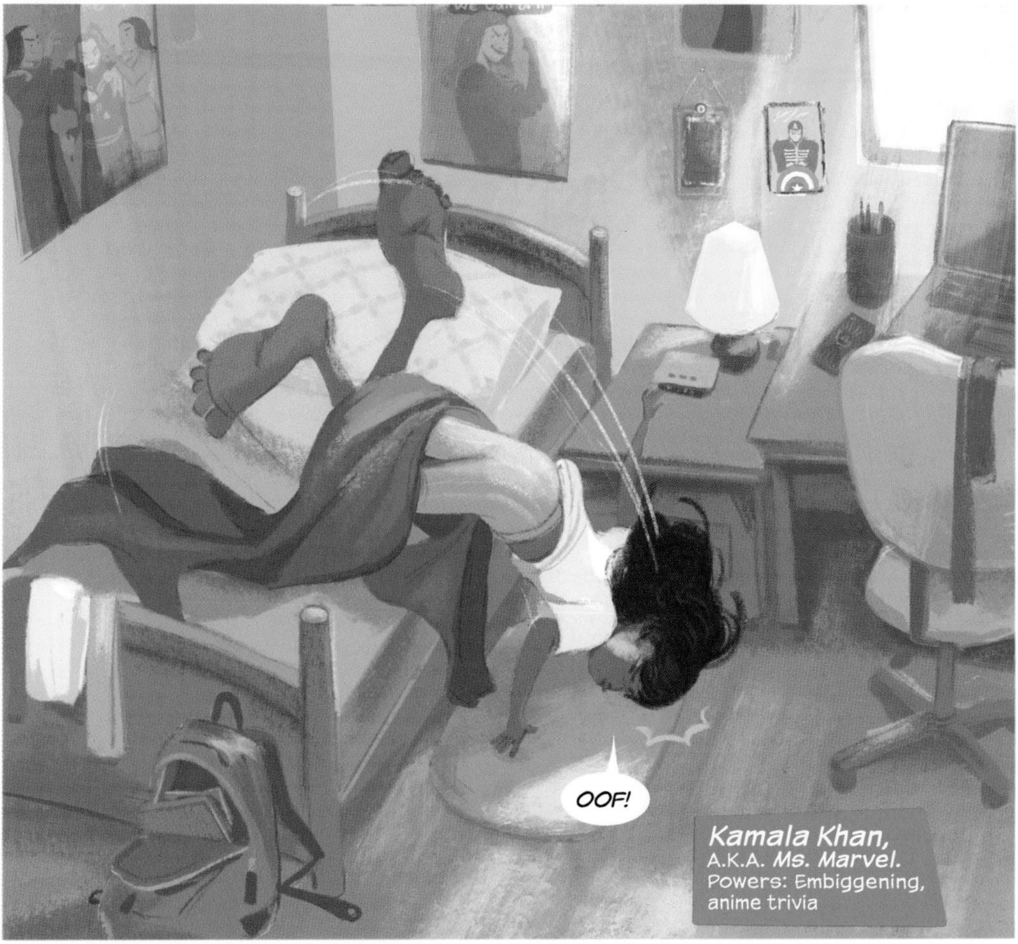
OOF!
Kamala Khan, A.K.A. Ms. Marvel. Powers: Embiggening, anime trivia

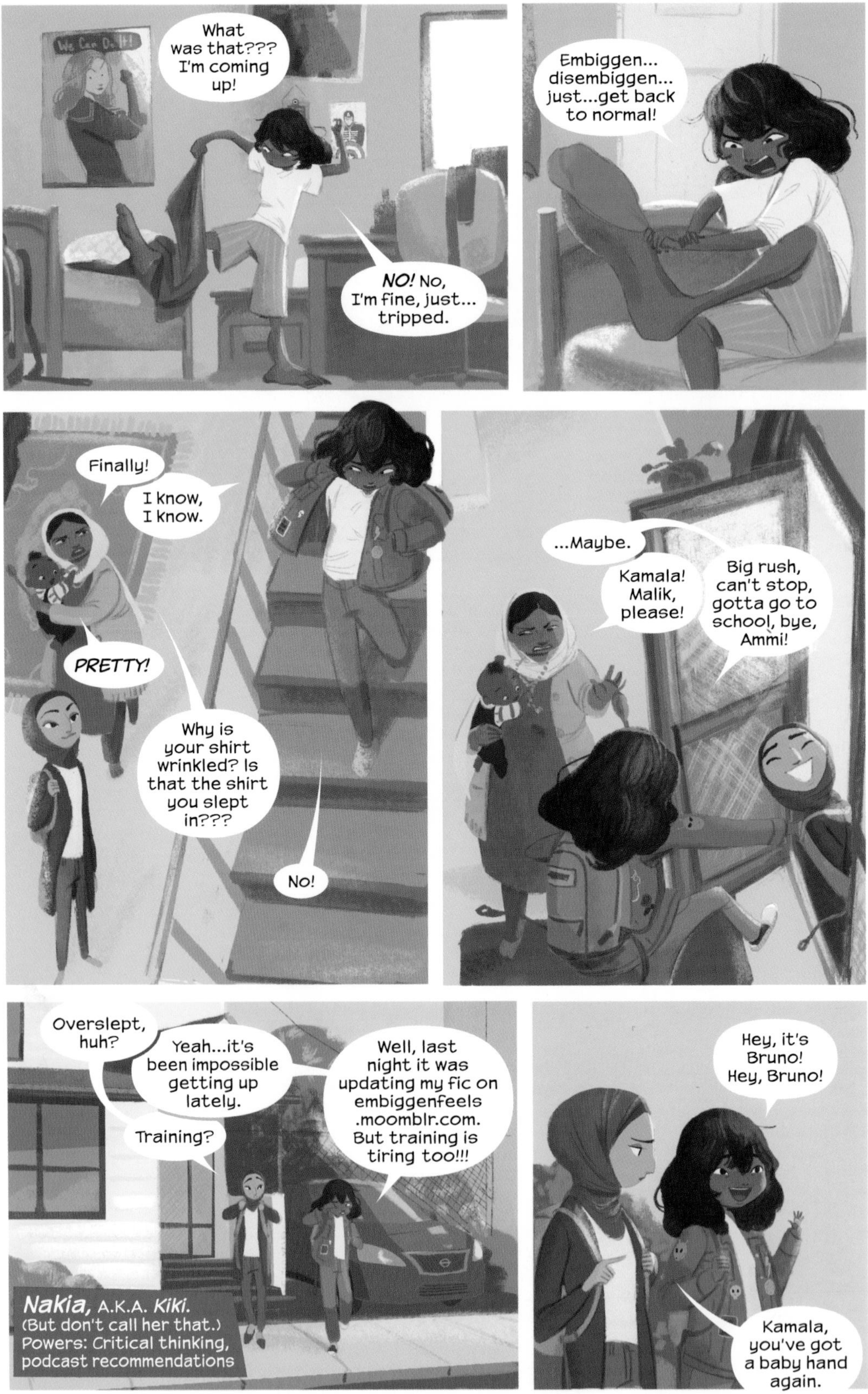
We Can Do It!
What was that??? I'm coming up!
NO! No, I'm fine, just... tripped.
Embiggen... disembiggen... just...get back to normal!
Finally!
I know, I know.
PRETTY!
Why is your shirt wrinkled? Is that the shirt you slept in???
No!
...Maybe.
Kamala! Malik, please!
Big rush, can't stop, gotta go to school, bye, Ammi!
Overslept, huh?
Yeah...it's been impossible getting up lately.
Training?
Well, last night it was updating my fic on embiggenfeels .moomblr.com. But training is tiring too!!!
Nakia, A.K.A. Kiki. (But don't call her that.) Powers: Critical thinking, podcast recommendations
Hey, it's Bruno! Hey, Bruno!
Kamala, you've got a baby hand again.

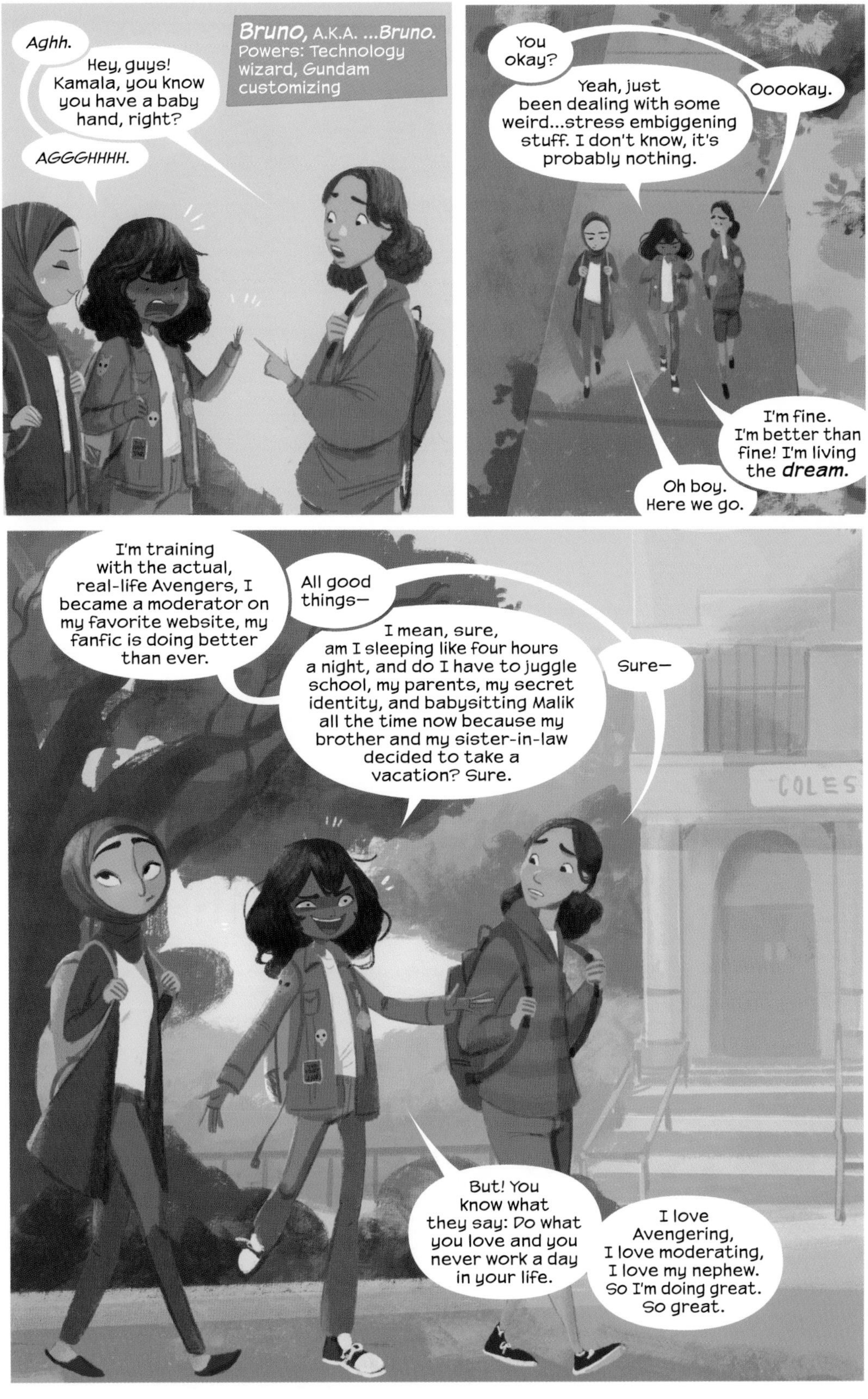
Aghh.
Hey, guys! Kamala, you know you have a baby hand, right?
Bruno, A.K.A. ...Bruno. Powers: Technology wizard, Gundam customizing
AGGGHHHH.
You okay?
Yeah, just been dealing with some weird...stress embiggening stuff. I don't know, it's probably nothing.
Ooookay.
I'm fine. I'm better than fine! I'm living the *dream.*
Oh boy. Here we go.
I'm training with the actual, real-life Avengers, I became a moderator on my favorite website, my fanfic is doing better than ever.
All good things—
I mean, sure, am I sleeping like four hours a night, and do I have to juggle school, my parents, my secret identity, and babysitting Malik all the time now because my brother and my sister-in-law decided to take a vacation? Sure.
Sure—
COLES
But! You know what they say: Do what you love and you never work a day in your life.
I love Avengering, I love moderating, I love my nephew. So I'm doing great. So great.

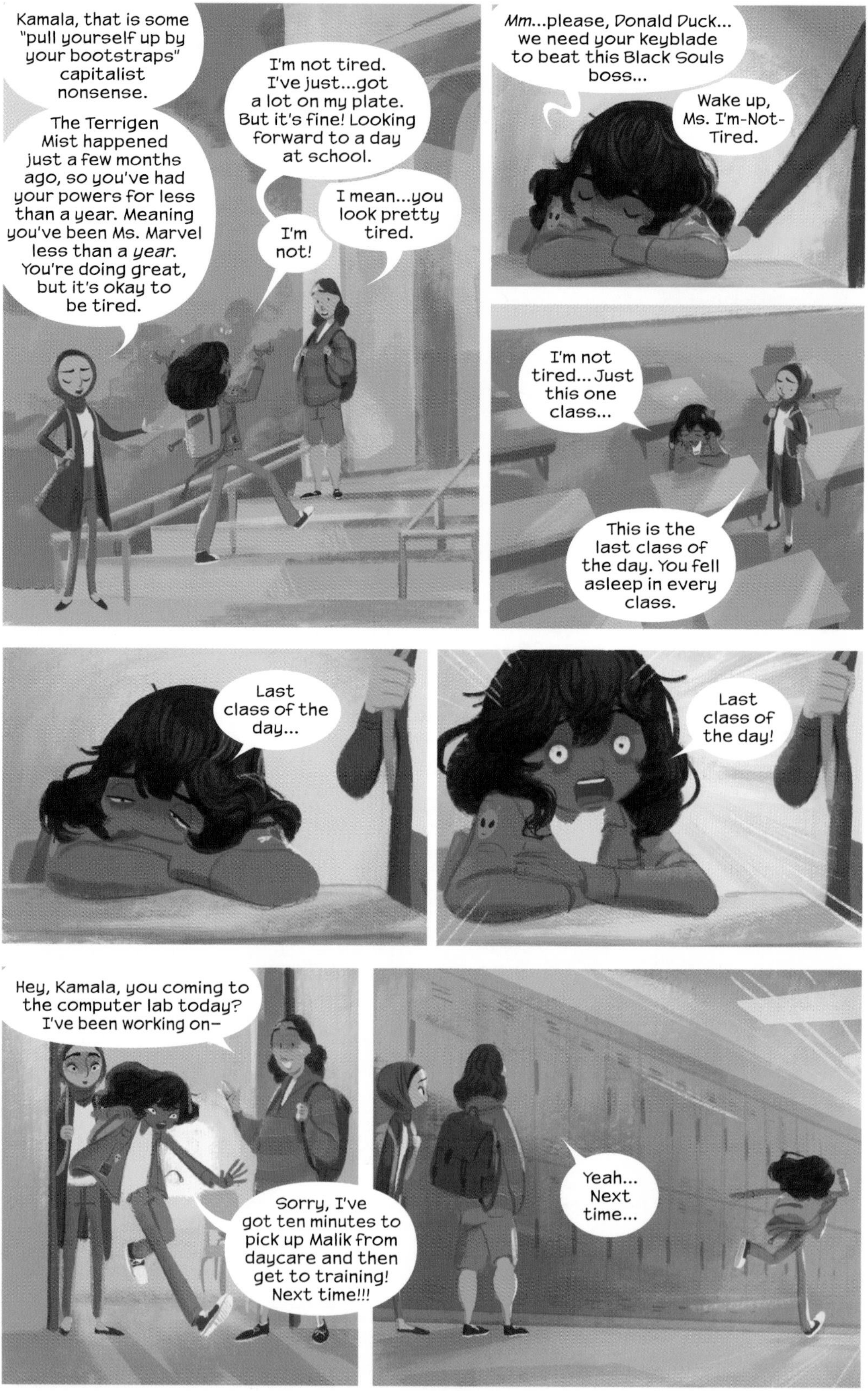
Kamala, that is some "pull yourself up by your bootstraps" capitalist nonsense.
The Terrigen Mist happened just a few months ago, so you've had your powers for less than a year. Meaning you've been Ms. Marvel less than a *year*. You're doing great, but it's okay to be tired.
I'm not tired. I've just...got a lot on my plate. But it's fine! Looking forward to a day at school.
I mean...you look pretty tired.
I'm not!
Mm...please, Donald Duck... we need your keyblade to beat this Black Souls boss...
Wake up, Ms. I'm-Not-Tired.
I'm not tired... Just this one class...
This is the last class of the day. You fell asleep in every class.
Last class of the day...
Last class of the day!
Hey, Kamala, you coming to the computer lab today? I've been working on–
Sorry, I've got ten minutes to pick up Malik from daycare and then get to training! Next time!!!
Yeah... Next time...

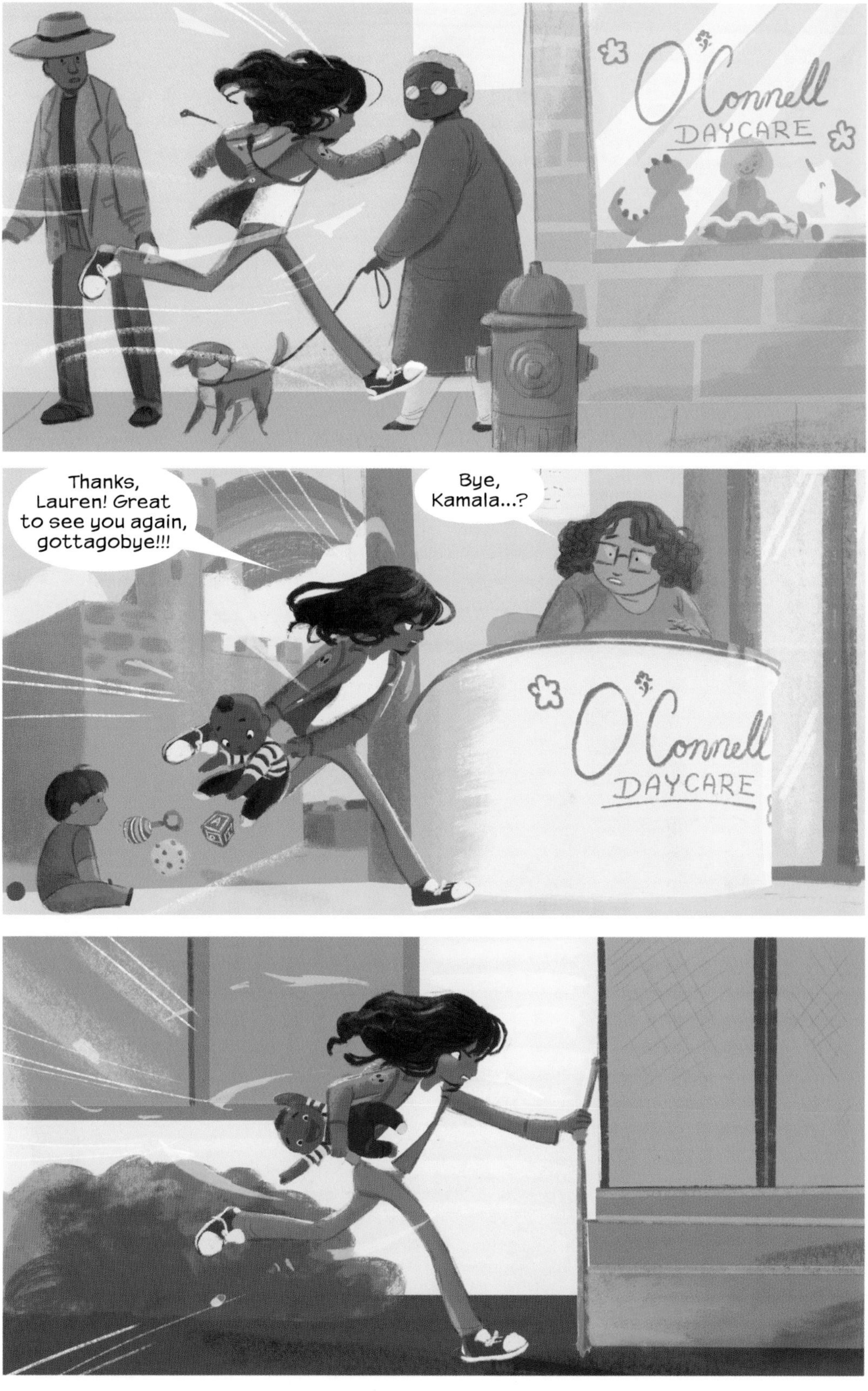
O'Connell
DAYCARE
Thanks, Lauren! Great to see you again, gottagobye!!!
Bye, Kamala...?
O'Connell
DAYCARE

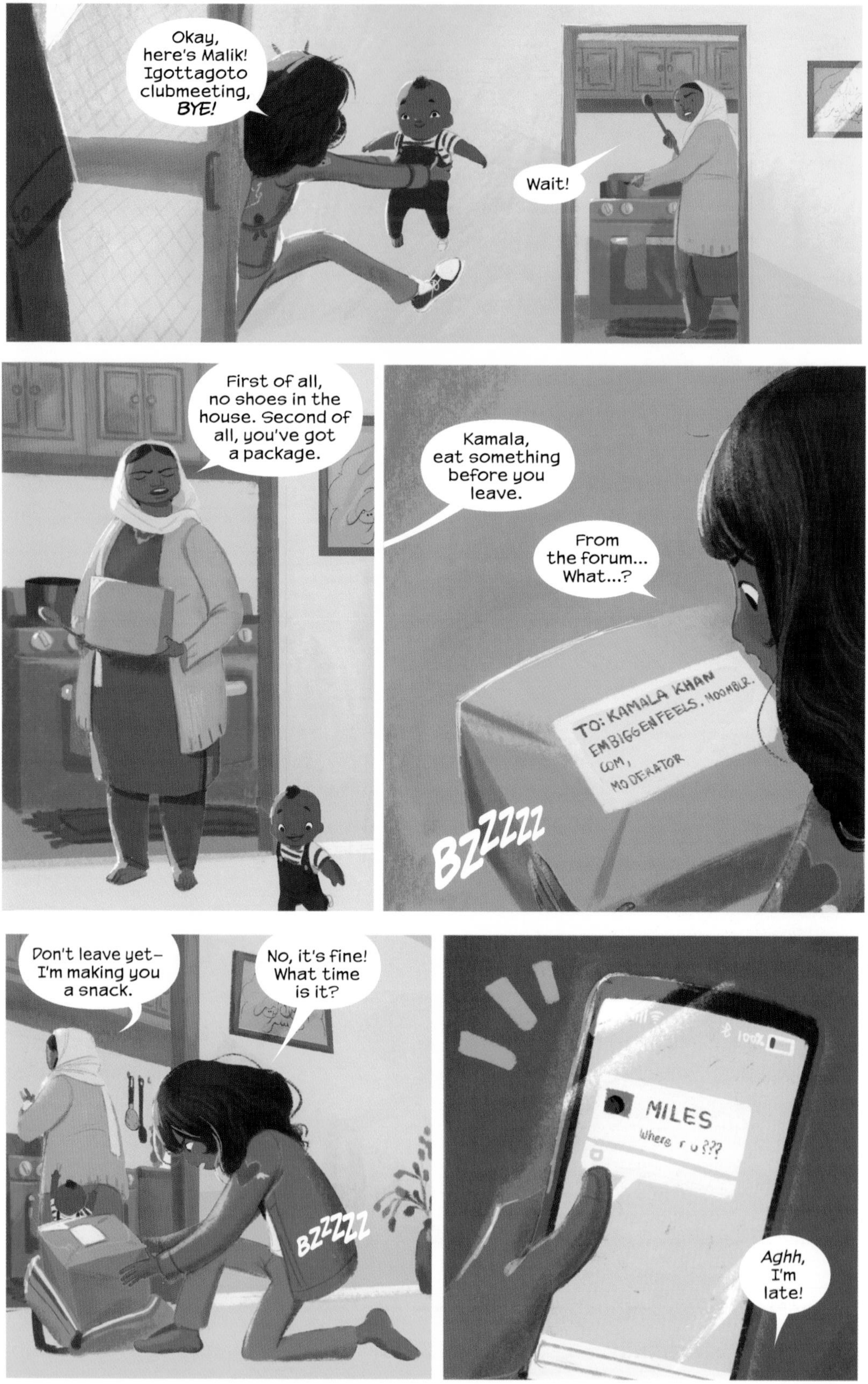
Okay, here's Malik! Igottagoto clubmeeting, ***BYE!***
Wait!
First of all, no shoes in the house. Second of all, you've got a package.
Kamala, eat something before you leave.
From the forum... What...?
TO: KAMALA KHAN EMBIGGENFEELS.MOOMBLR.COM, MODERATOR
BZZZZZ
Don't leave yet— I'm making you a snack.
No, it's fine! What time is it?
BZZZZZ
MILES
where r u???
Aghh, I'm late!

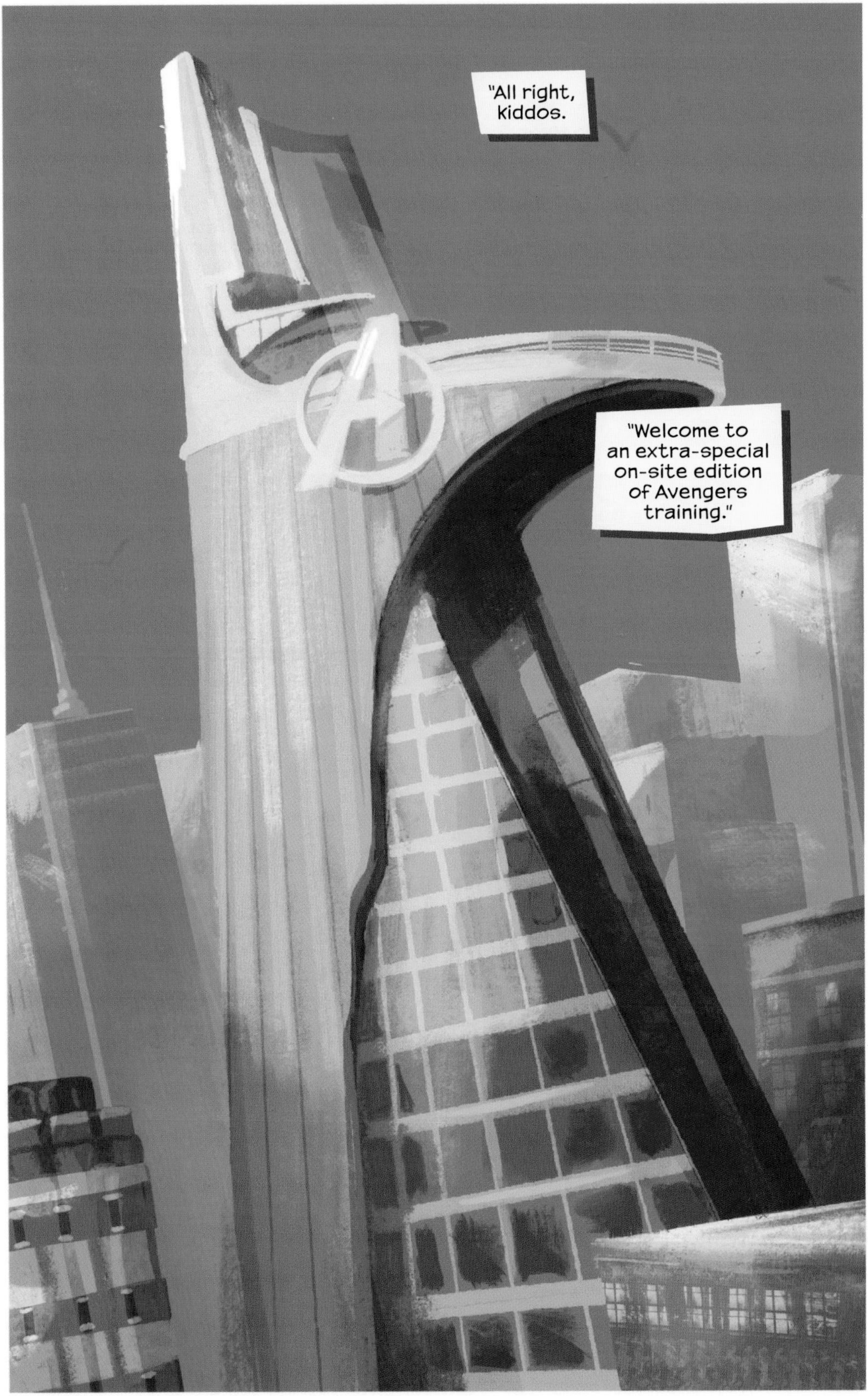
"All right, kiddos.
"Welcome to an extra-special on-site edition of Avengers training."

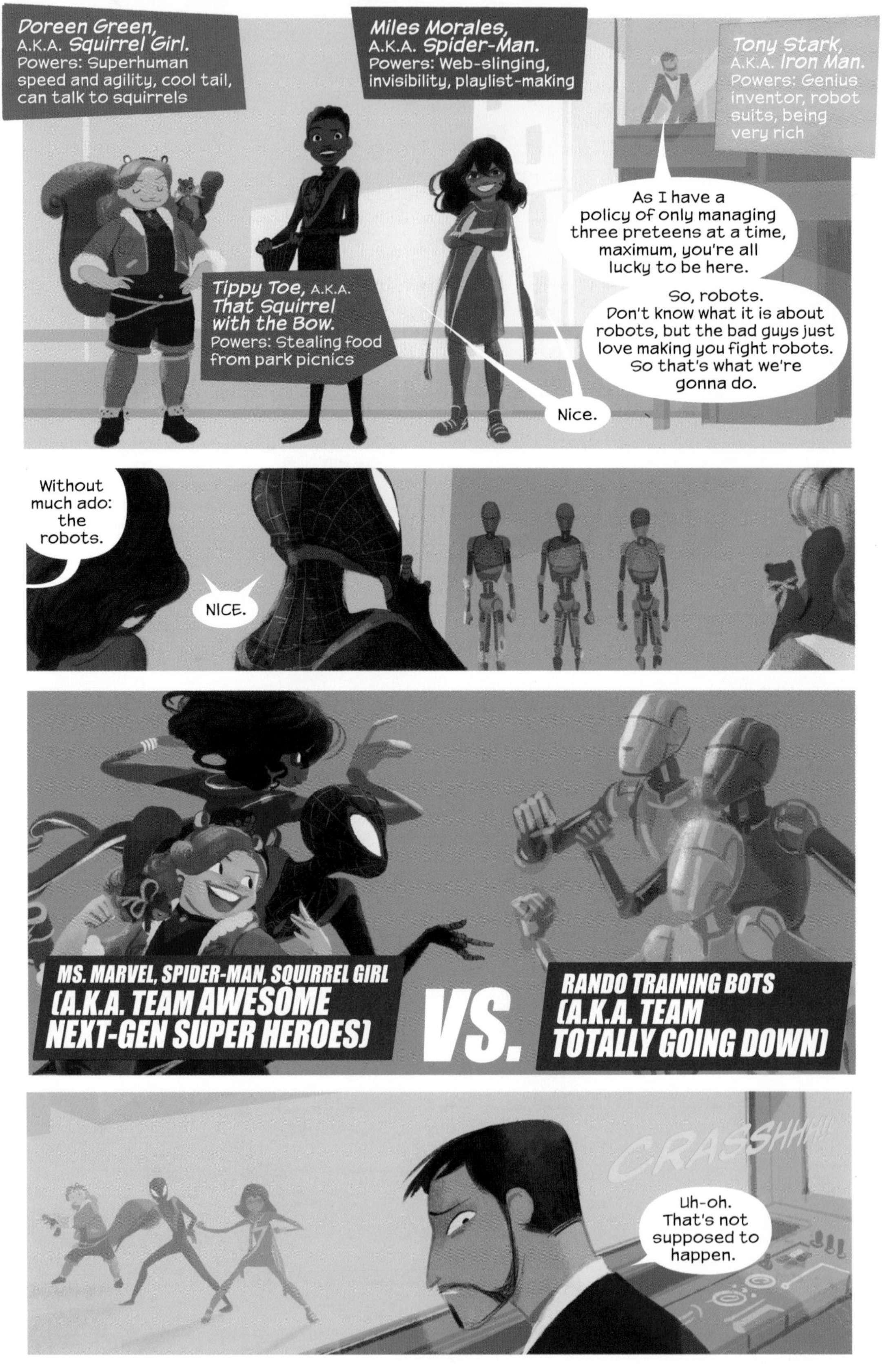
Doreen Green, A.K.A. Squirrel Girl. Powers: Superhuman speed and agility, cool tail, can talk to squirrels
Miles Morales, A.K.A. Spider-Man. Powers: Web-slinging, invisibility, playlist-making
Tony Stark, A.K.A. Iron Man. Powers: Genius inventor, robot suits, being very rich
As I have a policy of only managing three preteens at a time, maximum, you're all lucky to be here.
So, robots. Don't know what it is about robots, but the bad guys just love making you fight robots. So that's what we're gonna do.
Tippy Toe, A.K.A. That Squirrel with the Bow. Powers: Stealing food from park picnics
Nice.
Without much ado: the robots.
NICE.
MS. MARVEL, SPIDER-MAN, SQUIRREL GIRL (A.K.A. TEAM AWESOME NEXT-GEN SUPER HEROES)
VS.
RANDO TRAINING BOTS (A.K.A. TEAM TOTALLY GOING DOWN)
CRASSHHH!!
Uh-oh. That's not supposed to happen.

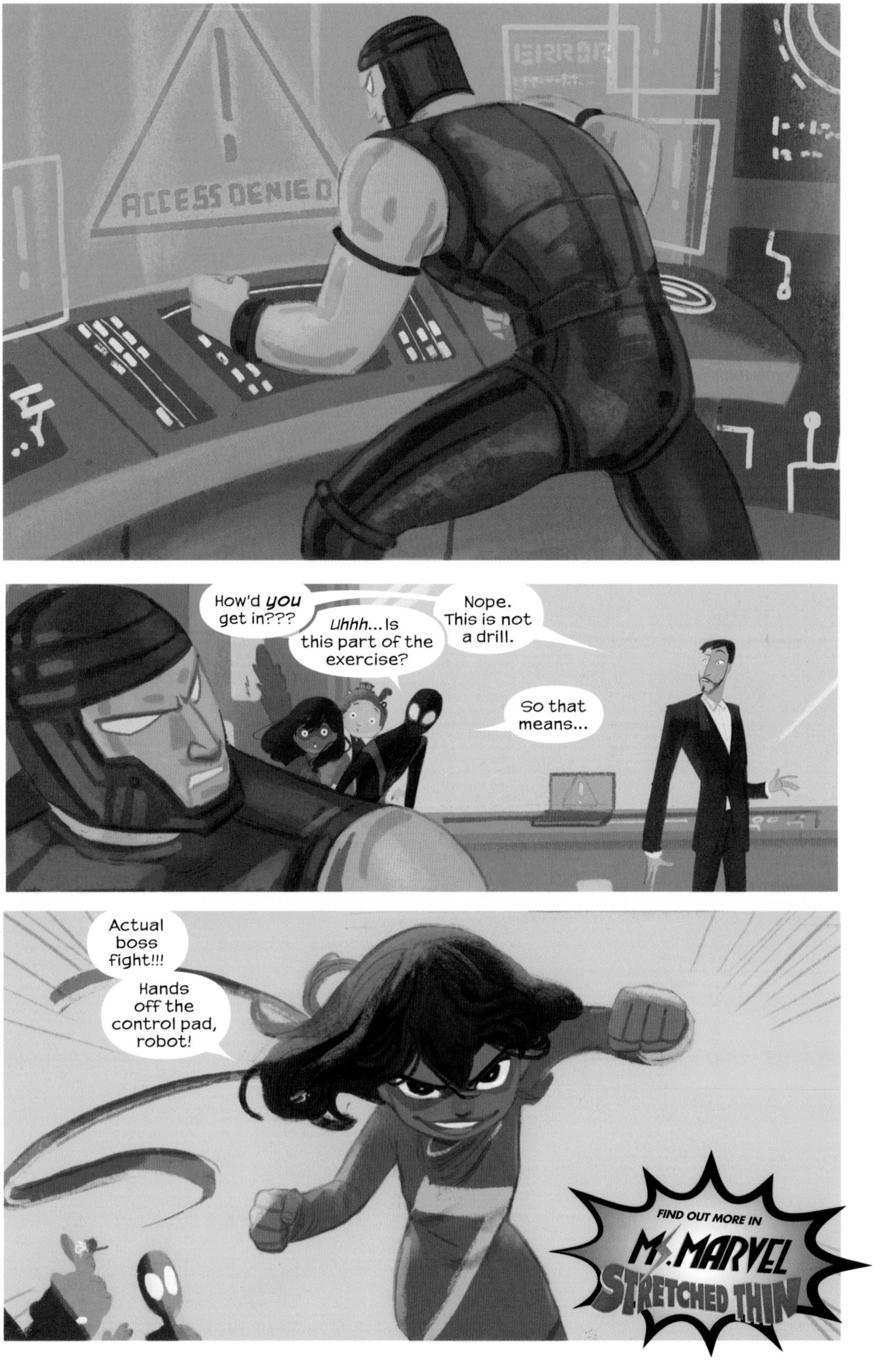
ACCESS DENIED
ERROR
How'd *you* get in???
Uhhh... Is this part of the exercise?
Nope. This is not a drill.
So that means...
Actual boss fight!!!
Hands off the control pad, robot!
FIND OUT MORE IN
MS. MARVEL
STRETCHED THIN